PRAISE F[OR THE NOVELS]
OF KAT [RICHARDSON]

Downpour

"Harper is one of my favorite paranormal detectives. In my opinion, this series is one of the best examples of true urban fantasy.... If you like mysteries that really make you think, I highly recommend Kat Richardson's Greywalker series."
—Night Owl Reviews

"A fabulous paranormal private investigative thriller.... The story line is fast-paced and filled with action."
—Genre Go Round Reviews

"[The] Greywalker series is a must read for those who appreciate entertainingly dark urban fantasy that is light on the romance and heavy on the unique."
—Smexy Books Romance Reviews

"The Grey continues to be unique, the series subplots get a boost, and the banter is fun to watch. This series is one of the few which truly feels as if it could exist in our world."
—The Ranting Dragon

Labyrinth

"Richardson's once-playful Harper is clearly evolving into a supernatural force to be reckoned with." —Publishers Weekly

"Richardson pulls out all the stops, making this novel a fast-paced and terrifying ride. Richardson's ability to spin a complex and riveting story is undeniable, and the proof is on the page." —Romantic Times

"A dynamic investigative urban fantasy saga pitting ghosts, vampires, and other paranormal entities against Harper Blaine—PI extraordinaire. Dark and fluid, the story line flows."
—Smexy Books Romance Reviews

"This is one urban fantasy series that is not to be missed."
—SciFiChick.com

continued ...

"Harper continues her metamorphosis into a grave paranormal entity in this delightfully evolving urban fantasy. The story line is action-packed.... This is a complicated, superb entry in an evolving series growing stronger and deeper."
— Genre Go Round Reviews

"A wonderful, unique heroine ... [and] a compelling place ... a wonderfully intense ending."   — Night Owl Reviews

Vanished

"Full of thrills, chills, and mystery ... easily my favorite in the series so far. Greywalker is a unique urban fantasy series that won't disappoint."   — SciFiChick.com

"Richardson has such a natural knack for storytelling ... completely captivating. I think Harper is one hell of a protagonist, and I can't get enough."   — *CrimeSpree Magazine*

"Richardson hooks readers from the start with her storytelling talents, and offers up a multifaceted mystery that's sure to keep fans riveted."   — Darque Reviews

"A terrific tale ... the story line is fast-paced and filled with plenty of action."   — Genre Go Round Reviews

"This fast-moving tale boasts lots of action, a complex plot, and meaty characters."   — *Booklist*

"Richardson continues to develop strong, intriguing plots."
— *Publishers Weekly*

Underground

"In many ways this is a book that brings together all that Harper has learned and felt over the previous books. She's stronger and more centered.... She's a very human and humane character."   — SFRevu

"Following in the tradition of Tanya Huff and Jim Butcher, this is a strong addition to the growing body of urban fantasy mysteries."   — *Library Journal*

"If you are looking for a new addition to your urban fantasy collection, then look no further than Kat Richardson.... The hair on my neck was standing up almost from the very beginning.... This is a tight, taut mystery wrapped in the paranormal; what more could a girl want? Ms. Richardson, keep 'em coming!"   — Night Owl Reviews

"This was a great addition to the Greywalker novels. . . . The actual concept of the Grey is brilliant, and I can't wait for the next novel." —The Witching-Hour Inquirer

"This powerful urban fantasy whodunit will appeal to fans of Charlaine Harris. . . . There is a lot of action as the chewing killer leaves his bite in Seattle, but the tale is character-driven by the protagonist as she goes from one escapade to another trying to end the Underground murders." —The Mystery Gazette

"Part Indian folklore, part detailed urban history, part PI procedural, part monster-from-the-depths horror story."
—*Booklist*

Poltergeist

"Richardson's view of the paranormal has a nice technological twist and features intriguing historical notes that lift this whodunit a cut above the average supernatural thriller."
—*Publishers Weekly*

"The story line is fast-paced, hooking the audience from the onset . . . and [it] never lets go until the final altercation."
—Alternative Worlds

"Gripping, stark realism . . . a truly excellent blend of detective drama and paranormal thriller." —*Library Journal*

"Richardson is really striking out into new territory with this series. . . . This is urban fantasy at its best with new ideas, crisp dialogue, great characters, and exciting stories." —SFRevu

Greywalker

"Nonstop action with an intriguing premise, a great heroine, and enough paranormal complications to keep you on the edge of your seat." —Charlaine Harris

"A genuinely likable and independent heroine with a unique view of reality." —*Library Journal*

"Contemporary fantasy meets urban noir in Richardson's intriguing debut . . . well produced, pleasingly peopled, with a strong narrative and plenty of provocative plotlines."
—*Kirkus Reviews* (starred review)

"This book kicks ass. . . . Like Charlie Huston's *Already Dead* and Simon R. Green's Nightside series, *Greywalker* is a perfect blend of hard-boiled PI and supernatural thriller. It'll grab you from the first page and won't let you go until the last."
—*CrimeSpree Magazine*

DOWNPOUR

||||||||||||||||||||||||||||||||||||||||||||||||||||||||||||||||||||||||||||||||||||

KAT RICHARDSON

A GREYWALKER NOVEL

A ROC BOOK

ROC

Published by New American Library, a division of
Penguin Group (USA) Inc., 375 Hudson Street,
New York, New York 10014, USA

Penguin Group (Canada), 90 Eglinton Avenue East, Suite 700, Toronto,
Ontario M4P 2Y3, Canada (a division of Pearson Penguin Canada Inc.)
Penguin Books Ltd., 80 Strand, London WC2R 0RL, England
Penguin Ireland, 25 St. Stephen's Green, Dublin 2,
Ireland (a division of Penguin Books Ltd.)
Penguin Group (Australia), 250 Camberwell Road, Camberwell, Victoria 3124,
Australia (a division of Pearson Australia Group Pty. Ltd.)
Penguin Books India Pvt. Ltd., 11 Community Centre, Panchsheel Park,
New Delhi - 110 017, India
Penguin Group (NZ), 67 Apollo Drive, Rosedale, Auckland 0632,
New Zealand (a division of Pearson New Zealand Ltd.)
Penguin Books (South Africa) (Pty.) Ltd., 24 Sturdee Avenue,
Rosebank, Johannesburg 2196, South Africa

Penguin Books Ltd., Registered Offices:
80 Strand, London WC2R 0RL, England

Published by Roc, an imprint of New American Library, a division of Penguin
Group (USA) Inc. Previously published in a Roc hardcover edition.

First Roc Mass Market Printing, July 2012
10 9 8 7 6 5 4 3 2 1

This is for the RAM–ily, with thanks.

ACKNOWLEDGMENTS

Many thanks to the ladies of the Clallam County Historical Society, who let me lurk in their archives for
hours, reading up on the history of the Lake Crescent
area, and who happily provided deliciously dreadful tales of
local horrors with which to haunt my readers. I'm really
sorry I couldn't work the steamships in. And more thanks
to Cherie Priest, who took the trip with me and is a delight-
ful research and travel companion, with or without the attack of the nose, ducks, and the Lady of the Lake.

Also thanks to David Feldman, who let me borrow his
name, and to Barbara Cox-Winter for supporting adult lit-
eracy in LA County and lending me the use of Jefferson's
and Erika's names. I hope their namesakes please you. And
Andrew Tripp — you know who you are — and "Aunt Jackie"
(sorry about that). A tip of the hat to Patricia Pederson,
who I hope won't mind the appearance of another Soren,
and much love to the RAMs.

To my Minions, Thea and Eric — Thing One and Thing
Two — I owe more thanks than I can express for Web sites,
art, tea, Voudoun, Chinese Alchemy, T-shirts, and garden
gnomes. I love you guys.

Special thanks to Ginjer Buchanan for the title — because
I didn't have one this time and probably won't have one next
time, either — and to my editor, Anne Sowards, and the edi-
torial and production teams at Penguin, who make me seem
very clever. And thanks to my friend Steve Mancino, who

convinced me it was all right to go my own way with the characters and not listen to other voices when they said stupid things. Also to Ken and Ana, who still think I'm cool enough to brag about.

And, as always, thanks to my friends and family, who keep putting up with me, beating up on me when I get lazy, helping me out when I need it, feeding me chocolate when necessary, and ignoring me when appropriate. Especially my husband—who is the King of Putting Up With Kat.

PROLOGUE

I have a habit of dying. I've taken the Big Sleep at least three times that I know of, though it never lasts more than a few minutes. Each time, I wake up changed, but not in any way normal people can see. Next time, I might not wake up at all, but between now and then, I have a job to do: to protect the Grey—the fringe between the normal world and the world of the purely paranormal, where ghosts roam and magic sings in neon-hot lines of energy across the empty space of the world between—and to protect the rest of the world from it. I am not a ghost or a vampire, not a witch or a sorcerer or a mage. I am just the unfortunate schmo who happened to touch death the right way and get stuck with the job. I'm a Greywalker.

Of course, I don't have that title on my business cards or my office door. Mostly I pay the bills by working as a private investigator in Seattle, because ghosts rarely have checking accounts and vampires are notoriously parsimonious. Some days I wish I could go back to just running down background checks and looking for missing kids—except that always seems to lead me right back to the Grey. Once you're in it, it doesn't let you go. It's hard on my friends, my family, and my love life, but it's necessary and, in the end, I'm good at it. And I can't really quit.

ONE

There was something deeply wrong with Lake Crescent; I knew it even before I saw the accident that wasn't there. The ground seemed to hum and mutter as if a current raged beneath it. Cobwebs of colored light leaked from the Grey—that slippery place between the normal and the paranormal where ghosts are real and magic gleams like neon reflected in wet, black streets. The unreal light stretched in patches and strands over the soil and low-growing plants or dripped from trees like Spanish moss. Sudden bolts and globes of the same transient energy darted across my vision, apparently unnoticed by anyone but me. Under the wan February sun, I could hear the whispering of ghosts I knew would appear as solid as living flesh once the sun went down. I hoped I wouldn't have to come back for them.

I could have written some of the weirdness off as the result of my altered interaction with the Grey since my most recent death, but I hadn't seen anything quite like it anywhere else since I'd gotten out of the hospital. It wasn't just me; the Grey itself was different there.

I'd come out to the Olympic Peninsula to work on a pretrial investigation for Nanette Grover—a lawyer who was a regular client of mine. I'd had to drive up into the mountains and try several sites around the lake before I caught up with the potential witness—an itinerant handyman/sometime carpenter named Darin Shea—whom she'd wanted me to talk to. He was a man of indeterminate age, race, and origin who spoke with a New England drawl as untraceable as the rest of him.

By the time I was done talking to him, I wished I hadn't started. He seemed to say little of value but took plenty of time to do it, his slow, molasses voice wandering off the subject in long, meandering asides as difficult to break through as a wall. We stood on the deck of the Log Cabin Lodge, the main building of the Log Cabin Resort, where he was working for the day, on the Piedmont end of the lake. Though I should have been paying more attention, his speech was so boring that I found my attention wandering out to the cold expanse of Lake Crescent as it lay behind him, struck with orange and pink by the fugitive sunset cutting through clouds above and illuminated from below by hints of the Grey's power grid in the depths of the dark, clear waters.

I listened to him with half an ear, taking notes while watching something burble out of the lake near the western shore—something dead white and man-shaped that seemed to slog ashore with the reluctant, spastic movement of a creature yanked forward on an invisible rope. I thought I saw a second figure on the shore, beckoning and calling in a voice that seemed to pluck the strings of the Grey and send a tingling electric sensation over my skin, but I couldn't be sure. . . .

I started to peer sideways at the strange scene, looking by force of habit for the eerie and hearing the hum and rattle of the grid swell as I did, but Shea waved a hand in front of my face. "Hey there, you listenin' to me?" he asked.

"Of course, Mr. Shea," I replied, reminding myself that I wasn't here in search of ghosts, but of reliable testimony for Nan's case—not that I was feeling positive about Shea's reliability by then. I pushed my attention to the Grey back and focused on the handyman instead.

It was cold, and dusk was descending fast by the time I was done with him. The ghosts around the shore began showing themselves as silver mist that moved in human shapes, and the sound of wind that breathed icy words. The uncanny queerness of the place made me anxious to get home—or at least down into the flatland and streetlights before full-on darkness hit—with the hope that I could let the strangeness lie for once. Of course, that is not the way my job works.

The road on the northeastern shore of Lake Crescent was narrow, twisting, and prone to dive down suddenly into unexpected gullies and through shadows of ghostlight. But even without the disturbing persistence of the Grey, the route was treacherous. Deep shade beneath the cedars and firs harbored dirty piles of snow between icy patches of bare ground and slicks of black ice on the asphalt surface of the road, so spotting a car rammed up against a tree beside the tarmac didn't even seem unlikely. The flames coming from under the hood didn't look quite right, but when a normal person sees someone struggling to exit a burning car, his first thought is not, "It's just a ghost," but something a bit more visceral, like, "Holy shit!" which was exactly what went through my own mind.

So I steered my Land Rover onto the frozen loam at the roadside and bailed out of the front seat to run for the other driver's door and wrench it open. But my hands passed through the flame-flickering material of the Subaru Forester with only a phantom sensation of heat while someone else's terror and pain washed over me. I flinched back from the melting face that stared from behind the unreal glass, and then I backed away. Was it my own fear I felt or his . . . ?

The ghost wafted out of the memory of his fiery death, following me, mouthing words without sound and bringing along the odor of searing flesh and melting rubber, hot steel, and burning cedar. I retched at the smell. I couldn't fall back any farther without standing on the road, so I put up my hands as if I could hold the smoldering specter at bay with the gesture alone. The ghost stopped, just touching my out-turned palms. A sparkle of gold and a flicker of Grey bent between us where his searing memory of fire struck against the shield I had unconsciously raised. I held my ground at the ragged edge of the asphalt.

The ghost's voice trembled off the Grey surface between us as if it were a speaker: "Not an accident. Not an accident."

I could feel the vibration of it in my head and chest. I nodded but still held him away. "All right, I believe you. What happened to you? What's your name?" He was not the first ghost I'd seen and he wouldn't be the last, but he was the first willful spirit I'd encountered in the nine months since I'd been shot in the back. This ghost felt horrible, exuding terror and fury and need while his memory burned in icy flames and remembered agony, resonating through the barrier between us and slicing into me.

"Steven."

The smell and sensation made my stomach flip, but I swallowed the lump of revulsion and held still. "What's your last name, Steven?"

But he didn't seem to understand me, or at least his answer didn't sound like a last name. "Blood Lake. My family . . . We should never have let them . . ." he said, then started fading away.

I forced my protections aside and pressed my hands into him, trying to make a stronger connection even though the feel of him made me gag. I couldn't grab onto him as I should have been able to do, so I let myself slide deeper into the Grey, closer to his own plane. He firmed up a little, but I still couldn't get much of a hold on him. He was thin and weak, as if whatever gave him substance was fading or distant and only his ardent need for help allowed him to manifest at all. "Steven. Steven, listen to me. Tell me your whole name or where you're from. Anything. Help me find you, or I can't help you."

"Le—" And he fell apart in a drift of dust and smoke.

The burning car remained a moment longer, sending memories of flame and sparks into the silvery air of the Grey. I stared at it, hoping to memorize the license plate before it vanished into the mist, but I got only part of it. I tried backing out a little and reaching for the temporaclines—the layers of time and memory that accrue in the Grey like silt—but they were slippery and knife-edged, and I couldn't seem to find the right one. I eased back out of the Grey and into the normal, looking for any sign of the accident, but I found nothing of it in the near-dark. It was long gone.

Disturbed, I returned to my truck and headed it back down the road that would connect to Highway 101 to Port Angeles and then to the ferry back to the Seattle side of Puget Sound. I felt haunted all the way home even after the strangeness of the area had faded away.

I spent the next morning finishing reports for Nan, but I couldn't get the ghost's words out of my head, and from the corner of my eye, I continually caught a flicker of something Grey that looked almost like a charred skull. Before I took my reports to Nan's office, I gave in to the phantom harassment and ran a search through the Department of Licensing database. From the partial plate number and the first name, Steven or Stephen, I got about two hundred hits; filtering for the make and model of the burning SUV, I got three.

A bit more poking got some additional background information on the three names and I printed out the pages to read at Nan's office. Since she was prepping for a trial that looked to be lengthy, it was hard to guess how long I'd have to wait for her to be free to talk to me.

I walked from my office to Nan's, liking the feeling of moving through a familiar place again where the Grey seemed less volatile and dangerous. After some chitchat and paperwork, Nan's secretary set me up to wait in the firm's library. The space was about twice the size of Nan's office and lined with floor-to-ceiling shelves filled with mostly outdated law books and periodicals. Most firms have no need for an extensive library anymore—they just subscribe to the LexisNexis system online and do their research from their computers, as I do a lot of the time—but Nanette's firm kept the room intact, using it as an additional meeting room. The acoustic deadening of a foot of leather-bound pages lining the walls made it an ideal space for recording depositions and discussing sensitive matters. No sounds penetrated in or drifted out of the room once the door was closed, and the few spooks around the place were as dull as tax law. I huddled over my printouts and drank coffee until Nan came in.

"Is that my report, Harper?" She was as uncreased and unemotional as a slab of ebony.

I looked up, tidying my pages into a pile and pulling out the folder full of reports from my bag. "No. This is your report."

I slid the folder across the table and watched her read it. Nan reads frighteningly fast. In a few minutes she looked up at me. "So, what are your thoughts on this witness?"

"He's a problem," I said. "I can't get a background on him so far—he won't even supply one himself. The best I could get was that he'd been in the area off and on since he was sixteen, but he wouldn't say how old he is now and he doesn't have a driver's license—though he does seem to have a truck, which isn't registered to him. He feels unreliable to me, even though he has a solid reputation as a worker with the locals. He was overly chatty in a way that made me think he'd been coached, so I don't feel confident about his information, and his manner of speaking would drive the judge and jury crazy. He volunteered some additional data I was frankly suspect of. With no fixed address or verifiable status, I think you'd be hurting your case if you put him on the stand. If your opponent wants to use him, all that might be in your favor, but he still feels shady to me."

Nan arched her brows only enough to notice. "*Feels* shady. Expand on that."

I gave it a moment's thought before I obliged her. "Well, to be crude about it, you can't tell what age, race, or region he's from and, unless he cleans up really well and changes his speech and mannerisms, that lack of identity will make a Seattle jury distrust everything he says. And at this point

I can't say they'd be wrong. He talks around the point pretty well, but when you tear it down, his information just isn't solid."

Nan nodded. "So you'll need to confirm or eliminate his facts and nail down his background."

"If you think he's worth it, I'll keep digging on Shea, but that's going to take me away from the King County side of the investigation."

"True. How long will it take?"

"I'm not sure. It's going to be legwork and combing the ground every step of the way. There's also another case that's come up out there—a cold case missing person that might be a homicide."

"Related to my case?"

"Doesn't look it, but it'll be a lot of the same interviewees, and I'd like to dog it down as long as I'm there."

Nan's face could have been sculpted from ice-cold bronze for all the emotion she usually displays. She didn't even raise an eyebrow this time, but I knew she was annoyed from the way ragged orange spikes flashed in her aura for a moment. "We'll be in court in less than a month, Harper. How long do you think the additional Clallam County investigation will take?"

"I'm not sure," I repeated. "I'd like to get David Feldman to take over the King County work. You know Feldman's solid. He did a lot of the background on that body on the freeway case a few years ago."

Nan nodded. "I've worked with him." She stopped talking and studied me a moment in silence. The wisps of blue and yellow energy that always coiled around her office stirred a cold draft and I shivered. "Tell me about this other case."

Relief spread through me: She hadn't decided to take a hard line with me about her own case taking precedence, at least not yet. I took a sip of my cold coffee and returned the cup to the table with care before I looked back at Nan. "Sometime in late 2005 or early 2006, a Lake Crescent–area resident named Steven Leung and his 2001 Subaru Forester disappeared. He was sixty-seven years old, retired from the Clallam County assessor's office, widower, two surviving daughters. A witness claims Leung was killed in a car fire on East Beach Road and the details he provided point to vehicular homicide. I can't find a record of any similar accident in that area in the past ten years, but the telling thing—the thing that persuades me this isn't a hoax—is that all information about Leung just stops by April 2006. There's nothing. It's as if the man stepped off the planet and no one cared—not even his survivors, who never filed a missing person report."

"Could Leung have moved out of state or entered some kind of medical care?"

"There's no forwarding address for him so far. Even if he was in a nursing home all this time, his mail would have to go somewhere. There's no death certificate or record of cremation or burial in Clallam, Kitsap, Pierce, or King County and no record of his car being sold or the registration renewed by anyone. There's no release of interest to indicate he'd transferred ownership to a wrecking yard or charity, either. The only other lead I have is that the witness said something about an area called 'Blood Lake.' It sounds like a local place-name, but I didn't have time to look for it before this meeting today."

"I don't find this missing person case that's five years cold particularly compelling."

She didn't ask what I wasn't telling her; she just fixed her commanding gaze on me and waited. I wasn't sure how to persuade her; I couldn't say that I had it from the ghost himself that someone had done him in and that there might be a lot more to the situation than a simple disappearance. I made up my mind and leaned forward.

The motion made me wince as the muscles in my back and abdomen pulled unevenly. I still hadn't rebuilt all the tissue destroyed by the passage of a .45-caliber bullet through my middle and I didn't move as fluidly as I once had. "I think it's murder, Nan. You know that every delay in pursuing something like this lowers the chance of solving it.

And yes, I know it's five years old already, but how long should anyone have to wait for justice?"

She studied me for a few long seconds before she replied. "Are you sure you're in condition to pursue an undetected homicide?"

"Am I in shape to chase down an unprosecuted corporate malfeasance complaint?"

Nan gave it some thought. "All right. Chase Shea for a few more days while you work your case, just to see where it leads. If you turn up enough to justify continuing, so be it. If not, I'll expect you back on my pretrial work immediately. In the meantime, call Feldman and brief him on the malfeasance case to date and get him to work before you leave town." She stood up and took the report file off the table. "Is there anything further on this witness?"

"Not from me."

"Good. I need a report Monday." She turned and strode out, which was pretty much the only way Nan walked. She was disappointed, but she didn't give any outward demonstration. She never showed an emotion outside the courtroom that I knew of, and I wouldn't have been able to guess what she was feeling if I hadn't had the ability to see the colors of energy that cling and swirl around most people.

Auras and energy lines didn't seem as blazingly bright or vibrantly colored to me as they had before I was shot. But they'd been getting a little out of hand by then anyhow, and I was just as glad that—except around Lake Crescent—the colors had faded a bit and I no longer heard a constant, inescapable singing and whispering in my head. It made me feel more human to know there were limits to what I could do and see.

There had been moments during that last, horrific investigation when I'd felt I *wasn't* all that human anymore at all. The power to sink to the grid itself and to move the threads of magic, to tear them apart and push them around with impunity, had been too seductive, too alien. I'd have been just as glad to have lost that, though I hadn't really checked the limits of my abilities yet. As I'd been warned, dying without direction had been like slamming a fist down on the magical Reset button. I believed I'd reverted to a lower, weaker state of interaction with the Grey or at least something on a less godlike scale. That was fine by me.

I gathered my papers and headed back to my own office to track down more information on Steven Leung. Outside, the February sky was the dull color of an old galvanized bucket, but it hadn't yet begun to rain and if I walked as briskly as I could, I'd make it back to my office dry.

TWO

It's amazing how much information resides in databases and on Web sites if you know where to look and how to pry. I do a lot of my investigative work from my computer or in records offices while someone else pokes their specialized electronic beast for me. Even a lot of my Grey work has clues and trails through the world of electrons flying through the void of cyberspace. Steven Leung, strangely, hadn't left much trace in the cyber world. He was survived by two adult daughters and had been predeceased by a son and a wife. He owned a house out in Port Angeles—or what was listed as Port Angeles, since the postal district covered most of the northern end of the Olympic National Park and unincorporated towns nearby. The property records showed the house was still in his name and someone had, apparently, been paying the taxes. It was too late in the day to catch up to the Clallam County payroll office to find out whether his retirement was still being paid out, but I'd have been willing to bet it was. Assuming the ghost I'd seen was not some spectral joker jerking my chain, it looked as if something quietly dreadful had happened to Steven Leung.

I paused in my electronic prying to call Dave Feldman to bring him up to speed on Nan's case. Since the case was a little complicated, the conversation took a while and I'd just finished faxing a lot of documents to Feldman when someone knocked on my office door. It was late in the afternoon, the glow of rain-diluted neon and the dregs of sunset creep-

ing in through my tiny window, and I thought I should be a
bit more careful than I had used to be and not just open the
door willy-nilly.

I called out, "Just a second," as I watched the last of the
pages crawl through the scanner and fall into the pile below.
I gathered up the papers and refiled them before opening
my door. I didn't like to risk confidential files being in sight
of other clients, and although I didn't have any more appointments on my schedule for the day, clients and my
neighbors in the building did sometimes drop in without
one.

Cops are particularly fond of making unannounced vis-
its, so I shouldn't have been too surprised to see Seattle PD
Detective Rey Solis in the hall. I had a lot of respect for
him, and we'd worked together a few times, but we weren't
friends and the messy ending of our last encounter hadn't
helped that.

At five foot ten plus boot heels, I'm taller than the taci-
turn Colombian, but he never seemed to care. I glanced
down at him and didn't smile. "Hello, Solis. What can I do
for you?"

"I'm seeking information. May I come in, Ms. Blaine?"

"Is this going to be the sort of information that leads to
subpoenas?"

"I'm tying up loose ends of the Kammerling case, largely
for my own curiosity."

"But not entirely."

"No."

That left me with the option of being rude or taking a
risk on the other direction of his curiosity. I didn't feel that
I owed him anything, but I didn't see any upside to annoying him, so I stood back and waved him in. "You might as
well sit down and ask what you came to."

He gave me a small nod and entered while I closed the
door. I noticed that he stood next to the nicer of my two
client chairs and let his gaze wander over the scarred oak
faces of my filing cabinets and shelves and across the
computer-burdened surface of my desk. The moisture on

his coat didn't run and puddle onto my floor, so I guessed the rain had started only a few minutes earlier. He patted the chair absently and took off his coat before sitting down with a satisfied grunt and a nod.

"What?" I asked, taking my own seat again.

"Your office is very . . . Raymond Chandler."

I found myself grinning; I'd read all those books, too. "I am from Los Angeles."

"The file cabinets are antiques?"

"No, just heavily used. I got them cheap and refinished them."

He gave me a curious glance.

I shook my head. "I don't think you really want to talk about my office decor."

He inclined his head—my point. "I have been wondering what you're currently working on."

"I can't discuss my clients' business."

"Broadly speaking. Have you had any more of your . . . odd cases?"

I gave half a smile and shook my head, although the timing did give me pause to wonder what he was after. Whenever my Grey investigations have crossed his normal ones, he gets . . . annoyed. But I didn't have anything running yet that could have pinged his radar, and I didn't think there was much left from the previous case, either, no matter how awful and freakish it had been. And so far as I knew, Solis had no sense of the Grey and wouldn't have any idea that I'd seen creepy and disturbing things at Lake Crescent. "You know, Solis, this is getting to be a habit with you. But, no. Just paperwork business. Some pretrial work, a missing person search, financials, the boring, bill-paying stuff."

"When did you return to work?"

"Five or six months ago, but not full-time until recently."

"Why the delay?"

"Getting shot is not like in the movies." I noticed I was running one hand through my shortened brown hair—I'd had it cut to my shoulders again in the hospital so it didn't turn into one giant, greasy mat—and forced my hand back down to the desk.

He nodded as if he knew.

"Have you ever . . . ?" I asked.

"Sí," he replied, and raised two fingers. "Twice."

"Then you know . . . how it hurts, how everything just seems to be so much harder than it should be. . . ."

"And you regret what happened."

"No," I replied. "I don't think I could have changed it."

"What about William Novak?"

That startled me, but I only frowned and blinked at him. "What? What about him?"

"Your missing person is not William Novak, then?"

"No. Is he missing?" Of course I knew he was, and I knew what had happened to him. But the uncanny fate of my ex-boyfriend wasn't something I could tell Solis. Will wasn't exactly dead, but he wasn't with the living, either, and I would never be able to explain it to Solis or damn near anyone else. I hadn't killed him; that was for certain.

Solis cocked his head to the side and regarded me like a crow considering where to jab its beak into an unsuspecting mouse. "I would have expected Michael Novak to bring the case to you. But since you may have been one of the last people to see William, perhaps not. . . ."

I sat forward and studied him. "Will is missing and you think I have a connection. . . . Why?"

"It is a strange coincidence. Several, in fact."

"William Novak was my *ex*-boyfriend. I hadn't had contact with him in almost a year before my trip to London."

"But he seems to have followed you home from London and sought you out several times."

"He did contact me, but he was acting a little weird and I asked him to stop. I didn't see him after that."

"Are you certain?"

"Yes. We met twice and I think he called me once. But that was all."

"His doctors and his brother think he was obsessed with you."

"Will?" I made myself laugh and tried not to think about the past few times I'd seen him. "Will wasn't the obsessing type. He was pretty easygoing. If something wasn't working out for him, he stopped doing it. That's why we ended our relationship—he didn't like my job, and I wasn't going to change it. There wasn't any rancor; it just didn't work out. Neither of us had any problem with that. The last time I did see him, he was sick. As I said, he acted a little strange, and I thought he wasn't well enough to be out of bed. I told him to go home. So far as I know, he did."

"When was that?"

I shrugged and gnawed my lower lip, thinking. The days after I'd returned from London had passed in a frenetic daze of scrabbling to figure out what was happening and then to put a stop to it. It was hard to sort out how much time had elapsed between one terrible thing and the next. "I'm not quite sure. . . . Maybe forty-eight hours before I was shot?" I'd written most of it down after the fact, trying to understand it all better, but I wouldn't show that document to Solis; he wouldn't like it and I didn't want to relive it.

Solis tapped a knuckle absently against his lower lip. Then he stood up and unfolded his coat, keeping his eyes on me the whole time. "William Novak's DNA was found at the Queen Anne gymnasium."

I made a puzzled frown and lied. "Are you saying he followed me up there? I never saw him."

Solis said nothing. He probably wasn't taken in, but he didn't have any proof I'd had anything to do with Will's disappearance. All he could do was try to rattle me. There was no telltale orange flare of frustration around his head at my lack of reaction; Solis was just flying kites and waiting to see if I spooked at any of them. He'd need to have something a lot scarier if he wanted me to flip, and I doubted he'd be able to come up with anything worse than what I'd already seen and done.

I stood up as Solis put on his coat. Then I walked with him to the door. "I hope you can find him," I said, opening the door for him to leave.

He stepped out into the hall and turned back to look at me. "Do you?"

"Of course I do."

"And what if we find him dead?"

Knowing what I did, the words startled me a little, but I didn't try to hide my reaction. I caught my breath and bit my lip, feeling moisture prickle in my eyes. "That—that would be tragic. But at least Michael would know what happened to his brother."

His expression tightened, a somber pall of disappointment darkening his aura. "Michael Novak did not file the missing person report." Solis gave me a thin smile and turned away, clattering down the wooden stairs as I remained, stunned, in my doorway.

THREE

Maybe I should have felt guilty, but I didn't—not about Will. I knew what had happened and I couldn't think it was a bad ending—not the best, but far from the worst, though thinking of it made me feel sad and hollow. But in the time since I'd left the hospital, it hadn't occurred to me to wonder what Michael thought or felt—for that, I should have been contrite and I should have let him know what had happened. He must have guessed that I and my strange abilities had had something to do with Will's disappearance, so of course he hadn't filed a police report when his brother had vanished from the face of the earth—just like Steven Leung had vanished. I wondered if my snooping into Leung's affairs would cause the sort of reaction from someone that Solis had seemed to expect from me. If, as I suspected, Leung had been murdered, I should brace myself for worse than a polite escort to the door. First I'd have to start rattling cages on the Peninsula and keep out of Solis's path until I could talk to Michael, which I plainly wasn't going to do today.

I went back to the desk and checked the late ferry schedule to the Olympic Peninsula. The last ferry left Edmonds at eleven forty-five and there were several others between now and then. I rushed to get a hotel booked and pack up some things for myself and the ferret.

I could have left Chaos with Quinton, but with my uncertain powers in the Grey, I preferred to have my clever little pet along. She saw a few of the creepy things I saw, too, and was pretty fearless, so she made a good companion when ghost hunting. Besides, leaving her with Quinton would make him suspect I was up to something dangerous, and I hated the quickly concealed worry that settled on him now when we talked about my work in the Grey. He hadn't said anything in a while, but I knew he was still a little freaked and unhappy about seeing me die. I wasn't pleased with it myself, but I knew, in spite of my momentary lapse at the lake, that I couldn't ignore the Grey cases: They were my duty; there was no one else to fix them. Still, they laid an awful weight on my personal life and I couldn't let them ruin what I had with Quinton.

When I was nearly ready to go, I left a message for Quinton to call me—he refuses to have a cell phone, so a numeric message was all I could do. He called back just as I was putting the last things into the Land Rover. I closed up the back and got into the driver's seat as I answered the call.

"Harper Blaine."

"Hey, beautiful."

"Hey, yourself. Wanted to give you a heads-up: I have to go back out to the Peninsula on some more work."

"Do you want me to look after Chaos?" His voice was just a little hesitant. I can't "see" voices, or get any sort of magical sense from them, but I can hear just fine, and Quinton was nervous.

I chuckled as if this were nothing important. "No. I'll take the carpet shark along—it's just the usual kind of thing, but the drive's too long to make two or three days in a row, so I figured I'd stay out there a couple of days. I'll be back Sunday or Monday." I figured I'd either have a good handle on what was going on by then, or I'd need help. I didn't like the idea of being out in whatever caused the Grey strangeness in Lake Crescent for too long and I still had other, ordinary work that needed doing. I'd lost my perspective too easily in the recent past; I didn't want to lose myself again.

He took a long breath and sounded much more steady

when he spoke next. "Oh, well, then I'll see you Sunday or Monday. Don't bring back any sparkly bloodsuckers."

"The regular kind are bad enough and I'm not planning to bring any of those back, either."

"Suits me." Something made a sizzling sound followed by a series of sharp pops. "Oh ... crap, gotta go!" And he disconnected without further chat about what I was doing, leaving me unfairly relieved.

Chaos stuck her head out of my purse, as if demanding to know the source of the delay. "Sorry, fuzz butt. Don't tell on me, OK?" I murmured, and rubbed her ears until she huffed at me and burrowed back into the bag to continue her mandatory eighteen hours of beauty sleep.

The ferry from Edmonds was full of cars, but almost none of the passengers left them to go above the car deck. The main passenger deck looked like a deserted bus station awaiting the announcement of tragedy. A few huddles of humanity were scattered along the windowed edges and a single hairy man circled the deck again and again like a caged bear. The blackness outside the windows seemed to have no division between sky and water; lights and stars scattered through them both as if the one were the same as the other. There were no ghosts on the ferry, and nothing rose from the Sound below to make itself known, but the boat still had a haunted feeling as it slipped through the night waters to Kingston. Perhaps it was my mood, but everything around me seemed colored with the strange, even where the Grey lay quiet.

The highways out to Port Angeles were narrow and twisty, a single, unlighted lane in each direction until the 101 passed the turnoff to Port Townsend, after which the road widened occasionally and looked like any other. Until then, trees and overgrown fences lent the darkened route a tunnel-like aspect punctuated by the looming shapes of buildings in the moment my headlights passed over and then left them to slink back into the dark. I was glad to reach the better-lit sections of 101 as it approached Port

Angeles and seek out my hotel, leaving behind on the road the sense of something lurking just out of view.

It was almost midnight by the time I got settled into the hotel room and let Chaos out to explore a bit before bed, knowing that if I didn't let her romp about, she'd rustle around all night in her travel cage and give me no end of dirty looks for most of the next day. As soon as I put her on the floor, she began zooming around the edges of the room with her head down and her front legs folded back, racing along with her front half flat on the carpet, as if herding some invisible thing with her nose. I cocked my head to the side and peered into the Grey, looking for the telltale motion of something barely glimpsed in the corner of the eye.

In the silvery mist of the Grey, I saw a bright blue line of energy cut through the room near one of the walls. A column of white haze darted along that line just ahead of the ferret, who harried it without mercy until it hit the corner and seemed forced to turn against the wall, sliding along the next straight line it encountered until it had made a circuit of the room. I bent over and caught Chaos on the next pass as she came near me. The white cloud of energy snapped back to the blue line and stopped as close to me as it could get, wavering like a shred of fog on a windless beach. I sank closer to the Grey, feeling myself grow thinner and less connected to the normal world as I concentrated on the misty shape.

The closer I got to being purely in the realm of magical things, the more defined the thing became, starting to look more and more like a person. I pushed deeper into the whispering, buzzing world of ghosts, reaching for an appropriate temporacline—a layer of time—where I might be able to talk to this one, but though there were several cold-edged shards of memory, none seemed to hold the specter. So it wasn't a loop or shadow of history, but an actual roving ghost, though one that seemed stuck on the gleaming blue wire of magical energy at the moment. I took a deep breath, letting the Grey rush over me completely. And there she was.

She was Caucasian, small and pretty and young, maybe eighteen or nineteen, but bearing a weight of sorrow that aged her face before its time. She wore a long, high-waisted dress like something straight out of a Jane Austen novel, which struck me as rather strange since Washington hadn't been settled by white people until much later in the nineteenth century. In my hand, Chaos made an aggravated chuckling noise, wriggling to get free and have another go at the spirit, which cringed away at the sound.

Even in the Grey, she was a little ragged and incorporeal, as if she were fading with the passage of time. She steeled herself against her fear and spoke, her words trembling out into the air on a cold breath that made the sounds sharp and brittle on the ear, but totally incomprehensible to me. From years of hanging around Ben Danziger, I recognized the language as Russian, but I didn't know what she was saying. I tried to let the words roll over me, to speak their meaning into my mind as some ghosts do, but I could catch only nonsensical snatches of what she was trying to tell me. She flickered and some of her substance was sucked away into the bright blue line at her feet.

"Who are you?" I asked.

Her mouth moved, but I didn't hear the whole name, only ". . . 'trovna . . ." Then she was yanked backward along the gleaming cobalt line, her face transforming in terror as her shape collapsed on itself, flowing away into a stream of white light, like sand falling through the throat of an hourglass. I tried to reach for her, to pull her back, but I couldn't catch a hold of her, and the only touch I felt ripped across my fingers and disappeared with the young woman's shade. Only a lingering shriek in my ear and a pain in my hand, as if it had been abraded by the ghost's passage through my grip, remained as the silver mist of the Grey stood momentarily empty around me.

Panting a little with surprise, I backed out of the Grey. As I returned to the normal world, Chaos heaved a sigh and started looking around for something else to bedevil. My ghost was gone. I put the ferret back on the floor and sat on the edge of the bed, watching her make several sniffling searches of the room's perimeter before she gave it the mustelid all clear. Then she ran back to me and put her front paws on my shin before scrambling onto my boot and trying to climb my leg to the top of the mattress.

"Lunatic," I chided, picking her up and plopping her on the bedspread. Chaos immediately began rolling around on her back, wiggling and rubbing her ears against the cheap comforter. I stood up and went to the bathroom mirror as the ferret bounced and writhed around on the bed, digging at the comforter until she could get under it and snorkel around, raising a moving, giggling lump like Bugs Bunny burrowing to Texas in a Warner Brothers cartoon.

Staring at my reflection, I mimicked the mouth shapes the ghost had made while she said her name. When I thought I had them right, I tried giving them voice. "Ahhh . . . llll . . . nnn. . . . Aaaannahhh . . . Anna." I sounded like an idiot and looked like a moron, but I kept trying. "Mmm . . . buh . . . puh . . . Buh'trovna. Puh'trovna . . . Petrovna . . . ? Anna Petrovna?" I called her name, reaching for the Grey as I did. "Anna Petrovna! Where are you?" But the only sound was a distant kind of gasp and then silence, as if something had disappeared and left nothing but a void.

It was a strange name to come from the Grey like that. I didn't like the coincidence of another weak ghost, like Leung, reaching out to me and vanishing, especially not a strange Russian girl who should never have been out on the Peninsula in that era. I'd dealt before with a Russian ghost who had no business being where and what he was, but he'd been strong, willful, and dangerous. Anna Petrovna was weak and helpless and . . . gone. Now there was a hole where she should have been, as if she'd been hacked from the fabric of the Grey with a dull ax. A chill ran down my back.

Chaos tumbled out of the bedclothes and thumped onto the floor, throwing herself into a frenzied war dance and baring her teeth at the blanket in her ire. I smiled, distracted from my unhappy thoughts, and picked the ferret up to toss her gently back onto the bed where she bounced around crazily with her fur on end, chuckling until she was exhausted and flopped flat as a ferret-fur rug across the nearest pillow.

"Well, I guess you're ready for bed, then," I muttered, scooping the limp animal up and depositing her in her travel cage. She flounced into her nest of old sweatshirt fabric while I finished setting up the cage. I could hear her issuing tiny ferret snores by the time I'd returned with her filled water bottle and food dish.

I shed my clothes onto the furniture and burrowed into my own ferret-disarrayed bed, falling asleep as quickly as Chaos had. I had a lot to do in the morning. . . .

FOUR

Six hours of sleep was less than I'd wanted, but I needed to start early since it was Friday and I wanted to get the paper trail wrapped up quickly enough that I could get back up into the mountains before dark. I did as much of a workout as I could manage in a hotel room with no equipment; then I showered and dressed while running interference in the ferret's plans for world domination through shoe theft.

I got to the Clallam County courthouse as the building opened for the day. The modern low-rise of glass and concrete was just behind and around the corner from the graceful brick-and-marble edifice of the original courthouse that had been converted into a small museum. All current county offices and services were housed in the new building, and every person who'd come to court, gotten married, lost his house to tax foreclosure, or come to file a death certificate had left shreds of emotion behind, until the modern cement buildings had accrued a thin, constant cloud of Grey energy. The new building was well lit with skylights and windows, but it still had a touch of gloom to it under the drizzling clouds.

Even though all the offices I needed were in the same building, it took most of three hours to confirm that there was no death certificate for Steven Leung and to get through the tax and property records for his house. No one was obstructive, but the county was, like all counties in

Washington at the moment, short-staffed to begin with and missing a few more who'd been furloughed for budget reasons or started their weekend a day early. The people who were at their desks were buried in paperwork and most were doing someone else's job as well as their own, trying to wrap up as much up as possible before four thirty. As I searched for information, I kept seeing the flutter of otherworldly flames at the edges of my vision. I couldn't quite catch a glimpse of Steven Leung, though. He seemed to have faded to the thinnest remains of a ghost—even more ragged than the mysterious Anna Petrovna had been before she vanished from my room the night before.

The assessor's office, where Leung had worked, kept track of property taxes, but with so much staff doubling up, I struck it lucky—the clerk in charge of deeds and property records was also the acting tax assessor's clerk. Property deeds and taxes are public records, so he was able to confirm that the house was still in Leung's name and that the property tax payments were up-to-date via automated payments direct from his bank.

The clerk gave me the location of the parcel on which Leung's house sat. I glanced at the slip of paper where he'd written the information and shook my head. "I'm afraid I'm not familiar with the area. Where is this?"

"It's up by the lakes." He pulled out a map of property lines and land parcels and opened it on a nearby table, passing a finger over the printed terrain until he came to the area around Lake Crescent.

On the map the big lake looked like the silhouette of a Chinese dragon puffing out a ball of flame in the direction of downtown Port Angeles. I followed his finger across the top of the dragon's head, past the stretch of East Beach Road where I'd seen the phantom of Leung's burning car, and across the highway to the irregular, elongated shape that seemed to have been spat from the dragon's mouth.

The clerk tapped the map. "Right here on Lake Sutherland. Just head up to Lake Crescent and turn left at the sign for Lake Sutherland Road. Pretty country even at this time of year, especially if you can be up on that end of the lakes when the sun's going down."

My interest was definitely piqued since I didn't recall anything unusual from my last viewing of the lake. "Does something happen at sundown?"

"If the clouds break right, the sun shines through a low point in the surrounding hills and turns the surface of the water pink and red and orange just before it goes under the horizon. It's right pretty, but you can't see it any other time of the year." He made a circle on the map with his fingertip, covering the western edge of Lake Sutherland and over onto the northeastern shore of Lake Crescent. A distant, muffled roaring sounded in my ears and the flickering flames that teased the corners of my vision grew brighter for a moment as the clerk said, "Someone tried to name the area 'Sunset Lakes' once a long time back when they opened up the first leg of the highway, but it didn't stick since you can't see the phenomenon during the warmer months. People don't want to hang around to watch the sunset when they're freezing their hind ends off," he added with a chuckle. "Even back in the day, tourists were big business. Not like the area's had a lot of settlement up there. Mostly lumbering in the early days, fishing, a bit of mining for a while, but not much, and the whole area's pretty much shut down from the end of October through April, when the resorts start opening up. A few hardy types live up there the entire time, but it's mostly just summer places and the big lodges in the national park property."

"Any idea if Steven Leung lived there full-time after he retired?" I asked.

He thought about it for a moment. "I'm not sure. It's hard to get by on a retirement salary if you have to pay rent in town *and* a mortgage at the lake, so I'd guess he did, but I don't know."

"Did you know him while he was working here?"

"Only to nod to. He started out in the surveyor's office and transferred here when he started slowing down a bit. But he still did a lot of the physical work on assessments

and I didn't work directly for the assessor then, so I didn't
see a lot of him. Seemed like a nice fella, but kind of quiet,
as I remember."

"Unrelated topic: Do you have any title records for a
Darin Shea?"

He looked but could find nothing to show Darin Shea
had any ownership or interest in any land in Clallam
County. Not that I'd expected any—roving handymen aren't
the sort to invest in real estate.

The clerk couldn't supply much more information on
Leung, either, and his paperwork was backing up while he
was chatting with me. I reluctantly let him go back to it. I
had a bad feeling about what I would hear next, but still I
went down the hall to discover what I could about Leung's
retirement checks.

The treasurer's office was responsible for the retirement
payments, and though the woman managing disbursements
wouldn't give me specifics, she was willing to confirm that
the payments still went out every month, direct-deposited
to Leung's credit union account—another case of no human hands touching a check. . . .

I wondered what happened when people died and how
long it took for the county to demand the overpayments
back from the family of the deceased. Her answer was complicated and not very reassuring. It seemed all too easy for
a dead man to keep receiving his pay until some other
authority—usually the IRS—got nosy. It occurred to me
that if Steven Leung had been dead for the past five years,
even a small retirement payment would add up to a big
chunk of money. If he'd been killed, would that—and the
taxes—have been worth the cost of murder?

I kept on poking, though I turned my focus mostly on
Darin Shea. I tried the licensing bureau, the office of business taxes, the DMV . . . but I couldn't find anything more
on Leung that I didn't have already; nor could I find any
paperwork for Shea, not even a suspended driver's license.
Neither man had any criminal record or fingerprints on file
that the county resources could turn up. That didn't surprise

me for Leung, but I had to hope I could find a crack in Shea's blank wall before Nan went to trial with him. I had to admit, though, that I was less interested in Shea than in Leung's disappearance.

Once I was done with the county offices, I went searching for a place to have lunch and compile my notes before I drove up into the mountains that loomed over Port Angeles. As I headed back to my truck, I mentally damned the systems that both invaded our privacy and made it possible for a man missing or dead for five years to continue to collect his stipend and pay taxes. Money is a remarkable motivator and unpaid taxes would have gotten someone looking for Leung a lot earlier than this, but with no human actually cashing or cutting a check, the organizations most likely to kick up a fuss and cause trouble hadn't even noticed. And someone may have profited by that.

I had coffee and a bite to eat at a tiny place called the Veela Café, while Chaos hung her head over the top of my bag and did her best to look cute and wheedle crumbs. The manager blinked at the ferret and then made a point of not seeing her as she handed over my plate.

"You might want to sit in the corner by the computer desks," she said, "so nobody gets freaked-out by your ... toy."

"Thank you. That sounds fine," I replied, taking the plate and sitting where she suggested, far from the window and slightly screened from the other patrons. I supposed she was concerned for her food-handling license, or possibly the reaction of other customers—some people mistake ferrets for rats and that wouldn't do her business any good. If it hadn't been so cold, I could have eaten outside, but today I would have frozen, so I was grateful for the woman's restraint and generosity. Once we were in our corner, I fed Chaos part of the meat from the sandwich. I'd have to give her some more food and water when we were somewhere more appropriate, but for now it was adequate to convince the furry kneesock that she wasn't hungry enough to eat my purse.

The Veela Café was just off the major intersection of the original downtown. The buildings were old brick and masonry from the days when Port Angeles was a thriving customs port exporting lumber and minerals from the hills. The customhouse had long since moved, the lumber was protected forest, and the minerals were mostly gone, so the businesses that now occupied the old buildings ranged from the traditional to the bizarre. My little coffeehouse was sandwiched between a fancy seafood restaurant and a shop that catered to fans of the Twilight books and films. Across the street was the venerable Lincoln Theater—now showing second-run films and community production plays—cheek by jowl with a Chinese restaurant of the red-paint-and-gilt-trim school. The eclectic collection made me smile a little even though the businesses were outnumbered by For Lease signs. County seat or not, Port Angeles, like a lot of towns on the Peninsula, was struggling under the unstable economy. It was a little depressing. By the time I'd finished eating, I was more than ready to head into the hills and look for the house. The ghost images in the corners of my eyes were growing dimmer and that worried me. While phantoms do fade over time or simply go away, they rarely do so at such a discernible rate of decay; they either linger and dwindle or they go completely in one fell moment.

Anxious to find an explanation for the vanishing spirits, I cleared up quickly. Then I put my notes and the ferret away, returned to the Rover, and pointed it up the road to Lake Crescent.

FIVE

Highway 101 hadn't changed since I'd driven up and down it a few days earlier, but I found myself alert for signs of the strange and ghostly. Not that they would be easy to spot through the glass and steel of the truck, but I felt unsettled by what I'd seen so far and the information I'd gathered. I kept expecting something else weird to happen.

Perhaps that was why I noticed the creatures beside the road. I knew that deer, bears, and the rare mountain lion lived in the Olympic National Forest. I'd seen plenty of deer on the previous trip and they didn't have any real fear of people—which wasn't too smart of them, considering that they weren't immune to bullets or speeding cars. They came right down into the ditches on each side of the road to graze the early plants that struggled up where the frost was thinnest next to the heat of the tarmac. At first, that was what I thought the things walking around on the other side of the road were—some kind of deer.

They walked on four legs and they had black horns, but deer aren't white all over like these things and their faces are long and narrow with the horns near the fronts of their skulls. These creatures were hard to keep my eyes on; I felt an unnatural desire to turn my gaze aside, and that alone gave them away as something paranormal. I wanted to get a better look, but I admit I was a little scared and wanted to observe them with caution.

The road was a single lane in each direction, but the verges were broad enough to pull into if you didn't fear the ice, so I stopped the truck on one of the wide spots and turned in the driver's seat to look back at the cluster of three large, white-hided, crook-horned things on the other side of the road. I couldn't tell too much about them through the glass, nor could I tell whether the area had the same strange, colored patches and lines of energy that I'd seen at the lake before, so I cranked down my window and peered at them through the Grey.

The ground seemed dappled with colored shadows that moved and re-formed without a visible source, the uncanny puddles of energy pooling most thickly near the white creatures. At first, the beasts ignored the Rover, continuing to walk a ragged circle around something in their midst. Their shape and movement had given me the impression that they had four legs, but when one of them reared up to bat at whatever they were surrounding, I realized they were two-legged creatures with a bent, brachiating posture. Their unusually long forelimbs ended in hands that sported black claws that dripped colors in the Grey. The one that rose up stopped walking and kept its weight on three of its limbs while it swiped with the fourth and made a shrieking noise like a heron caught in a wood chipper.

The thing they circled lurched aside, and another of the white creatures screamed at it and poked it back into the middle of their circle with its own raised forelimb. Their motion reminded me of school yard bullies shoving a smaller child around during recess. I opened my car door and stepped out onto the icy ground to get a better view, letting myself slide a little deeper into the Grey in hopes of figuring out what these things were.

One of my feet brushed a strand of wayward energy as I put it down. The third white creature suddenly jerked its head up in my direction, snorting as if it could smell me. The other two ignored it for a moment while they kept on tormenting their prey, shoving it back and forth while the third stared toward me.

Even at the width of the highway I could see that its eyes were tiny black coals under a heavy brow ridge, the kinked black horns growing out from its forehead like a cat's whiskers. It had the jaw of a bulldog and a complement of sharp, hooked fangs. It squealed and rose onto its haunches to slap at its nearest fellow, thin strands of red light flaying outward from its claw tips.

Suddenly, all three white things were staring at me and sitting stone still. Their quarry, forgotten, slumped to the ground in a mist of miserable green and scuttled away into the trees. It looked like a person dressed in black, but it moved like a spider along the strands of the energy web, and the sight made me shudder. On the seat behind me, Chaos exploded out of my bag and bounded toward the open door, scrabbling up my back and onto my shoulder. She made a harsh hissing noise into my ear and I jerked my head aside, breaking eye contact with the monsters across the street.

They let out a collective bark of excitement and leapt forward. A whining sound, like a generator winding up, vibrated through the Grey. Chaos barked back and tried to jump to meet them. I cursed and snatched her out of the air, diving back into the truck as the three . . . things halved the distance between us in two bounds. I slammed the door shut behind me. I shoved the ferret into my sweater and mashed down on the door lock—I wasn't sure how much like hands those big white paws were, but I didn't want to find out.

I'd just snapped the seat belt closed around me and the wiggling ferret and was twisting the key in the ignition when all three hit the outside of the Rover, rocking it hard. The engine caught and I yanked it into gear. The wheels thudded down again onto the dirt, throwing the truck forward and onto the road. Ice from the roadside spattered onto the surface. I tromped on the accelerator and felt the truck shudder before it dug into the road and leapt forward, racing up the hill toward Lake Crescent with the white things chasing after us.

I passed a sign for a general store with an arrow pointing to the right before I even registered the clearing it stood in. I didn't turn or stop. I figured it was safer to try to outrun the creatures than possibly drag them into the path of innocents. A few yards later, I glanced in the mirror and saw no sign of the white things. I dropped my speed a little to make a curve, half expecting them to bound out of the trees, but they didn't reappear. I didn't take the turn to Lake Sutherland but drove past, heading for the stretch of road next to Lake Crescent where the cliffs press in on one side and the lake on the other; the monsters would have to come out of cover there if they were still pursuing me.

The road remained empty behind and ahead. The white creatures had vanished into the forest.

I pulled into the first driveway I came to and turned the truck around before unbuckling my seat belt and removing the very agitated ferret from my clothes. Chaos glared at me and chittered her disgust. "Sorry, but you looked like you wanted to go have it out with those things and I don't think you would have won that fight." The ferret just wriggled around in my grip and scratched at my hand. I fought with her for a moment but managed to get her snapped into her harness and leash before stepping out of the truck for a breath of air; the fuzz butt wasn't the only one who'd nearly had the poop scared out of her.

Here, too, the strange manifestation of the Grey was evident in patches of color on the ground and a constant buzz from the grid far below, as if a hive of wasps went about their business beneath my feet. It seemed to bother Chaos less than it did me. We took a short walk around the picnic tables at what turned out to be a ranger station so I could calm my nerves and Chaos could heed the call of nature. The restrooms next to the parking lot were unlocked but no warmer than the outside air; I envied the ferret her natural fur coat as much as her ability to ignore the freakish behavior of the Grey. I noticed the little animal had given me a few scratches and made a mental note to clip her claws before I foolishly shoved her into my shirt again; given the magical state of the place, I feared I'd be doing that a lot. I was wishing I hadn't brought her along after all, but it was a little late to change the fact. After I cleaned myself up a bit, I fed the ferret and let her run around on her leash while I wondered just what the hell the creatures were that we'd seen.

They had a physical presence, so they weren't ghosts and they definitely weren't any animal I'd ever seen before alive or dead. Their movement reminded me of gorillas, but nothing else about them was apelike. Their faces were closer to those of dogs, but not really, and their horns looked almost like sharpened, burned branches. Their white hides were like a deer's shaggy winter coat; still short-haired, but thick, scruffy, and unkempt. I hadn't had much time to notice a smell, but, thinking about it, I remembered an odor as they rammed the truck—a bit like skunk and a bit like doused campfires. They were paranormal things for certain, but what type was still beyond me. They reminded me of hyenas: Not as intelligent as a human, they were still coordinated and smart enough to communicate and work together. They were fast, but they hadn't outrun the Land Rover, so either they couldn't, which I hoped was true, or they had decided to cut their losses. That made me queasy.

I'll be honest: I'd rather face a strong but stupid foe than a smart and vicious one of any size. I hoped they would prove to be passing apparitions, but I somehow doubted it. I'd have to figure out what they were before we met again. I wondered if they could have had any hand in Leung's disappearance. The thought didn't please me; if they'd been around five years ago, were they visiting again or had they stayed here all that time? How had they gotten here and what were they doing? Were they doing it for themselves, or under the direction of someone else? It was unlikely that the strangeness of the Grey here and the presence of such monstrosities were unconnected, but which was the chicken and which the egg? Everywhere I turned on this case I got more questions and fewer answers.

I kicked at a hump of crystallized snow that had banked

up next to a tree trunk and watched it shatter and crumble.
Chaos ran to challenge the snow to a fight, hopping up and
down in her weasel war dance and then biting the frozen
mess when it wouldn't play. She made a gagging sound and
spit out the mouthful of snow.

"Don't you know you're not supposed to eat dirty snow?"
I asked her, bending to pick her up.

The ferret gave me a look that clearly said she had
judged my intelligence and found it lacking. But she still
stuck her nose up against mine and tickled me with her
whiskers before attempting to climb up my scarf and under
my hair. I let her, and she flopped onto my shoulder and
sighed, tired out from her explorations and frosty battles.

"OK, stinky, you can sleep in the truck while I do some
more work. And this time, no teasing the monsters."

She just huffed at me. I got back into the Rover, carefully
tucking her into the travel cage in the rear compartment,
and drove back down the highway to the Lake Sutherland
turnoff.

I turned right just past the East Beach Road intersection
beside a double row of mailboxes mounted on a wooden
frame. I drove up a low hill until Lake Sutherland Road
petered out into a dirt track that burst out of the trees into
an open area that seemed to have been scraped clean of
vegetation. I followed the packed dirt until it entered another stand of trees with the glimmer of water beyond. A
small sign at the edge of the trees had a number on it and
the words FISHER POINT/FISHER COVE. I could make out the
roof of a house below the thickly treed rise, so it must have
been right down on the lakeshore, which was now below the
naked hillock I'd driven onto. There wasn't a mailbox—it
was probably among the collection at the edge of the
highway—but the number on the sign matched the parcel
number the assessor's clerk had provided me, so I guessed
that this was Leung's place.

I left the Rover at the tree line and walked down the rise
a little, toward the roof I'd spotted. I stepped onto a wide
wooden walkway that had been built through the trees

toward the faded-yellow house. When I reached the building, I could see it was a two-story affair with its top floor level with the bluff top and the lower one sitting on a platform on the shore, just above the water. The upper walkway crossed a short gap at the edge of the bluff to a deck that encircled the top story of the house. There was no other way down that I could see from there, short of a rough scramble along the bluff itself, so I walked across onto the deck and toward what I thought of as the front door.

I noticed that a couple of the deck boards had rotted a bit, but the rest of the path and upper level were otherwise in good shape. I guessed they hadn't been maintained recently but were well built enough to stand up to the abuses of time and weather. Snow had collected beneath the walkway, but the deck was clear, in spite of the forest shadow that fell on the house from the bluff side.

The red-painted front door faced west, into the trees. There wouldn't be a view of the famous sunset from Leung's house. I knocked on the door and got no answer, not even the rustling of startled birds. I would have peered through the nearest window, but all of them had been covered with winter storm shutters long ago. The house gave every appearance of being closed up on a long-term basis. I walked around to the side of the deck that faced the lake and glanced up and down the shoreline from my second-story vantage.

The shoreline of Lake Sutherland was lined with mostly small, older houses on the west and south. Larger, newer houses dominated the north and east shores with signs of a larger development at the northeast bend of the lake. Almost every house had a dock and a large porch or deck facing the water. The water-facing side of Leung's house was typical: more open, grand, and welcoming than the land-facing side, making the lake the focal point of life in the house. Most of the houses were shuttered at this time of year, just like Leung's. A few wood or fiberglass dinghies rested upside down on blocks along the abandoned docks, sheltering thin white patches of unmelted snow beneath them. I could make out the wide swath of a public boat launch beyond the big development on the northeast, but there were no boats out on the lake today and the water had a strange, submerged luminescence.

A fast look through the Grey didn't reveal a lot more from such a distance. The same strange shadows and threads lay on the ground and shore as I'd seen at Lake Crescent, but fewer of them, and the buzzing of the grid seemed softer at this lake. I did spot a bright strand of blue energy deep below the water's surface, connected to the shore on the east by a fan of silvery lines and smudges like glowing fingerprints and the spiderweb shape of windshield cracks. It would take a closer investigation to discover what the smears and threads were, and I didn't have the equipment to dive or row to them. I supposed I *might* still have some ability to grab a hold of such things, but . . . I let it go for now and turned my attention back to Leung's home.

I looked around the shore and the bluff on each side of the house and spotted a clearing in the trees just south of the house and facing the lake. It would have been impossible to see from almost any other angle along the shoreline. Dark shadows seemed to have drifted up on the ground in the clearing, defying the light that still penetrated through the trees. It wasn't moving, but there was something decidedly Grey about the spot, and I thought I'd best take a closer look, since I clearly wasn't going to get into the house.

I circled the house and found a staircase that led down to the lower deck a few feet above the water. From there I spotted a short set of steps that let me out onto the shore. The shore wasn't sandy but was made of mud and gravel and occasional larger stones. The short stretch of open shore just south of the house had been flattened a bit, leaving a hidden space big enough to drag up a couple of small boats or kayaks. A steep path of gravel and stones pretended to be a natural runoff beside the house, zigzagging from the shelf on the shore to the clearing, but the larger stones were too evenly spaced to be accidental, no matter how well they were camouflaged by the smaller gravel around them. I started for the makeshift stair.

"Looking for the owner, y'won't have much luck. It's just summer places round here." I knew that New England drawl. . . .

I spun to my left, seeking the voice's owner, and saw Darin Shea standing on the shore beside the next house to the south. He was wearing the same olive green parka and dirty work jeans as he had the first time we'd met and he kept his hands in the jacket pockets while he knocked his heavy hiking boots against the ground, shaking off a crust of icy mud. His aura was, as before, a weird mix of blue and gray with spikes of red, as if the world offended him in some degree and he was going to small talk it into submission.

"Hello again, Mr. Shea. You know the owner?" I asked, stopping where I was.

"That's Mr. Leung's place," he said, sauntering toward me. "Ain't seen him in a while, but the house is all wintered up. Safe guess he ain't around." He stopped a few feet from me, nodding as if we were just meeting for the first time. "Nice place, yeah?"

"Seems it," I agreed, slightly put off by his slow-paced chattiness once again. "Do you do any work for the Leungs?" I asked.

"Nah. His daughters and son-in-law watch out for the house."

"Do his daughters live nearby?"

"Yup."

I've rarely wanted so much to brain someone with a heavy object. Plainly he didn't feel like giving me the information yet. I tried a different tack. "Any idea when Leung left?"

Shea shrugged again. "Nope."

"So . . . you're staying on the lake?"

"Yes and no. I'm house-sitting one of my projects." He waved in the direction of the southeastern shore. "Down there a ways."

He had indicated south of the strange underwater lines,

but not on them. I considered asking him about the clearing, but if he wasn't volunteering information, I wasn't sure I wanted to call his attention to either thing. I didn't like the way Shea had just turned up, what with his weird aura and no visible way to have arrived here. I hadn't heard an engine, or a door, and I didn't see a boat at the dock or any footprints on the deck of the house behind him, though his boots had been muddy enough to leave some. There was also no boat in sight, and I didn't think he'd walked on water or scrambled down from the tree line above without making a sound. With the oddness of the world-in-between around here, I wouldn't have been surprised if he'd turned out to be a ghost. I wasn't sure why it felt so strange to meet him here, but it just seemed . . . odd.

"What business y'got with Mr. Leung?" he asked.

"My own business." Shea's eyes went a little cold and flat as I said it, as if he were about to do something I wouldn't like. I continued. "Just trying to find him; nothing sinister. But he's not here, so . . . I guess I'll ask his daughters." I turned and stepped back onto the deck, away from Shea, starting toward the stairs to the upper story, then turned back in a rush, expecting to catch him moving. But he was just standing the same way, with his hands back in his pockets. "You couldn't tell me where I could find them, could you?"

He chuckled, dismissing whatever danger he'd thought I posed. "Don't think you're too likely to catch up to Willa. Might have more luck with the older one, Jewel. You might not want to dawdle getting to her—folks say she's dying, though she's been doing it a while now." Shea didn't look broken up, and I thought I saw the tiniest flick of a smile pull one corner of his mouth as he said it. "She and her husband've got a big house on Lake Crescent. Ask anybody—they'll show you. I gotta get back 'fore the light goes." But he didn't turn to go. He held still and watched me go up the stairs and across the upper deck.

I'd have to come back once he'd left. I wanted a look at that clearing without Shea or anyone else around, but I didn't think he'd hang about long if he was seriously worried about getting home before dark; the shadows were already lengthening. I got back into the Rover and drove out to the highway, pulling in at the general store I'd passed when escaping the white monstrosities by the side of the road earlier. I checked on Chaos, who was still sleeping in her nest of sweatshirts, before turning the truck around and returning to Lake Sutherland Road. I left the Rover farther out this time, at the very edge of the scrubbed-clear space ahead of Leung's home, and walked along the edges of the tree line to get back to the house on the lake. Twilight had dyed the overcast sky ink blue and leached the colors of the world to indigo and navy with odd patches of bone white where the rocky ground was naked of cover. The trees around me looked like charcoal smudges and I found the footing treacherous in shadow.

Nervous about what might happen, I let myself sink into the Grey where the world between worlds was bright with silvery mist and colored lines. I braced for any attack, noise, or the invading reach of the magical grid. But aside from the rattling whispering of the grid and the muttering of ghosts, nothing came for me this time. I couldn't see the lakes, but the whole area within my view was like a more intense version of what I'd seen on the shore of Lake Crescent a few days earlier: Strange bolts of colored light shot horizontally through the mist, dodging the shadow-shapes of corporeal trees and diving suddenly downward toward the lake. Something gave a sharp laugh that came from no human throat, but no shape loomed from the Grey fog with it.

Ghost whispers grew louder as I worked my slow way back to the house, skirting the time-worn memory of the trees, and fell away as I emerged just south of the house, on the edge of the rise. I saw no sign of Shea or anyone else living—though there was a thin, boiling fog of ghosts along the shore. I caught my breath while my heart settled back into a normal pace.

I made my way to the hidden clearing next to the house

with the quietest tread I could muster on the frosty loam, touching trees as I went, as if they would protect me from danger. Even out of the Grey, the effects I'd seen as I approached lingered. The lake below and the wooded hill I moved across seemed menacing and otherworldly in the still, cold dusk with a strange, sparkling light flickering from deep below the lake's surface. I stopped at last at the edge of the weird clearing, peering at it through the Grey.

A hair-thin line of blue energy encircled the clearing and a thin sheen of silver stretched over the ground within, unmarred by other energy colors or strands of magic. The dark shadows I'd spotted before still lay there, and just beyond them a roiling haze of color with no defined shape that seemed to be tied to the circle in some way I couldn't see. I stayed on the outside of the circle and moved around, trying to figure out the configuration of the shadows and colors and if they were meaningful. But the more I studied it, the more it looked as if the persistent Grey shadows were the residue of people working magic here for a long time, and some hadn't bothered to clean up after themselves.

I pulled out my pocketknife and flipped open the long blade—it wasn't ideal, but I thought it would do in a pinch—and squatted down. Then I drew the blade through the hairline of energy, breaking the circle's edge. The Grey sighed a little, the colored haze dispersed, and the circle dimmed a bit, but nothing spectacular happened. Nothing active was going on there. That was fine with me. I stepped into the clearing proper and started looking for clues to the area's purpose. Magic, of course, but to what end and what kind? I didn't see the angry red and black accumulations of blood magic or necromancy, but the feel of the place was unsettling nonetheless, like unseen cobwebs fluttering against my face.

I poked at the dark hummocks of Grey shadow, trying to get an idea of what they were. One of them felt cold and wet and sharp against my fingertips, a bit like the edges of a temporacline. I put my hand flat on that one and pushed on it, careful not to step into it if it should suddenly open into a layer of time. The dark thing unfolded and I could glimpse a bent view of something happening in the circle sometime in the past.

A figure too warped to discern was casting a spell of some kind, holding up a rectangular metallic object and slowly moving it over a bowl with great effort, as if it weighed more than it possibly could. The mage struggled a bit with it. A second figure, something wavering and bright, not human, joined the first, seeming to step into it and add a green, energetic glow to their combined shape. The joined figures dropped the metal oblong with a grunt and it splashed heavily into the bowl, sending up a huge gout of liquid. I could feel it sting my face and I flinched, hoping it wasn't blood or something worse. The figures broke apart and finished their spell, the first chanting and lighting a candle that sparked oddly, before it began sputtering and smoking, then burning furiously until it was just a puddle of dark wax on the gravelly ground. The second withdrew to the edge of the circle, waiting. Once the flame was out, the original magician picked up the bowl and carried it to the edge of the circle, to a hole dug just inside the line, where the contents—including the metal thing—were dumped into the shallow pit and buried. Then the mage scuffed a foot over a dusty-looking symbol on the ground. . . . The loop of memory and magic shuddered to a halt.

I let go of the crumpled bit of time and started looking for the place where the spell's remains had been buried. I found it at the edge farthest from the lake where the dirt that had collected under the trees had become thick over time. It took a bit of digging with my knife and hands, and my fingers were scraped and stinging with cold by the time I found the metal object.

It was the front license plate from Steven Leung's car, badly rusted, burned, and bent but recognizable. From the condition, I assumed the plate had been on the Forester when it had burned, so the mage had taken it off the car afterward. I frowned, not sure what the spell had been meant to do. . . . I shivered and stood up, holding on to the license plate. I was too cold and not just a little paranoid about the place to want to risk hanging around in someone's magic circle any longer. I kicked dirt back over the hole and tramped it down, covering it with a scatter of junk and gravel. It wouldn't deceive anyone who took a good look, but it would stand a casual glance, especially from a distance. Tucking the license plate into my jacket, I made my way back to the Rover as fast as discretion would allow.

It was full-on dark and beginning to sprinkle by the time I got to the truck. I could hear a few nocturnal creatures moving about in the forest, heading for cover from the incipient rain, which made the place seem a little more normal. I just hoped none of them were the white things. There was nothing unusual near the truck and I was grateful to get inside and leave the area. I still wasn't sure what the spell I'd observed in the crumpled bit of Grey memory was meant to do, but my best guess would be that it somehow hid or moved Leung's burned car where it had, so far, gone undiscovered. If I could figure out where, I might be able to lead the authorities to the car and lay the ghost to rest.

The road back to Port Angeles hadn't changed, but it seemed lonelier and more dangerous in the wet and the dark. I kept an eye out for the white creatures, but I saw no sign of them, and I got back to the hotel without further strange events.

Chaos, having napped while I'd scrabbled in the dirt, was ready to run around the hotel room. I preferred to take a hot shower and check the damage to my hands. It wasn't bad—mostly scratches and a couple of ragged fingernails— but I was more tired than I'd expected. The lake was only at five hundred feet or so, but the thinner air and the adrenaline burn of being chased, as well as my paranoia and effort in the Grey, had taken a toll I wasn't used to. I was out of practice at being a Greywalking hard-ass. Of course, I'd probably feel better once I dressed and ate. Before I could do that, I'd have to call the Danzigers and see if they could make any suggestions about unraveling the meaning of the loop of magical memory I'd watched up at Leung's lake house.

The ferret had no such problem with priorities; she was busy slurping up water and crunching kibbles while I dressed. Apparently she'd started by hiding some food for later . . . in my boot. I dumped the crushed stash into the wastebasket while she ignored me. To hell with it—I would emulate my pet and eat first. The Danzigers were probably having their own dinner now, anyway.

My hotel didn't have a restaurant, but there were several in walking distance, and though the early darkness made it seem much later than it was, they were all open. I promised the ferret a longer romp when I got back and took myself out for food.

When I returned, Chaos gave me the poor-pathetic-ferret look, lying flat on the bottom of the travel cage and sighing at me, but she ruined the effect by bouncing up and wiggling impatiently as I opened the cage door to let her out again. She danced around, nipping at my toes and chuckling as I sat down on the edge of the bed to call Ben and Mara.

"Ouch," I said as someone answered the phone.

"Pardon?" asked Mara.

"Hi, Mara. The ferret nipped me."

"Have you been insisting on wearing your shoes yourself instead of letting her have them?" Ben and Mara had been stuck ferret-sitting for a while last year and they were well aware of her kleptomaniacal shoe fetish.

"Yes."

"Well, you know how she gets about that."

"To my toes' eternal, ferret-gnawed sorrow, yes."

Mara whooped a laugh, easing the discomfort I'd felt ever since I'd gone up the mountain. She wasn't given to decorous, careful enjoyment; if she was amused, she let her pleasure out into the world, wide and open for anyone to share. "You'll be hobbling come summer if you don't give in." She chuckled.

I tucked my sock-clad feet up under my hips and out of the dancing weasel's way. "Pray for sandal weather."

"Aside from the depredations of carpet sharks, how've you been?"

"Still a little sore and slow, but I'm back to work full-time. I'm out at Port Angeles right now and I wanted to ask you some questions about something I saw."

"Would it be geology or magic?"

"Magic, though geology might enter into it, I suppose." Since I was the expert on the Grey itself, there was no point in asking her what might be causing the strange colors and streaks I'd been seeing at the lake. It might be linked to something geologic, but the manifestation was something only I would know about. So I stuck with the most immediate questions.

"Just a moment, then." Mara moved her mouth away from the phone and called out to Ben to keep an eye on their son, Brian, while she spoke to me a while longer. "All right, then. What was it you saw?"

"I found a dormant spell circle—someone's been using it over a long period of years, so it's worn a pattern into the Grey—that had a strange accumulation of memories, but they weren't like regular temporaclines. They were more like residue that hadn't been cleaned off, kind of crumpled up and piled around the edges."

"That's slovenly of them."

"Convenient for me, though. I was able to replay part of one of them and I'm trying to figure out what was done. An object was moved somewhere and hidden by magic, but I don't know where and I need to find it. Can I tell that from what I saw in the image?"

"Possibly, depending on the spell and the residue. How big an object are you talking about now?"

"A car."

"Oh. I'd imagine something that size would take a bit of doing. What sort of spellcraft was it?"

"Well, that's what I'm not sure of. I didn't see the setup, but there seemed to be some candles, some designs drawn in powder or herbs or salt, a bowl of water, and a piece off the car. I couldn't see the spell-caster very well, so I don't know the sex or race, but he or she had some kind of magical help—like a double or a ghost of some kind—that lent some additional . . . lifting power to the spell near the end. They picked up the metal from the car and dropped it into the bowl of water. It looked like the movement took a lot of energy and was difficult for the magician alone, so the other one pitched in. Once the metal was in the bowl, one of them lit a candle—dark but I couldn't say what color— that burned down abnormally fast. When they were done, the human one buried the water and the metal in the circle and then smudged out the power symbols. What does that sound like?"

"No blood or body parts?" Mara asked.

"No, I'm glad to say."

"Well, it's kitchen magic of some kind."

"Like . . . what *you* do when you're cooking?" I asked, uncertain.

"Oh no. It's a category of spell work that's done with herbs, candles, household items. . . . It's symbolic and sympathetic: An object stands in for the one you want to effect, and the herbs or powders you use in casting the spell, drawing the symbols, anointing the candles, and so on, influence varying elements and actions in the world. It's the sort of working that led to alchemy and modern pharmacology. So when your caster moved the bit of the car into the bowl of water, he was moving the car into a body of water—or asking for some spirit to do it for him."

"So the car's in a body of water?"

"If the spell worked. And judging by your description of the candle's burning down, it most likely did. The candle represents work or effort turned to your task—though you should also be looking for the source of that much power as well. Was it a very fat candle?"

I thought about it. "Yes, I think it was. And dark colored."

"So you said. May have been black, which can mean a lot

of things, but certainly it would imply that your caster wanted to obscure something. If he'd wanted to reveal a lost thing, he might have used a white candle instead. D'you see?"

"I think I do. So the fatter the candle, the more effort can be put out?"

"Potentially. If the candle burns out before you've got what you wanted done, you can't just light another; it has to be the same candle—or a lot of them—burning continuously from start to finish of your spell work. The spell-caster in this case needed a lot of energy to move something as heavy as a car. So he used a fat candle and got some help, too."

"Who or what was the helper? It glowed green and I was pretty sure it wasn't human—or not a live one at any rate."

"Green? Could be an elemental or some kind of a loa, though I'm not very versed in Voodoo and such. . . ."

"Voodoo?"

"Don't make that face I know you're making. It's a religion, y'know. They call on spirits, called 'loa,' for knowledge and guidance, and the loa speak through human conduits during the ceremony. I don't know much more about it than that except that there are several related religions with slightly different ceremonies and names. But the spell work—it's called 'hoodoo'—is from an even older school and a lot of other practices have adapted it."

I sighed and picked up Chaos, teasing her with the corner of the blanket. "So this unknown person, using a non-specific magic and pulling a lot of power from an unknown source, hid the car in the lake."

"That would be very likely."

"But which lake? There are two."

"Which lake is closer to where the spell circle is?"

"They're both nearby, though one was very close."

"Hm . . . Which one was the caster facing? Which way did he direct the magic?"

"Um . . . west."

"Then it'll be in the lake to the west."

"Damn."

"I take it that's a problem?"

"Yes. The lake to the west is Lake Crescent. It's twelve miles long and I don't know how deep, but pretty deep."

"Well . . . someone truly didn't want that car found, did they?"

"No. . . . Not at all. Mara, one more thing . . ."

"Yes?"

"Do you know of any monsters associated with this sort of kitchen magic? Not just the loa."

"Elementals, I suppose. . . ."

"Any of them look like . . . sort of large, white, horned apes or dogs with hands?"

"Not that I've ever seen. Elementals vary, though. They tend to resemble that from which they're drawn, so a white, horned ape . . . sounds unlikely. At least in the tradition I know. Shall I ask Ben to look through his books?"

"Not right this second," I replied, thinking of the time I'd spend just waiting on hold while Ben sorted through his collections of myth and legend.

Mara laughed again. "Oh no! Not now, indeed! I'll have him try after Brian's gone to sleep, then, shall I?"

"That would be great."

"It'll give him an excuse to find some new stories to frighten the boy with. I swear that child has an evil genius for trouble," she said. "I'm sure I don't know where it comes from."

"Oh no?" I asked. "It couldn't possibly come from having a witch for a mother, a mad paranormal researcher for a father, and growing up in a haunted house?"

"Sha! 'Tisn't haunted anymore! Except by the boy-beast himself."

I chuckled at her. Brian did have a talent for raising Cain, but at least it had mostly been of a normal kind. I thanked Mara for her help and disconnected.

Then I sat frowning over the problem of the car in the lake. If the car was or contained evidence of foul play, hiding it in the depths of Lake Crescent would have been attractive. Normally, I'd have thought the use of magic for such a mundane task as moving a car was ridiculous, but if it meant keeping your secrets between yourself and some spirit you controlled, then it didn't look so utterly wasteful and stupid after all. Even if the wreck had been reported and someone had been sent to look for it on the road, the car would have vanished without a trace—no tire imprints or tow truck records to show how it had disappeared. If the site where I'd seen the image of Leung's burning car had been the actual scene of the accident, it was only a few dozen yards from Lake Crescent, which teemed with wild power. Even a magical lift wouldn't have to move it far.

But no matter how it had gotten there, if Leung's car really was in the big lake, I had no idea how to find it or prove it.

SIX

I started my morning at the Veela Café once again, using one of their ancient computers to look up some information about Lake Crescent and Lake Sutherland. The ethereal flames of Leung's presence kept up a dim flickering in the edges of my vision, fading further the longer I delayed. Sometimes the Internet is not your friend when you want to be reassured about the job at hand. The more I read, the more I wished the car had wound up in Lake Sutherland. The smaller lake's average depth was only 57 feet with a maximum of 86, leaving a possibility of spotting the car, if not of sending divers to it.

Lake Crescent, on the other hand, was huge and its bottom topography mostly unknown. Maximum depth had been given as 624 feet in the 1970s, since that was as deep as the equipment used by the college fisheries project doing the survey could measure. But the depth fell into dispute when a power company had decided to lay cable across the lake. The dropped cable had continued to sink until it hit the equipment's maximum at 1,000 feet, but it still hadn't struck the bottom. Since the lake's surface was at an elevation of 580 feet, the glacially formed lake bottom might lie hundreds of feet below sea level. If Leung's car was in one of the deep crevices, it was gone forever.

I started to go, tucking Chaos down into my bag so she wouldn't attract too much attention. One of the coffeehouse workers walked by, picking up unbused dishes. There were two employees in today—a boy and a girl, both dark-haired, young, and funky-cute, probably high school kids working the weekend shift. The girl paused to take my cup and glanced at the screen I'd left up with the physical information about Lake Crescent.

"I really like your scarf," she said.

It was cold enough outside, even though the sun was out in the watery blue sky, that I'd wrapped an improbable red velvet muffler around my neck under my wool overcoat. It was more froufrou than I usually went for, but it was wide and soft and warm, and I could always put it over my head if the weather turned wetter or colder while I was out in the woods.

"Oh, thanks. It was a Christmas present."

"Figured."

I raised an eyebrow at her. "Oh?"

"Yeah, y'know—the kind of thing you never buy for yourself 'cuz . . . um . . ." She cut herself off, blushing. Then she changed the subject. "So, did you get what you wanted?"

I pulled a rueful face. "Not really. I got information, but it's not heartening."

"Oh? What were you looking for?"

"Hope that something lost might be found."

"Where'd you lose it?"

I laughed a little at her earnest inquiry. "It's not something of mine. It's a client's car. It may have been dumped into Lake Crescent and . . . well, the lake's just too deep to hope anyone can haul the car back up. Nothing's coming back from that lake."

She shrugged and picked up the bus tub she'd been putting dishes into. "Maybe, maybe not. Stuff comes back sometimes. The Lady of the Lake did."

"Who?"

She turned her head and called to the boy behind the counter, who was tinkering with the espresso machine. "Jeff, what was her name, the Lady of the Lake?" She glanced back at me and said, "That's my brother, Jefferson. He's, like, the biggest ghost-story guy you'll ever meet. He knows *everything* about the Lady of the Lake." She rolled her eyes a little, but she was smiling nonetheless.

"Hallie," the boy called back. "Hallie Latham Illingworth."

I looked at the young man and started walking toward him. His sister tagged along with the tub of dirty dishes. It was almost too heavy for her to carry, even half full, but she swaggered under its weight and I didn't dare offer to help her.

"Hi," I said, and offered my hand. "I'm Harper Blaine. Who was Hallie Illingworth?" I asked. Business was a little slow at the moment, so I didn't think anyone would mind if I chatted up the kids.

The young man glanced up from his work on the machine, wiped his hands, and shook mine. "I'm Jefferson Winter. That's my sister, Erika." He was a good-looking kid, with wavy black hair and an unseasonable tan. He barely looked old enough to have a food handler's license and I guessed he was about seventeen. He leaned against the counter and gave me a grin. "Hallie's a legend." I could tell he liked the attention and would probably drag the story out as long as he could, but that was all right with me—for now.

"But it's true," he added, "and it's a real cool story. See, Hallie worked up at the lodge—it's the Lake Crescent Lodge on the park property now, but they called it the Singer Tavern back then. She worked up there in 1937. She was like a cocktail waitress or something. Anyway, she was married to this jerk named Monty Illingworth and they had a totally messed-up relationship."

"Messed up how?" I asked.

"He used to hit her," Erika cut in, carrying the bus tub around the end of the counter toward the kitchen door. "I mean, with a name like Monty, he had to be a real dork. Totally abusive, right?"

Jefferson nodded. "That's what the newspapers said. They lived in an apartment down here in town and they used to keep the neighbors up, fighting and throwing stuff.

Hallie used to show up at work with, like, black eyes and bruises and that." He paused to look over his shoulder as his sister took the dirty dishes into the kitchen. "Hey, Erika, could you bring me the other foaming cup when you come out?"

"Sure," she said, tossing her long dark hair back from her face as she rounded the doorway. "I live to be your minion, y'know."

"You *are* my minion."

Erika scoffed. "Whatevs."

"Yeah, whatever." Jefferson shrugged and looked back at me. "Anyway, so, like, it's Christmastime back in 1937, right?"

I nodded. "OK."

"And Hallie goes home from the tavern after work. It's really late, like eleven or twelve o'clock. And she leaves the lodge . . . and she never came back."

The pronouncement didn't have quite the impact on me that he'd obviously hoped for: I just made a doubtful face at him. "So . . . ?"

Jefferson frowned. "So, like, she doesn't come back, and Monty says she took off with some other guy and everyone's all, 'She musta left that creep and moved away,' and that's what they thought until . . ."

I rolled my eyes, but played along. "Until . . . what?"

"One morning in 1940, these two fishermen are rowing up on the lake near the burned-out remains of the Log Cabin Hotel—that's the far northwest part—and they see this thing floating on the water, so they go get it and it's . . . a body!"

"Hallie."

"Yeah. But here's the good part: She's all turned into soap." He was grinning and his eyes sparkled, kind of undermining the spooky effect he'd probably hoped for.

"Soap?" I asked.

Erika came back from the kitchen with the milk-foaming cup and put it down on the counter beside the espresso machine. "Yeah! Isn't that gross? They must have been all, like, 'What's this?' and then they get her up in the boat and all—"

Jefferson interrupted her. "And they thought it was a hoax, at first, like maybe someone had carved a person out of soap and thrown it in the lake for a joke, except her face and fingers are all eaten off, so they don't know who it is. So they take it down here. And there's this medical student who figures out it's a real dead person and her body fat all turned to soap because the water in the lake is real cold and real pure, and down at the bottom it's more alkaline than at the top, so she saponified and got lighter and then . . . she floated up."

"OK, that's kind of creepy," I agreed.

"It's kind of cool," Jefferson said. "This medical student, he's like that forensic lady on TV and he figures out that someone strangled his soap lady and bashed her head in before they wrapped her up in some old canvas and ropes and dumped the body in the lake. And then he figures out who she is because she has this dental thing in her mouth— he finds the dentist who made it and that guy says, 'Oh yeah, I made that for Hallie Latham.' And everyone says, 'Who'd kill Hallie? Everyone loved her!'"

"Except Monty!" Erika added.

"So Monty strangled his wife and threw her into Lake Crescent," I said, "and three years later—"

"Two and a half," Jefferson corrected. "She died at Christmas in 1937, but the fishermen found her in July of 1940."

I nodded. "All right. Two and a half years later, her saponified body bobbed to the surface of the lake. It's a really weird story, but I don't think my client's car is going to turn into soap and float to the shore of Lake Crescent anytime soon. And *he's* been missing for about five years, now."

"Your client is missing?" Erika asked.

"How do you know the car's in Lake Crescent?" Jefferson asked at the same time.

I ignored Erika's question, because I really didn't want to start down that explanation's road. Instead, I turned my gaze on Jefferson and gave him a slightly crooked smile. "A ghost told me."

They both stared at me for a moment, and I took the opportunity to lay an extra tip on the counter and get out before they could ask any more questions I didn't want to answer.

While it was nice to know that some things do come back from the depths of Lake Crescent, I didn't think it was going to help me prove something bad had happened to Steven Leung. If Leung had been burned as badly as his ghost looked, there wouldn't be enough of him left to turn into soap. I'd have to find another way to draw the right kind of attention to his disappearance.

I got into the Rover and headed back up the mountain. This time I kept a lookout for the white things by the side of the road, but they didn't show up on this trip. With the complexity of the legal jurisdictions that overlapped around the lakes, it wouldn't have been surprising if the case had been mired in buck-passing and paperwork. But there simply had never been a case opened. For some reason no one had said anything to anyone in authority about Leung's disappearance. His daughters were both alive and in the area, according to Darin Shea, but neither of them seemed to have done anything about their missing father—and it seemed strange that they hadn't noticed. Nor had anyone else said anything to the authorities. The small size of the year-round community and the Grey weirdness around the lakes made me think there may have been a more sinister reason for silence than jurisdictional uncertainty. I was going to have to step carefully until I knew what the situation around "Sunset Lakes" really was.

I decided first to take another look at the spell circle near Leung's house and left the Rover in a different location from the last time before walking down. I didn't see any sign of Shea, but I did notice that even in the daylight, the area on the west side of Lake Sutherland had a strong gleam of magic to it—not as colorful as Lake Crescent, but well beyond normal. But this was not the orderly grid configuration I was used to; it was more as if an unseen current running deep between the two lakes created a wellspring in the area that seeped upward until it was detectable as a thinly spread general presence, rather than a single source. The strange glow I'd noticed the previous night was easier to see today, even without sliding into the Grey. I had a harder time seeing the bright bolts of colored energy that had darted around me before; they were there, but not as numerous or energetic, and I couldn't see the spidery white lines in the lake at all from this angle. I was used to an orderly grid of magical feeder lines; what arises from the Grey is shaped by the human minds that manipulate it, so the density of humans in a city might cause the grid to reflect the shape of the city. Here, however, there weren't enough people to push the lines of magic around so easily—or at least that was what made sense to me at the moment.

When I reached the edge of the clearing where the circle was, I was disappointed: Someone had been there and done some cleaning up. The rest of the shadowy memories of spells cast had disappeared, and the circle itself was fading back into the wild stream of magic below the ground. Even the traces of herbs and dust had sunk into the ground or been swept away, so I didn't stand a chance of identifying them.

I swore quietly and at length.

Something crunched and shuffled in the frost-blackened bracken beneath the trees. Then a light voice with an odd undertone of distant rocks grinding together spoke just ahead of its owner appearing at the edge of the clearing. "I have not met him, so I could not say, but I'm quite sure that if Shiva had dog breath, it wouldn't be able to do *that*. But it is a blasphemy I've never heard before. May I keep it?"

I spun around to stare at him, the red tails of my scarf flying. When you're standing beside a magic circle in the woods between one lake that vomits up saponified murder victims and another that's floored with lines of magic, you should expect to see a few strange things. To most people, the strangest thing about this man would have been that he was wearing a European designer suit to go walking in the

forest. To me, it was that he wasn't actually a person—
though he was definitely male. Whatever he was, I guessed
he was some relative of the things I'd seen beside the road
yesterday; in the Grey, his skin was the same shade of otherworldly white and he had a smaller version of the burned-
black-twig horns poking out of his forehead. I preferred
seeing him in the normal, where he looked like a tall Asian
man with unusually red hair and broad shoulders. His eyes
had a disquieting glitter to them in both views, as if reflecting a fire the same unnatural color as his hair.

"You're welcome to it, if you'll tell me who you are," I
said. I didn't think the magic circle belonged to this creature; he didn't look as if he needed anything as crude as
herbs and candles to push magic around, much less magical
protection. Judging from the way strands of blue and yellow
energy reached up from the ground to cling to him, it was
more likely people needed protection from him than the
other way round.

He made a closed-mouth smile that let the impression of
small, curved, interlocking fangs crease his lips from within.
"It's an interesting bargain, since you know I won't tell you
my real name. People here call me Jin, so that will do, if you
like. You are . . . Hm . . . What are you . . . ?"

If I concentrated on the normal, the grinding noise in his
voice faded. I wasn't sure if that meant he had two forms or
was just very good at projecting his normal-world one. But
I did know "normal" wasn't his home.

I gave him a thin smile back. "My name's Harper." I
made a sweeping-up gesture at the fading circle. "Did you
do this?"

"Some people don't take proper care of their things." He
shrugged and his massive shoulders made the stitching at
his armholes strain, and the sound of it made him wince just
a little. He wasn't entirely a projection, then, which was
good and bad for me if we got into a tussle.

"So you know the owner," I said.

"Of course."

"Of the house?"

"Leung? Yes. But he's dead, you know."

"Do I? That doesn't seem to be common knowledge."

"I prefer *un*common knowledge—it's much more interesting than the sort that's lying around everywhere. And more valuable." His eyes gleamed with a light I recognized at once—avarice. I'd have to see what I could do with that....

"How do you know Leung is dead?" He didn't seem to think the fact was worth a lot, since he'd already tossed it at me; I wanted to know what else he considered cheap enough to give away.

"Oh, ghosts," he said with a dismissive roll of his eyes. "They always have something to complain about." It wasn't as much of an answer as I could have liked, but it was interesting, nonetheless. As he said it, something cold brushed through me. Startled, I shivered, shifting my focus to the Grey to see a ghost drifting toward Lake Crescent. It was an old specter, ragged and thin, but it moved toward the western lake as if drawn into the currents of magic, paying us no heed at all and giving me pause. The unconscious way it moved in a straight line through every obstacle intrigued me, but I had something more immediate to deal with and shook my curiosity off for the time being. "Do you have any real proof of Leung's death? Something I can show to someone?"

"Proof? Not the kind you mean. I could tell you who killed him, but you'd have to make it worth my while."

"Then he was killed by another person, not in an accident."

Jin frowned, both versions of his face creasing their brows for a moment and puckering their mouths as if the taste of slipping up was sour. He growled to himself.

"Jin," I continued, "I know the car is in Lake Crescent. I just have to get it out or get someone else to dredge it up."

"I could help you."

I wasn't averse to help, but I was pretty sure any assistance from that quarter came with a price—assuming he could do what he said. On the other hand, that he was wearing a very expensive real suit—not just the image of a suit—made me think he might be a little vain as well as greedy. "Sure you can," I replied with a deprecating smile. "After all, you've been so very helpful so far."

"I told you Leung was dead."

"Which I already knew, but you won't tell me who killed him, because you don't actually know." I started to turn and walk away. "You seem to be good enough to clean up after other people's messes, but you've done nothing to impress me. So far as I know, you're just the garbageman."

Jin bounded to catch up to me in one huge stride reminiscent of the way the white creatures beside the road had moved. "Wait!" He snatched at my nearer wrist and tried to pull me back around to face him.

I twisted my arm and danced sideways, pulling out of his grip and away to a stance that put my feet onto harder, less slippery ground a few feet from him. I flung the end of my scarf back over my shoulder and crossed my arms loosely over my chest. "Wait for what, Jin? My toes to freeze off? Because that's about all I've gained from this conversation so far."

He stood back and regarded me through narrowed eyes. "You want to know where Leung's body is. I can show you."

"I know where his body is. It's in the car, which is at the bottom of Lake Crescent. I'm not about to swim down there to see it, so unless you can pull that sucker up to the surface where I can show it to someone else and *prove* he's dead, you're no damned use to me."

He was still looking speculative. "Why do you want to prove Leung is dead?"

"Because you can't collect on a missing person, only a dead one."

"But I know who killed him."

"And are you going to tell me?"

He made a face. "No."

"See—you're still useless. Who killed him is irrelevant anyhow if I can't prove he's dead in the first place. I can't run off to the police and say some monster in the woods told me so-and-so killed Steven Leung and pushed his car into the lake with him still in it. Oh, yeah, that'll fly."

Jin sniffed in disgust at the word "monster" and muttered something in Chinese under his breath. "If you knew where to look—"

"Exactly."

He heaved an irritated sigh. "If I bring the car up where you can see it, what is that worth to you?"

Now we were at the crux of the problem. What did I have that Jin would want? I didn't think he'd want my scarf, I doubted I had enough cash to interest him, and the sex thing was not—ever—going to be an option. But . . . "I might have some uncommon knowledge. . . ."

Jin barely raised his eyebrows, but in the Grey his eyes glittered and his lips parted just enough to show the tips of his fangs. I love being right. "What would *you* know that I do not?" he asked.

"One or two things . . ."

"From across the water, from Seattle?"

"Yes."

"Hm." Jin fought a smile. "What about the Egyptians? Tell me about them."

"The asetem? Why should you care?"

"That's none of your business. Do you know something or don't you?"

"I know why they came here and why they left."

Jin seemed startled, his eyes opening wider. "They left?"

"There you go—the asetem have left the building."

He frowned; apparently Jin didn't get the reference. "Why? How?"

I shook my head. "No more freebies, Jin. I showed you part of my hand; now you get to show me yours. Let's go get that car and I'll tell you more when it's up where I can see it."

He narrowed his eyes and glared a bit, an expression that

was much uglier on the face with the horns and fangs, though it wasn't a delight on the human face, either. Then he smiled a little and made a formal little nod. "Very well. Do you know East Beach Road?"

"Yes."

"Take me there and I'll show you Leung's car."

SEVEN

I was a little reluctant to have Jin in my truck, but I didn't see an alternative that might not ruin the deal, so I shrugged and led him to the Rover. He made a face as I opened the passenger door for him, and the ferret—who'd been sleeping in her travel cage in the back—pushed her face up against the grille and hissed at him. Then she began pawing at the door and making angry little grunts.

"I don't think she likes you," I observed.

Jin didn't hide his distaste. "The feeling is mutual. Horrible little monster."

"I have my monster; you have your buddies by the road."

"Those pathetic guai? Strays, slip-gates. Not any friends of mine," he added with a sniff.

Even monsters have pecking orders. Apparently, Jin was higher up this mysterious food chain than his brachiating relatives—another tidbit to put in my mental file. If I ever figured out what sort of creature Jin was, it might come in handy. There was nothing I could do to pacify Chaos about his presence in the truck, though, so I ignored the ferret and hoped she wouldn't do herself an injury in her frenzy to take a bite of him. I drove.

The road I was already on turned into East Beach when it crossed Highway 101. About one twisty mile beyond that, Jin told me to stop only a few yards from where I'd first seen the spectral image of Steven Leung's burning Subaru and directed me down a dirt track so narrow and overgrown, it was visible from the paved road only as a thinness between the trees. The truck's paint was going to suffer, but I didn't care to leave the vehicle beside the road and walk this time. I wasn't entirely sure of Jin or what he was leading me into and I preferred to have as many escape options at hand as possible. The narrow way petered out only a few yards from the water. Once we were out of the truck again and standing on the shore of Lake Crescent, I could see a large house with floor-to-ceiling windows off to my left where the lake formed a sharp cove and a scattering of smaller houses along the shore to the right, past the Log Cabin Resort and nearly to the spot where I'd seen the ghastly figure rising from the water a few days earlier. The ghostlight and whispers were as strong as before and the colored energy mist still flowed and puddled along the shore. Straight ahead was nothing but deep, cold water for twelve miles to Fairholm.

Deep as it was, the lake was beautiful, not just along the heavily forested shore in a hundred shades of green, but the water itself was so clear, it reflected and intensified the colors of foliage and sky so the surface seemed to be made of colored glass.

Jin gazed at it with gleaming eyes and began taking off his shoes, revealing long, weirdly clawed feet. He handed the expensive shoes to me without another word and squatted down at the absolute edge of the lake, plucking fussily at the creases in his trousers as the water covered his toes. It must have been icy, but he didn't shiver. His illusory human form faded to a ghostly shroud and he stretched his arms out toward the center of the lake.

Jin crouched, his white monstrousness bizarrely clothed in his Italian suit, chanting in a low voice in a language that rose and fell, rose and fell, breeding lassitude and casting a green glow around him. The emerald energy brightened and burned as he continued to call to it, blues and yellows flowing into it like water from nearby patches of surface energy and the thin shadows of ghosts along the shore. Then he threw his arms out farther and gathered something in, as if bodily grasping the sunken car.

I could feel the strain of magic in my gut and across my skin as I waited, watching, sinking into the Grey to see what Jin was doing. The sun, a glittering disk in the Grey, shifted in the open slice of sky above the lake. Through the clear, colorful water I saw something moving, coming toward us, carried in the bright green energy Jin had cast into the lake. The colors around the thing writhed with strange shadows and as I stared, the green light showed a swarm of horrible, wax white things with gaping, toothy jaws and staring eyes pushing and lifting the shape toward the surface. I held my ground, though I wanted to recoil from the sight of this army of swimming undead coming to Jin's command. Slowly he unbent, standing, then rose to his feet and stepped back from the shore. . . .

The shadowy thing came up, broaching out of the lake like a whale from the sea as the hellish swarm burst to the surface and then plunged back into the depths, flinging their burden toward the shore. It was the car in double image—real and Grey—and it tumbled above the water for a moment before it fell back in only a few yards out from the edge where we stood.

I pulled back to the normal before Jin could see me and studied the car. Though dented and misshapen by pressure, rusted where the paint had burned off, it was still undeniably a Subaru Forester. It sank back into the shallow water on its side, leaving one door just below the surface, the rest covered by the clear water, but still visible.

Jin leaned back against the Rover, reassembling his human appearance in haste as a trio of ghostly shapes shivered and then blinked out of existence beside him as they were sucked away into the lake, leaving a moment's strange silence. In the Grey, Jin was panting a little, but the normal image wore a superior smile. "There is the car."

I made a show of peering toward the hulk in the water, shading my eyes from the sun that was much brighter in the real world, and taking a surreptitious glance at my watch. It seemed ridiculous, but an hour had passed and it was nearing noon. The Grey has a strange way of warping time, but

I felt as if I'd labored every minute of the elapsed time, even though Jin had been doing the real work. "How do I know it's Leung's?" I asked, hiding my own relief that the magic and its ugly cohort had dissipated.

He rolled his eyes and snapped at me. "How many of these do you think there are in this lake? You're oblivious trash-mongers, but even your kind don't go tossing dozens of these stinking conveyances into water like this!"

I put up my hands to calm him. "All right, all right. I'll assume you're as good as your word. It does look like Leung's car."

Jin resettled his face in a disdainful sneer. "Of course it's his. Now you tell me about the asetem. Why did they leave?"

"Because I killed their king."

Jin straightened so fast, the air cracked. "You what? You what? You what?" he babbled, rushing close to me.

I shrugged and pushed away from him, getting back into the Rover. "I killed him. Whacked him. Discorporated his nasty, manipulative hide," I replied, closing the door between us. Jin reached for me through my open window as I started the engine. I pushed his shoes into his elongating black-clawed hands. "Tell you the rest later. Gotta go get someone to haul this car all the way out of the lake before dark." I pushed the power window switch and let the window roll closed as I put the truck into reverse. Jin stared at me. Then he sat down hard and howled. I backed the Rover the hundred feet or so onto East Beach Road at a dangerous speed and pointed the truck toward Highway 101 and the nearest ranger station. Jin didn't pursue me and I could hear his uncanny, grinding howl for miles as I drove away. I wondered why he was so upset and if I would later regret giving him that piece of information. The ferret made a huffing noise in her cage and I hoped she wasn't privy to something I didn't know, since she sure as hell wasn't going to tell me what was making her chuff. But I had promised Jin I'd tell him the rest and maybe that would hold him off for a while. I hoped.

The closest place I thought I might find anyone was the

Storm King ranger station where the ferret and I had taken our break the day before. Technically it was closed until May, but there'd been signs of life around and there was a pay phone. The mountains cut off cell service, so the old landline was the best bet I had. If that failed, I'd have to drive to Fairholm or Piedmont. At least it wasn't raining at the moment; that would have made getting the waterlogged car out of the lake nearly impossible.

By the time I reached Storm King's ranger station, Jin's howling had died away. Once I parked in the lot, I got the ferret out of her cage again and wrestled her into her harness for a walk around the station in search of a ranger or any other help, hoping Jin hadn't followed us or wasn't interested in taking a piece out of me if he had. Chaos was nonplussed about the recent encounter with whatever he was, but she settled down to some intense exploring once I got her leashed and on the ground.

Chaos headed straight for the water, hopping and scampering across the chilly clearing in front of the ranger station. She diverged twice to check something on the ground, each time pausing only long enough to dig at a bright knot of Grey-stuff that had buried itself in the dirt. She lost interest in the hot spots after a few paws full of gravel and skipped back to her original path, but I noticed that the lake and the ground that sloped down into it had an unusual gleam, similar to the intrusive Greyness I'd seen near Lake Sutherland in the morning. I'd have expected so much effort to have drained, rather than added to, the freakish energy around the lake. The area near the car had seemed quieter and more normal. But here, near the ranger station, there were actually more bright lines shooting southwest than I'd seen the day before. The phenomenon seemed to ebb and flow to some rhythm I didn't know. The power lines in the lake were apparently the source of massive energy, but . . . where did it come from in the first place?

A white pickup truck bearing a green stripe and the U.S. National Park Service emblem on the side was standing to the left of the boat ramp and dock that pointed at the northeastern shore, just a few degrees west of where Jin had raised Leung's car from the depths. I couldn't make out the spot from the dock as Chaos humped and skipped her way along the planks, but I found myself straining to see if there was an angry white monster on the other side. I didn't see anything. The ferret looked over the side of the dock at the water and I did the same.

Below us, scattered branches and stones rested on pale green sand and gravel a dozen or more feet below the surface. Looking straight down into the incredibly clear water, I could see every bump and knot as well as if the branches still grew in air. As I stared down, Chaos—the ferret version of Kipling's 'satiable Elephant's Child—made a barking noise and jumped into the water.

"Damn it!" I spat, hauling her back up by her harness and leash as she attempted to paddle across the lake. She squirmed and wriggled as I picked her up and tried to brush the worst of the water off her, but she was soaked and shivering and stopped fighting me as soon as the cold really penetrated her skin. Then she wanted only to burrow into my clothes as quickly as possible.

"Moron tube rat," I muttered, turning back and heading for land, just in case she tried another fool's leap. I yanked off my scarf and started wrapping her up in it. "What are you trying to do—turn into an otter and swim out to sea?" I glanced up, gauging the distance back to the Rover, and saw a man in a dark green park service uniform and heavy jacket walking toward the white pickup. "Hey," I called out. I wished I could wave to get his attention, but I had my hands full of wet ferret-in-velvet. I started running toward him, cradling Chaos against my chest and calling out again.

The ranger shot a glance over his shoulder, then stopped and turned to face me, waiting patiently for me to catch up. He was a middle-aged man, wings of gray spreading from his temples into his brown hair, though judging from the way his uniform hung, the park service kept him pretty fit. His nose was a little crooked, and constant cold had made the veins spiderweb across it, but there wasn't much else about him that stood out. His aura was small and neutral yellow; he seemed totally normal—dull, even.

"Hey," he said as I drew near. "What happened? Your dog fall in the lake?"

"My crazy ferret wants to join the Polar Bear Club, I guess," I said, unwrapping the miscreant's face so she could wave her whiskers at the man. She didn't react to him at all except to sniffle piteously, so I wasn't missing anything Grey about him, and that was reassuring: I'd begun to wonder if I'd lost more ability than I'd realized. "She jumped right into the water."

He chuckled. "That water's so clear, it's like glass. Maybe she didn't think it was there."

"I have no idea. I'd think she could smell it, but maybe it's too cold for her nose to work well."

"It's been colder. It's above freezing today." He glanced at a long, low building beside the water, nearly hidden by shore grass and winter-dead water iris. "Why don't you come in here and I'll find you a towel for her."

I thanked him and followed him into the building. It was only a little warmer inside than out and the long open room held two long water-filled troughs. "What is this place?" I asked.

"Fish hatchery. We keep the lakes stocked with trout and a couple of other sport species so they don't get overfished. We almost killed off the native trout with introduced species and overfishing in the past. We try to learn from our mistakes." He took a small towel out of a cabinet near the door and handed it to me. "I was just up checking on the tanks, making sure they hadn't frozen over. Lucky for you we had a spate of subzero temps last week or I might not have come out here today."

"I do seem to have really good luck," I agreed, taking the towel and unwinding the ferret from my now-wet scarf. Actually, I don't have luck, according to another Greywalker I'd met in London; I have a gift of persuasion, and that includes persuading circumstances to favor me. I think that's probably bull, but I've learned not to let my natural cynicism ruin perfectly good magic: I'll take all the luck I can get.

I wrapped Chaos in the dry towel and rubbed the water out of her fur while the ranger held on to my wet scarf. "So, do you just do fish or do you take care of the whole lake?" I asked.

"No, I do pretty much the whole lake. Name's Ridenour," he added, starting to offer me a hand to shake, then realizing I didn't have one of my own free and stuffing it back into his jacket pocket. "Brett Ridenour. I'm the senior ranger for this district of the park."

"Well, then you're probably the man I need to see."

"About what, Miss . . . ?"

Chaos was shivering in my hands and I paused to stuff the mostly dry ferret inside my coat to warm up. "Harper Blaine." Now I shook his hand and went on. "I'm a private investigator and I was up here doing some pretrial work for a lawyer in Seattle when I noticed a car in the lake."

"A car?" Ridenour questioned, half frowning and half smiling. "There aren't too many places in the lake where a car would be visible if someone were fool enough to drive one in. It's pretty deep out there."

"So I hear, but there certainly is a car up near the northeast shore, about a hundred feet off East Beach Road."

"Seriously?"

I nodded. "Yes. Bit of a lonely stretch just west of where the lake comes to a point behind that big house . . ."

"East Beach. Well . . . yeah, I suppose that's about the one place a car wouldn't just sink all the way to Hades out there. That's an old landslide area; filled in part of the valley about eight thousand years ago and formed the two lakes here. The rest of it's all glacial and deep as hell. I wonder what cabin-crazy son of a bitch drove his damned car into my lake."

I made a clueless face and shrugged. "No idea."

"You didn't scare someone into the lake, now, did you, Miss Blaine?"

"Hell no. I was just looking for my witness and someone

said he might be farther out along the shoreline. I got a little lost and ended up going down the wrong tiny dirt road." I'm not too proud to make myself out to be a fool if it serves my purpose. "I got down to the end, realized I was in the wrong place, and got out of my truck to see if I could turn around or if I'd have to back out. And there's a car in the water—just under the water, really, but, as you said, the water's so clear that you can see down a long way. This isn't even down more than two feet on the highest bit."

Ridenour's frown deepened. "Huh," he grunted, staring into the distance. "I guess you'd better come show me, if you think your ferret's all right now."

"She's dry enough to warm up on her own now." I handed him the damp towel and he returned my wet scarf. "Thanks."

He opened the door and we left the hatchery, heading for our respective trucks. "Do you need to take that critter home first?"

"No, I'm staying at a hotel in Port Angeles tonight. I have her cage in my truck and it's warm enough. She'll go to sleep no matter where she is—kind of like a kid."

Ridenour's stride faltered and for a second his face paled; then he caught back up to me. "I'll bring my truck around and join you by yours. Then we can both drive out to the site."

"All right." I'd half expected him to ask me to come with him, but something had distracted him enough that he didn't question whether I was leading him on a snipe hunt.

I walked back across the clearing and past the ranger station to the visitors' parking lot. Chaos was more than happy to snuggle into her dry nest and give me the cold shoulder as if her aborted attempt to be a Popsicle were my fault. I rolled my eyes at her and shut the back hatch. By the time I was in my seat, I could hear the ferret crunching away on her kibble as if swimming in icy, haunted lakes was nothing unusual for her.

Ridenour pulled up and waited for me to get my engine started and pull out ahead of him. He followed me all the way to where the dirt track down to the lake lay exposed and churned up by my abrupt departure earlier. I rolled down my window and pointed to the road. Then I drove a bit past it, to the place I'd first seen Leung, and parked the Rover so I could walk back and join Ridenour, who'd parked his own truck beside a stand of frost-burned bracken ferns on the other side. The area now seemed almost unnaturally dull and quiet, the bright Grey overlay faded to thin mist for the moment.

"This it?" he asked as I joined him.

I nodded. "Just down there. You can see I made a bit of a mess."

"Well, I won't cite you, this time," he said in a forced jocular tone. "This path is supposed to be cleared up in the summer, anyway, so we have access to as much of the shoreline as possible without having to bring out the boats." We both glanced down the track and I was relieved to see no sign of Jin. "Stick close," said Ridenour, starting down the trail. "I heard a cougar across the lake earlier and it might still be around."

"You mean that awful screeching sound?" I asked.

"Yeah. Some people say it sounds like a woman screaming. Me, I just think it sounds like cougars."

I wasn't sure if he'd made a really horrible joke or no joke at all, so I said nothing and followed him down to the water's edge, back to the place I'd last seen Leung's car. It was still there, just visible as the daylight began to slant onto the lake from the west, illuminating the intrusive rust color of the wrecked car in the glowing greens and blues of the lake.

Ridenour glanced toward the water, apparently not quite convinced I'd really seen a car, and did a visible flinch when he spotted it. "Jesus!" He started forward as if he was going to jump in and swim to it, but the knowledge of how cold the water was must have stopped him at the brink. He hovered at the edge, rocking from foot to foot as if he could barely restrain himself from action but wasn't sure which one to take.

"I'm pretty sure there's no one in there," I said, not sure

at all, but the last thing I wanted to deal with was a ranger with hypothermia. "The car looks like it's been in the water a while."

He stopped his indecisive swaying and turned back to look at me, his expression mournful. "If there was someone in it, they'd be dead by now," he said with a sad nod. "I guess all we can do is have it hauled out."

"How are you going to do that?"

He bit his lip and frowned at the ground. When he spoke he seemed to be talking to himself more than to me. "This road's too narrow and soft to support any truck that could pull a waterlogged car out of the drink. We'll have to get the barge. It's docked down at Fairholm, but it'll take an hour or more to get it up here and then another hour and a half to haul the car on board and take it to the boat ramp where we can get it on a flatbed and out to the county yard. We've got about three hours of light left. Then the sun goes behind the hills and it gets darker than the inside of a grizzly out here." He rubbed one hand through his hair. "They're not going to like working on Sunday . . . but I can't give 'em a choice. They're just going to have to do it. Can't let that sit there any longer than we can avoid—it might slide down and sink."

"*Who* aren't going to like working on Sunday?" I asked.

He stopped staring at the drowned car and turned his head to talk to me. "The boat crews don't work weekends in the winter—usually they don't work up here much at all this time of year. Most of 'em have other jobs in the off-season. Damn it, I wish I had a diver with a dry suit up here! I want to know if I've got a body in that car." He glanced up at the sky and muttered, "Don't let this be a goddamned crime scene. I do not need a murder in my park!" He turned his gaze back toward the lake, rubbing his hands over his face and muttering something I couldn't quite hear, but I thought he said, "Kill you my damned self."

I stepped closer and put my hand on Ridenour's shoulder. "Hey, you all right?"

Ridenour jumped as if he'd forgotten I was there. "Yeah,

yeah. I'm just . . . I gotta wonder what the hell a car's doing in my lake. It doesn't look like it drove in here recently, so . . . I have to think the worst, and I've already got the culprit in mind. . . ."

"Don't start fitting someone for handcuffs. Wait until you have some real information before declaring this a major crime." As if I could talk. So far, everything was pointing to the ghost having told the truth, and the car *was* evidence of murder. But it wouldn't be reasonable of me, a stranger, to agree to Ridenour's visions of the worst.

He took a deep breath and straightened his shoulders. "OK. All right. We'll assume it's just an abandoned car for now, but it's got to get moved tomorrow. I'll head back to the center and put in calls for the crew and equipment. I'll get the county in on it so they can take the car once it's out of the lake and then we'll see. . . . Which hotel are you staying at, Miss Blaine? If I need you, can I call on you?"

"Sure," I said, and I gave him the name of my hotel. "I'll come back tomorrow, if you don't mind. I'd like to see what's in that car myself, if that's OK."

Ridenour nodded absently. "Yeah, sure. First thing, about eight in the morning, then."

"OK. Eight tomorrow."

I followed him back up to East Beach Road, watching him shake his head and mutter the whole way. He plainly took the situation personally and was angry as hell at someone.

EIGHT

I gave up on the day earlier than I'd intended, returning to the hotel to check the ferret out more thoroughly—she was fine, naturally—and put her down to romp somewhere safe. Then I sat down on the bed for a few minutes, which turned into falling asleep for a couple of hours. I woke up with every muscle in my chest and abdomen protesting as if I'd been the one to haul the car out of the lake myself and my stomach rumbling hunger even louder.

Clouds had rolled in once again while I slept, and getting food meant a trip in the downpour. It was cold rain that sliced in on the wind through the Strait of Juan de Fuca like a million tiny daggers. By the time I was back in my room after dinner and some quick shopping, I was feeling as miserable as Chaos had looked coming out of the lake. The already-wet velvet scarf had been useless, and even the baseball cap I'd snatched out of the Rover had only slowed the penetration of water to my head. I took a hot shower and lurked under the duvet to save my toes from predation by ferret while I made another phone call to the Danzigers.

Ben answered the phone. "Danzigers' House of Paranormal Pancakes." I could hear Brian chanting in the background, "Ghost, ghost, ghost!"

"What?"

"Oh, hi, Harper. We're having potato pancakes with dinner and the boy wants them ghost shaped. We're having some trouble disambiguating latkes from flapjacks."

It took me a second to puzzle out "disambiguate" before I could reply. "At least you aren't trying to explain the difference between blintzes and the Blitz."

"Oh God, I fear the cream-cheese-filled barrage balloons...."

I laughed. "So, did Mara ask you about monsters?"

"Oh, your elemental white apes? Yeah, but I haven't had a lot of luck narrowing that down. Technically a lot of things fall into the 'elemental' category, from brownies to the yangant-y-tan."

"A what?"

"It's a Breton creature of evil omen—it has candles instead of fingers. Your monsters didn't have waxy hands, did they?"

"No, they had black claws. But I have another clue. I met another ... thing that seems to be related, same kind of coloring and horns, but no fur. It's an intelligent monster, essentially human in shape and size, male, but it can project a human form over its own. This one looks Asian when he's pretending to be human, has red hair on his head, and he called the other ones—the smaller, dumber ones—'gwhy' or a word that sounds like that. Any bells?"

"Gwhy..." he repeated. I could imagine him staring at the kitchen ceiling and thinking, going through his mental catalog of monsters until he asked, "Could that word be ... guai?" His tone had the same odd rise that Jin's had had.

"Yes! That's what he called them."

Ben paused. "Ah. That's Chinese. I'm not so good with Chinese—I don't read either of the text forms, so what I know comes from translations and broad-stroke references. And the Chinese myths got around along with the rest of Chinese influence and conquest. For instance, a lot of Korean and Japanese demonology is based on the Chinese legends and myths that came with Buddhism—though of course it's impolitic to say that in some company. They have a bunch of demons and ghosts in common but for the name-change, such as the kitsune, the kumiho, and the huli-jing, which are all the same shape-shifting fox-demon, essentially. The three mythologies get tumbled together a lot, and it's sometimes kind of hard to pick out which version is which."

"Hey, Ben," I suggested, "could we just go back to 'guai'? What's that? Because that seems to be what I saw, if Jin was speaking truthfully."

"A djinn?"

"No. The articulate, manipulative one calls himself 'Jin.' He's also vain and kind of greedy."

"Oh . . . Interesting . . . I think that's the word for 'effort' or maybe for 'gold'. . . . I should learn some Chinese. . . ."

"Getting off track here, Ben."

"Oh. Sorry. Chinese is tough. It's contextual and tonal and it's easy to mistake one word for another—it's a great language for puns and jokes and embarrassment—but in this case, I'd think he meant it as a bit of an insult. See, the word I think he said can mean 'ghost'"—the word brought on a new spate of chanting from Brian in the background until the noise stopped with an abrupt yelp—"or 'spirit' or 'demon' or 'freak' or 'monster.' Probably a few other words as well . . . You get the picture. But I think what you've seen is a couple of different types of Chinese demons, since these plainly *aren't* ghosts. They'd be 'yaoguai' or 'yaomo,' depending on which shade of meaning you intend. If your big guy is smarter and more sophisticated, he'd naturally look down on the smaller, dumber ones, so calling them 'freak' would be about right."

"OK. So, what's the skinny on these yaoguai?"

Ben sighed. "Unfortunately, I really don't know. They *are* elemental in nature—or at least a lot of them are. The Buddhist legends say the smart ones used to be humans who died in some particular sinful way and became demons when they descended to hell. I'm not sure how they get to be demons, but they do, and then they sort of embody their sin, and their way out of hell is to acquire the power of a very magical or truly enlightened man—to the Taoists and Buddhists, enlightenment and magic are closely related. Anyway, the demons acquire this power by literally consuming it—they eat the power, usually by eating the man who has it. The demons trick people by using illusions and making bargains, because these are both considered degraded uses of the powers that lead to enlightenment. They get more sophisticated and powerful as they consume more, but they always remain tricksters at heart until they can devour a truly enlightened man. You see the general trend?"

"What happens after the demon eats the Buddha or whatever?"

"I'm not sure. I think they become humans again, because it doesn't make a lot of sense that they'd get to go straight to heaven after eating people. I'm going to have to look this up. . . ."

I had to say his name twice to get his attention back. "It's OK for now. I get the general gist of the thing. Is there a way to destroy these demons?"

"Oh, you can't really kill them—they're already dead. You can banish them back to Diyu—that's the Chinese underworld—though, if you know the right spell. You write it on a piece of yellow paper and . . . I think you make the demon eat it. I think—"

"Yellow paper?"

"Or silk I think will work, too. Yellow is the Buddhist color of sanctity and enlightenment. Red for happiness and luck, white for death."

"What about green?"

"Not sure on that one, either, but I'd make a guess at the earth or living things."

I humphed, trying to absorb all the information, match it up with what I'd seen and heard in the past two days, and let my mind look for connections to other magical things I was more familiar with. I'd stand a better chance of using this information to my advantage if I could relate it to things I already had some facility with.

"OK," I said, "I think I have a general idea about this. I'd like to know more, but I think that's all I can take in right now. Can I drop in on Monday and pick your brains some more?"

"Sure. Oh! And I have some great news! But I won't tell you now. I'll tell you on Monday."

"Tease."

Ben laughed. "Mara says that, too. Do you want to come for dinner?"

"No, I need to get back out here to Port Angeles as quickly as I can turn it around, so I hope not to be in town late enough. And if I ruin one more meal at your house with some problem of mine, I don't think Mara will forgive me."

"She's had to forgive me and Brian."

"With an emphasis on *had to*, Ben."

"Well, yes. . . ."

I smiled. "Can I call you before I come over?"

"Sure. Brian should be at day—um . . . *play* care until two, so if you come before that, we won't have to chase him."

"All right. I'll see you before then."

We disconnected and I leaned back into the pillows, still remarkably tired and sore, and turned on the TV, looking for something mindless. I wished Quinton was with me; we still didn't live together or spend all our free time together, but I realized I'd become used to his being around. It had been a while since I'd had to run a case completely alone and I missed his input. I also just missed him. Snuggling Chaos wasn't as satisfying, besides being a bit smellier.

After an hour of animal shows interrupted by explosions of ferret dancing, Chaos wound down and curled up next to my knees for some sleep. I stared at the screen until my brain went mushy. Then I put her back in her cage and went to sleep myself, wondering what, if anything, we'd find when the car finally came up from the lake.

NINE

My first impression at the lake in the morning was that this was going to suck. I was still achy and the sun was still on the shy side, the light it shed being thinned and turned platinum gray by the churning clouds overhead. It had stopped raining, but the air was colder than it had been the past two days and a crust of ice had formed on everything. The most interesting part of the morning was the behavior of the Grey near Fairholm where an array of magical power lines in every color seemed to have grown up out of the lake to shoot off across the ground to the south since my last time through the area. They made an electric singing as they stretched across the highway to vanish into the cliffs. They piqued my interest, and I would have cut my losses and pursued their mysterious terminus if I hadn't needed to keep an eye on the car-raising circus.

I might as well have stayed in bed on that point, though. Nothing seemed to move as quickly as Ridenour expected and he'd become a bossy, irritating martinet. He dismissed my questions about Shea's background and was on his phone or radio continually throughout the morning, issuing orders, corrections, or demands. I did my best to stay close enough to see what was happening without being in his sights much, but for the most part it was a lot of hurry-up-and-wait.

The barge crew had trickled into the store at Fairholm, but they weren't all there until after ten o'clock and each

refused to get started without the others for various safety
or legal reasons. Then the big diesel engine on the barge
had been reluctant to start, coughing and dying several
times before the three-man crew got it warm enough to
keep on running. Finally, the barge cast off from the dock at
Fairholm about noon and began its slow trip up the length
of the lake. Ridenour had pointed out that the barge, while
powerful and heavy enough to carry a crane and dredger,
wasn't fast; it would take about an hour for the barge to
reach the car on the northernmost shore. With yet more
time to kill, Ridenour and I returned to the ranger station
at Storm King to meet the deputy sheriff the county had
sent.

Deputy Strother turned out to be the lowest man on the
totem pole—barely out of training and still unsure of his
authority. The county administration wasn't convinced that
a truck was actually needed, and they wanted Strother to
give his opinion first. I thought I smelled politics in the
county's action and I wouldn't have been surprised if there
had been a few toes stepped on and noses bent out of shape
in the past. Ridenour tried to cow Strother from the first
minute, taking a much harsher tone with him than he'd used
with me. "When can you get that truck up here?" he demanded.

Strother glanced at his watch and looked up again without meeting the ranger's eyes. "Pretty quick. There's a flatbed already out at Piedmont, and the driver's on his way
there. I'll give him a call when the car's up on the barge so
I can see if there's really a need for the truck at all. Shouldn't
take him but ten minutes to drive over. No sense in his just
sitting here and freezing till then, not with the way things
have gone so far."

Ridenour scowled. "It'll move along fine now, but you
should light a fire under your man soon. That road's pretty
narrow and slick from here to Piedmont. Tell him to drive
around to the highway instead. It'll be longer, but safer, so
he'd better get to it soon or we'll all be standing around in
the cold waiting for him next."

Strother shifted his gaze to the side, hunching his shoulders a bit. "I suppose. . . ."

"Don't 'suppose,' Strother; get it done."

Strother shrugged and sighed. "Can I use your phone?"

"Can't you radio him?"

"Driver's coming in on his own time. He won't have the radio on until he's in the truck. Better to call his cell phone before he gets into the mountains."

Ridenour seemed to resent letting the younger man into the ranger station, but he unlocked the picturesque little cabin that stood across the open ground south of the boat ramp and ushered us inside. "Keep an eye on that pocket-edition otter of yours," he warned me. "This building's full of crannies and holes she could get into."

The interior of the small ranger station wasn't a lot warmer than the exterior, but it had a fireplace at one end and electricity, as well as the phone Strother wanted. Ridenour pointed him to it with a grunt that gave me the idea he might have been enjoying this job more than the rest of us, but it still wasn't anyone's idea of a good time.

Chaos chose that moment to decide she needed to get out of my pocket and explore. The way she scrambled around made me think she—and the cabin—would be better off if we went back outside. Though I loathed missing the phone call and whatever exchange the two men might have, I excused myself and took the ferret out to the frozen grass and skinny alder trees before she pooped on the floor.

I looked around while the ferret did her business and began exploring the place. She didn't like the cold on her feet, but she was intrigued by the area. I glanced back to be sure the cabin door was closed before letting myself slide a little closer to the Grey to see what she was so excited about.

The area around the lake was bright in the Grey, and the same sort of whizzing energy balls I'd seen around Lake Sutherland were much more active and numerous here. The air seemed to be thick with spirits that weren't quite differentiated from one another, as if a crowd of specters had been blendered into a ghost milk shake and poured into the valley around Lake Crescent. But in spite of the sense of their cold presence all around, pervasive as oxygen, the lake's shore seemed weirdly empty. I shuddered, disturbed by the expectant loneliness of the Grey around me, feeling as if something was waiting just beyond the edge of what even I could see. Was that connected to the sudden growth of energy lines near Fairholm? I walked around the verges of the clearing, looking for anything that might give me a clue about why the area was this way, but after half an hour I still didn't have so much as an inkling.

Chaos had found a hole in the ground and was frantically digging in it to get at whatever tiny creature cowered inside; I decided she'd had enough exploring at the lakeside for now. I picked her up and wiped the dirt off her paws, glancing back toward the northeastern shore for a moment. I could see the barge just coming into view on my left past what a map on the ranger station wall labeled Barnes Point. The barge wasn't fast, but it was making steady progress. In twenty minutes or so it should be in position to start hauling the car up onto its platform. I wanted to be as close as possible to it before the disputed truck took it away.

I returned to the ranger station and interrupted an intense staring contest. Neither man spoke, but their expressions indicated an unpleasant topic had been cut off in midsnipe. They weren't going to pick it back up in front of me, so I went ahead and announced that the barge was passing the point.

Ridenour jumped up from the desk, cutting his gaze away from Strother's with a sharp twist of his head. "Well, then, we should go up to the north shore and keep an eye on them."

Strother lowered his inquisitive eyebrows into a scowl. "I should stay here and wait for the truck."

Ridenour returned the annoyed expression, but he couldn't argue much since he'd been the one to insist on sending the truck the long way. "All right. You coming or staying, Miss Blaine?"

I was a little conflicted. On the one hand I wanted to be as close to the action as I could; but I'd need to be here when the barge unloaded the car—that would be the best chance I'd have to get an up-close look at it and what might be inside. But I didn't need to watch the preliminaries and I wanted to talk to Strother without Ridenour's overbearing presence, so I said, "I need to use the ladies' room. I'll follow you up in a minute."

Ridenour looked slightly appalled, but he shrugged and went out. I held Chaos out to Strother. "Would you hold on to her for a moment? She likes to eat soap, so I don't want to take her with me."

Strother looked a little nervous, but he took the ferret in both hands. Chaos sniffed him and flicked her whiskers. "She doesn't bite," I said, handing over the leash as well. "She's very friendly. Just don't let her get near your pant cuffs."

I went out to the restroom and returned in a few minutes to see Strother tickling Chaos's belly and trying to wrestle a pencil away from her at the same time. The ferret was adamant about keeping the pencil, but she wiggled around on her back on the desk, her head going one way and her butt going the other. She didn't growl or squeak, because ferrets don't, but she would have if she'd thought of it. She seemed to be having a good time playing with the deputy.

"You guys doing OK?" I asked.

Strother looked over his shoulder and Chaos took the opportunity of his distraction to hop onto all four feet and try to yank the pencil from his grip.

"Hey," Strother replied. "She sure is feisty."

"That's her stock-in-trade. There's not a lot of back-down in a ferret." And there didn't seem to be much in park rangers or deputy sheriffs, either.

He nodded, twitching the pencil out of her mouth as soon as she tried to get a better grip. Chaos launched into a weasel war dance hopping all over the empty desktop, waving her open mouth and showing off her tiny fangs. Strother laughed. "Damn, got some muscle there. She's a lot tougher than she looks, too."

I just smiled and picked the ferret up from the desk. She wiggled around in my hand for a moment, then resigned herself to having lost her pencil and scrambled up onto my shoulder to get a better view. "What did I interrupt?" I asked, keeping my eyes off him.

"It's a personal matter," Strother said, glancing around before looking at me again. "So, is it true you found this car in the first place? Ridenour said some investigator found it."

"That's me. I don't know that I'm the first person to see the car in the lake, but I'm the first to have reported it. I didn't mention this to Ridenour, but I suspect the car might belong to a man who disappeared a few years ago. There's no missing person report, but he's definitely not where he ought to be and no one seems to know where he is."

"Why wouldn't you tell the ranger that? This is his territory."

"He seems a little biased. And proprietary. I'm afraid he might not be entirely honest with me about the people and situation up here if I asked."

"I can understand that impression. He's got the park's welfare to think of and sometimes he does . . . uh . . . take things a bit personally."

I nodded. "That's what I was thinking. So I'd like to get a look at the car when it comes up, before it gets into the yard where things might be tampered with. Ridenour might not like that. Will you help me get a look at it when they bring it back to unload?"

Strother gave it some thought. "I don't see any harm in it, so long as you don't touch anything. But you see anything odd, you sing out. Hard enough trying to juggle the paperwork on this multijurisdiction crap without any cross-agency accusations of incompetence down the road."

I smiled at him. Strother was young, but he wasn't a fool, even if he didn't do much to dispel that initial impression. "I'll do that."

We shook hands on it and I went out to my truck to drive

up and join Ridenour while Strother stayed behind, waiting for the truck. I envied him the quaint little ranger station—it wasn't warm, but being there was more comfortable than standing on the frost-hardened shore was going to be.

Ridenour had gone back to the spot I'd taken him to before and I joined him, walking down once again from parking my truck next to the road. The pools of yellow and blue light were back, glowing like something radioactive in an old science fiction film. But though the energy was back, no ghosts had returned to the spot where Jin had squatted to raise the truck.

When I reached the edge of the water, the barge crew was already firing up the dredging crane and trying to maneuver into position to grab the car. They seemed efficient, and I imagined the cold was spurring them to get the job over with as quickly as possible, but it still took quite a while to get the barge and crane aligned to someone's liking. Ridenour, standing back from the water's edge, kept his words to himself, but I could see his jaw clenching and unclenching as he watched.

The clawlike extension on the crane arm descended, but the car was a weird shape for the tool and they only ended up pushing the wreck deeper into the water. We could hear the cursing from the barge as the crew repositioned to try again. Eventually, a small boat with an outboard engine cast off from the barge with a man in heavy-duty dry gear towing a hook and cable out from the crane. He got up close to the car and reached out to catch the hook on the nearest bit of doorframe. He had to stick his legs through some straps on the opposite edge of the boat and let the outboard engine act as a counterweight while he leaned out to get the hook seated a little more securely.

The small boat tipped up as if it were going to spill the man into the lake, but he didn't quite go far enough, and he righted himself before turning back to wave at the crew on the barge. Then he steered the workboat to the side about twenty feet.

Once the smaller boat was out of the way, the crew

reeled up the hook until the slack was gone and the car had begun to rise off the slippery bottom. The car turned and rolled a little as it came free, dragging along the gravelly slope for a few feet, and then stopped. The man in the small boat came in close again and motioned the crane operator to let the car down a little. As the cable slowly lowered and slackened, the car settled and stood still. It took several tries to get the hook on and the car moved into a position that pleased everyone. Ridenour plainly found it tedious.

I mostly noticed the cold, some of which had nothing to do with the ice on the ground. The edge of the lake had the same weird silver covering in the Grey up here, and the colorful balls of errant energy stung me when they hit, like small electrical shocks to my already-sore belly. I spent a lot of that time on the shore biting my lip and holding back from wincing.

Finally the barge crew members were satisfied with the disposition of hook and car and began to reel in the cable. This time the car came straight out of the water as the cable was taken up. Once the barge crew raised the car a little and saw it was stable, the man in the dry suit returned the work-boat to the barge. When he was safely aboard and the smaller boat secured to the back of the barge, the crew lowered the claw again. This time it grabbed onto the mis-shapen car, the lower jaw sliding under while the upper bore down. The metal of the waterlogged Subaru groaned as the claw closed up and the crane began retracting. As the car rose, water poured out of it. Even with the gush of water, anyone could see the crushed front end and burn-scarred metal, but to me the lake seemed to be reaching up, trying to keep hold of the vehicle with a web of ice blue and moss green energy that clung to the car as it rose.

The crane slowed its ascent and the crew watched it with anxious expressions. "Must be something awful heavy in there," Ridenour muttered beside me. I didn't give him a glance; I just stepped closer to the water's edge, feeling an urge to reach for the car as if I could help pull it free from the lake.

"Come on, come on," I murmured. "Let it go."

Leung's flames leapt in the corner of my eye as I started to raise my hand. I could feel the water lap at the toes of my boots and I turned my head toward the ghost. Encased in the red and orange of remembered fire, he also stared up. We both turned our sights on the car, willing it to keep moving, to clear the lake. . . .

The crane gave a squealing sound and lurched back into motion, the web of the lake's hold on the car falling away as the car suddenly lifted free of the surface. Water rushed back to its source from the broken windows and crooked doorframes, and the noise sounded like the heavy sigh of a giant. Leung's ghost turned toward me. Then he flamed up in a sudden bolt of red energy visible even in the wan sunlight of the afternoon and vanished with the stink of burned hair. I felt the same sense of emptiness that had accompanied the disappearance of the Russian girl's ghost. Was the last remnant of Steven Leung now gone forever . . . ?

I felt a hand on my shoulder and turned a little farther to find Ridenour reaching to pull me away from the water's edge. "Come on back. We don't need you in the drink, too. It's getting damned late and we'd never get out of here before dark if we had to fish you out as well."

I nodded and retreated with him a few feet to watch the barge crew swing the car over the side and into the well of the craft.

When we returned to the Storm King ranger station, Strother was standing in the parking lot, keeping watch for the flatbed, which drove in about thirty minutes behind us. The barge was also nearing the dock by that time and the pointing and parking, shouting and maneuvering of both the barge and the flatbed took longer than I'd have expected. The two men and the truck driver did eventually get the flatbed backed a few feet down the boat ramp and the barge tied up just right so the barge would have a shorter distance to move the crane arm when unloading the car. The truck driver didn't seem happy about the water; he hadn't brought hip waders and he took pains to let us all know he didn't see how he was going to secure the load without getting wet. With the wind finally coming up along the lake as the sun tilted toward the western rim of the valley, the barge crew and the truck driver were especially eager to get finished and headed back toward home soon.

More shouting and pointing went on until the problem was solved by the man in the dry suit who'd worked the smaller boat around the sunken car. He jumped to the dock and did the wading end of the business himself, though not without a show of annoyance. Strong words were exchanged in all directions, and the driver looked relieved when he could move the truck up onto the gravel above the water and tie the car down to his own satisfaction. The man from the barge rolled his eyes and returned to the craft after trudging back up the short dock to untie the vessel and jump aboard across the widening stretch of water. The jump wasn't so good this time and he had to scramble to get in, but he made it, and the barge began chugging away from the dock and out into the deeper water to head west and south to Fairholm.

While the trucker was checking on the straps he'd used to secure the car to the flatbed, and Strother and Ridenour were arguing between them, I took the opportunity to climb up on the bed of the truck and look into the remains of the car.

A skull, some dying fish, and a litter of bones floated in a puddle trapped on the floorboards. Ridenour shouted as he noticed me leaning in through the broken driver's window.

"Hey! Get out of there, Miss Blaine! It's not safe."

I turned back to shout over my shoulder at him, but I didn't leave the car. "There's a skeleton in here." I looked back into the car and saw something gleaming green and gold through layers of Grey in the back footwell. "And some other things on the floor." Besides water, the car seemed to leak a Grey mist. I wanted to take a closer look, but now was probably not the best time to try it, with tempers running a bit high and the hour growing late.

Ridenour and Strother both scrambled up to join me while the driver protested that they were keeping him from leaving. They told him to wait while they shoved up beside me to take a look.

Strother looked a little green as he spotted the skull, sticky with bits of soapy flesh still sticking to it here and there.

Ridenour shook his head in annoyance. "Damn it, now there'll be a bunch of damned investigators up here, making a mess in my park."

"Any idea whose car this is?" I asked. I knew exactly whose, since the license plate currently sitting on the desk in my hotel room matched the plate barely clinging to the front bumper. The whole front end had been folded into a V by impact with something I assumed was the cedar tree I'd first seen the ghostly car burning under, but I wasn't going to hand over that information. Someone might or might not figure out the tree connection, but as far as I was concerned, the most important thing was done: Leung's disappearance and death would now be investigated by someone. I just had to make sure whoever had hidden it in the first place didn't have power enough to bring the investigation to a halt.

Ridenour and Strother both backed up and began looking the car over until Strother shrugged and Ridenour scowled. "That's Steve Leung's car. I haven't seen or heard from him in . . . must be five years. I wonder—"

"I'm wondering the same thing," I said. "Don't you think it's unlikely that the skeleton found in a missing man's car would be anyone other than the missing man?"

Ridenour's expression went darker. "He could have killed someone, and then have run off and hid. . . ."

I gave him a doubtful look. "Do you really think so? Do you think a man in his sixties is going to just dash off and leave a body in the lake?"

"No, I don't guess so. . . . Hey, how would you know how old Leung is?"

"He's one of the guys I was looking for while I was up

here. But I didn't find him and no one knew where or when he'd gone. He didn't change his address with the post office or the people who send him his retirement checks. Looks like I've found him now."

"Hell," Ridenour swore. "I guess I'll have to go talk to Jewel."

"Is that one of his daughters?" I asked. I knew but couldn't let on.

"Yeah. Why were you looking for him, anyway?"

"I'd rather discuss that with his daughters."

"Well, you won't have any luck catching up to Willow—no one from law enforcement's been able to catch her in years." Ridenour's tone was pointed and bitter.

"So she's a troublemaker?" I asked, making a mental note of the name—Shea had called her "Willa," and I now assumed that was just his accent in play, not her actual name.

Strother made a wry face and answered before Ridenour could. "Bit more than that. County and city both have standing warrants on Miss Leung for various violent and property crimes. So far, no one's had any luck bringing her in on any of them."

I'd have to find a way to get to her, even though every local authority had failed. What fun. But I said, "I guess I'll just have to go with Ridenour to see the other sister."

Ridenour didn't seem eager to bring this particular news to the Leung survivors, so it wasn't too much of a battle to get him to agree, but he didn't like it. He also wanted to take a deeper look into the car before we left; however, the doors were jammed and Strother pointed out that any additional poking about wouldn't be appreciated by whoever had to investigate. Unhappily Ridenour jumped back to the ground and offered to drive me to Jewel Newman's once the truck was safely on its way to the county yard with Strother in tow.

The truck driver rechecked his straps once we were all off his flatbed. He didn't seem too pleased with any of us and I wondered if he was just grumpy in general or if the

Grey oozing from the car was affecting him in some way. We watched him climb inside and start the truck rolling. Strother waved the flatbed out to the highway as I stayed behind with Ridenour.

"Who's Newman?" I asked him as Strother walked away from us.

"Jewel's the oldest of Steven's kids. Married a fella named Geoff Newman back quite a few years now. They were in high school over at Piedmont together, but you couldn't have called them sweethearts. The Leung kids have been trouble since they were little. The girls got a lot worse once their mother and brother died. Not that the brother was a prize—he was argumentative and arrogant."

By now the flatbed had made it to the road and disappeared, heading for Port Angeles. Strother waved to us and then took off in his own car, leaving me and Ridenour to lock up the ranger station. As we walked toward his park service pickup truck, Ridenour continued the story. "I don't know what Newman's got—aside from money—but when he came back from college, he and Jewel hooked up and got married in a big hurry. You might be thinking he got her pregnant, but there never was a child, and she settled down to doing a lot of community work around the area— busybody stuff, if you ask me. The residents treat her like the queen of the lake. What she says goes with most of them. Except with her sister and a couple others."

We got into his truck and Chaos stuck her nose out of my pocket to sniff the warm, weird smells, but decided she wasn't too crazy about them and burrowed back down to nap some more. "What's the story on Willow, then?" I asked.

Ridenour ground his teeth as he started the engine. "She's just plain-ass wild. Half-crazy and all dangerous and no way to know how she got that way—both her folks were fine people." He started driving and I kept on asking questions.

"Strother said there were warrants—for what?"

"Well, aside from a couple of homicides, there's the petty

stuff like smoking pot, trespassing, and vandalism, and then she got into breaking and entering, burglary, robbery, and a few other unsavory things. Most of it's been down around Lake Sutherland and below—which is outside the federal park property—but not all of it. I can't say I'm pleased to have a few federal charges to press if she's ever caught—I don't really like that aspect of my job when you come down to it—but Willow is dangerous. Unpredictable and crazy enough to do damned near anything. Something goes bad around here that isn't caused by bears or tourists acting stupid, you can bet it's Willow.

"She's the best damned woodsman you'll ever meet, though. That's the mixed blessing of her having been born and raised here. She can track and hide in this country like no one's business, which has made her impossible to catch. You'd almost think the trees and animals are on her side or something, and she's as crafty and as mean as one of our mountain lions. Wouldn't be at all surprised if she hadn't killed her dad herself over some damned thing. She's that mean and crazy. And she's killed before, so it's not like she's squeamish about it."

"Who did she kill and why?"

"Well, we're not entirely sure she killed her brother—though that's the general belief—but we do know she killed a telephone lineman who was working out around Lake Sutherland one summer." His voice dripped disgust. "She claims he raped her and she shot him in self-defense when he came round for a second try, but she never reported the first incident, and the man was shot with her rifle from one hell of a distance, which sounds like lying in wait, not self-defense."

"How did you get this statement from her?"

"Well," he started, but the rest of his words were cut off by a squeal from the truck's radio and a voice calling out for him to respond at once. Ridenour snatched the hand piece off its hook and barked back. "What the hell is it?"

"This is Metz out at Hurricane Ridge station. We have a situation."

"What sort of situation?"

"You're not going to believe this, Brett, but . . . we've got animals in the parking lot attacking the trucks, and that damned Leung girl seems to be with them."

"Willow?"

"Yep. I've never seen anything like it—it's like the critters are working for her or something. You need to get out here ASAP. There's just me here and the rifle's in the truck. I think I'm OK in the visitor center, but the rest of the station's getting a hell of a mauling."

"What sort of critters are we talking here?"

"Bunch of those crazy white deer, including some big bucks, couple of pissed-off bears—"

"You sure it's bears?" Ridenour asked. I was wondering if the bears and deer weren't ugly white guai instead.

"Damn it, Brett, I know a bear when I see one! One of 'em's old Blaze, and I don't know what got that grizzled old bastard out of his cave this early, but he's having a ball ripping the doors off the compost shed. Those bucks are ramming everything he hasn't ripped into yet and I don't know why he hasn't tried to eat one of 'em, but if you don't get here soon, we'll be knee-deep in mulch and bear poop!"

Ridenour swore. He turned to me with eyes slightly too wide and wild. "I'm going to drop you off at the top of the road down to Jewel's place. You'll be perfectly safe walking down to the house, and her husband can drive you back to the station at Storm King to pick up your truck when you're done."

"Done?"

"Yeah. You're going to have to give her the bad news about her dad yourself. I gotta go catch her crazy-ass sister!"

TEN

In a few minutes I found myself at the top of a steep graveled road with Ridenour's park service truck vanishing
into the distance. He didn't seem to think it was odd that
Willow Leung was apparently leading wild bears around —
bears that should have still been tucked up at the end of
winter hibernation, not rampaging around ranger stations.
Frowning over the strange behavior of bears and park rangers, I started down the road to Jewel and Geoff Newman's
house.

It turned out to be the big glass-fronted house at the end
of East Beach that I'd spotted down the shoreline from the
sunken car. The place was impressive: two stories of wood
and glass that spread across half the wide lot directly on the
waterfront at one of the few locations with any beach to
speak of. Remnants of an old dock clung to the shore at the
extreme southeastern end of the property where the wedge
shape of an ancient landslide had filled in the ground between Lake Crescent and Lake Sutherland. I didn't even
have to move toward the Grey to see the glimmer of blue
power that ran under the ground to the other lake. The
power lines and smears of color were stronger here, closer
to the source, I guessed, than at Lake Sutherland.

In the Grey, the house was darker than the surrounding
landscape in spite of being well illuminated with electric
lights, as if the house somehow defied the energy — or drank
it without a trace. Something magical lived here. The mem-

ory of an older, more rustic building flickered over the modern house. I was thinking I should take a deeper look at the area, when the front door opened.

A man stood silhouetted in the bright doorway and called out to me. "You can come in or you can go away, but you can't just stand there."

I shrugged and started walking toward him. His shape changed as I moved closer, and I realized he'd picked up something from inside the house. The long black shape set off a nervous stirring in my chest—it was a rifle. He didn't shoulder it, though. He just waited to see what I would do.

I kept on walking toward the steps that went up to the door. "Hello," I called out. "Ranger Ridenour sent me down to talk to Mrs. Newman."

I went up the steps, keeping my eyes on the man with the rifle. I wanted to put my hand in my pocket to keep the ferret from doing something that might upset him, but I didn't think he'd like it if I hid my hands suddenly. As I got closer I could see him better in spite of the backlighting: He was about my height, middle-aged, judging by his posture, a little stocky. . . . Details were still hard to see with the bright electric light behind him, but when I reached the open doorway, I realized he was black and wearing dark clothes. Clallam County was so overwhelmingly Caucasian that it was almost startling to see him.

I nodded and offered my hand. "My name's Harper Blaine. I'm a private investigator and I'd like to speak with Mrs. Newman."

The man put the rifle down just inside the doorway. He looked me over but didn't take my hand. "What do you want with my wife?"

"It's about her father."

Newman crossed his arms over his chest. His energy corona was a dull, unhealthy olive green fired with jagged bolts of frustrated orange. "What about him?" He clearly wasn't going to let me in without more information—if he let me in at all.

"Mr. Newman, you may have noticed some activity

down on the lake this afternoon, just a hundred yards or so down the shore."

"We certainly did. Jewel's been agitated ever since. She's sick and she doesn't need any more upsets today, so if you've come to make any more trouble, you can go back where you came from right now." The orange sparks around his head went red as he glared at me.

"I'm sorry, Mr. Newman, but I'm afraid I may need to upset her further. The car they removed from the lake was her father's. I can go away and let Mr. Ridenour come speak to your wife tomorrow if you prefer, but I don't think he'll be any easier on her. He's currently pursuing her sister and he doesn't seem to have a very positive attitude about the family."

Newman snorted. "That's the truth. But you won't be coming up here and upsetting her, either. Whatever's happened to that old car, it's nothing to do with Jewel."

"Mr. Newman, there's a body in the car."

"Well, it hasn't got anything to do with us." Everything about him seemed to darken and pull in.

Distantly, a noise moved through the house and a weak voice tried to call out, but the words were too hard to hear. I could see something that sparkled with magic skitter across the floor of the open second-story balcony and down the stairs on my right. Whatever it was died out as it got halfway down. A rhythmic thumping started. I could tell from the slight tightening at the corners of his eyes that Newman heard it; he just refused to acknowledge it in front of me.

I tried again, this time leaning a little on the Grey to persuade him. "Mr. Newman, I really think your wife will prefer to hear this from me. I know a few things about what happened to your father-in-law that Ridenour doesn't."

He frowned, considering. I think he still would have slammed the door in my face, but the thumping had grown closer and now the voice called out again, strong enough to make itself heard and shivering with the sound of power. "Geoff, let the woman in."

Geoff Newman snorted in disgust, but he stepped back and let me enter the house.

From the entry, the living room's two stories of glass windows flooded the room with the light of late afternoon. It was gray with thin streaks of pink today as the clouds broke, but it would have been spectacular in summer sunshine with the colors of the lake reflecting onto the white and scrubbed-wood walls. But as arresting as the view was, the woman on the staircase landing was far more commanding.

Given her family name, I had expected her to be purely Chinese, but one of her parents plainly hadn't been. She was only slightly lighter-skinned than her husband and wore a vintage silk housedress that made her look like an image from some other time and place. She wasn't tall or beautiful; her posture was stooped and broken far beyond mere age, and she held herself steady with two heavily carved canes. Her face was broad and dark, lines of pain destroying the once-graceful arch of her brow and obscuring the tilt of her eyes. No, she wasn't pretty and probably never had been more than "exotic" with her Asian features in dark brown skin, but a dim nimbus of energy strands in blue, green, yellow, and red reached out from her in every direction, touching a million things, even though the power of each strand individually was weak. She coughed like someone who'd smoked two packs a day since age five, and the energy around her retracted for a moment, pulling back into her as if it sought to keep her going just a little longer.

Then she caught her breath again, a glow of sweat on her face, and looked down at me and her husband. "Come up," was all she said, her voice quiet, but as it rode down to us on the amplifying effect of magic, we had no difficulty hearing her. Then she turned around, lurching in a pain-wracked half circle, and went away, her canes thumping on the hardwood floors as she vanished into the upstairs hall.

I stepped inside, watching her disappear. I felt as if I'd walked through a net of electricity, sensing the persistent pulse of her power in the very walls of the house. The energy the building had seemed to soak up from the lake was plainly the source of some magic of hers.

Newman huffed and closed the door behind me. "You can follow me," he said, orange and red sparks jumping from him in the Grey.

He led me up the stairs on the right, though now that I was inside, I could see there was a second staircase to the left that led up to the open gallery running across the otherwise-open vault of the living room. A closed hall at each end led to private rooms that gave off the dull, cold radiation of emptiness. The house had been designed for a lot of people, but it housed only two.

"Don't get the impression I'm in favor of this," Newman warned me as he started up the stairs, ignoring the heavy rail of a chairlift installed on the staircase's back wall. "Whatever you've got to say, you'd best say it quick and get out. I don't want you upsetting Jewel any further. She adored Steven. Don't you believe anyone who says otherwise. Especially not Ridenour. That is one angry, bitter man, and you can't trust a word he says."

I raised my eyebrows, but I didn't say anything. Newman cast a hard look at me as we reached the top of the steps. "Are you listening to me?"

"I am. But so far you haven't said anything."

"You have a fast mouth."

I just used my fast mouth to smile at him.

He snorted again and led me down the hall to a door that stood ajar on the left—the water-facing side of the house. He tapped on the door and said his wife's name. "You ready for us?"

Her voice came back, much softer this time than before. "Come in, Geoff. Ask our visitor to wait."

Geoff looked at me and I shrugged, leaning back against the opposite wall in a show of patient nonchalance. He nodded and, for the first time, he didn't scowl. The spiking energy around his head dimmed and he entered the room, taking care to block my view and close the door completely once he was inside. I loafed in the hall, watching the play of

strange energy along the floors and shooting at random
through the open spaces. It was a lot like what I'd seen on
the shore outside the ranger station farther down the lake.
I wondered whether it was the standard configuration of
magic here, or if there was something special about the
places where I'd spotted it so far. A few of the strands
crawled toward me and started to curl around my body,
stroking at me like the tentacles of a curious octopus. That,
I thought, was not normal, so I caught one between my fingers, taking a cold electric shock for my pains, and flicked it
away before I bent an edge of the Grey around me, making
a thin, silvery barrier between me and the sneaking strings
of energy. They pulled away with a jerk and disappeared
into the walls.

I let go of my temporary shield as the door opened.
Geoff waved me in.

I stopped in the middle of the room to look around before I went any farther. The space was dominated by the
odor of illness and a large hospital-style bed that stood near
the wall-wide window on the lake-facing side of the building. The center of the room was empty, but the edges were
lined with various medical equipment and aids, including an
unused wheelchair, a few locked cabinets, and shelf after
shelf of big old books. A table stood against the wall opposite the bed with two dining chairs. Another, cozier chair
sat near the head of the bed, away from the view and next
to a bank of medical monitors and machinery with flickering lights and glowing switches. The last bit of wall between
the bed and the window held a smaller table with a large,
closed wooden box on top.

Jewel Newman sat in the bed, propped upright by the
mechanism under the mattress and a buttress of pillows.
She'd changed out of the antique housecoat and now wore
an equally old silk bed jacket over her plain white night-
gown. It made her look like a Hollywood ghost. I could see
how crabbed and skeletal her hands were as she rubbed one
over the other in her lap.

"Come over here," she ordered.

I don't care to be commanded, but since I wanted to get closer to her, I went. Up close, I noticed she was rubbing one particular, bent finger as if it hurt and she was trying to hide a slight swelling. She'd wiped the sweat off her face and I could smell powder. Apparently she still cared about her appearance.

"So," she started, "you're a private investigator—among other things." She didn't look at me. She kept her head straight, facing the wall opposite the bed, but her eyes strayed to the half-drawn curtains that covered the windows on her right. Her weak, colorful strands of energy reached out, waving in the air but never touching me. I guessed she hadn't liked what I'd done to the one that had tried to curl around me in the hall.

"Yes," I replied.

"And you have some news about my father."

"He's dead. But I think you know that."

She bowed her head and stared at her feet under the white coverlet.

"They pulled his car out of the lake today," I continued. "I assume you saw it."

She took a slow breath. I could hear Geoff stir and start to move toward me, but she put out her left hand, waving a little to hold him off.

"I wasn't at the window when they . . . retrieved it. How did they make the identification?"

"They haven't yet. But it's his car and I know the skeleton in it was his."

Now she finally looked at me. "How? How do you know?"

"He told me." I looked at her bruised finger—it was swollen and reddened as if the injury had just happened. It hadn't been that way when she'd leaned on her canes earlier; she hadn't favored one hand or cocked the finger up to relieve the pressure.

She followed my gaze and covered her misshapen hand. "You have a strong grip."

I nodded, figuring she took physical control of her extruded energy and had taken the pain for it as well when I had pinched it off. "I didn't realize that was you or I would have been gentler."

She scoffed. "Don't coddle me—I don't like it. Now, I know you can touch the power and that you don't like being poked and probed any more than I do. All right. Why did you come? What did you know? That's what you need to tell me."

"I don't need to tell you anything, but your dad might appreciate it if I spoke up."

She made a face as if she smelled something foul, but waved at me to continue.

"I saw his ghost on Tuesday. Down on East Beach Road. He said his death wasn't an accident and he mentioned you and your sister."

"Hah! I'll bet he didn't."

"He said 'my daughters.' But he didn't mention your names, which is why it took me a few days to find you."

"More likely you were looking for some way to profit from what you knew. What did you think, that I'd give you a reward for finding the body after all these years?" Jewel snapped.

"No. Mostly I hoped your dad would go away if I found out what happened to him and got someone to do something about it. I haven't seen him since we first pulled the car out of the lake. He went away. But it didn't seem to be easy; the lake tried to keep the car."

"It doesn't give up its treasures readily," she agreed.

"It gave up Hallie Latham."

Jewel gave another of her dismissive snorts. "That was before the others came. That was before . . . all of this turned into so much filth and corruption." She waved her bruised and shaking hand toward the half-drawn curtains, now turning a strange pink. She glanced toward her husband. "Geoff, you can go."

He stepped up to the side of the bed and reached for her hands. "I won't. Baby, you shouldn't be alone with this . . . woman. You don't know what—"

She batted him away with impatient swipes. "I know *exactly* what she wants, Geoffrey! Now get out."

He stepped back, shocked, and then started for the door.

Jewel relented just as he touched the knob. "I'll call for you, dear. It won't be long."

He nodded, still dejected, and went out.

Jewel sighed. "He's a good man. But I suppose it isn't easy living with a witch like me. I'm a horrible old woman, sick and dying, and I want my own way. I want my way about this, too."

"You can't be very old, Mrs. Newman. Your father would have been seventy-two this year. So what are you . . . forty-five? Fifty?"

"I'm forty-nine. But I might as well be a hundred." She picked up a small white remote from the table on the far side of the bed. "That's what this lake has done to me. What pride and stupidity made of me." The curtains drew back as she pressed on the remote with shaking fingers. "Do you know what they call this place? What they should have called it if they were telling the truth?"

"Sunset Lakes," I answered, remembering the story the clerk at the county offices had told me.

The curtains stopped moving at the extreme edges of the window, revealing the lake, carmine red in the reflected light from the sunset below the western peaks. The water lay so still and deep, the colors of the landscape washed away completely in the darkness beneath and the ruddy light from above, that it looked thick, as if it had poured down into the basin from some giant's wound.

"Blood Lake. That's what they should have called it," Jewel said. "For all the blood it's swallowed and all the horror it's spat right back." She stared out at the lake as if it mesmerized her. "The Indians say there used to be a beautiful river valley here, the Valley of Peace. But the people in the valley got to fighting and Storm King wanted to shut them up, to punish them for making war, so he tore off the peak of his mountain and threw it down into the valley—right here, right where we are now—and he dammed up the river. All the people in the valley drowned and the lakes formed over their corpses. That's what this is, a valley full of blood, a lake full of death."

"Is that what you think killed your father? Some kind of curse?"

"What do you think, Miss Harper Blaine? Don't be so surprised. I'm sick and broken, but I still have ways of knowing what I need to know."

"I don't doubt that, Mrs. Newman. But your father—"

"Was killed by one of *them*. By one of the mages who came flocking to our lake and drank in the power like greedy dogs. One of those . . . bastards killed my father. All of them, maybe. And all of them are going to pay."

"What about your sister, Willow? Couldn't it have been her?"

"It might well have been. The Powers know she didn't have any love for our father or any care about the lake. She's as bad as the rest." Jewel collapsed in a fit of coughing, her near hand scrambling like a spider over the coverlet for an oxygen mask that lay on her pillow as an alarm began squealing on the monitors beside the bed.

I picked up the mask and put it in her flailing hand. I watched her clap it onto her face and suck in the gas to regain control of her breathing. I thought I should have felt more moved by Jewel's condition, but something about her chilled my sympathy.

The bedroom door banged open and Geoff darted in, heading for the bed, but drew up short when he saw that Jewel already had the mask to her face. He glowered at me, but Jewel waved him away again, lowering the mask for a moment to say, "I'll call you, Geoff. Go away now."

"Jewel," he protested.

She took the mask down again, but this time her voice was tender. "I *will* call for you."

Newman stiffened his jaw, his mouth turning down as he tried to hold it steady and his eyes got wet. Then he wheeled and marched out, back and shoulders stiff.

I waited a while for Jewel to be ready to speak again,

watching the fast-fading sunset color the lake darker and darker, like a stain.

Finally she put the mask aside. "Miss Blaine, I don't have the luxury of beating around the bush. I'm sure you wonder why I didn't make a report when Daddy went missing. But I knew he was dead, and I also knew it would only make things worse for me if I said anything. I didn't want to be the subject of a murder investigation—my family's had enough of that. I tried to discover what had happened on my own, but I couldn't, and in trying . . . this was the result," she added, waving at the machines and the hospital bed. "There was—there is—no one here I could trust to carry on the investigation. Not anyone with any power, at least, and I'm sure you understand that any normal person would be eaten alive by the things that drink from this lake. I think my father tried to stop these things—these poachers and despoilers and their filthy familiars—and I am sure one of them killed him and dumped his body in the lake to feed the power. I want to know, but more than that . . . I want them all to stop. I want them to stop using the lake. I want them all to die. At the very least I want them broken, driven away from here forever. Do you understand?" She stared at me, unwavering, the colors around her head clinging close, weaving into a snowy veil of white.

White: the color the Chinese used for death and mourning.

"I can understand that," I replied, noncommittal. I knew it would get ugly and I wasn't sure I needed to be the one to do it. I was pretty sure I wouldn't want to do it, either. The proprietary fury that rolled off Jewel made me sick and her desire for bloody revenge repelled me.

Something yellow touched the distant side of her face and she cocked her head over as if listening to it, still watching me the whole time, calculating. She straightened up with an effort and nodded. "You do understand. I know that. I know your own father was driven to death by magical things." Her voice had a disturbing singsong quality, carried

on a thread of magic. "You can sympathize. You understand. I know you'll do this. For me. For both of us."

She was trying to play me and that was the last straw. I
slammed down my mental doors and narrowed my eyes,
letting cold disgust flow out at her. I took a step back. "Not
for my sake," I said. "And not for yours, either, you bitter
old woman. You don't understand one thing about me." I'd
already done my time with family vengeance. I wasn't going
to shoulder that gnawing burden for someone else, especially not for her.

I turned on my heel and started out, in that moment not
caring if the lake drank up another hundred life forces before it finally destroyed whoever was using it—and I was
sure it would, judging by the toll it was taking on Jewel
Newman. I didn't care who'd killed Steven Leung any longer. I told myself the county or the feds or the city of Port
Angeles would find out eventually and that was no longer
my job. I'd done what I'd come to do.

"I'll pay you," Jewel called out from the bed.

She couldn't possibly pay me enough. I ignored her and
reached for the doorknob.

"You can do whatever you feel you must—I'll make sure
of it. I'll protect you," she cried. "I *can* protect you from the
police. Just break their power! Make the sorcerers and
houngans go, and I'll pay you."

I ground my teeth and turned the knob.

"You'll be saving us—all the rest of the people around
the lakes. You'll save them. You have to. You have to try.
You have power and . . . and the Guardian will demand it."

That stopped me. I knew that she'd been fed the information by some kind of Grey spy, some magical snooping,
whispering thing, but unfortunately, she was right. That's
my job: Hands of the Guardian—the human instrument of
the thing that keeps the Grey safe, and the rest of the world
safe from the Grey. That was indisputably my role ever
since the last job, when I'd unwillingly helped to destroy the
previous Guardian and then watched a new one take form

once I'd shut down the threat of an unfettered Grey—at the expense of my life and the lives of others. Damn it all! How dared she use that against me?

I halted at the door, indulging in a fit of mental cursing, but I didn't turn back. "I'll think about it," I said. Then I left.

ELEVEN

The ferret woke up with a frantic need to scratch her ears as I was trudging down the darkened road toward the ranger station. I had forgotten to ask about Shea, and I didn't think that query or a request for a lift to my car would have been well received after the way I'd walked out on Jewel Newman, so I'd just kept walking. Geoff Newman tried to brace me at the door, but I am good at slipping out of physical holds—especially when the person trying it has no idea what he's doing.

In the falling darkness, the lake's uncanny presence impressed itself on me as an ululating whisper of song, half-heard. The phenomenon that had lit Lake Crescent bloody red had faded as the torn clouds closed up again, gathering their stormy menace, and the sun set completely. Now I felt the sparking tingle of minuscule raindrops against my face like tiny ice needles.

"Great," I muttered, grabbing the ferret as she tried to leap to the ground. "What odds will you give me that we don't make it back to the truck dry?"

Her only response was to squirm harder and paw at my hands. I stepped off the road and let her down, holding her leash tight so I didn't lose her. I could hear her scratching her ears and I knew she was propelling herself around in a backward circle like she always did, one back leg going a mile a minute, while the other made a pivot for her to scoot around. As soon as she was done, she hopped up onto my boot, apparently finding the slippery frozen ground too chilly for her liking. Sighing, I bent and picked her up again, putting her on my shoulder, since she was now too awake to go peacefully back into my pocket.

I got my phone out and pressed a button to illuminate the screen and check the time. It was only six p.m., but it was as dark as midwinter midnight. I started walking again. A mist-form darted out of the trees on my right, gleaming in my sight like a cloud of tarnished silver. It trailed streamers of color and darker smoke as it crossed the road, and a trio of the white doglike demons I'd seen on Friday chased it, letting out unearthly howls. Not wanting to be seen by them, I backed up into the line of trees beside the road until I felt a shaggy cedar trunk at my back. Chaos tensed and crouched, her tail moving rapidly along my neck as she prepared to leap at them, but I clamped a hand down on her and wrestled her inside my coat before she could make the weird, challenging bark she'd issued the last time. I did not want these creatures after me again.

The white demon dogs caught the cloudy form near the opposite edge of the road and locked their jaws on it as if it were a thing of flesh and bone. They began yanking it back and forth between them while they made noises that sounded like laughter.

Two more shapes ran out of the bushes on my side. They trailed water as if they'd just come from the lake, though no one would swim voluntarily in that frigid water day or night at this time of year. The two new creatures headed for the ring of demons. I shifted my sight deeper into the Grey, looking through the gleaming mists in hope of seeing the creatures better.

One I recognized as Jin—a yaomo, according to Danziger—but this time his human form wasn't wearing a fancy suit. Like his companion, he was stark naked and streaming wet. I concentrated on the other newcomer. It was a slim woman who lit up the Grey with her aura of dancing, brilliantly colored lights that gave off the odor of incense. The lights looked like small, captive versions of the bright energy bolts I'd been seeing all around the lakes and inside the Newmans' house. The woman's actual face or form was hard to see in the moving illumination; all I could tell was that she was slender and had long dark hair.

She moved with incredible speed and grace, stopping a hairbreadth from the monsters that worried at the spirit in their circle. She thrust a finger at them and snapped some words at Jin that I couldn't understand.

The yaomo waded into the circle of smaller demons, slapping them aside and snarling at them, manifesting his inhuman form as he snatched the ghostly thing away from them. The guai didn't like that and attempted to bite at him and fight back, but Jin shook them off, letting out a shriek that sent a shudder up my spine.

Holding on to the struggling mist-shape, he turned back toward the woman while the smaller demons lurked behind him, heads down, but beady eyes watching Jin for any chance to snatch the spirit back from him. The woman reached out and grabbed it from him. Then she tilted her head and let out a thread of sound that gleamed with color, twisting and coiling around the struggling Grey form, binding it and drawing it back toward her body. . . .

Headlights swept down onto the asphalt and struck across the figures as a car turned onto Highway 101 from East Beach Road. The woman gasped, snatching at the silvery cloud, and the entire group of demons bolted into the bushes on the east side of the highway, the spirit thing wailing as the woman dragged it away and slipped into the darkness in their wake. Her brilliant aura and smell faded swiftly into the distance beyond the edge of the trees.

I'd had enough. I stepped back into the normal and out to the edge of the tarmac, waving one arm while I clutched the ferret securely inside my coat. A dark red Mercedes SUV pulled to a halt in front of me.

I walked to the passenger-side window, which was already on its way down, and glanced in. The driver turned on the courtesy light and looked over at me. It was Geoff Newman and I wasn't even surprised.

"Get in, Miss Blaine."

"Is that an order, Mr. Newman?"

He fumed. "It's common sense, woman! You don't know what sort of things run in the night here."

"You mean like those demons that just cleared the road?"

His eyes widened a little, but he just said, "Whatever they were, wouldn't you rather not meet them again tonight?"

"That depends on what other monsters you might take me to."

"Goddamn it, I'm trying to help you! Get in and I'll take you to your car or your hotel or wherever you like, but let's not just sit here like sheep!"

The flashes of anxious orange were back in his dim green energy corona. He was genuinely worried. I took a deep breath, making up my mind, and got in.

Chaos poked her head out of my coat and gave me a dirty look as I buckled the seat belt over her.

"Jesus! What's that?" Newman yelped when he saw her.

"It's a ferret. Don't worry—she's a pet, not some wild animal I picked up on the road."

He huffed and forced his attention back to driving. "I know what a ferret is. I just wasn't expecting one to come bursting out of your chest like an alien."

I laughed. I hadn't pegged Newman for a science fiction fan, though I certainly didn't know enough about him to have made that leap, anyway. "I'm sorry. I'll try to keep my aliens to myself."

"Well," he said, but he seemed to switch thoughts as he finished his sentence. "So, where can I take you?"

"My truck's at Storm King ranger station."

"You drive a truck?"

I nodded. As far as I'm concerned, the "SUV" thing is a load of marketing crap: It's either a sport vehicle or a utility vehicle. His Mercedes was more of a luxury utility vehicle while mine was definitely just plain utility, but neither one of them was "sporty."

As we rolled down the dark highway, he started to talk, flicking on the wipers as slushy rain finally arrived. "Miss Blaine, I don't want you to have the wrong impression. . . ."

"What impression do you think I have?"

"You may be thinking Jewel's a little . . . unstable. It's not true. She's just . . . put a lot of herself into the community here and she has some odd ideas sometimes."

"Trust me, Mr. Newman. Your wife's ideas are not that far off the beam. There is something very unsavory around here."

"Ridenour's gotten to you."

"No. Not the way you mean, at least. I don't think your wife's crazy, either, but that doesn't mean I trust either one of you—or anyone else from this place—as far as I could drop-kick the pair of you."

"Is that why you told her no?"

I made a show of thinking about it. "Yep. That would be it."

"Jewel didn't kill her father. If—if anyone were to say she had, they'd be wrong, and if either of us were to have done it, it would have been me," he babbled.

I sighed and rubbed the ferret's ears. "Mr. Newman, I'm not the one you need to convince, and I'd advise you not to say anything that stupid when Ridenour—or whoever gets the case—comes around with questions. I cannot be involved in an active homicide investigation and especially not one that might end up on the feds' plate. I could lose my license."

He chewed his lower lip. "What about the rest . . . ?"

"Were you eavesdropping on our conversation?"

"No, but if it were just about the homicide thing, you'd have said so to Jewel just like you did to me. So that's not what's put your tail in a twist."

"Do you believe in ghosts, Mr. Newman?"

He stared at me. "What?"

I pointed out the windshield. "Deer."

He looked up and slammed on his brakes. The phantom herd of long-dead deer ambled across the road, through his front bumper. He stared at them; then he turned his head and stared at me.

"It rubs off after a while," I said. "When you spend enough time with someone who sees ghosts and works magic, even a normal person starts to see the freak show. And then you start to think like them, too. You might want to drive on now."

Newman got the Mercedes moving again.

"The problem I have here, Mr. Newman, is that the unsavory elements are running the show, and I don't know the players or the play, but I'm reasonably sure I can't do what your wife wants without becoming as bad as the rest of them. Now, why would I want to do that?"

He turned in at the ranger station and said nothing until he'd pulled up next to my lonely Rover. Then he looked at me, keeping his hand on the automatic door lock, holding me in the Mercedes until he'd said his piece. His aura went an ugly chartreuse shade. "You kicked over the wasps' nest; it's up to you to clean it up."

I unbuckled my seat belt, but I didn't try to leave yet. "I didn't kick over anything. This rotten situation was already brewing, and it was what killed Steven Leung as much as any person did. All I did was bring a light."

"And now that you've shined your flashlight on the problem, you think it'll go away."

I shook my head, disappointed. "Not exactly. See, when I said 'a light,' I meant something more like a match to gunpowder. You don't want to see what will happen if I accept your wife's proposal. Because I won't be dictated to about my methods; I'll do it my own way, and that way is not pretty. Now, please unlock the door and let me go."

"No." He looked sick and scared, but I had to give him credit for balls.

What I didn't have to do was give in. I rolled my eyes and reached under my coat for my pistol. "Let me out or I'll have to shoot your car." I let him glimpse the hard shape of the slide and sight as I drew it, carefully keeping it pointed away from him. I placed the P7's muzzle against the passenger window. It made a hard clink as the metal touched the glass. I glanced back at him.

He looked about to faint. Then he pushed the lock release. I had to keep one arm across the ferret—which was tricky—as I opened the door and stepped out. Once I was standing on the ground between the two vehicles, I reholstered the gun—I hadn't even cocked it, but Newman didn't know the difference. I turned and started unlocking the Rover as half-frozen rain worked into my collar and hair. I refused to hurry, to give him the impression I was afraid or anxious, but I was still relieved when I got into the seat and closed the door on the weather.

Newman watched me the whole time, rolling down the window as I started to pull out. He shouted, "A quarter of a million dollars!"

I just drove away.

It wasn't that I wasn't tempted by the money, but I didn't want to think about it right then. I wanted to go home. I didn't even want to stop at the hotel and pick up my things. I certainly didn't want to spend another night here. I could still catch a ferry and be home before midnight. I could even drive all the way down to Olympia and back up the other side of the Sound if I had to. In my gut I knew I wasn't going to escape, but for now I'd do whatever it took to get home and away from Blood Lake.

TWELVE

Between the packing, checking out, and waiting for the ferry, I reached home about eleven o'clock. Quinton was hunched over my computer, typing madly, when I came in. Even though he'd said he'd see me when I got back, I hadn't really expected him to be right in my living room. He shut his session down and came to greet me as soon as I closed the door.

He slipped his arms around me and hauled me close for a kiss and a lingering hug before either of us said a thing. "Hey. You're back," he started.

"I brought my front, too."

"Mm . . . I could tell," he said, squeezing me a little closer so my breasts flattened against his chest. I gave him a smile, but it was a little less enthusiastic than usual. He noticed. "Are you OK? You seem wrung out."

I shrugged it off. "Oh, yeah. Just tired. Long day watching a bunch of guys haul a sunken car out of a lake."

He leaned back, loosening his hug, and gave me a curious look. "Sounds weird. What was the car doing in the lake?"

I tucked my chin and pressed the top of my head to his shoulder. "What cars usually do—sink. I really don't want to talk about it right now. Can we go to bed?"

He pulled me close again. "Sure, sweetheart. Sure we can."

Of course, we had to unpack the ferret first and she

wasn't ready to go back to bed, so our desires had to wait on her pleasure. But we did manage to fall into bed around midnight. Not that we did a lot of sleeping....

In the morning, we both got up earlier than we wanted to, but I had work to do and Quinton had some mysterious project he had to get back to, so we gave up on attempting to unmake the bed from the inside out and returned to work.

From the office I started on the business that was still hanging over my head from before I'd left. First I called Nanette Grover and, once I had her on the line, she argued that having found the car and body and turned further investigation over to the sheriff's department, I was now free to come back to work for her. I hadn't found anything on Shea, though; he was still as much a blank as ever. I needed more time on him and, much as I'd have liked to, I couldn't walk away from the broader problem of the lake, its monsters, and its magicians. I knew the police wouldn't get into it—it wouldn't even register in their minds and whatever motive they eventually found for Leung's murder would be as mundane and sordid as for any other normal-world homicide. And there was the matter of the Grey itself.

There wasn't much doubt in my mind that Jewel Newman's job was at least akin to the best interests of the Grey and the Guardian Beast. There might have been a loophole to get me out of the situation, but ignoring Grey jobs tended to be a lousy idea. Like the proverbial bad penny, it would keep turning up and causing problems until I gave in and dealt with it, anyway. I was also a bit on the fence about the quarter of a million dollars. Certainly it was a tempting amount, but taking the money would imply my doing Jewel's bidding, and what she demanded in the heat of grief and anger—or in cold calculation—might not be so wise once things began coming apart under my prodding. Her avowed preference was that I kill the competing mages, but I was no assassin. Her second choice—to drive them away—was more to my taste; better still if I could get them to turn on one another.... I was still a little unsure of my powers in the Grey now, but I was reasonably certain I could make a damned fine mess if I tried. And after a night to think about it, I wanted to try, no matter how much I despised Jewel.

Even with these twisted thoughts, I carried on talking to Nan. "I still don't have any information on Shea's background, and the family of the dead man is still very concerned about the situation at the lake. It's complicated by the overlapping jurisdictions. There's still a lot of information to be found on both cases. I'd like to go back out and work them both some more. You know how the family becomes the last concern when agencies start bickering over who's stuck taking out the garbage," I said.

Nan made a noise of disgust. "Yes, I do, but that's a distraction, and it doesn't make me any happier about this. Stick on Shea and make sure I have something before we hit trial or I will start contracting with Feldman in the future. Don't let this become a habit, Harper."

"I understand, Nan."

"I hope you do. I hire you because you're reliable. Whether we're friends or not makes no difference to me."

If we *had* been friends, that would have hurt, and it stung more than I liked to admit, but I nodded at the phone, repeating, "I understand."

"Good." She hung up.

I wasn't sure if I was burning a bridge or opening a door to something else, but I didn't have a lot of time to ponder it. My phone rang within seconds of my putting it down.

Wishing I'd stopped for coffee on the way in, I picked up the phone again. "Harper Blaine."

"Rey Solis. I wanted to ask you a few more questions."

"Can it wait a few hours? I have a ton of paperwork to catch up on since I spent the weekend out on the Peninsula." He rarely called—usually he just showed up if he wanted to grill me—so I guessed he wasn't yet ready to arrest me for making Will Novak disappear, but I still thought maybe I ought to be considering the money end of the Newmans' offer a little more seriously. If I had to dodge Solis until I could find a plausible way to convince him I wasn't a good suspect, a quarter of a million dollars would certainly come in handy. . . .

"So I understood."

"Understood what?"

"That you have been busy around Lake Crescent finding sunken cars with human remains in them."

I sighed in annoyance. "It wasn't exactly a plan."

"So Steven Leung was your missing person case."

"Yes, and now he's found—I'm assuming it is Leung's body in the car. But how do you know about the car and Leung?"

"The Clallam County sheriff's investigator called me this morning to vet you."

"To vet me? Why?"

"Professional courtesy. And I suppose he is curious what a King County–based PI was doing in his territory."

"I think I told you it was a coincidence. I was in the area on some pretrial work for Nanette Grover. I assume you know her."

"Professionally only."

"Not surprising; she's not a social butterfly."

"How did you come to be involved in this case?"

"One of the witnesses I was looking for mentioned a car accident in the area a few years earlier. It just sounded odd, so I looked it up, but there wasn't any record of the accident and . . . you know how I like to poke my nose into anything weird," I said with a heavy dose of sarcasm. "The more I looked at the information on Leung, the more it seemed like he'd simply disappeared, and with that and the accident information, I thought I should find out if they were connected, since no one else seemed to give a damn. The more information I got, the more it looked like I was right. So I poked around the lake a bit on the weekend and found the car. That's all. I'm more than glad to turn over my research on Leung's financial and property situation to the investigator if he wants it."

"I'm sure he will."

"Then I'll be sure to send it over, if you give me the investigator's name and office address."

"I would also like to speak with you myself."

"Why? What business is Leung's death or his family's misery to you?"

"They aren't. But I am still concerned with the matter of William Novak."

There it was. I wanted to swear, but I held back. "Solis, I'll talk to you all you like in a few hours, but I have to get some work done here first. We can meet after lunch if you like. Wherever you want."

"That will do. One o'clock here at the police department. I'll meet you in the west lobby."

I would have objected—if I had any intention of turning up—but I'd already given him the choice of place and time; throwing a fit wouldn't change anything. "All right," I replied. I think I sounded snappish and I didn't care. Nor did I put the phone down politely. I just dumped it into the cradle and got ready to go out.

Before I could go on with anything else, I needed to talk to Michael Novak. I'd let it slide, and now with Solis breathing down my neck, apparently thinking I was somehow responsible for Will's disappearance, I had to face up to it. I also had to find out what Michael had already told Solis and if there was any hope that I didn't have to duck and run.

The pressure from Nan and my own sense of paranoia about both the situation at the lake and Solis's sudden interest in Will's disappearance swamped my brain, and I dove into the nearest of the impending disasters without noticing I'd forgotten all about meeting with Ben Danziger.

It didn't take very long to hunt Michael Novak down. He and Will had been in London for almost two years and he'd been back in Seattle for less than one, so he'd gravitated back to the parts he knew best and the jobs he understood. I found him at a motorcycle repair shop in the industrial part of Ballard. I recognized his shaggy head of blond hair even streaked with grease and at a distance. The shop was noisy, full of metallic bangs and loud engines, but in spite of the cacophony, the energy around the place flowed in calm blue lines and concentrated swirls. I didn't think I stood much of a chance of being heard over the din and I didn't want to pick my way through the work area nor yell my business at full volume, so I walked to the customer counter and waited for one of the men in coveralls to come talk to me.

The guy who walked up to the counter was in his mid-thirties, tanned so leathery, the creases at the corners of his eyes looked as if they'd been stitched into his skin. Even with the nearest engine barely idling, he had to raise his voice. "Do for ya?"

"Michael Novak?" I asked, pointing.

"Why?"

"Personal business about his brother."

The mechanic winced slightly, the creases beside his eyes deepening to canyons for a moment. "Ahhh . . . yeah." He turned his back on me and let out a piercing whistle, waving his arms over his head.

The volume in the place dropped in a wave moving from him to the rear wall, and all eyes, including Michael's, turned toward the front. His gaze flickered over me and the corona of pleasant blue around him sank down to a narrow band I could barely see at this distance.

"Novak!" the mechanic at the counter yelled. "You good for fifteen minutes?"

"Yeah," Michael called. He put his tools down with care before he started walking my way. The noises started up again as Michael passed each workstation.

The man at the counter looked at me. "S'all right?"

"Yes, thanks."

He nodded, but he also didn't return to work until Michael had stopped beside me and turned to give him a reassuring nod. "Back in ten, OK?" Michael asked.

"No problem, man," the other guy replied, heading for the bike he'd been working on.

I glanced toward the narrow strip of graveled parking outside and Michael shrugged, leading me out. He kept going around the corner of the building and stopped to lean back against it. Cold wind channeled between the buildings and pushed the sound of the shop into the canal ahead of us. Michael started to cross his arms over his chest, but then he dropped them to his sides and pressed his palms against the cold wall, letting his gaze fall to the ground.

It was a strange posture, as if he was afraid of me but couldn't or wouldn't bother to hide it. The thin line of his aura flickered blue, then orange, and back to blue. "I wasn't sure you'd ever come around," he started.

"I'm sorry, Michael. I should have come sooner."

He shrugged, still not looking at me. "I think I understand. Will . . . really screwed things up. After all you did, he couldn't let it go. He got so crazy at the end. . . ."

"That isn't why," I said. "I was just being selfish, pretending everything was all right everywhere, just because it was all right where I was."

"How all right was that?" he scoffed. "I heard you got shot and it was pretty bad." He snuck a glance at me, as if looking for evidence of the wound or some change he could spot with his ordinary vision.

I worried my bottom lip a second. "Yeah . . . it was bad. But I'm still here. And Will's not."

Michael finally looked up at me. "What happened to him? I mean . . . I know he's not coming back, but . . . He really isn't, is he?"

I shook my head. "No, he's not coming back."

"Not even . . . like a ghost?"

I knew there was something even worse than ghosts in his mind, but almost a year after London, he seemed to be trying to soften what he knew about the Grey and its horrible denizens. I didn't know if I was going to make that easier or harder for him.

"Not like any of those things," I said. "Not at all."

He looked relieved, yet he still asked, "But what happened? Why can't they find any trace of him?"

The words hurt as I said them, as if each syllable had barbs. "I'm not sure you want to know. Because if you do, you may want to tell the truth when . . . someone asks you for it, and they'll think you're crazy if you say something like that at my trial."

"*Your* trial?"

I nodded. "Detective Solis thinks I killed your brother. Or am responsible, at least, since I was the last person to see him alive."

Michael pushed himself off the wall, standing straight and wide-eyed. "No, he doesn't! He doesn't think it's you; he thinks it's me!"

I blinked at him. "What?"

"Solis thinks *I* killed Will. He thinks it was an accident, that I was angry at Will or scared of him or something like that. He thinks that because Will hit me, I—I hit him back. But I didn't! I didn't, I swear to God. I swear. . . ." His voice broke and he covered his face with his grease-stained hands, his words coming out in hard, gulping sobs. "I don't want to be here. I want to go back to England. I tried to hold out here, but I can't make it—I can't stand the pitying stares and the horrible memories. I was going to leave, but that detective started asking around and then he told me he would find out." He lifted his face. "I can't go while he thinks I did it, but I *want* to. I want to so bad. I just want out of this place. I just want to go back to where I had a life I understood. I want to make my own life."

I grabbed onto his shoulders, keeping him from sliding to his knees from the weight of his despair. "Michael, I know you didn't do it. I *know* it was nothing to do with you. But you can't run while you're under suspicion, and why would anyone believe you killed Will?"

It took him a moment to catch his breath and rein his emotions in, but he managed. "Because . . . he broke my jaw. And then . . . he ran off."

"He ran off?" I questioned, not because I didn't believe him, but because something wasn't adding up: Wygan had made Will call me to come to the gymnasium on the night I'd most recently died. Will had clearly been a prisoner and in their clutches for hours by the time I saw him. He certainly hadn't run to Wygan and the asetem. How had they grabbed him?

"Tell me what happened, Michael. Just tell me in sequence. When did Will hit you and why? What happened before that and what time was all this?"

Michael sucked in a shaking breath and looked ill. "It was about four, I think. In the afternoon. I came down here to drop off my references—I was trying to get a job. I'd been sticking to Will or trying to keep him with me, because every time I didn't, he'd slip away or do something horrible to himself. I'd taken him to the doctors when we first got here and they said he shouldn't be left alone, but . . . I needed a job—we needed the money so badly. I was here that time you called me—remember?—about Charlie Rice's shop. That was when Will socked me in the eye. I thought he couldn't hear me talking to you, but he did, and he asked if you were going to Charlie's and I lied and said no. But he didn't believe me."

"He was your older brother and you've never been a good liar, Michael," I said.

His face crumpled and he squeezed his eyes shut for several seconds until he could open them again without leaking tears. "I know. He knew I was lying and he tried to go after you. I told him he should leave you alone, that we should go back to the hospital. But he didn't want to go and he hit me. I—I was so shocked, I couldn't stop him. He'd never hit me before. Will was like my dad as well as my brother, but he'd never even yelled at me, and now he'd gone and smacked me one right in the face and I didn't know what to do. The crew here tried to help hold on to him, but Will got away, and then they tried to help me, which kept me from doing anything to find him right away. Then Charlie called me when he had Will arrested for harassing you. He was pretty worried about him, too.

"When I got him out of jail, I tried to make Will go to the hospital, because he was acting so strange, but he wouldn't go and he gave me the slip again. He kept doing that—I'd find him and then he'd get away again. That last day, he got a phone call and said he needed to go somewhere, but he wouldn't tell me where. I figured he was stalking you again and I said I wouldn't let him go. I needed to come here and drop off my paperwork, but I couldn't leave him alone, so I made him come with me—I even locked him in the car like a little kid while I came inside. But he got out and when I tried to hold on to him and make him go home, he fought with me. He hit me in the face with a piece of steel pipe from one of the workbenches. I already had the black eye from earlier in the week, so I didn't see him swing at me until it was too late. And then he was out of here so fast, no one could catch him.

"Mencez and the crew wanted to send me to the hospital, but I wouldn't go—I didn't know I had a broken jaw. I just had to find Will, so I went after him, but I didn't know where he was. I just kept looking everywhere I could think of. Then I got smart and I called the rental car company—"

"Why a car rental company?"

He paused, catching his breath. "We didn't have our own car—we sold it when we moved to England—so I had a rental. The rental company has those tracking things on the cars in case they get stolen. So I finally remembered that and called them, and they said the car was up on Queen Anne Hill. I went to get it and look for Will—"

"What time was that?" I asked.

"I don't know . . . like seven o'clock? It wasn't dark yet."

That had been before I arrived, when the vampires were only just waking. The asetem and their pharaohn would have been hungry and greedy for their particular food—fear. I shuddered at the thought. I tried not to let Michael see my distress; he was upset enough already.

"All right, so what then?" I asked.

"I kept looking for Will, but I couldn't find any sign of him and I was . . . having some trouble. People wouldn't talk to me because of how I looked, and I couldn't see on the left side and I felt kind of sick and dizzy. . . . I didn't know how bad I was hurt and I don't think I'd have cared. I drove the car around, looking for Will everywhere, anywhere he might have walked to from there. I wound up down in Myrtle Edwards Park—you know, that park along the bay front where they used to have the Hemp Festival. I don't know how I got the car in there, but I guess I made a turn somewhere and ended up on the bike path instead of a road. About then I just stopped driving. I think I passed out. Things get pretty hazy about then. . . ."

"Where in Myrtle Edwards?" I asked, fearing the answer. The long narrow park with its winding twin bike trails borders Elliott Bay from a few miles south of the ship canal where we now stood, all the way to downtown. There are plenty of train yards, commercial ship docks, industrial Dumpsters, and unwatched bends along the shore where a body could be dropped.

Michael bit his lip, his brows knitting down and telltale sparks of sick green fear shooting off his aura. "Near the grain elevator . . ."

I swore softly: Solis must have seen the grain elevator as an ideal place to dump a body—or even a live person who couldn't fight back, if he thought Michael had given as good as he got in the fight the mechanics had witnessed. I supposed the detective was hot to talk to me because he thought I could nail the timing for him and help put a noose around Michael's neck whether he could find a body or not. And if I'd been Solis, I'd have been thinking the same way.

I knew Michael hadn't done anything but try to help his brother, even while he was in pain, half-blind, and probably bleeding, but it wouldn't look like that to an outsider. It would look like a crime of the moment driven by overwhelming rage and complicated by pain and a traumatized memory. Considering all the injuries and arguments the brothers must have had while using it, the rental car probably had plenty of blood samples from both of them. Those blood traces would have been hard to get so long after the fact, once the car had been cleaned and rented out over and over, but not impossible. All the records would have been there for Solis to put together, much like I'd put Leung's pieces together: police reports, hospital records, impound receipts, rental agreements, witnesses. . . . Michael hadn't helped himself with his actions and evasions, nor with his desire to skip town, which was probably no secret to anyone.

"Michael," I asked, "why didn't you file a missing person report on Will?"

"What could I say? I knew Will's disappearance had to be tied up with whatever you were doing at the gymnasium— all that business with the kidnapping—and that it had to be more of what happened in London, and how could I explain that? It was rough enough with the English cops. I couldn't do that again. The gym—that was the end of it all, wasn't it?"

I nodded.

Michael looked teary again. "See, I knew you knew what had happened to Will, but you hadn't said anything and he hadn't been found, so I knew he was gone. I didn't *need* to file a report. And if I had, it would have just been as bad for you. And why should I when I just want to leave here?"

"Oh, Michael. You should have just thrown me to the wolves and saved yourself. Now Solis has every reason to think you killed your brother and dumped the body in the grain elevator—from which it's now long gone. He doesn't have to have a body to build a circumstantial case and now he's got a damned good one against you. A decent defense will break it down, but in the process, you'll be spending a lot of time in jail over something you didn't do and Solis and the rest of the department will try everything they can to persuade you to confess to it. Because that's the easier route for them."

"I may not have done it, but I deserve to be blamed—it's my fault he's gone. If I'd been a better brother, if I'd called the doctor, or the cops or . . . anything but what I did, he wouldn't have gone and he wouldn't have followed you and whatever happened to him . . . wouldn't have happened."

"That's not true. He didn't follow me to the end. He was brought there well before I got there. That must have been the phone call he got, probably from Goodall, telling him some irresistible lie about me. They used him as bait and they would have used you, too, if you'd been able to stop him from going. You were a good brother; you saved him once in London and you were trying to save him again twice over here. You did everything you could and more than most would even try to do. You didn't fail. You don't deserve any blame."

"But I didn't save him. . . ."

One of the mechanics stuck his head around the corner and glanced at us. "Hey, man, you about done?"

Michael waved at him. "Yeah. I . . . just need another minute. I'll be right in." He looked back at me with an intense gaze and whispered, "I didn't save him and he's gone forever. And I just want to go home." He started to turn away and go back into the garage.

I caught his arm, feeling the shock of his despair leap like a spark through my hand and into my heart. "I know it won't be enough for you yet, but Will didn't die horribly at the hands of monsters. He didn't even die as you think of it. He was alive at the end and he *chose* to go on to something else."

Michael gave me a bitter look. "This isn't the 'he's gone on to a better place' speech, is it? Because that's just so much bull."

"Then listen to what I'm actually saying. You remember all Marsden and I told you about the Grey and the things that live there?"

He nodded, wary, but listening.

I took a slow breath before I tried to explain. "There's a sort of gatekeeper for that place. It keeps the monsters on their side of the line and us on ours."

"Well, it didn't do a very good job." Michael's voice shook.

"No, it didn't. Not this time. Because Wygan destroyed it." I was surprised at how easy it was to tell Michael these things. The Grey had always tried to muzzle me in the past. But perhaps I'd surpassed the need to be regulated. Or maybe it just couldn't stop me. So I went on. "There's no time for the details—you probably don't even want them— but without this guardian, things fall apart. The monsters get loose in the world. At the end, someone had to take that job and Will chose it for himself. *Chose.* No one forced him.

You know he was breaking, and what happened up in Queen Anne would have left him a wreck in this world. He had a chance to be better, but he had to leave here completely."

"So . . . he *is* some kind of ghost after all?"

"No. He can't haunt you, or be haunted by the memory of life. He's not some kind of remnant of his former self; he's something else. I can't even explain what it is—I don't really know—but it protects us . . . from things even worse than what you saw and heard and fought against in London and again here. That's what became of Will."

Michael didn't look a lot happier, but he did seem less afraid and angry. The greenish tinge around his head faded a little and the orange sparks sputtered out. He seemed to be thinking about it, but hadn't made up his mind if he believed it or if it comforted him any.

"Are you sure, knowing all that, that you want to go back to England?"

He bit his lip until it bled, but he nodded. "I had friends who didn't look at me like I'm going to break any minute. Even—even with the things that are there, like Marsden and the vampires," he added with an expression so bitter his mouth could barely shape the words, "I'd rather be there than here."

A sour cold twisted through me and my throat felt harsh as I said, "All right. I'll take care of Solis." Then I added, "I'll find some way to get him onto another track. I promise he won't arrest you."

Michael nodded, still abstracted, and headed back inside to work, still trying to make something better of the situation.

I breathed a few long breaths, trying to loosen the ache in my chest. I didn't know how I was going to keep that promise, but I would. I owed Michael at least that. And I owed it to Will, too.

THIRTEEN

After leaving Michael, I found a place to eat lunch and think. Obviously, I wasn't going to skip out on my meeting with Solis after all, which was a relief, but also a problem. I had to find out if Solis really did believe that Michael had a hand in his brother's disappearance, and if so, I had to turn him off that idea without telling him the whole truth of the matter. He'd never have believed it if I did, anyway, and I didn't need to be suspected of being any crazier than he probably already thought me. But I had to have a plausible story that would cast a different light on the evidence he had. Once that light was on, I'd have to let him reconstruct a satisfying scenario on his own; if I gave him a tale that was too complete and whole, he'd become more suspicious, not less. He had to persuade himself.

I finished my lunch and drove back to my office. Parking at the municipal garage is ridiculously expensive, so I left the Rover in my own parking lot and walked to Seattle police headquarters at Fifth and Cherry. The usual afternoon rain hadn't started up yet and it wasn't as cold in Seattle as it had been around Lake Crescent, so I didn't mind the hike, even if Cherry was one of the steepest slopes in downtown. I let my mind wander a little as I went, trying to decide what angle I'd take with Solis, but also just letting the problem of the lake tumble around in hope of some inspiration as to what I should do and if I should take Jewel Newman's money.

The differences in the Grey landscape of Seattle reminded me that whatever I chose to do, I would not have the advantage of knowing the magical lay of the land any more than I knew the physical geography around the lake. I'd need help up there. But I wasn't sure whom I could trust. I didn't even know who the other mages that so upset Jewel were aside from her sister, Willow, and I hadn't met her. I wasn't sure about Ridenour's involvement, but while he wasn't a mage, he could still be trouble. I didn't know who else was in the game; the only player I had any kind of line on was Jin, the yaomo. . . .

Thinking about the problem of Chinese demons, I paused for a light at Fourth Avenue and spotted a familiar-looking black coat and hat in the crowd on the opposite sidewalk. I thought about trying to call out to Quinton, but the distance was too great to expect him to hear me. I'd barely formulated the thought, though, when he turned and went across in the other direction, heading north toward Marion Street and the library. I would have liked to catch up to him, but I didn't have the time, so I contented myself that I'd be able to page him once I was done with Solis and not have to tell him I was going on the lam from the cops.

The cliché from a dozen old crime movies made me smile and I was still smiling when I entered the police headquarters lobby. Solis and his dour expression wiped that off my face soon enough. He escorted me through the security checkpoint and deep into the building to a small room with a sign beside the door that read ATTORNEY CONSULTATION ROOM—NO UNAUTHORIZED RECORDING. That was more reassuring than having our chat in an interrogation room, but only a little, and I experienced an unpleasant jolt of alarm at the thought that Michael might have been wrong about Solis's suspicions. The decor wasn't any nicer, either, but at least the chairs were clean.

Solis closed the door behind us and dragged his chair to the short end of the table so he could sit at an angle and closer to me than the usual face-to-face formality of interrogation. I cocked an eyebrow at him.

"You're not here under any sort of charges, Ms. Blaine," he offered. "This is not a formal meeting."

I made a show of glancing around the room. "I feel like I ought to have my lawyer. . . ."

"I assure you, that's not the case. Now, in the matter of William Novak—"

"Who filed the missing person report?" I cut in.

Solis blinked. "Mr. Novak's doctor."

"Which Mr. Novak and which doctor?"

"William's attending physician, Dr. Booth, at Harbor View. According to his report, he became alarmed when his patient missed several appointments in a row. Mr. Novak was considered psychologically fragile. Is that all you want to know?"

"It'll do."

"Tell me all of your interactions with William Novak from the time you returned from England, please."

"I've already gone over them with you once."

"I am aware of that, but I want to hear it again. Please include as many particulars as you can remember." He took a notebook out of his jacket pocket and flipped it open to a marked page. I assumed he wanted to check my new statements against the old, and that irritated me for an instant, until I thought what a good opportunity it really was to color in some persuasive bits of truth. . . .

We fenced back and forth for a while, him picking at details, me filling in petty information that revealed little. Finally, he sat back, giving me a long, considering stare. "We should give up this pretense. I do not want to know what Michael Novak told you earlier today. What I *do* want are details that prove or disprove his tale. So, again, what can you tell me?"

So he knew I'd seen Michael. I wondered which of us he was having watched. . . . "Do you really believe Michael Novak is responsible for his brother's disappearance?" I asked.

"Like you with your interest in Steven Leung's case, I find myself plucking at threads, looking for a pattern. There are more pressing cases that should occupy me, which is why I asked you here. I can spare very little time for this, but I cannot put it aside. There is a shape of a crime, but no clear picture. It is so much smoke and mirrors without substance," he spat. Frustrated whips of orange energy around him punctuated his unhappy words.

"I honestly don't remember some of the details," I said. Some things *had* scrubbed themselves from my mind; others were too bizarre to describe.

"I believe you. But what more can you bring to mind? If there's a fact that will cement the cause of William Novak's disappearance, I want it, whether it implicates Michael Novak or not. I do not wish to lay a charge on an innocent man. But I must know who is innocent, even if I cannot prove who is guilty." I'd rarely seen Solis so annoyed by a case. He took them all seriously and did his best, but this puzzle seemed to bother him at a personal level.

"I don't know what else will help you. I saw Will only twice after I returned from London. Once at Rice House Antiques, and I told you he came to see me before the incident at the gym. At that meeting I asked him to go home and stop trying to get in touch with me. He seemed less agitated and I thought he was going to take my advice, but the next evening, when things went to hell up on the hill, it was actually Will who called and got me to go up there."

"Why did you conceal that from me before?"

"To be frank, I was in no condition to tell you at the time. I thought I'd explained everything when the FBI questioned me, but I guess I didn't. Later, I didn't mention it because I thought you'd blame me for Will's disappearance. You came very close to accusing me of being involved in Kammerling's kidnapping and Todd Simondson's death, so why not an apparent-stalker ex-boyfriend, too? And I wasn't thinking quite straight after getting shot. Most people don't. As you know."

Solis pressed his lips together and kept silent while he thought and drew his frustration back down. In a minute he asked, "Why did Novak call you?"

"Maybe because Goodall had called him."

"Why?"

"To make sure I showed up so Goodall could frame me for what happened. Goodall was a power-hungry monster, but he wasn't stupid. It wouldn't have been hard for him to spot Will following me, find out who he was, and get his number. Beyond that, I'm just guessing that he must have fed Will some story about me that convinced him to sneak away from Michael and go up to Queen Anne. After that, Goodall just had to wait for Will to turn up, and then force him to call me with a cry for help. It's the only thing that makes sense."

"Did you see William at the gymnasium?"

"Yes. Fleetingly. Then I lost him in the confusion. I did try to find him, but that was about when things went to hell. I will tell you this and it's the truth whether you believe it or not: Will was alive when I saw him last."

"It might still be possible that he left the gymnasium and was found by Michael."

I gave it only a moment's thought to calculate the times before I said, "No, it isn't. The timing doesn't work. Unless Michael lied about when he picked up the car and when he left it at the park. The car rental company might be able to tell you where the car was at what time by looking up the tracking device information, but even without that, I saw Will later than Michael claims to have picked up the car. So unless he found Will totally by luck, wandering around *after* the FBI and SPD broke into the gym, that idea won't hold water."

Solis sighed heavily and leaned back into his chair. "I'll check the records. I do not *want* to arrest the young man. I hope that you're right, even though that leaves the mystery of William Novak's disappearance unsolved. You know I hate mysteries."

"Some things never get solved, Solis. There are more than a hundred thousand missing persons cases that have never been closed in the U.S."

"There are as many where I came from, in a country a tenth the size. And this is no better than any of those."

"Except that you aren't going to put an innocent man in jail. Isn't that worth something?"

His brow furrowed, but he didn't reply. He wrote something on a page of his notebook and tore it out, handing it to me. Then he stood up suddenly, tucking the notebook under his arm. "You can go, Ms. Blaine."

"Thank you," I said, picking up the paper and rising to my feet to follow him to the door.

He showed me out and watched me go, and I had no idea what he was thinking as I walked away.

FOURTEEN

I did some more work at the office—the sort of mindless mechanical grind that isn't hard if you have the tools to do it. It wasn't much, but it generated billable hours and I spent the end of the day making up those bills and their accompanying reports. But my mind wasn't on the paperwork. I worried a little about Michael, but not that either of us would find ourselves in jail. I worried more that he was now alone in a haunted world and I could offer him no more comfort. I had to admit, guiltily, that I was glad he wouldn't want any such thing from me. I am not a good family person. I don't have much and I'm not particularly fond of what family I have, for the most part, but I don't wish to build another one from the wreck of someone else's. Michael didn't need me and I hoped he was right about finding his own life again in England. We'd both be better off without the other nearby.

More than Michael's problem, though, I thought about Blood Lake and wondered what I was going to do about it. The paper Solis had given me bore the name of the Clallam County investigator, Deputy Alan Strother. I didn't have a lot of confidence in Strother's ability to get to the truth—not even a normal-world facsimile of it. He seemed like a nice guy; however, no one I'd met around the lakes was likely to take the young deputy and his questions seriously and he was not equipped to deal with the magical world at all.

The differences I'd seen in the Grey as I'd walked up to
the police station had sparked a lot of new questions in my
mind. Their unknown answers left me at their mercy and
could do me harm if I returned to the area—and I was still
trying to decide if I would. I knew the Grey and its grid of
magical energy responded to the pressure of human belief
and desire in strange ways, making way for the manifestation of monsters and ghosts that matched the concepts of
the local people, but rogue elements could also exist—after
all, I'd seen Native American monsters coexisting with pure
thought-constructions and ghosts displaced through time
and space to places they never should have been. Strother
was going to be even further out of his depth with that than
I was.

There was also a problem of culture. Clallam County's
population was more than ninety percent white and about
as middle-of-the-road in terms of belief as any group of average Americans. Strother fit in perfectly. But, according to
the records, Steven Leung had been Chinese and, though I
was guessing from Jewel's dark skin that his late wife had
been black, his daughters probably got some of their own
beliefs from him. That would explain the presence of the
yaomo and yaoguai. But that didn't seem to be the sum of
Blood Lake's strange powers. What else was in the mix?
Mara had suggested that the spell circle and casting I'd seen
were something akin to hoodoo spell work. Jewel had alluded to the native's legends about the area, and the Winter
kids in Port Angeles had been more than passingly interested in the later mysteries around the lake. There were also
the strange puddles of light around the shores and the singing lines that had erupted near Fairholm. . . . All that was
part and parcel of the complications I might have to deal
with.

It didn't appear that I had any real need to flee Seattle to
avoid Solis, but I wasn't enthusiastic about getting deeper
into the problems around Lake Crescent even without that
impetus. I found myself chasing the arguments around and
around in my head: Should I go or should I stay away? Did

I have to go? Was the situation potentially damaging to the Grey? Would I find myself hounded to go? Or could I slip off this hook? I just couldn't come to a clear decision. I wasn't even sure about what I *wanted*.

I pushed myself back from my desk in disgust and stood up. Moving around sometimes helped me think. Even though it had started to drizzle outside, I locked up and went down to the street to walk until I could figure it out.

At first I went around the block and up and down Pioneer Square, but after a while I stopped paying attention to where I was heading and just walked. The sidewalks were empty in the unwelcoming weather and I didn't pass another living human being until I was nearly up to the Seneca Street off-ramp. Without thinking, I'd walked up to the area of Quinton's hidden home beneath the street.

I wondered if he was there. It would have been nice to talk to him about the situation . . . but, given the way he'd vanished earlier, I thought he didn't want to see me. The sun was going down, bruising the clouds darker shades of blue and gray and laying directionless shadows over everything. I turned and walked toward the waterfront.

As I went down the Seneca stairs, I had the sensation of sinking, as if the city were swallowing me. The rain took the remaining light and turned it into twisting strands of gleaming white and silver. I reached the bottom and turned left onto Post Avenue, which would eventually take me back to Pioneer Square. The rain seemed to fall down in wavering curves, filling the narrow road with something that seemed too thick and shiny to be water. . . .

A cold ache burned along the ravaged muscles of my abdomen. I adjusted my sight a little and caught a spinning lurch of vertigo as the air flashed and thickened into the formless ghostlight of the Grey. The long silver strands of rain coiled and writhed, making a sound like wind chimes of glass and steel as they wove into a shape: a long dragonlike head on a slender neck and body that ran in looping undulations into the mist, rippling and cutting it here and there with claws and bones connected by spiderweb sinews of ghost-stuff. Light slipped around the shape of mist and shadow, leaving an impression of vitreous scales. I didn't think I had any power to call it up, but here was the Guardian Beast, looming in the Grey outlines of Post Avenue, breathing cold down onto my face.

It wasn't the same bone-spined monster I'd seen the first time I'd entered the Grey; this was the new version, a younger, sleeker thing built of the remains of Will Novak and the Grey's own memories of guardians past. It didn't have the clattering ruff of spines around its head or the accompanying sense of bone-jelling terror when it came near that the old one had possessed, but it was already different from the barely sketched form of mist and silver I'd last seen. For an instant I wondered how much of Will resonated in the creature, but the thought was knocked away as it lowered its massive skull and butted me in the chest hard enough to send me onto my back in the cold, roiling cloud-stuff of the world between worlds.

The Beast rumbled a growl and churned up the mist with hooked talons as if it were trying to pick me up and put me back on my feet. The power lines of the Grey—the grid—strobed in sudden flurries of red energy that illuminated the face of the Guardian Beast with a suggestion of flesh that bore an angry expression and then vanished back into nothing. The Beast began circling me, laying coil on coil around me like a boa getting ready to squeeze. . . . Then it shrieked and launched upward, dragging me into the air for several feet and swatting me violently toward the water with the whiplike end of its tail and the sound of a ton of steel pipes crashing to the ground.

I hit the wall on the other side of the narrow street with my arms up to protect my head, but even in the Grey mist, the impact hurt and now my whole body ached. I held myself up by digging my hands into the cracks between the bricks. I started to turn and the Guardian spun around, coming back to shove me again, westward. It put its long snout against my spine and pushed as if the building had no more substance than fog and the creature could force me through it. But the wall was a hundred years old and even its ghost memories were solid and resisted my passage.

"Stop it," I yelled, twisting and batting at the Beast's head, trying to get away before it crushed me. It was a little slower than the old one, which was all the hope I had. As it reared to get another run at me, I dropped down flat into the rising silver mist of the Grey, my hearing suddenly clogged with whispers and muttering.

The massive head of the Beast passed over me and the movement pulled sound from the grid like fingers plucking a chord on a harp. "Go."

I rolled onto my back and propped myself up against the flickering wall. "OK, OK! I'll go. Gods, you're as subtle as a train wreck."

The Guardian Beast moved its head through the mist and the Grey laughed at me. I felt the sound roll over me and swim outward into the rippling incorporeal world until it died on distant shores of memory and broken time.

Was this better or worse than the old version? I couldn't decide. The old Guardian hadn't told me what to do, but it hadn't really been communicative at all; it was mostly a bundle of inchoate fury drawn by need alone to whatever threatened the Grey. It had been strong and driven, but incredibly stupid, which had made catching and killing it comparatively easy. This version wasn't so dumb—in either sense. Not that it was exactly chatty, and it certainly didn't have Will's reticent personality.

It gave me another look. Then it whipped around and shot away, through the wall, sucking the chuckling mist with it. I found myself sitting against the brick wall of the Post Alley Pizza Company, thin tendrils of ghost-stuff trickling around me while water started soaking into my clothes. Most of the bruised and battered sensation in my body had gone, but not all, and I still felt tender along my belly and where my limbs had hit the not-so-incorporeal bricks of the building.

I picked myself up and brushed the mud off, muttering, "Oh, yeah, that was graceful. Thanks so much."

But at least I had an answer. It was not an answer I was thrilled with, nor was I thrilled with the manner of its delivery, but still, I couldn't argue that it was ambiguous. I hoped the Guardian wasn't going to make a habit of such assistance to my decision making in the future. Among other things, I must have looked like a drunk at the moment; I was glad no one seemed to have observed my sudden stumble, fall, and flop.

But I was wrong about that. As I turned to walk back out of the narrow street, I saw someone at the base of the stairs, watching me. Great. Swallowing my embarrassment, I headed back the way I'd come, toward the person in the long black coat and hat. . . .

Quinton.

I stopped, feeling a flush on my cheeks. "Hi. . . ."

He raised an eyebrow at me. "Traction problem?"

"Slippery planar problem."

"Ah. Do you need a hand?"

"Not with that, but . . . maybe you could see me home?" I added with a grin.

His face went utterly blank, startling me. I'd seen that lack of expression only once or twice before from him and it was still as opaque to me now as the first time. "No."

I frowned. "Is there something—"

"I have to get back to work. I can come by later."

"I'll be out of town for a while."

His eyes flashed wide for a moment as if in panic and he started to say something. Then he clamped his mouth shut and bit his lip, swallowing hard. "The same case as before?"

"Same area."

"I'll come to your place to get the ferret." He turned from me with a twitch of his shoulders and started off, away from his hidden door.

"Hey," I called out.

He glanced back over his shoulder. "Not now." And he strode across the street and turned to dash up the steps of Post Alley toward the multiple paths of the Harbor Steps complex.

It was clear he didn't want me to follow him or question him, so I didn't pursue, but I stared after him, confused and bothered. What had he nearly said? Why was he being so cryptic?

This had been a day for the books: First Solis's phone call had put me on edge and ready to flee; then Nan had made noises as if she was going to fire me; Michael had flipped my perspective over and driven me right back to Solis, whom I'd had to steer into different lines of investigation; and now I'd had a rough-and-tumble with the new Guardian Beast that dumped me practically into my boyfriend's lap, where I'd been set down as if I were radioactive. What. The. Hell?

The upside was at least I knew where to go from here. But nothing else made any sense at all.

FIFTEEN

I went home and let the ferret out to "help" while I packed up again. Her assistance was more amusing than useful, but at least something made me smile. Watching her romp in my duffel bag and "redistribute" half my spare pair of shoes to her stash under the TV, I hoped Quinton would actually show up to take care of her. I just couldn't risk taking her with me again. I liked having her along and she'd been a small amount of help, but she was a liability even in the Grey world, where I'd expected her to be of more assistance. She was as much a stranger to whatever was loose around Lake Crescent as I was, and she'd almost gotten us munched on by the dog-demons with her aggressive attitude.

At least I wouldn't have to tell Quinton what I was doing; by the time we had the luxury to discuss it, it would be a moot point. I was still confused and annoyed by his behavior. He'd been a little ... protective since I'd gotten out of the hospital, and while it hadn't become a problem, I didn't like it. But now he was acting like a stranger and that didn't add up. I didn't want to cause him distress, but I wasn't going to run my life differently to save him from it. The Guardian Beast had given me the strong impression I wasn't going to be allowed to anyhow, even if I'd been inclined. Whatever was going on with Quinton would also have to wait until I was done with the immediate problem of Blood Lake.

As I plucked Chaos out of the laundry basket, I considered what I knew and what I might need for this investigation. Money wasn't going to be an issue—not with the Newmans' offer—and that alone could grease a lot of wheels, even magical ones. But I was going to need some kind of native guide, for lack of a better description. I wouldn't get any kind of assistance from the Beast—the Guardian's duty wasn't to help me; it was my duty to help *it*—so I'd have to figure out something else or find someone at the lakes. I half hated this job already, but I was stuck with it. It was my role and I'd do my best, but I was definitely going to take the money.

Once I got packed up and had teased Chaos into exhaustion and locked her back into her cage with food and water, I headed, once again, to the Olympic Peninsula. I'd dawdled so long, I barely made the last ferry, and the rainy passage across the sound was more empty and haunted than before.

The ferry seemed to hold a darker body of ghosts this time, the corners and companionways shadowed even in the sad yellow light of the ship's overhead lamps, and an impression of watching eyes staring from reflections of invisible faces lingered in the window glass.

I saw a ball of greenish energy rolling across the floor of the main deck, weaving from side to side in the walkways and skittering over the chairs fixed to the floor until it crossed my own wandering path. The energy ball flared blue and turned decisively to follow me, keeping a strict distance, but sticking to me no matter where I went. When the docking announcement came over the PA and I returned to the Rover, the ball followed me until I got into the truck, when it fizzled away in desultory sparks spent against the steel doors.

Even the road to Port Angeles seemed more haunted. Black shapes swooped across the road and flirted with my headlights, more numerous and nearly recognizable as I got closer to the lakes. Again and again the shapes of great birds, bears, and some sort of flying lizard that spat lightning back into the stormy skies drew close to my truck and then fell aside. The hollow eyes of the dead seemed to stare and watch me as I passed, their host growing until, when I left the safety of my truck for the quiet of my hotel, I had a cortege of ghosts pressing close in my wake. I wondered if they were following to assist me, to hamper me, or were merely drawn to me like moths to candle flames. They gave no indication; they only watched. Even as used to phantoms as I'd become, these unnerved me, and I had difficulty falling asleep.

In the morning, I discovered that the Newmans didn't have a listed phone number. With the dead-slow Wi-Fi connection at the hotel, I gave up on the cross-directory and realized I'd just have to drive up the mountain to their house. When I stepped outside, my entourage of ghosts had thinned but was still there.

As I drove up Highway 101 to Lake Crescent, several of the ghosts in my train fled past and vanished in the direction of the big lake, leaving trails of yellow energy sparkling behind them for a few minutes. I didn't exactly recognize any of them—they were individually quite weak—but they didn't look like local spirits; they looked more like shades that had somehow followed me from the city or joined the strange parade along the route. I found the thought disturbing.

With the sun up, I saw Geoff Newman's Mercedes SUV parked to the side of the house when I arrived. I guessed that meant they were home and I climbed the steps to knock on the front door.

Geoff opened it and stared at me for a moment, blinking as a beam of sunlight pricked at his face. "Miss Blaine?"

I nodded.

He made a couple of indecisive mouth shapes before he stepped back and asked me in. "I'll take you upstairs."

I put my hand on his arm, stopping him. "Which of you made that offer the other night?"

He clenched his jaw and ground his teeth before he answered. "Jewel did."

"And you don't know if you're glad to see me or not, do you?"

"That's about it, yes."

I assumed he meant he'd be as happy if I lived or died, as long as I did it elsewhere. This job didn't look any more attractive to me today than it ever had, but there was a big mouth full of Grey teeth that would make the rest of my existence hell if I didn't take it, and that was considerably more compelling than any other point. Not that I wasn't going to bear some of those other points in mind ...

I nodded again, thoughtful and not making any moves or expression Newman could interpret as eager. I studied him a moment. Then I said, "I'm not finding the prospect much more pleasing than you are, but something does have to change here, before someone else goes missing."

He scoffed. "So long as the tourists are still out of town, no one's going to 'go missing' here. They'll just show up dead."

I raised my eyebrow.

He continued. "I don't begin to think I understand the ... craziness that's going on here, but I do know this for a fact: Once the resorts reopen for the season, the battles change. They get subtler. Until then, it's cutthroat and damn it all. Jewel can't hold out against that anymore. She's too sick. Whoever's got control of the lake come May, that one'll hold the rest in the palm of their hand until October when the park shuts down again and the knives come back out. I don't think she can last until May and unless something changes, she won't get any stronger by October even if she did last that long. Something's gotta give and much as I don't think I like you or this plan of hers, I would rather the 'give' be in my wife's favor, and you seem to be the one she thinks can make that happen."

"She may be right, but if I can do it, the cost won't be small."

He snorted in derision. "You're that greedy that a quarter of a million dollars isn't enough?"

"That's not the cost I mean. You say the magic users around here fight dirty in the off-season. How dirty?"

"Used to be they just did what they were going to do and

pretended everything was free for the taking—even if it was someone else's. They'd at least say sorry if they stepped on one another's toes, though that was about *all* they'd do. Now they're getting mean and trying to control things, and whatever they need to do it, they will. Even if it means doing some serious hurt. There used to be more of 'em."

"What happened to the rest?"

"Some left of their own accord. Some of 'em . . . I don't want to think about it."

"What do you think I'm going to do about them? Your wife wants them to go away, but originally she told me she wants them dead. It sounds like she's not the only one to have that idea. She even suggested that one of them killed your father-in-law and dumped him in the lake for the power. If the rest of the crooked magicians around this lake think the best thing to do is kill people and one another, what alternatives do you think I'm going to be able to offer?"

He stared at me and I stepped past him, going up the stairs on my own to Jewel's room.

Jewel Newman didn't seem much more excited to see me than her husband had. Maybe she'd had time to reconsider . . . but I doubted it. Probably she just didn't like me any more than Geoff did; an ugly necessity is the least loved thing in the world. She didn't turn to see me as I let myself in. She just sighed heavily as she sat in the chair between the bed and the window, staring at the lake outside with a tray resting on her lap. Tarot cards lay in a random spill across the surface.

"I knew you'd come back."

"I imagine you know a lot of things you don't talk about."

"What good would it do me?"

"Probably none. The people who believe would use that knowledge against you. The rest would just laugh and think you've lost your mind."

She made a noise that might have been a laugh or might have been a cough. "As if some of them don't already think I've lost that."

"I don't think you've gone around the mental bend, just that you've lost control—or want to grab it."

She sniffed. "You're brash, but you're not foolish, at least."

"Oh, I'm definitely foolish. Only a fool would take this job."

"Oh really?" she asked, finally turning her head to look at me. "If you're a fool, then what good will you be?"

"What else is a fool good for but walking into danger? Of course, I'm not a complete fool, just enough of one to say yes to this insanity."

"And to my money."

"Certainly to that."

"I think I liked you better when you weren't so venal."

"No, you didn't. Because you couldn't figure out what handle to twist me by. But I'll tell you, the money's not enough."

"I won't go higher."

I walked closer and pulled one of the hard little chairs away from the table at the end of the bed and sat down on the other side of the window so I could face her. I noticed in passing that the card topmost on her pile showed a man in motley about to step off a cliff. "It's not money you have to give me," I started. "I want your promise—the most binding promise you can give—that you'll let me do what I consider necessary." I started to press on the Grey, letting the black needles of compulsion and persuasion grow between us. I didn't try to hide them from her, but I wasn't sure she noticed as I continued. "You'll back me if I ask you, even against your family or your husband or the law. Do you understand?"

She shivered and pulled back from me. "What? How dare you ask that of me? Don't you know who I am, what I can do to you if I choose? I may be sick and dying, but I'm not gone yet and I don't—"

I cut her off, pushing harder as she resisted. "I know exactly what you are." OK, I was lying, but I bluff well. "But if you could do this yourself, you wouldn't need me. I'm not afraid of you and I won't be hampered and hog-tied by any sudden regrets or attacks of conscience from you. If you want this done, it will be my way. It was your father's ghost who got me into this and it's his murder I have to solve. After that, this whole nasty web of magic and murder has to be torn down. I won't kill these people for you—I'm not an assassin—but I'll make them go away. I'll break their hold on the lakes and find a way to take down whoever killed your dad. After that . . . it's on you. Because I'm not here to build anything: I'm here to destroy something. Do you understand that?"

She straightened up defiantly, though I could see it cost her to do so. The cold black points of my demands pressed against her and I could feel her shudder through the Grey. She could resist the geas—the magical contract I was building between us—if she tried hard enough. I wasn't pressing it with any great weight or determination. I had no interest in forcing her: I *wanted* her cooperation. It was in both our interests, I hoped—unless she was lying to me, in which case, I'd have to deal with her, too.

Jewel breathed heavily, fighting, I supposed, against her impulse to be in control and plow me under like a weed. I could feel her distaste for this agreement as a burning in the back of my own throat. She didn't like having to play by anyone's rules but her own. I felt evil for the way I'd done it, but I had her and she knew it.

She glared at me, settling back in her chair and letting the black points of the geas cut into us both. I twitched at the sudden cold, piercing sensation of it and she gave a satisfied smile that lit her eyes with malice.

"All right," she said. "You do what you must and I'll back you. But you'll stay till the last dog's hanged. No running out."

"No running out," I agreed. "But I will need the money up front."

She struggled in the web of the geas. "What?" she screeched.

"You offered it and I'm accepting. And that's how we'll go. Geoff and I can haggle the details of how it's paid out."

Her narrowed glare should have cut me to ribbons, but she was not at the height of her powers anymore and she had already tied herself to me. She was stuck with it. "Agreed," she ground out, choking on her rage.

I let the pressure off, feeling the icy shape of the geas ease into an invisible but unbreakable binding between us. "Call Geoff up and we'll do the paperwork, unless you'd rather you didn't have to watch. . . ."

Jewel growled, but she caught her breath and pressed a button on the remote that rested on the bed beside her. "Geoff, bring up the checkbook and some writing paper." She didn't bother to exert herself to send out a voice of command. She knew her husband would do what she wanted.

I nodded and got up to wait on my feet for Geoff. I knew it would make Jewel happier if I weren't posing as her equal when her husband came in. Her pride was still a formidable power on its own and it didn't hurt me to let her keep it— for now.

The smoldering glare she kept on me while we waited let me know she hated me. I'd have disliked me, too, for knowing what a calculating liar she was; it hadn't slipped past me that she'd never said a damned thing about finding her father's killer in her proposal.

Suddenly she grabbed my hand, her expression tense. "Draw a card."

"What?"

She pointed at the messy pile of tarot cards. "Pick one. Now."

I plucked a card out and flipped it over onto the top of the pile. Jewel's eyes widened, but she said nothing, staring at the image of a stone tower blasted by lightning.

SIXTEEN

Geoff Newman wasn't pleased with the arrangements, but he played the role of secretary without audible complaint. Once things were settled, he followed me back into Port Angeles and to his bank where we made appropriate financial arrangements that left me with a nice chunk of cash and a check with a hell of a lot of zeroes on it. I wished I had Quinton's devious tinkerer's brain at my disposal to figure out where I could hide the stuff, but I'd have to make do with my own.

Before he left me in the drizzly parking lot, Geoff turned back and gave me a hard look. Then he glanced around and held out a key. "You might want to use my father-in-law's cabin instead of staying all the way out here. Be more convenient and you wouldn't have to be driving up and down the hill all the time."

"And I'd be a lot easier to keep tabs on."

He didn't deny it. He just kept standing there, staring at me, the key to Steven Leung's house in his hand.

I shrugged and took the key. "Thanks. I'll think about it."

"Keep your ferret out of the vents—that's all I ask."

"I wouldn't want to leave a mess for Mr. Shea."

Newman snorted. "I've done all the maintenance on that house myself. I wouldn't ask that pie-sucking liar into my place, much less give him the keys."

I nodded, filing his comments under "volatile." "All right."

He glared at me for a moment as if I were a friend of Shea's before he finally turned away and headed for his Mercedes. I waited him out. He didn't need to know where I went next or what I did. I might have been on the payroll, but I wasn't hired to be the entertainment.

As I was already in Port Angeles, I thought I'd try the sheriff's office first and see if Strother was in, since he was so interested in me. I found him at his desk in an aluminum cubicle that had the charm of an upholstered soda can.

Without his hat, Strother reminded me a bit of a baby mouse—the scalp showing through his fine blond hair was pink and the skin on his face was just as pink. I hoped there weren't any big ugly snakes around waiting to swallow him whole.

I walked into his view and waited for him to look up. When he did, I said, "I hear you've been asking about me."

He turned an even brighter shade of pink. "Sorry about that, Ms. Blaine. I was just . . . interested."

"I understand. Are you the investigator assigned to the case?"

He looked slightly nauseated at the reminder. "Yeah. I'm not qualified—I know that. But Ridenour kind of insisted that since I was already on it, I should stay on it. 'Continuity of evidence,' he said."

"Ridenour insisted? Is the sheriff's department normally on such . . . cordial terms with the park service?" I asked, sitting down in the ratty, rickety typist's chair nearby. The seat lurched and leaned, but I perched on it as if I didn't notice.

Strother turned his own chair to get a better view of me and leaned close. "Not really. I don't know why he wants me on this. I don't know why my boss didn't overrule him. We have a good investigative team here. Do a lot of drug work and missing persons stuff in cooperation with the Canadian authorities—the Mounties and the Canadian Coast Guard—along the Strait. People going overboard, stuff washing up on beaches . . . You know. Remember those feet last year . . . ?"

"The shoes that floated in? Wasn't that a hoax?"

"Only the one. The rest are the real deal. But so far only one's shown any sign of unnatural separation from the body. The rest are just poor souls lost at sea and the feet float in when the body falls apart—because athletic shoes are full of foam. It's not any conspiracy or serial killer—" He cut himself off before he reached full rant and shrugged to apologize. "Anyhow, the investigators here are damned good and the cadaver dogs are the best. They didn't need to put me on this. 'Cept there's not much to investigate, I guess."

"How do you guess that?"

He shook his head. "This case is so cold, you could store fish on it."

"You guys ID the body?"

"Yeah, had to ship it to King County for further forensics, but the ID was easy. Steven Leung all right, like you thought. He was a local guy, so a local dentist matched up the records with the teeth in the skull and the rest recovered from the car. The ME said it was the fastest ID on a body so badly decomposed that he'd ever done. Got the ID back last night."

"What else are they looking for? Why send the remains to King County?"

"We don't have a medical forensic lab. We don't even really have a morgue. The county prosecutors act as coroner to certify death, but they don't have any medical expertise for a cause-of-death investigation. If there's a question or need for an autopsy, we send 'em to KC. Otherwise they just go to the nearest mortuary until the family can pick 'em up."

Strother continued, a little self-consciously. "In this case, the body was decomposed to bones and bits of flesh, but . . . there were signs of fire in the vehicle, and the doctor who looked at it to recommend we send it on said most of the flesh was"—he gagged a little—"burned away. He also thought there might have been some kind of injury to the head, and with most of the rest of the flesh ei-

ther eaten up by fish or . . . sappo-saffo— I can't manage
that word."

"Saponified?" I asked, echoing the voices of the Winter
kids in the cozy comfort of the Veela Café.

"That's the one." He nodded and looked even sicker. "I
guess it means, um . . ."

"Turned into soap." I'd had to look it up to be sure.

Strother cleared his throat and licked his lips, looking
pale. "Yeah. It's the craziest damned case. They don't know
anything about how it happened yet or how the car got in
the lake, but I was wondering . . . what you were doing up
here, looking for him."

"Just doing some pretrial for a lawyer in Seattle. Back-
grounds, story check, that sort of thing. Nothing in your
field—it's a corporate case."

Strother nodded, his mouth open. If he wanted to look
like an idiot, he was doing a good imitation, but I wasn't
sure I believed it. "So you don't know Mr. Leung?"

"I don't," I said, but then I had a thought. "But it looks
like I might get to, in a manner of speaking."

He raised his eyebrows and pursed his lips, which made
him look comical to the point of something drawn by Walt
Disney. "Oh?"

"Much as I hate to say it, it appears the family doesn't
have as much confidence in the investigative powers of the
county as you do, so they've asked me to poke around a bit
as well."

Strother gave an ironic laugh. "You mean Jewel has. And I
suppose she's already got someone picked out for the deed."

I cocked my head. "Why would you think so?"

"Best I can tell, she'd make a damned fine prosecutor:
Jewel Newman never has done anything that didn't benefit
her first and she never asks a question that she doesn't already know the answer to. When she asks 'a favor,' she's
already got a way to make sure you do it. The Newmans
may be of a minority color, but let me tell you, their money
isn't, and in a county this close to the edge, money talks. She

wouldn't be talking to you unless she thought she already knew how the whole thing was going to go down."

"How well do you know the Newmans, personally?"

"Feh," he scoffed. "I don't know them at all in person. Just the common knowledge."

"What about the rest of the Leung family? Did you ever know any of them? Go to school with Willow or her brother?"

His eyes widened, but he quickly forced the expression into amusement and shook his head. "I grew up on the other side of the county, actually. Out near La Push, where the *Saint Nikolai* ran aground."

I didn't corner him about his evasion—though I was a little surprised that he had grown up on an Indian reservation. Instead, I took his bait to see where it might lead. "The what ran aground?"

Strother laughed with a touch of honest embarrassment. "Where the first white woman in Washington came ashore. It was our obscure claim to fame—aside from the Quileute reservation—before that vampire movie up in Forks. So, anyhow, back . . . 1809 or so, this Russian ship was coming down from Alaska and foundered out near Destruction Island—it's a rock, really, but 'island' sounds better—and the crew came ashore at La Push. Everybody got off, including the captain's wife, Anna Petrovna, so she was the first white woman in Washington."

A cold stab of memory lanced through my chest. "What happened to them after that?"

"Some were killed and the rest were captured—probably by Makah—and they sold 'em as slaves. Anna and the captain finally died in captivity after about a year or so, but most of the surviving crew were found out around Quileute and the Hòh River and bought back by an American sea captain. Kind of tragic and ironic, huh?"

Anna Petrovna . . . a Russian lady who died near La Push in 1810—I wondered if she was the ghost I'd seen in my hotel room on Thursday night. And if she was, why had she been so far from her resting place?

"Strother," I asked, "do the Newmans know the regular investigation team?"

"I imagine so, what with Willow's way of causing trouble and all."

"Maybe that's why you were assigned and not one of them. You don't have any past association with the family or the area, so you're less likely to be influenced by them."

Strother seemed to consider it. "Could be. Maybe." He nodded to himself and repeated, "Maybe."

I pulled an envelope out of my bag and offered it to him. "These are the background notes I took to find Leung. I don't think they'll be a lot of help, but they're what I've got. Since this is an active case now, even though it's pretty cold, I can't, technically, investigate it. But I can keep you in the loop if I find information helpful to you while I'm on my job. Would you feel uncomfortable reciprocating?"

"You mean tell you what I find?"

"Yes."

"I suppose I could, mostly. I mean, not everything, of course, and not if you might tell your client something that could derail the investigation, you understand."

I nodded, noticing he suddenly sounded a lot less "hick" than he had a few minutes ago. "That'll be fine. My cell phone number's on the paperwork. You might want to start with Leung's bank records and see if all his retirement money's accounted for, less his taxes, of course. If it's not, that might be an interesting angle. . . ."

He sat up straighter. "It certainly would be. And you might want to keep an eye out if you go back up the mountain anytime soon for a fella named Costigan—Elias Costigan. Seems to have some noisy parties and he's what you might call 'a practitioner of alternate lifestyle.' Got a place almost directly across from Jewel and Geoff's on the west shore of Lake Crescent. Near Devil's Punch Bowl. They say he and Jewel have been heard to scream at each other across the lake—though I imagine that's not really possible. He's not exactly what you'd call a friend of the family."

That was interesting. If I had the location right, Costigan's place would have been close to where the white things I'd seen rise from the lake had come slogging into shore while I was interviewing Shea. "Anybody else I should keep an eye peeled for?" I asked.

"Not sure," he said, picking up a yellow legal pad with neat rows of writing. "Kind of funny—there seems to have been a little housing boom up at the lakes about the time Steven must have disappeared. A half dozen families in a year or two sold up and moved on. Now, could be they foresaw the market collapse, but I'm thinking not all of 'em could have been that smart."

"You have a list?"

He made a clicking noise with his tongue. "I could do." He flipped the first few pages back and wrote himself a note.

"Could you indicate which of the newcomers are year-round residents and which are seasonal visitors only?"

"I think I could, but it'll take a little while longer."

"I'd appreciate it."

"I'll call you when I've got the info, all right?"

I nodded and smiled a little. "Thanks. And I'll let you know if I find anything that might help you."

"All right, then."

I noticed he didn't offer to tell me what he found out from the bank, but I figured he'd trade information with me once I got anything he could use. He wasn't quite the native guide I might have wanted, but he was at least a useful source of local information. And he seemed disposed to be friendly, which I couldn't expect from a lot of others if there was, indeed, a nest of tricky mages around the lakes.

I thought it unlikely that everyone on Strother's list was a magic user of some kind, but I could see where his thinking and mine intersected: Carefully-planned murders don't happen out of the blue; something in the status quo changes and that triggers the violence. It could be something big, like a crime or an indiscretion, or it could be something small, such as the weather or one too many humiliations. Or it could be that someone comes to town and blows the whole thing up. Steven Leung's ghost had said something about "them": "We should never have let them." His daughter Jewel was also concerned with "them." I felt pretty confident that one of "them" was—if not the trigger—the one who'd pulled it. I just had to figure out which of "them" it was—once I met them—because, even if it wasn't my case, I wanted to make sure that someone got special treatment when the flak hit. It takes a dangerous lack of empathy to set a man on fire.

Having picked Strother's brain for ideas, I thought my next stop should be Ridenour to see what he thought of the names on Strother's list and whom he might add to it. Between Strother and Ridenour, I stood a good chance of getting many pieces to this puzzle I'd never get on my own, since there weren't a lot of neighbors in residence of whom to ask questions. Most of the houses were still closed up at this time of year and I'd have to spend some time with the tax records to figure out where the owners actually lived.

I opened my cell phone and called the main ranger station for the park; it seemed most likely Ridenour would be there or that they'd know where he was. I wondered how much damage Willow and her creatures had actually wreaked on the place Sunday evening and how she'd gotten the bears to do her bidding.

The ranger who answered the phone thought Ridenour was at the southwestern end of his territory, near the Sol Duc Hot Springs resort. That was beyond the big lake by a couple of miles, heading toward Forks. The ranger offered to call Ridenour on the radio and have him meet me at the hot springs tollbooth, which sounded like a good idea to me.

It took a while to drive to the far end of the lake and then on down the road toward Sol Duc. A sign at the edge of the road informed me I was entering the Hoh Rain Forest and another sign pointed toward the hot springs. I followed it. When I got to the quaint little booth in the middle of the road with its red and white striped traffic barriers and blinking stoplight, I found Ridenour's pickup truck parked at the bar, but there was no sign of the ranger. I stopped the Rover and stepped out, thinking he might be in the booth itself, but no dice there, either.

As soon as my feet were on the ground, I felt a flush of sourceless heat and a strange noise took over my ears.

SEVENTEEN

I t felt much too warm for February, yet the air had the crystalline sharpness of ice and it rang in my ears like a chorus of glass pipes singing through an electronic filter. I took a step away from the truck, and the heat plunged and cut across me in bands. It was like standing in the ghost of an electric fence. Looking down and around, I saw a rainbow array of lines much like the spectrum of energy lines I'd seen on the Fairholm shore Sunday morning. I wasn't quite sure of my position, since the road from the lake to the hot springs had twisted and turned all along its length, but I thought there couldn't be two similar sets of energy lines. . . . Could there?

They felt strange, and the high, uncanny singing pulled me toward it, away from the little guard shack and deeper into the site. I wondered where they went and started to follow.

The deeper I went into the rain forest around the hot springs, the more the sounds resonated on my chest in uncomfortable disharmonies that tweaked up and down as if someone were adjusting the tuning of a giant harp strung with souls. The colorful lines of magical energy kinked and took on odd angles, curves, and spirals that looked like screws lying along the road. Wherever the lines crossed or knotted together for a space, the chiming cry of the magic formed a chord of Grey voices that rippled colors outward. I could see them even without sliding into the Grey.

The road bent away, but the lines stayed their general course south and I stepped out of their influence for a few steps. I stumbled and felt disoriented and deafened as I stopped on the ice-packed verge of the tarmac. Looking at the lines on the far side of the road, I could still hear their noise and feel their compelling pull. In the background, if I concentrated, there were other sounds, normal and Grey, that continued without reference to the bizarre orchestra of light and noise, clashing against it in head-aching discord.

Cleaving to the Grey I recognized, I looked around, sinking as deeply as I dared toward the grid, hearing its murmur and whine. The aberrant lines and sounds continued, but in an echoing distance, as if they were in another plane somehow, or in another room. I turned slowly, trying to gaze into the more familiar structures of the Grey and see what the cause was of this unsettling development.

But I was distracted by more familiar things. Not far from me, back toward the gate, I could see two tangled energy shapes, one more radiant and red than the other, but while they both showed some connection to the deeply buried grid and not to the freakish sound and light show, neither seemed particularly strong. I'd bet one of them was Ridenour. As much as my curiosity was piqued by the strange array of energy, I wanted to know who his companion was more, so I pushed myself back up to the normal and started back along the road as quickly as I could without too much clatter and concentrating on staying out of the singing, enthralling construct that had led me down the road to begin with.

I walked toward the tollbooth through icy ground fog, still hearing the echoes of the ethereal noise in my head, which masked the voices of Ridenour and his companion. As I was rounding the last turn, coming out of a stand of trees and nearly to the gates, the sounds fell away and I could just make out the words, "Over there before she slips out," but I couldn't quite place the voice.

"On my way! Thanks!" Ridenour replied.

I caught a glimpse of his companion turning and jogging into the trees, but I still didn't know who it was.

Ridenour saw me and glared, his hands on his hips. "Miss Blaine, what the hell are you doing out here?"

"I was looking for you. Didn't the station radio you to meet me here?" I still couldn't quite throw off the Grey completely and saw him through a thin veil of silver where the trees around us seemed to be moving without wind, shifting in the ground and glowing with green, blue, and yellow light. Their branches appeared to reach for Ridenour, the naked alders and birches looking like bony hands among the furry greenery of the cedars. I shivered, thinking the trees were aware of me, too, in some way foreign to humans, as if they watched with incorporeal eyes. Whatever strangeness was going on farther down the road had set my imagination running in creepy directions.

"I had other business and now I've got some more that's more pressing than whatever it is you want," Ridenour said, walking the last few feet to meet me. "You should have just waited by the gate until I got back."

"I meant to, but . . . I thought I saw something and assumed it was you."

He snorted, heading back to his truck. "Lots of people think they see things up here. The rain forest has a lot of fog this time of year, especially out here near the hot springs. It's too easy to misstep and fall into something, so I'd appreciate it if you didn't go wandering around off the road here." He looked at the way my Rover blocked his truck in the narrow road. "Damn it! Move this truck of yours!"

"Where are you headed in such a hurry?" I asked, walking past him to get into the Rover and digging through my pockets for my keys. Ending up with the hotel key card first, I held it in my other hand as I pulled out the truck keys and unlocked the vehicle.

"I got a tip that Willow might be up at one of our greenhouses and I'd like to catch her, if you don't mind, since it is on park property."

I stopped and turned back to him from the open door of the Rover, tossing the hotel key onto the passenger seat. "I'd like to go with you, then."

"What the hell business is it of yours?"

"I'd be there if you catch Willow. I'd like to talk to her and I'm not sure how long she'll stay in custody."

He slammed his truck door closed again and stomped to me. "Are you implying I can't keep a prisoner?"

"No. I'm saying she seems to be hard to hold and, if nothing else, her sister may bail her out. And when you do catch her, won't it be better if you have an unbiased witness around? Her family seems the litigious kind."

He glowered but gave in. "All right. You'd better come along. I called Strother for backup, but he isn't close enough. I can't miss this opportunity! Just hurry up!"

I got in and started the Rover while he went back to his truck and lifted the barrier on the tollbooth. I backed the Rover into the interpretative center parking area a short stretch back up the road beside the sign and got out again, locking up and running to the side of the narrow road to catch up to Ridenour.

He'd turned the pickup truck through the tollbooth's gates and lowered them again, but he was only just getting back into the driver's seat, so I ran around and got in on the passenger side before he could do anything about it.

He rolled his eyes and buckled up. "We have to get up to the old watchtower on Pyramid Mountain. Road's pretty rough, and it'll take about fifteen or twenty minutes. Hang on and pray we catch her."

The pickup lurched and leapt along the road and out onto the highway. Ridenour pointed it northeast toward Lake Crescent. I thought now was the time to ask a few questions, while the road was still smooth.

"What's Willow doing at a park service greenhouse?" I asked.

"Forestry service and I have no idea. Maybe checking on something she put there herself. Forestry has a few greenhouses scattered around on the ridges to grow native plants for replanting in slide areas and where we've had to do redevelopment and construction. That way we anchor the soil and get the ecology back on track faster. But none of us check up on them frequently in the winter and one extra planter full of something might not be noticed. I wouldn't put it past Willow to plant something illegal or dangerous and not worry too much about the consequences."

"So you trust your tipster to have steered you right? It sounds like those greenhouses would make a pretty good spot for an ambush."

Ridenour snorted. "Willow is dangerous and crazy, and there's no love lost between us, but I can't imagine she'd go out of her way to try to kill me."

"That's not quite what I meant. . . ."

He turned the truck sharply off the highway and onto the road that led to Fairholm where the barge was kept. I could see it tied up at the dock as the road rose a bit and turned to the west, toward the ocean and Pyramid Mountain. And there was the same bright array of energy lines that sprang out of the water and headed south toward the hot springs. It was just as it had been on Sunday, just as I'd seen it near the springs.

Ridenour interrupted my thoughts. "I'm not much for guessing what people aren't saying, so whatever you're thinking, you'd better spit it out."

"I'd imagine everyone around here knows you're pretty hot to catch Willow. What if one of them wanted to get you out of the way? Telling you Willow is someplace isolated and dangerous where you might nab her seems to get you moving pretty fast."

Ridenour made a growling noise. "Now you're assuming I've got enemies around here who'd like to see me dead. You have one hell of an imagination, Miss Blaine. Mostly we're all pretty friendly up here."

I reserved judgment on that. I'd garnered the impression that the Newmans weren't great friends of Ridenour's, and certainly Strother didn't think as well of him as Ridenour might imagine. According to Strother, the Newmans didn't get along with their lakeshore neighbor Elias Costigan, and no one seemed to trust Willow Leung, who probably returned the sentiment in spades. Even if Jewel Newman hadn't said so, the strange things I'd already seen around the lake had convinced me there were other magic workers in the area. It was a safe bet there were rivalries and grudges galore between them, and I knew they'd be downright thrilled if Ranger Ridenour stopped keeping such a close eye on "his" park and let them get on with their casting and calling without needing to be discreet and sneaky about it. Not that any of them seemed overly concerned with being sussed out, so far as I could see. The lack of population gave them a fairly open field most of the winter.

Ridenour changed the subject. "So what the hell did you think you'd seen out at the springs to make you go wandering round like a pie-eyed idiot?"

"I'm really not sure," I replied. "It's a little strange out there, if you don't mind my saying so, and once I was walking around, the place seemed a little spooky. It doesn't have a reputation for being haunted or anything, does it?" The weird effects of the energy lines I'd seen could just as easily be written off to some generic ghost story as to magic, though I knew the difference.

Ridenour turned the truck onto a dirt road that headed up the steep slopes that ringed the west side of Lake Crescent, and I had to hold on to the armrest as the surface got rougher.

"Not haunted as such, though you could say it's got its share of spirits. Used to be a fancy resort there in the early nineteen hundreds. It burned down after a couple of years and then it was just a ruin for a while. Then it was rebuilt and the water went bad. The new buildings were built in the seventies and the filter problems were fixed, so it's been back in seasonal business since. Before that, the hot springs used to be a special place for the local Indians — maybe that's why the resorts have always had such hard luck there. People claim to see all sorts of crazy stuff out that way: Indian ghosts, walking trees, lightning fish — "

I interrupted him, puzzled. "What's a lightning fish?"

"Sort of a Native American dragon," he said, not slackening the truck's pace much over the rutted dirt track.

"They fly around in the clouds and spit lightning during storms. The Quileute claim the red fulgurites that show up in the ground at the site of lightning strikes are bits of the lightning fish's tongue. They also say the hot springs are made of the tears of two lightning fish who fought over which one owned the mountains and lakes here. They battled for days on end, tearing off each other's skin that dropped to earth to make the tree ridges, but neither one could win, so they hid in caves under the mountain in their frustration and cried hot tears that worked up through the ground. Really it's volcanic seeps coming up through the sandstone around the springs, but, hey, that's nowhere near as entertaining a story.

"Anyway, related geologic phenomena are what makes the nitrogen level in Lake Crescent so low—that's what keeps it so clear and colorful. It's also the reason animal remains that sink to the bottom saponify and float back up sometimes. The Indians claimed that white whales would swim into the lake once in a while through an underground river from the ocean, but I think it was probably dead elk or bears resurfacing. People imagine a lot of wild things when they don't know the real cause."

I gave a show of thinking it over. "The soap bodies I can sort of understand. But do people really think they see lightning fish flying around?" Had I seen one during the night? I remembered a shadow-shape in the wind that looked like a flying lizard, but maybe that had been my imagination. . . .

We were jouncing around a little more violently as the road dipped and rolled over the ridges, climbing toward the top of the triangular mountain that overlooked Lake Crescent from the west. I thought I spied a building on stilts ahead, but it was hard to get a look as the pickup lurched along.

Ridenour huffed. "When there's a storm, some of them do. People can get a little cabin-crazy up here during the winter. It's not so bad at the lake elevation, but it's a lot worse when you get up in the snow line around Hurricane Ridge and the tops of the mountains here, like this one."

"How about the walking trees?"

"You'd be surprised what some people think they've seen when they've been indulging in various substances. We get plenty of folks up here who seem to think nature is less scary with the application of medicinal herbs and alcohol. And there's always someone willing to supply it," he added in a grim undertone.

"Maybe Willow Leung?"

"I'm hoping not, but we'll have to see what she's up to with the greenhouse."

He spun the truck onto an even smaller dirt track that cut away at an angle to the mountaintop, keeping us hidden from the crest. Ridenour pulled the pickup under a stand of trees and set the hand brake. He was panting a little as he turned to me. "You should probably stay here with the truck—it'll be safer."

I shook my head. "I'd rather come along. Besides, if you need backup, I'll be right there, not way out here."

He looked me over. "Strother said you've got a hell of a rep with the Seattle PD."

"Good, I hope."

"Fella he talked to seemed to think you're a good hand—if a little crazy."

I nodded. That would be Solis's opinion.

Ridenour sucked on his teeth a second, thinking. "Maybe Willow won't bolt so fast if she sees a woman. . . . Got a piece on you?"

"Yes," I replied, touching the grip of my HK pistol for a fleeting moment to be sure it was where I'd put it: tucked into the holster at the back of my hip—I'd never had a lot of luck with shoulder rigs. I hoped there'd be no need for them, but I had a spare magazine and my cell phone in my coat pockets, and I thought I was as ready as I was going to get for whatever Ridenour had in mind. I had no intention of shooting anyone or letting Ridenour do so, either, but this wasn't my show, and I had to go along with his paranoia if I was going to get a chance to talk to Willow.

"All right," Ridenour said. "We'll have to walk up from

here. If Strother can make it, he'll join us in a while, but we need to get a look at the place and see what's going on. The greenhouse is just below the old observation tower and slightly to the west of the ridge, so anyone up there can't see us down here, but we'll have less cover while we're near the tower. I'll have to shut off my radio so it won't squawk, so stick with me, move fast, but stay quiet."

That was going to be a bit more of a challenge for this city girl than for Ranger Ridenour, but I could always slip into the Grey if I had to. I nodded and followed Ridenour out of the truck and into the brush.

The ice and snow on the ground were harder and thicker here near the top of Pyramid Mountain. It wasn't the tallest peak in the area, but it was the farthest northwest, and even on the ground it had a mesmerizing view toward the ocean in one direction and back down into the lakes on the other. A spindly wood-and-steel tower poked out of the ridgetop. I guessed it was some kind of fire watch station, but no one seemed to be in it today. Glancing back toward Lake Crescent, I could see a sheet of white reflection off the windows of the Newmans' house and starlike gleams from the buildings at the Lake Crescent Lodge resort near the Storm King ranger station. I could even spot the blue glimmer of Lake Sutherland from this height and, peering sideways through the Grey, see the thick river of magical energy flowing between the two lakes and sending thin creeks of power out over the ancient landslide toward Storm King Mountain on the east.

Ridenour ushered me off the ridgetop and into a stand of trees, the lower trunks of which were buried in chest-high seedlings and ferns sprouting from an old, dead log. He pointed through the undergrowth to the south of our position and whispered, "That's the greenhouse."

I looked through the leaves and saw the low building of wood and glass just on the ocean side of the ridge. I didn't have the time or privacy to try to look down at the lake again through the Grey, so I concentrated on the task at hand.

The trees around the building had been cleared away when the tower was erected years ago and had not grown back, leaving an open field of low-growing scrub on the rocky ridge. The greenhouse roof stuck up a bit on the east side to catch the early hours of sunlight the ridge would otherwise block.

I couldn't see into the building, the glass walls being steamed with moisture, but I could see the silhouette of a human shape moving around inside.

I patted Ridenour on the shoulder and pointed him toward the shadow.

"Do you think that's Willow?" I whispered.

"Hard to say."

He sized me up again before he said, "I feel funny asking, but would you head down there first? I'll move around to come from the blind spot on the left of the door. Make all the noise you like. I'm thinking she'll concentrate on you and maybe even come outside to see what you want. Then I can catch her from behind."

I shrugged. "It's worth a try. If she doesn't come out, I'll try going in. If I don't come back out in ten minutes, you can assume Willow's still in there with me and make your move."

"I'm beginning to believe that 'crazy' thing," Ridenour muttered as I started off to work my way around to the tower and walk along the exposed ground to the greenhouse. I didn't have a pack and I didn't look like a hiker, but I figured that anyone really suspicious wasn't going to care. If Willow bolted, we'd have to give chase, but I thought I might be able to get inside and talk to her before Ridenour came barging in like the cavalry. Either way, I didn't think the risk to me was that great—I was just a civilian getting into as much trouble as she was by breaking and entering the greenhouse.

The bare, scraped rock of the mountaintop was slippery wherever there wasn't a patch of the stubborn, nubbly ground cover that had made a few inroads on the surface chinks and pits. I had to watch where I put my feet, trying to step on the hardy little plants only enough to keep my footing as a chilly breeze rushed over the mountaintop. I hoped the greenery wasn't some rare species of something Ridenour would have to cite me for trampling. I could see him from the corner of my eye, edging around to his own position until he disappeared behind the legs of the tower. I kept going for the door, making a little ordinary noise and swearing under my breath—as you do when you're out walking on the top of a mountain and thinking your feet are going to slide out from under you any second.

My angle on the greenhouse didn't give me a view inside now, but I could see something ripple through the Grey, like the visual representation of a single sonar ping across a dead sea. Willow—or whoever was inside—had noticed me. It would have been hard not to. No one came out to evaluate me, so I stumbled up to the door and pulled on the handle.

The door opened, making only a tiny squeak as the long rubber flap over the hinge rubbed against the glass wall beside it. The warmth of the greenhouse and the smell of mulch and cedar trees made me shiver with pleasure. I hadn't realized how cold my walk had been until I was inside again. I rubbed my hands together and cast a glance into the Grey, looking for Willow or whoever was lurking in the greenhouse with me.

The power lines of the Grey seemed distant here, deep in the strata of rock and dirt between me and the ocean that looked like a dark blue ink stain spreading to my right as far as I could see. But the zipping, whirring bits of energy I'd seen down closer to the lake were here, if a bit less active and numerous. In the silver mist of the Grey, a whirling column of colored threads and spinning lights, wound in a whiff of scent like incense and hot brass, hovered near the back corner of the greenhouse. It was dense enough to cast a sort of shadow onto the rolling fog of the world. "Get out," it said.

I adjusted my view and turned my head to look toward the corporeal source of the voice. The young woman oc-

cupying the swirling cloud of energy had to be Willow
Leung. Her skin was much paler than her sister's and she
was distinctly more Asian in appearance. She also looked
a lot younger—mid-twenties—and I wondered about the
differences, but not for long. She moved toward me with a
swift gliding motion, dodging the long tables full of seedlings like a feather on an updraft, her loose-fitting dress
fluttering behind. The balls of energy around her flushed
blue and green and glowed brighter as she started to thrust
her arms out at me.

I ducked and swung around under Willow, pushing on
her arms so I came up behind her. She spun to face me
again so fast I was barely straight when she glared up at me.
I had a good six inches on her as she dug her bare feet into
the ground to hold her balance. "You must be Willow," I
said before she could make another gesture.

Even with her clothes on, she was still easy to connect to
the quick-moving woman I'd seen trying to snatch a ghost
on the highway with Jin a few nights earlier. The round little
wads of energy were exactly the same. I wondered if she
always went barefoot, or if she had just dropped her shoes
someplace in the greenhouse for the pleasure of digging her
toes into the warm, feathery cedar mulch on the floor.

She reared back a bit and tilted her head to look at me,
her loose ponytail of long black hair brushing at the nearest
tiny treetops. I imagined she was very rarely surprised, but
she widened her eyes and raised her eyebrows as if she
were. "Who are *you*?" she asked.

I gave her a thin smile, but not my name. "Your dad
asked me to come find out who killed him. Your sister wants
me to run the rest of you wizards and sorcerers out of town.
While I can get behind that idea, I'm not sure I want to do
it her way. So I guess that makes me the monkey wrench in
the works."

While I'd been talking, I could see the glowing orbs of
energy brightening; Willow was gathering power to do
something. I wasn't ready for her to leave, so I reached out
and scooped the nearest energy ball out of the air, closing

my fist over it. It felt hard as a knot of rope and it hurt like hell; I may have contained it, but it hadn't gone out like a candle flame deprived of air.

Willow took a hasty step back from me, taking the rest of her glowing energy globes out of my immediate reach. "That's a nice trick. What do you do for an encore?"

"I break things."

She narrowed her gaze. "I'm not that easy to break."

"Maybe it's not you I'm interested in breaking. See, I'm a stranger in town, and though I'm not sure of all the rules or all the players, I can see things aren't as they ought to be. . . ."

"So, you won't kill me if I pay you better than Jewel?"

I shook my head. "You have the wrong impression. I'm not here to kill anyone. I'm just not quite sure which bit of trash needs to be thrown out to make this place clean again. I'm still trying to figure out how the system works, though I think I have a loose idea." The way she'd reacted to losing one of the spheres of energy had given me a clue: Although there were huge lines of power in the area, they were too deep for anyone on the surface to use easily—or almost anyone, I amended, thinking of the strange lines flowing out of the lake at Fairholm and taking on weird shapes near Sol Duc. That should have made the lakes the only source of power, and *that* should have been limited and difficult to draw on without care and effort. But something had happened: Somehow, the magic had gone wild and rambled loose like Saint Elmo's fire, seeping up to the surface like the tears of the lightning fish. The power lines still burned me when I touched them, just as her energy ball had, so my guess was that the orbs were extensions or encapsulations expelled from the grid. Of course, I still didn't understand what was going on at the hot springs, but it had to be related.

Willow pushed her face toward me, still keeping her body and the gathered energy globes back. "There is no system. Once upon a time, there was order. But when I was a girl, something broke. I didn't break it," she hastened to add, "but I'm not going to let a gift go to waste, nor am I willing to play handmaiden to one of the cardinals. And no one else would, either. If they weren't all such pigs, we could get along, but some people are greedy. Four parts would do—one better still, as it used to be—but no one is going to volunteer to give up the power. So I do what I want, and I do what I must to keep myself out from under my sister's heel. Or anyone else's thumb. You really should think twice about taking her money."

"I already have. And I'm still thinking. I'd rather straighten this mess out than make a new one."

"Then you'll have to restore the quarters. Or the center. And good luck with that."

Outside I could hear a commotion and angry voices. Willow turned her head toward the sound, letting one of the balls of energy spin away through the wall, trailing an unraveling skein of light behind it.

"I'd bet that's Strother," I said.

Willow gave me a sharp look from the corner of her eye. "Alan Strother?"

I nodded. "Probably talking to Ridenour. You might consider running right about now."

She flashed a tiny, mean smile and whipped one of the glowing spheres of energy toward me. "Thanks for the heads-up."

I ducked the orb and Willow vaulted over me with a diving roll that slammed the door open.

Someone shouted. Shots rang off the hard peak of the mountain and a few shattered the glass near me. I spun and bolted for the door, too.

"Hey! Hey, you idiots! I'm still in here!" I yelled, dashing after Willow.

Strother and Ridenour were both too far back to get a good line of fire at the fleeing Willow, but that wasn't stopping them from shooting at her as they ran forward to draw a better bead on her.

Running while shooting is stupid. You can't get a decent sight picture, and unless you're a damned good instinct shooter and your target does just what you expect, you stand no chance of hitting them except by pure luck. Ridenour had finally stopped and braced himself to take a better shot. So I rammed a shoulder into him and took us both down in a heap.

Willow zigzagged across the last of the open space and dove down into a copse of trees and bracken that seemed to close behind her like a door in a wall. I could hear her tumbling and scrambling down the slope, gaining distance vertically as she went. I tried to run forward and get a look to see if she was somehow flying or falling majestically downward like an actor in a Hong Kong fantasy film, but I was too tangled up with Ridenour. The plants that Willow had passed over so lightly tangled our feet and tripped us as we scurried to the edge of the cliff. By the time any of us got to it, there was nothing to see but the waving of branches in Willow's wake. Only the startled scream of a mountain lion halfway down the slope gave us any idea where she was.

"I hope the damn cat eats her," Ridenour muttered. Then he turned and glared at me. "What the hell were you doing in there? Why'd she bolt off like that? Did you tell her we were out here?"

I gave him an incredulous stare. "You must be kidding. You two are about as quiet as a band of five-year-olds with a set of cookware and metal spoons. Next time you open up shooting, make sure there's no one in the way. One of you guys nearly shot me! What the hell!"

I wasn't quite as upset as I sounded, but I really disliked the idea of getting shot again. And I was puzzled by the gunfire to begin with. Why had they opened fire on Willow? So far as I knew, neither had any reason to.

They both had the grace to look sheepish. I took a couple of deep breaths and closed my eyes for a moment before I glanced back at the greenhouse. "Maybe we should see if we can figure out what Willow wanted up here," I suggested.

Strother shrugged, but Ridenour lit up and hurried toward the greenhouse door to investigate. We all trooped inside with Ridenour in the lead.

It took a while to figure it out, but eventually Ridenour found a pot that had been ruthlessly plundered, the small, shrubby plant within ripped in half and lying dry and limp on top of the soil. Strother and I both gave him curious looks.

"What is it?" I asked.

"Kinnikinnik. It's a ground-hugging evergreen shrub. It grows pretty quick and they use it for securing soil in slide areas or where they've had to replant a hillside due to construction or damage. The natives used to smoke the leaves mixed in with some other stuff such as willow bark and blackberry. Some people say it gives you visions. While I can understand being kind of fascinated by this stuff when you're a kid, it's not something a grown woman should be fooling with."

"Is it dangerous?" I asked.

"Not unless you have asthma. It's also called bearberry because the bears love the little red fruit it puts out in early spring. But I can't imagine why anyone'd smoke the damned stuff these days unless they were so broke they couldn't afford a pack of cigarettes."

Strother made a noise through his nose. "With the way the economy is, plenty of people can't afford a pack of smokes. But I can't see why they'd come up here to steal this stuff."

"Does Willow smoke?" I asked.

The men glanced at each other, as if each sought the answer in the other's face. "Probably not tobacco . . ." Ridenour said.

Strother's face hardened a moment as he frowned at the ranger. Then he shook his head. "No idea. But who knows what habits she might have picked up, living rough out here?"

I suspected there was something else to it. The odor around her hadn't been that of a smoker of any kind and she hadn't taken a lot of the plant—only about half the small growth from the planter, which would have fit nicely in her pocket. I didn't think she was stealing it to ease a nicotine fit. Though why steal it at all when it literally grew wild? I guessed I'd have to find her again and ask her.

"Does anything else look tampered with?" I asked, but neither Ridenour nor Strother could see anything more that had been disturbed.

I heaved a sigh and headed for the door, buttoning up my coat. "Then I guess we're done here. I'm going to walk down and see if I can pick out Willow's path. If I can figure out where she went, maybe we can find her again."

"I'll go with you," Ridenour said. "After all, you're no woodsman and you don't know your way around the area."

I gave him a hard look and leaned into it through the Grey. "You need to drive back down to the bottom and start at that end. There are two trucks here and I can't drive either of them, since they're official vehicles. And we need to start while the sun's still up. I don't want to be scrambling down that trail in the dark."

Both men looked at me as if I'd gone insane. They argued with me for a while, but I finally talked them into heading down the mountain on their own before we lost any more light. I had a gun and some brains; if they gave me my purse, I'd also have my flashlight and other useful things. I was the obvious choice to follow the trail down since I didn't have to drive.

And I wanted to get a better idea of how Willow had made it down the mountain. If I was lucky, I'd be able to see where she'd headed long before I got there—or either of the men did.

EIGHTEEN

I wasn't halfway down when I wished I'd ridden back to the lake instead of hiking by myself. Surely I could have figured out where Willow was headed without having to stumble along in the brush. . . . There was a trail, but it was steep and treacherous with loose scree. I couldn't see where I was headed half the time and only the fading glimmer of Willow's energetic trail told me I was on the right path. Here and there, I lost it and had to take a recon in the Grey to find the steadily fading sign of her passage—a hint of dimming colors on the silver mist. It was also growing dark a lot faster than I'd expected and I realized I'd lost track of time. It was past noon and the winter sun was heading for the notch in the mountains before it sank into the sea. Yet another meal missed . . . For a moment, I thought I should have started carrying protein bars or some kind of snacks in my bag. Then I remembered the bears and cougars prowling in the hills and was glad I hadn't.

I continued, hoping I would make it to the populated levels soon. After a while, I came around a switchback on the trail and suddenly had a view toward the lake. I was lower than I'd thought, with maybe thirty feet of elevation yet to lose before I'd be down on the dirt road that connected the houses and campgrounds along the northwestern shore with Fairholm on the far west and Piedmont on the north.

The trail had brought me out closer to the Piedmont end,

and I found myself looking down toward the hook at the lake's most northern end on my left and a deep, round miniature bay on my right. A delicate-looking bridge crossed the tiny bay from arm to arm. A rambling log building stood just northwest of it. I stared at the odd hole in the shoreline, thinking I knew something about it, but not quite bringing it to mind. I started walking again, knowing the information was more likely to pop into the front of my head if I didn't work so hard at it. With only four switchbacks to go, the information came: The hole must be Devil's Punch Bowl.

Strother had said Costigan—no fan of the Newmans—lived there. I wondered if he was a friend of Willow's, since the trail she'd taken down the mountain seemed to end just a quarter mile from his house. And did he have anything to do with the lurching thing that had come up from the lake a week ago while I'd watched at a distance? I'd have been willing to bet he did. That made him the fourth magic flinger I'd found around the lake—if I counted whoever was making the Grey do strange things near the hot springs.

I stopped and thought about the location. Jewel's house lay in the mouth of the dragon-shaped lake, to the east and slightly north, with Lake Sutherland farther east behind it. Turning, I could see Fairholm down to the extreme west and a couple of miles south of Devil's Punch Bowl. The lake wasn't actually very long from north to south and had, in effect, two north shores, the top of the dragon's head being the more northern and eastern shore where I'd found Leung's ghost the first time; and the dragon's back stretching nearly level from just below my position at the back of the dragon's head to Fairholm at the tip of the dragon's tail on the extreme west. The only landmark on the south shore—which wasn't very far south—was Barnes Point, where the Lake Crescent Lodge and Storm King ranger station sat, the rest of the southern shore—the dragon's belly—being steep and mostly barren next to Highway 101 all the way to Fairholm. The bright lines that ran toward Sol Duc were barely threads seen from here, but I could tell they were pointing south, exactly as I'd expected.

Willow had said something about cardinals. At first I'd thought she meant something like the Catholic kind, but she'd also said I'd have to restore the quarters and I didn't think that was a coin. I'd seen enough spell work in the past four years to have picked up a few principles, and one thing I knew was that the points of the compass—the four cardinal directions—turned up again and again. Many traditions start ceremonies and spell casting asking for the protection and attention of the powers of nature by addressing each of the directions; it's called "calling the quarters."

I sank into the Grey, past the level where the seeping puddles of light and color lay, down as close to the humming and muttering of the grid as I dared, and looked out at the lake without the distraction of buildings and roads. I studied the lines of power that lay in the matrix of rock and water, searching for the crossing leylines that would tell me if I was right or wrong. There was the throbbing river of blue that crossed through Lake Sutherland, shooting straight from the curve of Devil's Punch Bowl. And across it, gleaming green sparked with gold, I could see another power line. It was harder to pinpoint where this one crossed the edges of the glacial trench that contained the lake since I was looking at it from the side, but it seemed less focused and slightly crooked, like a line painted by a drunk and then walked over while it was still wet. At the tail, seemingly unconnected from the power line, but dragging it in a loop as if it were a garden hose caught on a stake, the sudden fan of energy struck out toward Sol Duc.

There was something wrong about the geography of the big power lines. . . . They should have connected four cardinal points by two straight lines that crossed in the middle. But they didn't. It looked as if both lines crossed just offshore of Jewel's house. And while the Newmans' house and Devil's Punch Bowl seemed to be in a straight line, that line lay imperfectly west to east, and there didn't seem to be any anchor points for the other line that should have run north to south. It just meandered from about where Steven Leung's car had come ashore at last to someplace near the ranger station at Storm King, then sent its lazy, looping tail off into nonsense directions that touched the cliffs, Fairholm, Pyramid Mountain, and points south and west without any pattern I could make out.

Maybe this was another reason magic ran wild here: The power lines not only weren't a neat grid, but they didn't run straight for some reason. It looked more as though the east/west energy had become anchored by Jewel's house and the Devil's Punch Bowl than that the houses had been built near a naturally occurring nexus on the power lines. I'd seen misplaced power lines before, but not anything as big as these. And the last time I'd seen such a thing, it hadn't been a good sign. No wonder the Guardian Beast had practically shoved me through a brick wall to come here. And I was sure that, somehow, this connected to the death of Steven Leung. How was what I needed to discover.

I eased away from the grid and back toward the normal. Pausing a moment in my ascent, I could see the puddles and streamers of wild magic that lay around the lake. As I watched, they seemed to grow and change shape and size, drawing together like beads of mercury and sucking in other loose bits of energy from whatever they touched, before spilling into the lake in lambent streams. Even the ghosts that seemed to swarm in impossible numbers along the shore drew inexorably toward the water. Did the lake rebuild its power by literally sucking up ghosts? Was that the fate of Anna Petrovna and the other spirits I'd seen moving helplessly toward Lake Crescent? I turned away from the unsettling idea and pushed back toward the normal.

Coming out of the deep Grey, I shivered and staggered a few steps. I'd lost track of time in the Grey and been standing still for so long, my limbs had stiffened in the cold. I needed to get the rest of the way down to the road before it got dark, or I'd never get back to my truck.

Ridenour and Strother were probably put out with me for taking so long to get down the mountain. I wondered if they'd found any trace of Willow at their end. I hadn't found

much and now the trail was literally too cold and faint to
follow. I was still certain she'd headed for Costigan's place—
it seemed too big a coincidence otherwise—but they might
have some other ideas, since they knew the area and residents better than I did; you don't have to know anything
about magic to know what people may do. I got moving
again and found myself on a comparatively wide, groomed
trail following the curve of the shoreline. I headed north
because, although it led away from Fairholm and the most
likely direction to find Ridenour and Strother, it was a
shorter distance to the road, and I'd driven that stretch of
East Beach enough to feel confident I could find my way to
someplace with a phone—possibly Costigan's house. . . .

The trail finally died out at a tiny parking lot a few yards
from the river that was the lake's only outlet. A sign told me
my wide trail had once been the right of way for the Spruce
Railroad and now connected the head of the Lyre River
with Camp David Jr. I wondered for an irreverent second if
people sent aspiring presidents there to summer camp. I
turned toward the Devil's Punch Bowl and Costigan's
house and began trudging.

Along the short bit of road was a line of small lakefront
houses. Most boasted short docks for tying up sporty little
boats, just like the houses on Lake Sutherland did. No boats
currently swung from any of them nor did any of the houses
pour light out onto the road. This was strictly seasonal housing. I was almost to the end of the road that could actually
be called one when I saw a cluster of people huddling at the
edge of the pavement, nearly hidden under the long shadow
of Pyramid Mountain and the boughs of alder trees near
the water. The smears and strands of colored energy that lay
across the ground and plants seemed to crawl toward them.

"You should go," the group whispered. "Get out of here.
You'll end up like us, like *him*. . . ."

I frowned and walked closer to them. One of them
strained to pull away from the others, walking a few steps
toward the nearest house and then falling back, flickering
and jerking like a film running backward.

They weren't people; at least not live people. But they weren't thin and fading like most of the ghosts I'd seen recently around the lakes. These were almost present, almost . . . alive, and they seemed to become more solid as the sun dropped. I stopped close to them, but not close enough for them to reach me—I hoped. They were far more disturbing than most ghosts I'd seen. They were . . . wrong. And they had a smell like something that had lain bloating in water for a long time. One of them swayed and turned eyes like rough, unpolished marble in my direction. I recoiled. This one looked like the white things I'd seen come up from the lake a week ago. It was not a ghost but a sort of walking corpse, half-eaten away by whatever lived in the lake, the remaining flesh and bone dull white and rot gray. It made a low noise but didn't move any closer.

"What—" I started, but had to stop and swallow hard before I could go on. "What are you . . . doing here?" I asked. Were they zombies, ghosts, ghouls? I didn't know, but they sent some part of my brain screaming in horror and I had to work hard to keep from letting that part run the show.

They knotted themselves closer together and seemed to speak from a single breath that rattled through all of their decaying throats. "Drawn, tied. Run away."

"Who's keeping you here? How long have you been here?"

"Him . . . Days on end. Run. . . ."

They were dead. The dead don't know everything, but sometimes they know something. Much as the conversation sickened me, I asked them, anyhow, "Do you know what happened to Steven Leung?"

"In the lake . . ."

"Not anymore," I said. "Do you know how he got there, who put him there?"

They were silent, staring at me for a few moments. I hesitated to call what they did thinking, but it seemed to be something of that nature. "Because . . . the anchor."

"Is that a person?"

"No. . . . Cause. The anchor . . ."

"An anchor was the cause of his death?"

They let out a collective sigh and one slumped to the ground in a wet heap, a noxious odor bursting up as it hit. I jumped back, closing my mouth and holding my breath. "Run," the rest reiterated as dusk deepened under the ridge in the shadow of the setting sun.

Then they lurched toward me and I could hear something like a snake moving swiftly through dry grass. I back-pedaled as fast as I could, gaining ground without taking my eyes off them. The slithering noise stopped with an abrupt whipcracking sound, and the standing dead were suddenly free of whatever had restrained them. They staggered and began shambling toward me, gaining speed the longer they stayed upright.

I swore and whirled, breaking into a full run toward the narrow bridge that crossed the Lyre River. I was a few feet ahead and I thought my living legs were probably more powerful than their dead ones, but I didn't want to turn my head to find out. I'd know I was wrong when I felt their rotting hands on me. And that thought goaded me to run faster.

I pelted down the road in the lowering darkness, the lake a momentary red flash as the clouded sun tipped beyond the edge of the mountains on my left. I didn't pause to admire the effect. I just bolted in the direction of East Beach Road. Whatever Costigan might have been able to tell me, I could try for it another time.

I ran like hell. I could hear them—or I thought I could—gasping and thrashing across the ground after me. I aimed for the bridge. It couldn't have been more than a hundred feet away. . . . I thought maybe, if I crossed it, I'd be safe. I hoped so, at least.

As I ran, I saw something moving in the trees on my left where another small road came down toward the bridge from the mountain. Friend or foe? I couldn't slow down to find out. I'd have to deal with it when it hit me. I didn't hear an engine, so it wasn't a truck, though right that second I'd have been thrilled to see Ridenour or Strother, no matter how freaked they might be by the zombies in my wake. I dodged a little to the right, to make room for whatever was coming.

A flash of black and white and then a confusion of shapes and colors burst from the intersecting road. For a moment I thought I saw a swirl of black hair, but I didn't look too hard. Something barreled into me, almost shoving me into the lake, and then snatching me back at the last moment and pushing me toward the bridge again. The thing closest to me howled and I knew that sound.

I turned my head a fraction, glancing at the big white monster next to me.

Jin, a double exposure of white demon and black-suited man, grinned back. "Hello!"

"Hi," I panted, feeling a stitch knitting tight in my side.

"Cross the river. They'll stay back after that."

"Goody," I gasped, stretching for the last few yards to the bridge.

I almost lost it and fell down when my feet touched the wood and steel of the short span across the Lyre. Jin grabbed me under the arms and flung me the last ten feet, jumping to join me on the far side.

Then he turned back and looked across the bridge. I picked myself up from my undignified sprawl and rushed to my feet, ready to keep running, but seeing Jin standing still and grinning back at the other shore of the river, I turned back, too.

With gruesome black liquid oozing from them here and there, the undead things on the other side milled back and forth in their lurching, teetering manner. They shambled forward one by one and fell back, turning their dead eyes on us to stare for a moment. They twitched and re-formed their strange, pressing cluster as if they were too weak separately to speak until they had compiled themselves into one mass. "Not safe." Their common voice sighed. "Don't return for us."

Then they separated, turning individually and shambling back the way they'd come.

I shuddered. They knew I'd try to come back and let them go and they didn't want me to. Being told not to release them from whatever dread enchantment held them in their rotting flesh was worse than making the decision myself. I wanted to throw up at the feeling of helplessness and the pain in my side.

Jin laughed at them as they left. "Senseless, useless things."

"They're pretty good guard dogs," I panted. "That's hardly useless around here."

"Hah! That depends on what one wants." He glanced around; then he turned and faced me, composing his human features into a pleasant expression while his white demon face leered in hunger. "Now you owe me two stories," he whispered.

NINETEEN

I was pretty sure I could have fought out if the zombies—
or whatever the appropriate word was—had caught me,
but I was just as glad not to have had to. On the other
hand, now I was in debt to a demon; not the brightest or
pickiest demon, but still . . .

I watched Jin while I caught my breath, thinking about
how I was going to slip out of this problem. Jin had helped
me out twice, but it wasn't from altruism. He would always
want a quid pro quo; that seemed to be how he worked,
though I wasn't completely sure. He could think for himself,
so it was possible he might play a longer game if he had a
reason to. There was no doubt in my mind that he was
working with or for Willow Leung—I'd seen them together
on the highway and he definitely took orders from her—but
the purpose was what made no sense to me yet. How could
I get him on my side?

First I needed to know why he'd come along just now,
though I thought I knew. "Thanks," I said, turning and starting up the narrow road in the general direction of East
Beach.

Jin caught up to me in a single easy bound that almost
looked like teleportation. He waved a clawed hand in front
of my face and spoke in an urgent, low voice. "No, no. You
owe me some information and I shan't let you walk off
without giving it this time."

My feet felt unusually heavy as he said it and I glanced

down, seeing green tendrils of magic wiggling out of the earth to hold me in place. I glared back at Jin. "Do you really think this is the best location for an exchange?"

He shushed me and scowled, making a gesture like a conductor cutting off the end of a song. All noise seemed to drop away.

"What are you doing?" I snapped. "We're apparently only a quarter mile or so from the zombie keeper," I said. Pointing upward, I added, "And it's probably going to start raining again as soon as the sun's all the way down. I'd like to be inside and dry before that happens."

"He won't come for us. And rain doesn't bother me, but we need some quiet or others may overhear. I've just made it much harder."

"Harder? Marvelous. Then we can stand out here and chat in the storm, since you no longer care how pretty you look in that nice silk suit."

He frowned. One gambit shot down, he tried another. "You have a truck."

"Not right here and it's a long walk to get back to it, so unless you want to turn yourself into a unicorn and let me ride you all the way to Sol Duc—"

Jin looked startled. "Sol Duc? What were you doing down there?"

"Looking for Ridenour and that's where I found him."

Jin looked thoughtful. "Interesting . . . I didn't know he had business—down there."

I wondered what he'd meant to say, but I was pretty sure I'd get it out of him later. For now, I wanted to get moving before the clouds opened up and poured water on us. I tried moving my feet, but they seemed to be well stuck to the ground.

"Why did you leave your truck there?" he asked.

"Because it was easier to take one truck than two, though right now I wish I'd stuck with my own ride."

"This is inconvenient."

"Damned right it is. Next time Willow wants to do me a favor, tell her to send a cab."

Jin started to object, but I waved him down and bent over to snap off the viney tendrils that held me in place. They stung a bit, but they were not as painful as holding on to Willow's energy globe had been, and I figured it was about time these two got the idea I wasn't just a flunky trotting at Jewel's heel. "Let's not play this game, Jin. I know you work for Willow—I saw you with her. Not saying you couldn't work for yourself as well, since you don't seem to want her to hear this conversation, but it seems an unlikely coincidence that she's around this area and so are you, just when I need some help. So you're in a bit of a tight spot here if you want to negotiate."

Jin sniffed to hide his surprise at what I was doing. "You think too much of yourself."

I laughed at the irony of such a claim coming out of Jin's mouth. "I think that your . . . friend is a more honorable woman than the local authorities have given her credit for. She probably is a thief, a trespasser, and a troublemaker. She might even be a murderer, but like you, she knows about paying debts. Ridenour and Strother would have trapped her in that greenhouse if I hadn't said anything, and at least one of them wants her dead, even if they say they don't. Because they weren't shooting at me."

Jin looked annoyed, pursing his human lips and furrowing both brows. "They might have been."

"Why? What sort of threat do *I* hold for them? Neither one's a mage of any kind, so they don't have any interest in the energetic properties of Lake Crescent, unless you think one of them killed Steven Leung. . . ."

"Ridiculous. Neither of them could have moved the car."

"So . . . whoever killed Leung is the same person who moved the car."

"Of course."

"And you're sure of this . . . how?"

Jin looked smug. "Wouldn't you like to know."

I nodded and started walking again. Jin strolled along beside me. "Yes, I'd like to know, and it would be easier if you told me, but I can find out on my own."

He stopped and narrowed his eyes at me. They gleamed amber like hot coals. "It won't be as easy as you think, Harper Blaine. These aren't the soft, power-dead humans you chase down in Seattle. You could do it without my help, but you'll never do it if you make me your enemy. You owe me information. I do not like to be robbed. . . ."

I turned on my heel, letting down my guard against the Grey and allowing it to flow around me, free and raging with ghosts. I felt fury spark and set fire to the nearest seeping threads and pools of energy as I reached for him, a sudden blaze of incorporeal strength flowing through me. I closed my hands on his white demon form, pushing my fingertips into him, past the shell of seeming flesh. I knew I couldn't hold on to him for long or push much deeper, but I shook him and held tight for the moment. "Listen to me, yaoguai," I roared, spitting the word out. "I will keep my bargain, but never, never threaten me. Do you understand?"

I let go and shoved him backward. He slipped on a patch of ice and fell, just as the clouds chose to open up and let loose the rain.

Lightning burned the sky and thunder cracked over our heads. I could hear a sound like a rush of wings, and the ghosts along the shore screamed in unison. In the Grey, the fallen night was lit with flashes of color that leapt from the ground and the water of the lake, then subsided back into the ground and the mist. The ghosts fell back to whispering and muttering. Jin landed hard on his ass and stared at me as I stepped back.

I felt burned out and soaked through, but I refused to sag or stagger with the sudden draining of whatever power I'd momentarily held. Jin might want to consume me for whatever powerful creature he now thought I was, but he wasn't going to do it just yet. I wanted to huddle into a tired little ball and go to sleep, but I wasn't going to let him know that.

"Now," I said, "enough of this. Let's get the hell out of the rain. Then I'll tell you about the asetem. And you will tell me about the hot springs."

Jin picked himself up, brushing mournfully at his ruined suit. "I saved you from the shambling dead. You owe me more."

"You did what you were instructed to do. Don't pretend you did it for me. But, I can be gracious: I'll tell you more once we're someplace dry. With a functioning phone."

TWENTY

If I'd thought Jin would magically transport us someplace warm and dry, I was destined to be disappointed. Apparently he wasn't that sort of demon. But he did know where the nearest dry place with a working phone was. About a half-mile walk along the shore, through clouds of ghosts and pouring rain, we stepped up onto the porch of the Log Cabin Resort's main lodge.

Under the overhanging roof, it wasn't warm, but it was dry, and an old pay phone nestled in an aluminum hood on the wall near the front door. It wasn't working when we arrived, but Jin assured me he could make it work as soon as I told him what he wanted to know. He also knew where Darin Shea had stashed the spare key to the lodge. I think he would have tried to dicker over that information, too, but he still seemed a bit in awe, which suited me fine.

Frankly, I was a bit impressed myself. It wasn't that I didn't know what I'd done—I'd pulled on the strands of the Grey for a moment, letting the already-loose power of the local grid flash up like a grease fire—but I hadn't thought I still had any call on the grid itself. I certainly didn't seem to have it in Seattle, so it must have just been here, where magic oozed up from the ground like springwater. It hadn't felt the same as the seductive, leaching pull of the grid and its singing, near-sentient voices; it was just energy, not power, not knowledge. Knowing I wouldn't be pulled back down into the infinite everything-and-nothing of the grid relieved me, even if it meant I'd have to bluff and work all the harder to get what I needed.

So now we sat on the floor of the lodge, dripping, in front of an unlit fireplace. My coat was fairly soaked, but I was mostly dry under it, so I'd hung it up on a hook beside the door with my wet red scarf. I kept my boots on, just in case. Jin looked miserable and indecisive. His expensive suit and shoes were obviously ruined, but he didn't want to take them off, no matter how wet they were. We didn't want to start a fire, since we shouldn't have been in the building to begin with, but it wasn't a lot warmer inside than out, just drier.

So I told him a story to cheer him up. It was the kind of tale one ought to tell around a waning campfire on a summer night when even the bats have gone to bed and the forest at your back creaks and groans and whispers as if every word has conjured up the monsters named and they lie in wait just outside the ring of light. . . . It was a story about Egyptian vampires who came to Seattle because their king wanted to let chaos loose upon the world and how the tool he'd forged turned upon him and destroyed him and, with him, his brood and kin.

When I finished, Jin stared at me, as a child at that campfire might have done. "They can't all be gone," he whispered. "I hear of them in the wind."

I shrugged, though his words disturbed me. "Maybe, but if there are any left, their numbers are small and they haven't shown me their faces."

"They'll come back," he said, half-hopeful, half-convinced.

I just shrugged again. "Now, tell me about the hot springs."

He blinked. "Why? I don't owe you any information." He plucked moodily at his trousers and one of the fine black silk threads snapped and unraveled, leaving a hole at his left knee. He cursed in Chinese—or I assumed it was cursing, from the tone—and slashed his black claws through the remaining fabric of the pant leg, tearing the lower half off and flinging the tattered piece across the room.

"Stop that," I ordered. "You'll tear the whole thing apart and I have no interest in seeing you in your boxers."

He gave a disdainful sniff. Then he perked up and leered at me with an expression that might have been sexy if I hadn't been able to see both his faces. "I could take them off, too. You really don't know what you're missing."

"I'd like to keep it that way, thanks." An idea struck me: I might be able to get Jin working for me—at least at a low level—by assuaging his vanity and pique. I was out of exceptional information I was willing to share, but for the first time in my life, I had money—a ridiculous amount of money I didn't really care about.

"Jin," I started, "I'm sorry about your clothes. They were very nice and you look so"—I searched for whatever word would flatter a vain, greedy demon—"debonaire in them." A frown flickered across his face and I guessed that I'd hit another term he didn't know. "Very refined. Very rich."

He smiled but didn't say anything, apparently waiting for more compliments. But I wasn't going there.

"I know you can't just give out other people's secrets," I continued. "They have value and, of course, you can't just break any arrangements you have. Like the one you have with Willow. I understand. But . . ." I paused to see if the hook was going to set. Judging by the way his eyes lit up and he leaned forward to listen to every word, I was doing well. "I'm sure I could get you a much nicer suit. If you helped me while I'm here."

He frowned a little.

I felt slimy for it; I hate wheedling. "I wouldn't ask you to break anyone's trust, just to tell me a few things, answer some questions, show me around—that sort of thing. And you'd have to be honest—no trickery."

He didn't look happy about that, but his greed was greater than his caution. "What about the shoes?" he asked.

"That goes without saying, doesn't it?" What did it matter to me? I doubted Jin could go through a quarter of a million dollars for a single outfit. "But you'll have to earn the rest. . . ."

We sat on the dusty floor and dickered over the details for another fifteen minutes before Jin was satisfied. I knew he'd try to find loopholes and work-arounds, since it was his nature to deceive and devour, but I stopped up as many as I could think of and warned myself to keep a close eye on him. The seal on the bargain was that he agreed to turn on the phone so I could call someone to come get me and take me to my truck.

The only number answering was the sheriff's department. Strother wasn't available, but he'd left a note that he wanted to talk to me, so another deputy was dispatched to fetch me. It would be another half hour or so before he arrived, however, because the shift had just changed and there weren't any patrols nearby.

I decided to use the time I had to question Jin a bit more. "This problem is all about the magic," I started.

Jin nodded.

I thought about what the zombies had said concerning an anchor. What kind of anchor? Anchors stop things from drifting. The major north/south meridian of the grid in the area didn't flow in a smooth, straight line, but wandered. And its color wasn't strong and bright as it should have been. Earlier, from the side of the mountain, I'd thought it looked as if the east/west line was defined by the Costigan and Newman houses, not that they'd been built to take advantage of a nexus that already existed on the spot. But if Costigan's was the west and Jewel's house was the eastern cardinal point, then what were north and south? If Willow was the loose anchor, there should have been one fixed or semifixed point at one end. . . .

"What's at the hot springs?" I asked.

Jin raised his eyebrows and tried an innocent look, which didn't work on either face. "Water?"

"Come on. You told me that Leung's killer is a magic user. There are four quarters and one of them has to be involved. I know who three are, so once I know who number four is, I can pick this thing apart. Who or what is the southern point?"

I could see he was calculating something, appraising, measuring. "The southern cardinal is a ley weaver."

"A spider?"

Jin laughed and the sound scratched at the back of my mind like a nightmare. "No. It builds ... things. It shapes. You left your truck nearby. It's a good thing you're going to get it soon."

"What are you suggesting?"

Jin shrugged. "Only that metal gets in the way. If the ley weaver is making something, it won't like your truck blocking the flow."

"Why would Ridenour be down at the hot springs today? Would he have business with this ley weaver?"

"I can't imagine what use he would have for such a creature. Nothing the ley weaver builds could help him get his wife back."

"Ridenour had a wife?" No one had mentioned any wife to me, and if something tragic had happened, surely Strother or Newman would have said something about it.

"Yes."

"What happened to her? How did he lose her?"

"She was banished."

That sounded medieval. "What kind of wife are we talking about here?"

"She was a spirit wife, a huli-jing."

I had heard that word before. . . . Danziger had mentioned it. . . . Some kind of shape-shifting Chinese fox-demon, he'd said.

"How did a nonmagical guy like Ridenour end up with a demon bride?"

"She chose him because he was the only man alive who already had any power on the lake when we came."

"Who came and when?"

Jin bit his lip. "The first guai and I came through the gate between your years 1989 and 1994. May came before the gate closed in 1995."

"May?"

Jin nodded. "That's what Ridenour called the huli-jing because she came in the month of May. She liked it; it sounded like a Chinese girl's name, Mei. She liked to pretend she was a real woman, not a five-tailed fox. She helped him with his work. He got promoted and she got stronger — that was when she grew her sixth tail. She thought she could make him important and powerful. And when he was strong enough and she had nine tails, she was going to eat him."

"How very nice for her."

Jin gave another shrug. "We must consume enlightenment. Our souls are so weak, we cannot learn. We can only eat; we are demons. It is the only way to escape Diyu forever, to become human again, to leave hell."

If he hadn't been talking about eating people, I might have felt sorry for him, but I didn't.

"So . . . what happened? Did Ridenour figure it out and banish her before she could eat him?"

He laughed again. "No! He never knew her plans. He wasn't smart enough. He knew she was a fox-woman, but he thought she was one of the old people — an Indian spirit come to help him. He was so surprised when he found out she was Chinese."

"Who told him that? And what happened afterward?"

"Willow told him. She used to gather herbs with the hulijing and Ridenour didn't like it, so she taunted him with the knowledge. He was very angry — angry at May, angry at Willow. Then, when the telephone man died, May tried to help Ridenour catch Willow. When May disappeared, Ridenour thought Willow had killed her in revenge."

For a second I was thrown by his reference to "the telephone man," but I guessed he meant the lineman Willow had supposedly shot. Still, I caught his main implication. "But she didn't, did she?" I asked. "Willow didn't kill or banish May."

Jin looked startled. "No."

"Who did?"

"I can't tell you."

"You can't or you don't know?"

"I can't tell you."

"All right." I stood up and squeezed my scarf and the sleeves of my coat to see how wet they still were. The sheriff's car would be along soon, I thought, and I wondered how uncomfortable the ride to my truck was going to be. Judging by the squelching and dribbling, it would be awful.

"When she was banished, could anyone else slip through from Diyu?"

"The other little guai came, but the way wasn't open very long."

"Why not?"

"The one who banished her was very careful. Not like the one who opened the gate in the first place."

"So who opened that first gate?"

He spoke with care. "I am not certain."

"Could you guess?"

"I could."

It was frustrating that he would volunteer some information but make me work for other bits, and he seemed to enjoy the pure arbitrariness of it. Maybe he hoped that making me angry would lead to a mistake he could exploit. I put a lid on my irritation. "Tell me your guess. And be specific."

"Jonah Leung. He was Willow's brother. A middle child. I don't know that he opened the gate, but he was there when I came out."

I had a bad feeling, but I asked anyhow. "What happened to him? What did you do when you came through the gate and found him?"

The white demon face grinned, but the human face seemed surprised. "I killed him."

TWENTY-ONE

As I stared at Jin, I could hear a vehicle coming close, the engine grumbling while snow tires roared on the road's rough surface. I wanted to keep on questioning Jin, but I figured the only person who would be driving this way now was the sheriff's deputy on his way to pick me up. I grabbed my wet coat and scarf and struggled into them as we went outside.

"You'd better get out of here and lock up when I'm gone. I'll find you again tomorrow."

Jin made a face. "Bring something nice with you or I won't come."

I wanted to smack him with the heaviest object I could find, but I didn't have anything but my bag and I didn't have time, either. "I'll meet you at the hot springs gate. I need to talk to the ley weaver and you're coming with me."

The demon looked unhappy but nodded and slid away around the corner of the lodge, lopsided and strange in his torn, legless suit and limping, barefoot, past the soup of ghosts and lambent magic along the shore. I gave a bitter laugh and the ghastly shadows in the yard echoed it as headlight beams swept down from the road and caught me on the porch.

A white Crown Victoria with Clallam County sheriff's office stripes and decals rolled into the parking lot. I stepped into the rain and onto the asphalt, away from the building, hoping to discourage the deputy from inspecting the lodge and seeing any telltale boot prints.

The man, whose name tag read TRIPP, wasn't too pleased with his errand, especially when he saw how wet I was, but he bundled me in and drove the thirty minutes to Sol Duc so I could get my Rover. He waited with his lights on while I approached the car. The noise and light of the ley weaver's work had dwindled, banked like a fire for the night, I guessed. If it had been brighter or louder, I might have missed the lingering streaks of gray, red, and blue that clung to the edges of the driver's door. I paused and stared at it, not caring that I was getting further soaked in the persistent rain. I pressed the automatic lock switch on the fob, which I usually ignored since I'd long ago developed the habit of locking doors manually and hadn't broken it, in spite of the Rover's automated lock-and-alarm system.

The car honked once, already locked and armed. But I knew there hadn't been any tattered threads of Grey on it when I'd left it. Unless the ley weaver's work had rubbed up on the truck in some way and left the energetic shreds behind, someone magical had been in my truck.

I unlocked it from a distance—another thing I rarely did—and let myself in, checking for further signs of the intruder as I got into the driver's seat. A few things had been moved around, but I could have written that off to the rough road, if I hadn't seen the other indicators first. I checked the glove compartment and under the seats. Then I made the deputy wait while I got out and went around to check the back. I couldn't see that anything was missing, nor did there seem to be anything new. . . . But something had happened.

I checked my pockets. Something *was* missing: my hotel key card. I'd had it earlier. I could remember it in my hand when I'd been trying to persuade Ridenour to take me with him to the greenhouse. I'd tossed it on the passenger seat, but it wasn't there now. I got back out and walked to the Crown Vic.

Tripp lowered the window and gave me an expectant stare. "Something wrong?"

"Yeah, I think someone's been in my truck. My hotel

key's missing and I left it in there. Would you follow me to my hotel? Just in case?"

"I can do that. Strother wanted to talk to you anyhow, and I can have the dispatcher call him to meet us there. That way I'll know you got there all right."

"And didn't run away," he implied, but he was polite enough not to say so. "Thanks," I said. Whatever his motives, I would be glad to have some backup if anyone was lying in wait for me at my hotel. I was wet and tired and sore from my hike down the mountain, running from zombies, and sitting in an ice-cold cabin while bargaining with a demon. I was not too proud to ask for help. I'd keep an eye out for Grey things at the hotel while the deputy played tough guy. That suited me fine.

I took off my wet coat and grabbed a dry jacket from the rear so the drive to Port Angeles wouldn't be quite as itchy and miserable as the stretch from East Beach to Sol Duc had been. I cranked the heat up to maximum as I drove. The deputy followed me down Highway 101, keeping a safe but observant distance all the way to the hotel.

My room was on the back of the building and I drove around to park the Rover near it before walking up to reception. I don't know if Tripp was afraid I'd bolt or if he thought I was being silly, but he stuck with me every step of the way. He'd been chatting into his radio as I asked for a new key, and as the clerk handed it over, the deputy stepped up beside me.

"Pardon me," he said to the clerk. "Has another sheriff's deputy been in asking about this woman here?"

The clerk looked a bit nervous and gave me a sidelong glance. "Um . . . yeah."

"About when was that?" the deputy asked.

"'Bout an hour ago, maybe an hour and a half."

"Where'd he go after that?"

"He . . . uh . . . he headed on back to her room. 'Cuz he asked for her and she didn't answer the phone when I called her and he said he'd just go on back and try the door himself, so I told him the room number and he started walking that way."

Tripp nodded. "Thank you. And he hasn't come back up here to leave a message or passed by on the way out?"

The clerk shook his head.

The deputy bit his lip. Then he added, "All right, then. We'll go take a look ourselves."

This time, Tripp walked in front of me with his flashlight in one hand and his other resting on his gun. I looked for things in the Grey but didn't see much I hadn't seen the night before. The only things new in the thin soup of mist and a small cluster of ghosts were a few streaks of black and red near the jamb of my steel-clad door. There were no bright lines of magic or bolts of streaking light; no knots of pain or spiked figures of malevolent spells.

I stood to the side and unlocked the door. Tripp pushed it open and took a step inside.

"Ah, shit."

He stepped back out, trying to pull the door closed, but I stuck my foot in the way and swung it open again.

"Ma'am, don't go in there."

I just stopped in the doorway and doubled over, not from the sight, which was bad enough, but from the blast of recent death that hit me like a giant fist. I spun back out of the doorway and let the door slam closed, wishing I hadn't looked.

I collapsed in a crouch against the wall and put my head between my knees, trying to squeeze away the pain in my chest and gut and the nausea that twisted through me. I retched. I hadn't seen it coming. The steel door had blocked it, holding in all but the tiniest threads of horror.

Even in the dim light from the hallway, there'd been enough illumination to see the man lying facedown on the floor, a few thin strands of blond hair showing above the gruesome pulp someone had made of the back of his head. The uniform, the height and build, all told me who it was; I didn't even need the confused, aching tangle of ghost hovering there to know it was Alan Strother.

TWENTY-TWO

The problem with murder is that it makes a mess and attracts a crowd. I couldn't get close to Strother's lingering ghost and I could see it fading as I watched; sucked away into Lake Crescent the way the ghost of Anna Petrovna had been. The kid from La Push heading for the same silent end as the town's famous castaway. At least this time there was a body, but I didn't think I'd get another chance to look at that, either.

I wondered why he'd come to the hotel looking for me instead of staying on the mountain. And why was he looking for me at all? Had he been the intended victim or had I?

The cops and more sheriff's department people arrived in record time. The rooms on each side of mine were already empty since there wasn't much demand for hotel space in February, so the cops put me in one while they investigated the scene. As soon as the door was closed, I sank down into the Grey, pressing as close to the wall as I could to see if I could attract the attention of Strother's ghost. Even with the wall between us, the blunt, churning trauma of death reached for me, and I had to kneel on the mist-covered floor or risk falling from the nausea and pain.

I could see him as a dissipating scatter of red and blue beyond the cloud shape of the barrier between us. I put out my hand, hoping no corporeal person on the other side could see the apparition of a hand poking out of the wall.

"Strother," I whispered, willing him to notice, to have enough presence left to do anything.

The broken energy shapes stirred and drew together, making a sketch of the man that was fast unraveling. The ghost floated toward me slowly, as if weighted. I stretched myself harder against the wall, panting against the pain and pushing my hand toward him until I could feel the agonizing slash and stab of his remaining energy against my fingertips. I scrabbled in the mist, half-blind from the tears that welled over my lower eyelids, until I could hook my fingers into the waning coil of his life.

Held to shape by my touch, he firmed up a little and I had to swallow hard to keep from crying out or throwing up. He wasn't going to last; I could feel the energy slipping like sand from my grasp.

"What happened to you?" I gasped.

"Don't know," he said on a sigh.

"And you don't know who?"

"The list . . . recent . . . residents . . ." Then he fell apart, and the burning strands of energy tore out of my grip, leaving my palm feeling burned and raw.

I tumbled back onto the floor of the new room, gasping as even the sensation of recent, violent death yanked away and vanished. I dragged myself up onto the bed and hunched into a miserable huddle. My body didn't hurt as badly as it had a moment ago, but my mind was a startled mess.

Strother might have known who killed him or he might not have, but he'd tried to give me information he thought was more important. The list was the key to the murder of Steven Leung and it didn't matter whether I or Strother had been the intended victim; the killer's name had to be on that list.

I straightened myself out, trying to breathe deeply and slowly, pulling myself back together before I staggered to the door and opened it, looking for the nearest cop. I must have looked appalling if the guy's reaction was any indication; he stared and then jumped away from the wall where he'd been leaning to rush to me.

"Are you all right?"

I was shaking a little and my voice came out unsteadily. "I—I think I know why Strother was here. He was making a list . . . of the year-round residents at the lakes. The ones who moved in about the time Steven Leung went missing. Does he have it? I mean, with him?"

The cop glanced back toward the open door of the other room, and then back at me. "Why are you interested in this list?"

"We were going to discuss it. Strother and I. See if any of the residents knew anything about that time."

The cop gave me a narrow-eyed once-over, then pulled me with him to the edge of the other doorframe. "Hey, Faith, you guys find a list of any kind?"

A husky man with mussed hair turned away from his observation of the corpse to stand in the doorway and block the view. "So far, nothing like that. Why?"

"Strother told me he was making a list of the year-round residents—the people who might have been around when Steven Leung went missing," I explained again. "I'm working for the family on this and Strother was going to discuss the list with me. I think that's why he came here. He should have it with him. If he doesn't . . ."

"You think his killer took it?" Faith asked, rubbing the side of his head and revealing a glimpse of a long scar under his messy locks.

I nodded, feeling my knees wobble from adrenaline burnout. I wondered for a moment where he'd gotten the scar. He didn't strike me as a scrapper or a bad boy. He had a calm blue energy currently streaked with red that made me think he was the sort of solid, quiet guy everyone liked, until they were on the wrong end of his resolve.

"Why would they take the list?"

"Because his or her name's on it?" I suggested.

"Just one of many. Why would he or we make a connection?"

"I don't know. Strother must have had notes. . . . Maybe he knew something else that fit one of the names. This is a local problem, so I'd assume local knowledge is the key."

Faith nodded thoughtfully. "Could be. We'll look into it. You know, you can go now, if you like."

"I can? I thought you wanted to hold me. . . ." I knew I sounded like an idiot, but I'd assumed they suspected me—it was my hotel room, after all.

"Nah, you're clear. Doc says the time of death was about when you were up on the mountain with Tripp. I suppose if you were some clever criminal from one of those cop shows, you might have figured out how to make a phone call from the Log Cabin Resort while you were lying in wait for Alan, but this ain't a cop show and you couldn't have been sitting in Tripp's car at the same time you were knocking Alan's head in. You're free to go."

I blinked at him.

"Really. No bull," he added. "I've got your numbers. I'll call you to answer some questions, but not tonight."

"Oh. Well, then . . . could I have my suitcase?"

He thought about it, then had one of the guys in the room bring it to the door. He let me take a change of clothes out of the bag, watching the whole time and making a note of what I took. It was a little annoying, but it gave me a chance to crouch down by the door and look up into the room so I could see the desk. I was glad I'd put the laptop into the back of my truck that morning, since I wouldn't have to wait for it to be released from evidence, but it wasn't the only thing that had been on the desk: The license plate from Steven Leung's Subaru that I'd found in the spell circle beside his house had been there, too. Now it was gone. I didn't think Housekeeping had tidied it up, so unless the cops found it in Strother's coat, I would bet the murderer had it now.

I didn't mention the missing license plate. I didn't want to explain how I'd gotten it in the first place, and I thought it might be just what the sheriff's office would need when the time came to play pin the tail on the killer.

*　　*　　*

Do I need to say mine wasn't a restful sleep that night? Even after finding another hotel, I'd slept badly because I'd known I couldn't sleep anywhere near the activity—paranormal and otherwise—of a violent crime scene. I wondered what connection Strother had made, if any, that had brought the killer down on him and why he or she hadn't resorted to magic this time. Lack of preparation? Too far from the lake? Whatever it was, it looked to me as if the killer had panicked and acted on impulse, not with the care used in Leung's case. Strother or I had done something to frighten someone.

I also couldn't help wondering if Willow was involved in Strother's death. She'd known his first name and seemed surprised or frightened to hear he was outside the greenhouse. Could she have sent Jin, not to help me, but to make sure I stayed out of the way while she went after Strother? What would she have wanted to kill Strother over now rather than days or years ago? Of course, there was also her sister, Jewel, and her overly protective husband to consider, as well as everyone else whose name might turn up on Strother's list.

Was the list the key? Maybe the killer had just taken it on general principle. Maybe it was the license plate he or she had been after and Strother's appearance at the scene had just been a coincidence. Maybe Strother had caught the killer stealing the plate . . . but no . . . the ghost would have said so. Strother's lingering spirit hadn't known what had happened and he'd been hit from behind, so I'd have to believe Strother hadn't seen death coming. That, at least, was something to be grateful for.

I'd liked Strother and I felt angry at whoever had smashed in his skull. It looked as if the killer had the power to hide a car after the fact but couldn't kill victims from a distance. He or she had to—or liked to—kill up close. Or maybe both the murders had been impulsive, without time to plan ahead and cast a spell. Could someone actually cast a spell that would kill someone else at a distance? Would the killer have cleaned up after the death of Strother if there'd been more time? I didn't know, but the questions tumbled around in my head all night and left me sandy-eyed and tired in the morning.

I had to waste a portion of my morning buying some clothes, since I was pretty sure I wouldn't get my suitcase back soon, and shop for something to placate a greedy demon, too. Luckily, be it off-season or not, Port Angeles is a tourist town and I was able to find a couple of high-end shops near the ferry dock and the fancier hotels that had a few trinkets I thought might please him. I did wonder if a demon really needed a Swiss watch, but perhaps it would dazzle him into flat-out telling me who'd killed Strother. Much as I thought it necessary to solve the bigger problem of the lake eventually, at the moment, I was still angry enough to put that aside if I had the chance to grab the person who'd set Steven Leung's car on fire and smashed in Alan Strother's head.

Eventually I drove to the tollbooth outside the Sol Duc Hot Springs resort with a watch that cost more than my first car tucked into the pocket of my new coat—the old one, still pretty damp, was hanging up in the back of the Rover, making the whole interior smell of wet sheep. So much had happened the previous day, it seemed like more time should have elapsed since I was last at the tollbooth looking for Ridenour, but it was only a little more than twenty-four hours. It was less than that since I'd seen Strother alive for the last time on the top of Pyramid Mountain.

I wasn't in a spectacular mood when I arrived and Jin, dressed in a suit of dark gold silk with a brown stripe, only tempted my temper to flare by saying, "You're late."

I pulled my red scarf tight around my neck and swung toward him, pushing the loose strands and pools of magic outward with a vicious thought that flashed up white and bowled the demon onto his back. "Don't screw with me," I warned him. "I told you to meet me here. I didn't say when."

Jin picked himself up out of the icy bracken and brushed himself off with finicky little flips of his hands. He glanced at me warily in the normal, but I could see the demon face glowering with indignation. I caught my ire and clamped it back down before I could get myself into real trouble. The flash-bang trick was about the only one I had in my arsenal at the moment and I didn't want him to catch on.

I sighed as if disgusted. "I'm sorry," I said with clear insincerity. "I had a bad night."

He didn't look mollified, but I noticed he didn't say anything about Strother. Did he not know? I wondered as the sound in the Grey escalated to a warped chorus of untuned organ pipes and wailing musical saws. The lines that reached from the lake to the springs coruscated as if someone had turned up the wattage on an array of neon tubes. The ley weaver seemed to have noticed I'd borrowed some of his power. I wondered how long I had before he—or it—showed up.

"Do you know about Alan Strother?" I asked.

"The sheriff's man? I know a few things."

"Do you know where he is right now, or where he was last night?"

Jin looked truly puzzled. "No. Why do you care?"

"Because I suspect your . . . friend, Willow, will care that he's in the morgue—or what passes for one around here—until his body can be shipped to Seattle for investigation."

Jin frowned. "He . . . is dead?"

"Yes. He was murdered last night in my hotel room."

He blinked at me, leaned in, and sniffed me. Then he settled back onto his heels. "You didn't kill him."

"No—and here's the juicy bit you won't be hearing from anyone else—he was bludgeoned to death while I was going to retrieve my truck here last night. Since you seemed genuinely surprised to hear it, I assume you didn't kill him."

He shook his head and looked mournful on both faces. "No, I did not. I wouldn't. Willow was . . . fond of him. She would be angry if I had killed him."

It didn't take Willow off the hook since many a fond heart has been moved to murder the object of its affection, but it did put a different light on her interest in him at the greenhouse. Though that, in turn, left me wondering why Strother had shot at her . . . if he had actually been shooting at *her*. His aim had been improbably high and wide. . . .

The noise in the grid began to rise and play across my bones in uncomfortable disharmonies as the light and energy flickered.

"We've attracted the ley weaver's attention. But we're safe up here. He won't come out to the road where he might be seen," Jin said. He gave me a cringing glance, as if he was afraid I'd lose my temper with him again. "Did you . . . bring me . . . something?"

He was like a kid who wanted his birthday present but felt embarrassed to ask. Maybe that was the truth of it: He was a child in demon terms, not old enough to have much power and a little naive about how the rest of the world worked outside his playground. It would certainly explain his odd behavior a bit.

"Oh," I said, reaching into my pocket. "I did bring you a present."

I held out the box and Jin took it with care. I was surprised he hadn't snatched it, but if he was truly wary of me now, I guessed that wouldn't do. He looked at the box, turning it over a few times and reading the labels. He opened the white outer box and pulled out the black leather-covered inner box. He looked at the brand name stamped in gold on the top. Then he glanced at me. "Is it really?"

I just nodded.

He grinned and ripped the box open, hooking out the watch inside with one curved claw and holding it up to his face. He cooed at it, and I wish I were exaggerating, but there's no other word for the sound he made as he looked at the slim automatic watch and stroked the eighteen-karat-gold case with his fingertip. For a moment I'd been tempted by a flashier Rolex with diamonds and a case so heavy you could crack crabs with it. But I'd remembered the elegant lines of the defunct black suit and thought a lower bling factor and a more rarefied name would be better. Score one for me.

Strange noises, like a tarantula walking on a piano's strings, played across the grid and moved closer to us while Jin strapped on his new watch. Then he snapped out his well-adorned hand and snatched me forward, onto the trail down to the resort. "We have to meet him before he can sneak up on us."

"You can't call that sneaking," I gasped, running behind his remarkable speed down the road. "He sounds like a whole convoy on the move."

"You can hear that?"

"Better than you."

Jin giggled and dragged me onward for a few dozen yards before he stopped with a jerk and shoved me forward. "You have to go without me. He won't like you if he thinks we're together. Just go down the road and when the fire starts, keep going. Follow the lights."

I stumbled forward on my own and caught my breath, coughing on the memory of smoke. I let the mist-world rush in on me—not that it was giving me much choice. Ahead of me a silvery plane cut across the Grey: a single, shimmering temporacline from which the noise and heat rose. Surely Ridenour hadn't come down here before? And to what was Jin sending me?

I stepped into the temporacline and the world opened out into a vista of trees through which the light of a massive fire flickered. I walked forward into the slab of memory, down the road on which women in long, straight dresses and men in white trousers and striped jackets, all looking as though they predated the First World War, passed by me. The people—memories of people—ran from the flickering light, calling out in fear as they went toward the highway. I walked on toward the firelight until the trees opened up to expose a compound of wooden buildings engulfed in flame, facing a long, steaming body of water. The buildings had been elegant before they caught fire and, as I watched the loop of time replay itself, some of the smaller ones collapsed, sending sparks into the shivering air. The roaring of the flames was accompanied by the eerie, warped sound of an organ playing something funereal and grim while a handful of people tried to extinguish the flames with buckets of water. They were no match for the fire, and the inferno blazed while the organ played on.

There was a whiff of sulfur in the air that wasn't just a memory; nor was the smell of evergreens and soil that hadn't frozen over but churned with some unnatural life just below the surface. Stripes of colored light shot through the scene—power lines drawn from the grid—veering into the trees to my left. Bright orbs and streamers of color danced along the lines, heading deeper into the trees. I followed them away from the memory of the burning resort and into the rain forest.

Ahead, through the mist both real and not, I could see something rising and shining through the gloom. Echoing the mournful organ, a strange atonal song came from the brightness ahead, and I felt a frisson of cold fear run along my spine. Something was moving in the bracken nearby, something low to the ground and many-legged.

I stepped through a screen of low-hanging branches, feeling a curious buzzing in my blood as I crossed out of the temporacline and into a huge bubble of Grey separated from the rest. The cacophony I'd heard off and on near the hot springs shifted suddenly into tune and swelled, the harmonies of grid and ghost voices roaring in a chorus of sound that slammed me to my knees.

Where my hands and legs hit the ground, the mist and colored light rippled, adding a chime of silver bells to the uncanny choir and a wash of blue and gold lights to the weird construction ahead. Something scurried up to me and I raised my head. Then I recoiled from the thing that had paused beside me, making the song of the place waver and slide into a minor key as I stared in horror at what appeared to be a disembodied hand the size of a rottweiler with a sphere for a head where the stump of the wrist ended. The palm and back were a dark green color, fleshy, thick, and callused like the hand of a manual laborer, but the head was a round glob with only a pair of jabbed-in pits for eyes, as if they'd been made with the tip of a massive pencil; yet they moved together as if the thing were looking me over. The fingers were skeletally thin, knobby, and blackened, with short, pointed nails and rough skin covered in tiny hooks where the pads of fingertips should have been. It scuttled around me like a lopsided spider. The smell of sulfur and brackish water clung to the hand-spider-thing as it inspected me.

It turned toward the gleaming tower of woven energy strands growing in the center of the Grey bubble, and the singing dropped away to a musical whisper. "Ah, it's you," a voice said, riding on the back of the music and shaping the chorus into its own words. "Come to the center."

The hand-spider lifted a freakishly jointed thumb toward me as if it meant to help me up, but I rolled away from it, gulping against the desire to scream or vomit. I wanted to clap my hands over my ears and cut out the singing voices that reminded me too much of the voice of the grid, even though I knew it wasn't the same. But I fought my fear and disgust and scrambled to my feet.

Reflexively, I reached to brush mud and leaves from my knees, but the ground around me, while it seemed normal—if unusually green and warm for this place and season—had left no trace on my clothes except a thin sheen of energy, like a cobweb clinging to the fabric of my jeans and coat. The hand-spider stood still until I moved, when it scuttled around me, herding me toward the tower of light. The energetic shine on my clothes fluttered with my movement and dragged tattered edges through the thin mist of the Grey, swirling tiny vertices and contrails of color. Puffs of silver and gold dust and pale green vapor rose from the ground with every step I took.

My heart raced as I walked forward, casting my gaze around, looking for anything, any clue, any indication of what was happening or how to get out of it. A tree swayed near me, and I turned sharply to stare at it. The tree shifted its roots away from my plodding boots and gouged the soil as it moved aside, leaving a shimmering trickle of green light along its path. The boughs shook over my head, dropping laughter and a glitter of raindrops.

The hand-spider herded me along, bumping against my legs and scratching at my calves with one of its pointed black nails. I kept walking.

The area inside the bubble was misty, but not rainy, so it wasn't quite the real world, but it wasn't very far from it. The landscape was definitely the same as that around Lake Crescent and I could, if I strained my ears, still hear the crying of the burning organ in Sol Duc's past-tense conflagration. The thread of sound had been woven into the music of whatever the ley weaver was making. The area was deep with magic, not only the thick bright lines pulled from the grid, but pools and eddies of other energy that welled up from the ground. Trees really did walk here and I had no doubt that if I looked for them, I'd see plenty of Indian ghosts lurking in the mists. I wondered if there were dragons—lightning fish—somewhere under my feet, weeping boiling tears.

The hand-spider stopped at the edge of a circle of pale blue light that seemed to define the edge of the ley weaver's construction zone. Then it bodychecked me, shoving me sideways along the line. I guessed I was supposed to go the rest of the way alone. I turned, but caught myself up short with a surprised gasp. Someone had stepped out of the circle a few feet ahead of me.

Someone human shaped, but not human . . . Like the hand-spider's head, it seemed roughly made with no fine details, just the raw shapes of a body formed from the dense cloud-stuff of the Grey. This one had more of a face, with a pinched little nose, a thin-cut mouth, and gleaming eye pits under a suggestion of hair. But it seemed androgynous and unfinished. And whereas it had two feet, it had only one hand, the other simply missing, as if it hadn't been stuck on at all. I wondered if the hand-spider had sprung from the missing extremity, until I turned my head a bit farther and saw two more of the things scurrying up and down the scintillating, shifting construction in the center.

The human-shaped thing made a curve of its mouth that should have been a smile and wasn't. Then it opened its mouth and words came out on the whisper and song of the energy flowing nearby. "You have been playing on my instrument."

I clutched at the first conversational possibility offered. "Instrument?" I asked.

The ley weaver waved its only hand at the tower of light, and then at the lines that ran through the earth to feed it. "My art."

I looked toward the otherworldly construction. "What is it?"

The ley weaver nodded. "It is beautiful," it replied in the voice of the choir.

"It is," I agreed. The construction, woven of pure colors of energy that gleamed with magic, and singing in the voices of ghosts and nature and raw power tamed and trained into a living shape, was dazzling—breathtaking. I turned my gaze aside with effort, feeling my will and attention drawn toward it, into it, as more raw material. "But what does it do?"

"It does nothing. It is Beauty. Art does not need a function."

So close to it, I could feel the insensible hunger of the thing, drawing what it needed from every source, drinking in energy and power as the hand-spiders spun and wove, shaped and built still more and more of the singing, changing form. My body seemed to vibrate with the thrumming of its harmonies; I felt cold and loosened, as if I might fall to pieces and be swept up as so much gleam and fairy dust—raw material for the ley weaver's art. Then I saw a wisp slip by, a face elongated in a silent scream of terror as a ghost was drawn into the gyre. "But it does do something," I said, thinking aloud, holding myself together by mind and word. "It devours magic. It drinks the remnants of memory."

The ley weaver shrugged its shapeless shoulders and its chorus replied, "It requires. It takes. The lake gives. It is bountiful."

"But it's not unlimited. Others take from the lake, too."

"They are unimportant. Beauty is not harmed by what the puppeteer takes. He has even given me these hands to build with."

The hand-spiders stopped their work for a moment and turned as if looking toward us before returning to their tasks. The movement came from all around the shining shape of Beauty and I realized there were, perhaps, a dozen of the scuttling monsters at work. And each was different in color and size: some slim, some small, some large, some ghastly white or corpse gray, others mold green and rot brown. They were hands of the dead, crawling, reanimated, and enlarged to the size of dogs and men. That was what I'd seen creeping away from the dog-demons by the side of the road—one of the ley weaver's hands.

No wonder Jin hadn't come with me; the guai weren't his friends, but they were his party. I wanted to run, scream, puke . . . and my horror soured Beauty's music, throwing sweat onto my skin and pulling me back into myself.

The ley weaver made a furrow in its forehead and turned down its mouth. "You are hurting my song."

"I'm sorry," I gulped, holding back my urges and emotions and calming myself with long breaths until the sound soared back into a more pleasing mode. "If the puppeteer has given you hands, what did the others give you?"

"Nothing. They wish me gone."

"Do you fight?"

"No longer. There was one who fought, who tried to stop the flow, but he did not understand. He was broken. His energy joined the flow."

I thought I understood, but I wanted confirmation. "That one was the . . . parent of two others?"

"Of three."

Leung had three children, though one was dead, so he must have been the one who fought and was broken— killed—by someone so he wouldn't dam up the flow of magic. But if the ley weaver thought there was no battle, it was mistaken—or didn't recognize it.

"How was he broken? Who broke him?" I asked.

The ley weaver shrugged again and the music sighed blue and purple glissandi of light.

"Do you know how he could have stopped the flow?"

"He did not know to replace the anchor. He could not do it."

"Do you know?"

The sound of Beauty laughed as the ley weaver opened its mouth. Then it said, "I will not tell you. Those who know, will not try. Those who try, do not know."

I couldn't tell if I was getting somewhere or just going in circles, and I only felt colder and more torn apart with each moment I stood so close to the pull of the ley weaver's construction.

"Do you ever . . . travel from this place?" Could it even leave the hot springs? The ley weaver would never pass for human, so I doubted it could have walked around to the back of the hotel and bashed in Strother's brains. But could it have been involved in the murders another way? "Or send your hands?"

"No. I am content here." Not quite true, since I'd seen the harassed hand far from here, but it had the ring of truth in the moment. Perhaps "the moment" was all that existed or mattered for such a being.

"How long have you been here?" I asked, hoping I could figure out who'd come first, who had the biggest stake in keeping the lake as it was.

"A short time."

What was a short time to this creature? A decade, a century? I'd have to try a different tack. "Who was already here when you came?"

"The old nexus has always been here, and the rogue just before the anchor was removed. The east was taken away and the puppeteer came soon when the flow grew wild. The child was last."

Rogue and child . . . Which one was Willow? The east who was taken away might have been Jonah Leung. . . . But why "east"? I wasn't gaining much clarity and I felt more wretched by the moment. I had to get what I could and leave before I lost my focus and was torn into fodder for Beauty.

"If the anchor were returned to its place, what would happen?"

"Beauty would dwindle."

"What about the rest? Of them? Of you?"

The music whispered, "There must be one. There can be four. But starveling and squabbling. Perhaps the mountain will crush them again. . . ." Once more, the ley weaver frowned. "Beauty must not wither. . . ."

I started backing up, knowing I wasn't going to get any more that was useful out of this . . . thing. And the longer I stayed, the smaller my chance to leave. I eased one booted foot away from the blue line at Beauty's verge, then the next, putting a yard or two between myself and the ley weaver before I would turn and bolt. . . . The ley weaver put out its one attached hand and reached for me. I could hear the other hands skittering toward us. . . .

"Beauty sings when you are here. You must stay."

Even the trees began creeping toward the center, tearing green-weeping trenches in the earth as they tried to trap me. I ducked a swinging branch and rolled away, gaining ground, but not fast enough.

One of the hands scrabbled toward me and grabbed! It wrenched me to the ground and tried to move me, but it had no traction so long as it held on. Once I was on the ground, however, I had all four paws to dig in and crawl with, dragging the surprisingly light weight of the hand with me. I rolled onto my back to dislodge it and get a look at the oncoming things. I didn't like what I saw: The trees were slow moving, but the spiderlike hands were quick. They moved fast, but they stuck to the ground or scurried along lines of energy; none of them leapt the way a real spider would.

Because they weren't spiders. I wrenched the one that held me around so I could look at it, peering hard through the Grey and looking past the inflated size and freakish shape. The thing squeezed and pushed the breath from my

lungs, but it really was nothing but a hand: a rotting hand
bound together with magic and illusion. I worked one of my
own hands between the squeezing horror and my chest,
then pushed my fingers into it.

The feeling was repulsive, but I'd done it before and I
could stand to do it again. I didn't have the pheasant feather
that had been so useful the first time, but this time I wasn't
dismantling entire corpses, just a single disembodied hand.
Once I had my fingers past the shell of flesh, the feel of the
burning web of energy at its unnaturally animated core was
familiar. I didn't have to look to know which of the white-
hot lines of magic to rip loose; I closed my hand on the one
that hurt the most and yanked it free.

The hand-spider dissolved, leaving nothing but skeleton
fingers clothed in tatters of rotten flesh that crumbled away
as I watched. The voices of Beauty's chorus shrieked and
the harmonies shattered into noise.

The ley weaver and his minions stopped as I stood up,
holding out the gruesome trophy. I felt sick and it was hard
to talk, but it was the only thing I could think of. "He lied to
you," I yelled to make myself heard over the howling of the
choir. "The puppeteer didn't give you helpers; he gave you
spies and weak sisters. He wants the power you've been using to make Beauty. The demons try to destroy your hands
so they can stop you and the puppeteer, too. They're all like
that. They just want the power and they'll do what they
must to take it." I didn't know if it was true, but it seemed
likely, given the way Jewel wanted to destroy them all—
even her sister—to reclaim the lake for herself. I doubted
any of the rest were different.

But now I got it: Jewel was the old nexus that the ley
weaver had alluded to. The lake wasn't meant for four quarters; it was supposed to be anchored—nailed down—by a
single nexus. Willow, the child, hadn't been around long
enough to understand the original structure of the lake's
magic; she knew only the way it had been pushed and
pulled and manipulated after the anchor—whatever it
was—had been removed. Maybe there were four anchors,

but there was only one center and Jewel wanted it back. If I was to fix the problem of the lake, I had to get rid of the sorcerers and magicians who were using it. And it would be easier if I could get them to turn on one another—at least until I could figure out something better.

The hands stopped where they were, quivering as if I had struck the truth, and maybe I had. Why would Costigan, who kept everyone away from his property with a patrol of zombies, help another magic user? I didn't know the man, but if his colleagues were anything to judge by, he wouldn't unless there was some advantage to be gained for himself.

I threw the skeletal hand to the ground and it crumbled away, raising new dissonance in the sound of the construction behind the ley weaver. Then I bent and grabbed onto the nearest energy thread that led to one of the other hands. It wasn't a big power line or I'd never have been able to move it, but I hauled as hard as I could, bracing myself against the agony until it burst out of me in a shriek while I heaved and flicked the line. The spiderlike hand gripping the energy line was flung into the air and fell, diminishing as it did, losing its giant size and terrible shape.

Beauty screamed.

I staggered and barely kept my feet under me, nearly blind from the tears of pain flooding my eyes, pummeled and deafened by the construction's disembodied blast of fury. "None of them are your friends," I gasped. I turned away, risking my back, and hoping hard, and stepped through the unnatural bubble to the edge of the temporacline that led to the inferno of Sol Duc. I stepped across the barrier, into rain for a moment, then into the smoky, firelit memory of the burning resort. I kept going, pushing myself though I wanted to fall down and be sick, until I came to the rise at the top of the road's memory where I stepped back out into February.

That was where I finally fell down.

TWENTY-THREE

This time the ground was normal gravel and mud, and it stuck to my jeans and the side of my coat where I fell into it. I lay for a moment in the rain, blinking, sucking in wet, cold air that tasted like winter fir and cedar. "Get up," I muttered to myself, as much to test my ears as to reclaim normalcy. I didn't need to be soaked again; I had a lot of discontent to sow and I couldn't get it done if I had to waste time finding more dry clothes.

I picked myself up and leaned against an alder that gave a little under my weight. I turned and glanced at the tree, seeing a swirl of green energy around it and a pair of small hazel eyes that blinked between pale bark lids.

The shadow visage startled me. "I'm sorry," I said, starting to step away.

A breeze without origin pushed a slim branch across me and twigs brushed against my chest and arms, dusting off the muck that had stuck to me. "Slaves yearn for freedom," the breeze whispered and creaked on the tree boughs.

The rogue wind eased and the branches rose away, giving me a clear path back to the gatehouse where I'd left the Rover. I took a step out onto the road and turned back to look at the trees. In the mist and rain, shapes flickered, almost recognizable, then fell away. I could still hear the crackle of fire's memory and the discordant strains of the organ and Beauty weaving together; I could still smell the ash on the breeze and the crawling things in the loam, but they lay at a distance. A safe one, I hoped. I nodded at the trees. "I'll do what I can."

A deer walked across the road, paused to glance at me, then bounded away, its hooves breaking through old wood and frost-burned bracken, cracking words into the air. "Do. More."

I shivered as the forest went still and I looked around, expecting something more. But except for the feeling that I was watched on every side, that was all.

Then the rain came harder on the road, beating drums on leaf and limb. I turned up my coat collar, kept my mouth shut, and started up the road to the truck.

They say nature is a mother, and they're right about that. Now I was being bullied by trees. I would have grumbled, but it seemed a bad idea.

I spotted Jin lurking under the roof of the guard shack, huddling from the rain to keep his suit dry. I motioned for him to come with me to the Rover, but he frowned at the rain and shook his head. Goody—now the demon was feeling prissy. I went to the back of the truck and rummaged for a minute. I find umbrellas impractical most of the time in Seattle, but I had one. I found mine and a hat with a brim, which I crammed onto my head before taking the umbrella back to Jin.

I held it out. "Come on. I want to talk to Costigan before his zombies wake up."

Jin popped the umbrella open and grinned at it. "You should talk to Willow first."

"Why?"

He kept grinning but didn't say anything.

I sighed, annoyed but resigned. It was getting late, and I'd have preferred to get to Costigan today, but if I had to wait for another day, so be it. "Where is she?"

"Tragedy Graveyard."

The tiny cemetery was in Beaver, behind the old school-house that no one had used in ages. The drive took us most of the way to Forks. I knew I wasn't likely to get back to Lake Crescent before the sun went down; I only hoped whatever Willow could tell me would be worth it.

The rain was lighter in Beaver, but Jin clung to the umbrella as if we were stepping out into a monsoon. I made do with the hat, hoping to avoid getting any wetter where it really mattered. I had parked the truck in a patch of weedy gravel off the road that served as a parking lot beside the old school, and the demon and I walked around to the back of the rickety nineteenth-century building. A haunting melody whispered on the wind, twining strange rills and falls through the Grey as we entered the cemetery.

It wasn't much to look at—a sad collection of wooden crosses and slabs inside a hastily erected fence. There were thirteen graves and the markers were of a more recent vintage than the bodies under them—probably put up by a local group to ensure the dead weren't forgotten completely. Most of the markers were too weathered to read, but I didn't need to; the ghosts that lingered in the cemetery hovered around their graves like frightened tourists guarding their luggage. At one site, I saw a woman huddling over a child in her lap, crying eternally. Beyond the mother and her dead baby, we passed a group of four ghosts squabbling in thin voices. The shades of three men had gathered around the ghost of a pretty young woman. They were dressed like early settlers and each of the men tried to grab onto the woman and pull her to him. She smiled at each one, a horrible wound in her throat opening to gush blood every time she turned. They didn't seem to care. Each one yanked at the woman's arm in turn, shouting at the others, "Rose is mine!"

"She's mine!"

"Mine!"

"You're all stupid," Jin jeered at them. "She killed you all," he added, and laughed.

I grabbed his sleeve. "She killed them? She's the one with the neck smile."

"It's her fault they're all dead, the selfish little trollop. See, that one," he explained, pointing at the shortest of the male ghosts, a rough, bearded man with a shotgun in one hand, "killed her husband, that one"—he pointed at the tallest ghost—"because he wanted to marry her himself and she told him she was so horribly unhappy with her husband and her little cabin by the lake. Boo hoo. So sad."

"What about the other guy?"

"That's the lover she took while the ugly one was working to make enough money to convince Rose to marry him. When he found out what she was doing, the ugly one borrowed a boat and some guns and rowed across the lake—"

"Lake Crescent?"

"No. Lake Pleasant," he said, waving vaguely west. "He rowed over to her house, caught her lover in the outhouse, and shot him. Then he broke into the cabin and cut her throat. And then when he was rowing back home, he felt such remorse that he decided to shoot himself with that shotgun. But first he sat there on the lake and wrote it all down and apologized to the friend he'd stolen the boat and guns from. Idiots," he added, grinning. "If they were Chinese, they'd all be in Diyu for being lustful, greedy morons."

"Like you?"

He sniffed and turned his head. "There's Willow," he said, leading me away, toward the whisper of sound that haunted the graveyard as much as any ghost.

Under one of the few trees, Willow, wearing her dark loose-fitting dress, crouched next to a grave, singing under her breath. I could see her bare toes peeping out from under her hem as she used a small knife to scrape something from the edges of the one stone marker in the whole graveyard into her cupped hand.

She stopped singing, but she didn't look up as we drew near and paused beside her. The sound of rain seemed too loud now. "So," she said, "you've seen the ley weaver. Now what do you think?"

"That the lake has a problem."

"Didn't I say so?"

"Not exactly." I looked at the green-gray grit collecting in the palm of her hand as she scraped away the lichen that had grown on the small headstone.

She turned her head to glance at me and I saw her eyelids were red and swollen. She moved her hand a little toward me. "Grave mold." She put down the knife and picked up a small cotton drawstring bag that lay on the hem of her dress. Then she dumped the scraped lichen into it and pulled the bag closed before picking up another. She returned to the knife with her free hand and used the point to pick at the ground along the edge of the marker, scooping up the driest bits of dirt and dumping them into the new bag before tying that off, too.

"Graveyard dust?" I asked.

She nodded.

"Who's it for?" I had no idea what she was making, but I could guess it was some of the kitchen magic Mara had talked about; some kind of hoodoo or trick, in this case to do someone harm with the threat of the grave.

She stabbed the blade at my nearest hand and I barely jumped out of the way. Willow snickered at me. "I'm going to get whoever killed Alan."

"Do you know who it was, then?"

"No. But I can find out."

"How?"

She didn't reply, just kept at her task.

"How did you know Strother? Not just as a cop. You know him better than that," I said.

She made a noncommittal head wag. "Around."

I pushed on her and wasn't quite surprised when I felt her energy wriggle away from mine. She was stronger than she looked and I was tired. I sighed. "You were friends. Weren't you? He had to do his duty, but you were still . . . friendly at least. So you must have met him before you got into trouble."

She made a soft snorting noise that might have been sadness as much as dismissal. "We got into trouble together, to begin with. White boy from the rez, bad girl from the lake, hanging out in the hills, smoking weed." She cut me a sideways glance, wanting to see my reaction. "Ridenour caught us. We were fifteen, so off to juvie. No record. Alan went straight. I just stayed bent."

I imagined them as teenagers, outcasts together, lying in the sun on the mountainside and laughing at everything while they had the chance. I could see how Ridenour's animosity toward them had grown from that little seed of rebellion. Strother had toed the line afterward, but Ridenour probably had never trusted him—handing him the investigation of Leung's death had been a kind of dare to see where Strother's loyalty really lay. Willow, of course, hadn't even tried and had probably thrown her wild ways in the ranger's face at every opportunity, making friends with his fox-wife and flouting the law until she broke one in an unforgivable way. I wondered why she'd shot the telephone lineman—if she'd really done it—but I didn't think she'd tell me.

"Did you go back to school afterward?" I asked.

I guess that wasn't what she'd expected. She turned her gaze away. "No. I had other things to look after." She glared at Jin, who made a face at her.

She wasn't scraping or digging anymore, but she stayed crouched down on the ground, not looking at me, letting the silence grow longer.

Maybe it was the place, or maybe it was Willow, but I felt heavy and bleak standing there. "You know that whoever killed Strother probably killed your father, too."

She nodded.

"Did you use the circle near your dad's house?"

"No," she replied, her voice sharp with old resentment. "That was *Jonah's* circle, then. I wasn't *old* enough to use it. Once you broke it, I sent Jin to clean it up."

"Why didn't you do it yourself?"

She made a noise in the back of her throat. "I never learned to write enough Chinese to claim it. It was my mother's first. Someone stole it after Jonah"—she gave Jin a hard look—"after Jonah was gone."

"How old were you then? When he died?"

"Twelve. My mother had started teaching me the Tao Chiao and the characters when I was five, but she died of cancer on my birthday in 1990—I was eight. Jonah wouldn't teach me more." She made a face. "He said I was a child."

"What about Jewel?"

"She's too high and mighty to stoop." Her voice dripped bitterness so thick even the ghosts turned toward her. "She was busy building her house on the lake. I taught myself."

"Your brother died . . . when?"

Jin growled at me, but Willow flicked a gesture at him and he shut up. "It was Spring Moon in 1994. When Jin came. Mid-February. A dog year."

Spring Moon was what I thought of as Chinese New Year. It would have been a powerful time of year to be casting spells—and a stupid one if you weren't as much in control as you thought. Jin had come through and eaten him, so Jonah Leung hadn't brought Ridenour's fox-wife into the world and neither had Willow. Once again, there was someone else at work. Not the ley weaver . . . Costigan? Jewel? Someone I didn't yet know?

I crouched down next to Willow to think. It was an uncomfortable position—something cold and hungry drew at my energy as I came closer to the surface of the grave while the drizzling rain worked through the trees to chill my back. I touched the headstone and the sensation pulled away like a scalded hand from a stove. That explained the stone and why Willow gathered the ingredients for her vengeance here—something bitter and full of spite lay under it.

"You said order was broken in 1989. Did that have something to do with your mother's death?"

"I don't know. She was a happy creature. And then she was sick. As if the magic had suddenly poisoned her. She died so swiftly, they barely knew what killed her. Jewel and Jonah were already fighting—they never liked each other. *She* married Newman because he owned the land over the nexus and she left the rest of us alone."

"What else happened in 1989? What made the magic change?"

"I wish I knew."

"That must have been when the anchor got loose. . . ."

Her glance was sharp. "Anchor? Someone pulled an anchor out of the lake?" she demanded.

I was startled: I had thought *she* was one of the anchors. . . . Obviously I'd gotten the wrong end of that stick.

"You didn't know."

"No!" She was on her feet so fast, I didn't see her get up. She darted across the graveyard and I started after her.

"Willow!" I shouted, but I got only a few steps before something yanked my feet out from under me and I sprawled across the nearest graves. The ghosts pounced on me and I heard Jin giggling as he ran after Willow. I cursed him under my breath as I fought off the vicious, incorporeal hands that tore through me.

I tried to yank a shield between myself and the ghosts, but I couldn't keep it in place and get to my feet at the same time. I'd already lost sight of Jin and Willow, so I gave up trying to follow them and concentrated on getting away from the ghosts of Tragedy Graveyard.

They had no flesh to push through, and their structures weren't like the spells that had animated the ley weaver's hands. I pushed at them, but my hands went through their forms without resistance. I'd pulled the hand-spiders apart, but I couldn't even grab ahold of these, much less tear them apart. I had dismissed a ghost before, on an airplane, just swept it aside and it vanished. . . .

I tried the flicking gesture that had sent my dead cousin away; the ghost nearest to my hand wafted backward, losing shape for an instant before it surged back together and wound itself again around my body.

"Damn you," I spat.

I repeated the gesture, shoving outward violently, pushing the Grey the same way I'd slammed my force against it to bowl Jin backward. This time the flash was smaller, absorbed by the mist-shapes of the ghosts, but the forms and their tangled energies burst and scattered like leaves before an autumn gust until there were none left that menaced me. For an ire-filled moment, I considered blowing away the rest, just to be thorough, but they hadn't come for me and most were nothing more sinister than loops of memory, replaying their misery endlessly. And even as I contemplated it, I could see the air and Grey matter moving in the distance; the ghosts would come back, however slowly. It appeared I hadn't just lost something when I'd died—I'd gained a new trick, or accidentally applied an old one in a new way. I wasn't limited to pulling things apart. I couldn't make something out of the Grey or its energy, but I could push it around and pull on its lighter threads. But it did leave me feeling a little as if I'd been standing under a giant bell as it tolled.

I made my way back to the Rover, stumbling a bit on the wet, uneven ground and cursing Jin still more for stealing my umbrella, which would have been a useful prop against the fatigue that weighted my limbs after fighting first the ley weaver's hands and then the cemetery's ghosts. I needed to catch my breath and restore my energy. I'd hoped to talk to Elias Costigan before the sun went down, but the drive back from Beaver along the twisting thread of Highway 101 would take forty minutes and I'd arrive exhausted just as his powers were rising for the day.

I needed to regroup and think. And the closest place was Forks, just a few more miles down the road away from Port Angeles. Frustrated, I climbed into the Rover and headed for the once-sleepy little lumber town that had become a tourist mecca for dewy-eyed girls with vampire crushes.

TWENTY-FOUR

Food and a chance to dry out were welcome. While I was wolfing my meal—unladylike of me, but true—I kept turning things over in my head. Aside from the late Jonah Leung, the ley weaver had listed four mages: the nexus, the puppeteer, the child, and the rogue. Including the freaky, inhuman thing as well, that was five, not four as I'd expected. I'd been thinking in terms of four cardinal points and assuming the spell-flingers who occupied each virtual position *were* the anchors. But going from Willow's reaction, the anchors were physical objects that lay in the lake itself—or had until one of them had been shifted in 1989, causing the magical energy of the grid at the bottom of the lake to break loose. So in a way, maybe I was right in thinking that Costigan's house and Jewel's were now holding down two of the points, but it wasn't the way the system was supposed to work. What the hell had happened in 1989 and how had it moved the anchor? Surely an anchor was something pretty solid or magically resistant to change, something that probably dated back to whenever the landslide tumbling down Mount Storm King had dammed up the original valley and formed the lakes. It wouldn't be something easily shoved aside. And where was it, whatever it was? Leung must have had it or had some control over it if it was the cause of his death, but Steven seemed to be the only member of the family who didn't possess an iota of magical power. But he'd known about it. . . .

I put the gnawed remnants of my meal aside, frowning and wondering if I was chasing my own tail. It would be nice to know what sort of object was causing all this carnage, because then I might be able to discover who had one, but if I just knew who killed Leung, or Strother, surely I'd be able to find the anchor among the individual's effects. It was another chicken-and-egg problem—find one, find the other, but where to start looking . . .

The longer a crime goes unsolved, the harder it becomes to close, and the events of 1989 were now twenty-two years past. Clues were fading away. But now someone had killed Alan Strother, not just because I was in town—though that certainly was the catalyst—but because he was close to something that pointed at Leung's murderer. He hadn't been killed for the license plate, because no one knew I had it, not even Jin. No one would have confused Strother for me, either, so it wasn't an accident of time and place. On the surface, there was no connection between Alan Strother and Steven Leung except the investigation of the sunken Subaru. But there was one link, now expunged from the records: Willow.

Seventeen years had elapsed between the time the anchor was moved and Leung disappeared. It wasn't the wild magic that had taken him, as it had his son; it was a person who wanted to stop him from doing something with the anchor. Not Willow; she hadn't known the anchor was the cause of the wild magic or her father's death until I'd said something. Why had Leung waited so long to do something about the anchor? Hadn't he figured it out sooner? Willow hadn't, but she'd had other things to look after, as she'd said. Chasing and taming the yaoguai would be my guess. But Steven, alone in his house mourning his wife and son and missing his daughters, must have had a lot of time to think about what had taken them all away. . . .

And the anchor had sat wherever it was all that time. Could Leung have had the anchor all along and not known what it was? If he suddenly came to that information, would he think the anchor was the key to his problems and try to get rid of it or fix it? Jewel had indicated as much, and if she wasn't jerking my chain, then what had Leung tried to do? And who had known his plans and tried to stop them? I was still betting on a neighbor; someone Leung had trusted enough to talk to when he must have been scared—at least scared enough to try something crazy. What had he done, who knew about it, and where was the anchor now?

I sat at my table, puzzling over it all for a few more minutes, getting nowhere. Now that I was actually in Forks, my cell phone had started working again and it flashed a light at me to let me know I had messages waiting. I hoped they'd be more helpful than my current ruminations.

The first was from Soren Faith. The department had found an electronic file containing the list of resident home owners around the lake on Strother's computer. It had half a dozen names and addresses, going back to 1988. It looked as though Strother had been out trying to talk to some of them in person when he'd told Ridenour he wasn't nearby. I guessed he was buying time for Willow to leave the green-house but hadn't known I'd take his place and undo that gift. Faith seemed to think the list wasn't that useful, but he told me to call him anyhow.

But there had to be something to it. If Strother had found something interesting, maybe he'd gone back to follow up rather than coming to look for me on the mountain. Of course, he didn't know Ridenour hadn't picked me up, so he'd have assumed I'd be at my hotel once the storm came in after dark. He'd had no way to know about the zombies or how long it would take me to get back to Port Angeles. But someone could have followed him down the mountain and to my hotel.

I let the other messages wait while I called Faith back and asked for the list.

"Well . . . it is the homicide of a fellow officer, now, Ms. Blaine. Not sure I should pass it on."

"You know I'm not the one who killed him and he only made the list because I suggested it. My client wants some closure on the death of her father. I promise not to get under your feet. I just want to see the list."

Faith sighed. I could hear an ancient desk chair creak as he leaned back into it. "I wish I was working with a dog on this...."

"Excuse me?"

"Usually my partner and I spend most of our time with K-9 units, hunting down missing persons and dead bodies that float up off the Strait, chasing down marijuana smugglers, and picking up after idiots who drink and drive on the cliffs. No offense, but frankly the dog's a lot easier to work with than you. I know you're cooperating, but for God's sake, lady, you're kicking over rocks like you want to get yourself killed next. One freakin' homicide a year's more than enough. I'll give you this damned list if you can get yourself into my office by four thirty. But after I do, you tell Mrs. Newman that any more carnage on this account will not be ignored. She is not going to wave this off with the smell of money."

I found myself nodding at the phone. "Understood, Mr. Faith."

"Ah, that 'mister' stuff makes me think I ought to wear a tie." He said it as if he could already feel it strangling him. "Just 'Faith.' And you're not here by four thirty, I'm gone."

I didn't get a chance to reply before he'd cut the connection. I checked the time and thought I could listen to the next message and still make it back across the hill if I started right away.

The other message was from Quinton.

"Hey, beautiful. Um . . . sorry about the other day. But I'm done with my project and I thought I'd better come talk to you, so . . . I'm about to get on the ferry to Kingston. I'll call again when I get to Port Angeles." Strange—not only did he sound odd, but he wasn't in the habit of checking in on me or randomly showing up while I was working.

The next call was also Quinton. "Hey. I'm in Port Angeles, but the clerk says you checked out of your hotel. I'm just sitting in the lobby for a while, staring at this pay phone. . . ." He rattled off the number. "I'll wait here until four. I brought you something from Ben."

He sounded worried and I guessed the sheriff's department was still hanging around. Given his feelings about police agencies, I imagined he was nervous, and I wondered what had prompted his trip—I doubted that whatever Ben had given him was so compelling that he had to bring it to me immediately. He hadn't called very long ago, so I tried the number.

"Hello?" It was definitely Quinton's voice at the other end.

"Hey," I said. "What brings you out this way?"

"Hey. Um . . ." He cleared his throat but didn't say more.

"So . . . someone's nearby whom you don't want listening to this conversation?" I asked.

"That sounds right."

"All right. I have to stop at the sheriff's department. Do you want to meet me there?"

"Not so much. I met most of them already, I think."

"OK. Go down to the Canadian ferry dock and I'll pick you up there about four forty-five."

"Will do." He got off the phone without an endearment or good-bye, which was standard procedure for Quinton if he thought anyone might be too interested in what he had to say. Since having worked for a covert agency, he really distrusted phones.

I rushed to get back to Port Angeles before Faith's deadline. In the steadily increasing rain, it was going to be tight.

But I made it and found Soren Faith standing beside a desk in the sheriff's department, shrugging on his jacket. He looked up and waved me closer.

He picked up a file from the desk as I approached and held it out to me. "I don't think it's going to be much help."

I took the folder anyway. "Why not?" I asked.

"Well, most of the folks on that list are already suspects. The rest aren't around anymore. The 1990s were a good time for real estate investors, so most of the lake cabins were bought as vacation homes, not permanent ones. Aside from Elias Costigan, the Newmans, and a couple of Morganroths and Barnses whose families have lived here as long as Washington's been a state, no one's a year-round resident who isn't accounted for. Alan's car computer logged all his stops and times, so I marked up which houses he visited and when on that list. He pretty much covered everyone. The only thing that's unusual is that he drove back and forth a couple of times."

"Did he drive or did he stop?" I asked.

Faith smiled—a crooked, funny smile—as if I'd figured out something that pleased him. "That is the interesting feature, but I haven't been able to figure out what he was doing yet." He reached for the folder I held and I gave it back to him so he could spread the contents on the desk. He pointed to the car computer log, item by item. "Down here, he stops by Costigan's place. Then he stops a few minutes later at the Newmans'. That's not too strange since they lie along the same route. But then he goes back and stops at the Log Cabin Resort—isn't that a strange coincidence—about four hours before you called us from there. Then he turns it around and drives out to Lake Sutherland and goes around the back side of it and stops at three different houses, including Steven Leung's. All of them are unoccupied. He goes to Fairholm, around to Camp David Jr. and back, then heads to Lake Sutherland again. He was out of the car for about thirty minutes at that point, and he didn't log what he was doing, so I assumed he was eating or having a piss, but the car wasn't near any facility because all of them are still closed and there's no one resident at the small lake who'd have let him."

"So where'd he go and what did he do?" I asked, as expected.

"I don't know. Nothing else on the list or the log points to anyone specific," Faith replied, rubbing the scar under his hair.

I frowned and started to push my hair back, mirroring his movement until I caught myself. Faith gave me another of his crooked cat-smiles. "It points to no one," I said, disappointed. "I was sure it led to something."

A wry quirk twisted his mouth. "It does. We just don't know what. And that's why I'm giving it to you. I don't want you getting into trouble, but putting the extra brainpower on the problem won't hurt. You been up here most of a week, so I figure you might see something I'm missing."

I gave him a suspicious glance. "How do you know how long I've been in town?"

"I like to be thorough. I checked with the hotels and guesthouses, 'cause you don't look like the camping type."

I snorted. It wasn't that I wouldn't or couldn't go camping; I'd just never had much cause or chance to. Though I suppose surveillance details were kind of like camping, in a homeless-guy-living-in-his-car kind of way. And thinking about cars made me ask, "Hey, do you have a list of the items found in Leung's car? I'd like to take it to my client and see if anything stands out."

Faith glanced down, thinking. "I believe I do. Hang on a second." He banged around on the nearest computer keyboard for a moment and coaxed a page from a cranky laser printer that made grinding and coughing noises and shook as if the page were being generated by a hidden Gutenberg press tended by asthmatic souls of the damned. Faith handed the still-warm paper to me. "Good luck with that. And if you come up with any ideas, don't act on 'em. Call me first."

I agreed, knowing I was probably lying. "Oh, one more thing," I said as he shooed me toward the door.

Faith cocked me a look with raised brows. "Yeah?"

"What happened at the lake in 1989?"

"'Eighty-nine?" He gave it some thought. "Nothing. Nothing I know about at least. Ridenour'd be the one to ask. He would have been pretty new back then, but I imagine if anything significant happened, he's the one who would know."

I plunged back out into the rain in Faith's wake and watched him head deeper into the parking lot until the rain hid him from sight, reflecting light from the sodium vapor lamps into scrims and rippling swags of liquid gold streaked black in the fallen night.

*   *   *

The rain was no heavier by the water, but the wind off the Strait of Juan de Fuca blew it in at a cutting angle that filled the windshield with blurry white lines. I had to concentrate on the road just to be sure I was on it, and not wandering into some ghostly pocket of the Grey, but I found the Black Ball Ferry Line's passenger pickup zone without having to circle around more than once.

There was only one passenger at the dock at that time of night, since the last boat from Victoria hadn't arrived yet. The size and shape were right, but in the downpour it was hard to tell if it really was Quinton. After what had happened to Strother, I was a touch more paranoid than usual and moved my pistol into the center console. I kept my hand on it as I unlocked the doors.

He bounded into the front seat and shut the door, sweeping off his hat and dropping it onto his boots along with his backpack. Then he pushed back the hood of the sweatshirt he had on underneath the coat, and as the light fell on his face I almost shot him.

"Whoa!" he shouted, putting up his hands as he saw my hand on the gun. "Next time I'll say something first."

I let my breath out in a relieved puff at the familiar sound of his voice and drew my hand away from the pistol. I peered at him for a second, just in case it wasn't really Quinton but some kind of Grey trick. "What the hell happened to your hair?" I asked as I started to pull the truck back onto the road.

He made an embarrassed chuckling sound and ran one hand over his head. His long ponytail was gone and his hair was clipped into a neat, short style that probably looked boringly corporate when it wasn't damp and mussed. He'd shaved off his beard as well, and his face seemed too large and a little too hard around the jaw without it. He looked more like the old ID photo I'd seen of him when the NSA had come calling a couple of years earlier than like my beloved, shaggy anarchist. I recognized him from other details as well, but it took some restraint not to stare at his broad cheekbones and naked chin.

"Well . . . um . . . I had a need to change my look."

"Are you running from someone? Is that why you've been so jumpy? Is that why you're here?"

"Not as such."

"How 'bout you get to that 'such' and tell me what's going on?"

"Could we go somewhere drier and quieter for that? And private?" he added, reaching into his pocket for his pager. Then he popped off the back and removed the batteries, eyeing me with an unspoken suggestion that I do the same.

I pointed at my phone where it sat in one of the cup holders. Quinton took it and removed its battery also, putting the two parts in separate holes in the console. He seemed to breathe easier once it was done.

"What's the problem?" I asked.

"It's a long story. I'd rather tell it all at once. Where are you staying?"

"I was at a hotel a few blocks away, but I wasn't planning on going back there. One of the local cops—"

"Was killed in your previous hotel room. Yeah. I got that story out of the desk clerk. So you were going to take a different room tonight?"

"It sounded like a good idea to me."

"Is there some other place, not a hotel, we could go? Someplace a bit . . . off the grid?"

I thought about the key Geoff Newman had given me. The Leung place wasn't perfectly safe, but it wasn't likely anyone would come there by chance. It also was guaranteed to have no phone or Internet connections, and probably no cable, either, so if Quinton was being paranoid about electronic surveillance, it was the best choice we had, short of staying in the Rover. We'd done that before and I hadn't cared for it.

"I have a place. . . ."

TWENTY-FIVE

Leung's house was shuttered tight and silent as ever, and a strange luminescence swirled around the eaves like a flock of ghostly swallows, though the energy playing on the rise nearby had shifted lower and darker since I'd last been there. I hoped that was caused by Jin's having cleaned up the magic circle there and not by something more sinister. I'd had quite enough of sinister for the day and even though I knew there was something unpleasant behind Quinton's appearance in Port Angeles, I was hoping it wouldn't wreck all chance of a quiet night snuggled together under the pile of cheap blankets we'd bought in town. I was counting on Geoff Newman's wariness to have sealed his lips about lending me the house key, so no one would turn up to disturb us.

The hike in from where I'd left the Rover at a discreet distance from the cabin had left us more than damp around the edges, but the lakefront building with its big decks and upper-floor entry was sound and dry inside even after it had been closed up for five years. Most of the houses around the lakes were summer homes, but this one had been meant for year-round residence, so even though there was no water or electricity, it had everything else you could want, including some old canned goods and a couple of firearms—in case of rampaging bears, I supposed. The shutters kept any movement inside from being visible and it would be cozy enough so long as we didn't make a lot of noise or wave flashlights around like disco lights. We debated, but in the end Quinton started a small fire in the Franklin stove on the bottom floor and we took the risk that anyone would notice the trickle of smoke it put out the chimney.

We huddled in the dark together before the stove with blankets around our shoulders and sock-clad feet propped on a stool just out of scorching range. A couple of fat little candles provided enough light to see, but we hoped not enough to attract attention if a vagrant flicker fell through the storm shutters and onto the water outside. It was still too tense and soggy to be romantic, but the scene had potential.

"So," I started, teasing, "where's the ferret?"

"I left her with Brian Danziger. Oh, that reminds me: Ben gave me something for you." He scrabbled around in his backpack and handed me a small package swaddled in plastic wrap—not quite what I'd had in mind. . . . "I guess he was expecting you to come by on Monday, so when I showed up this morning, he gave it to me. Did he tell you about the book?"

I'd forgotten completely to go visit the Danzigers. I winced in shame. "Book?" I looked at the package—it wasn't big enough for a paperback. . . . "No."

"That's not the book. He's writing a book. Ben is."

"Yes, I know—a paranormal field guide. He's been working on it for a while."

"He got a publication deal. Some small press, but they're excited. Mara's taking a sabbatical at the end of the quarter and they're going to Europe and Asia for a year to finish up some research for it. She's going to write something about sacred rocks while they're out—petroglyphs and dolmens . . . I think."

"Oh," I said, feeling odd. I'd never thought about the book seriously or how it might change their lives—and mine. The Danzigers had been my lifeline through the Grey so many times that I couldn't imagine my life without them nearby. That was silly and selfish of me, and I didn't realize how much I'd taken them for granted—I'd taken most of my small number of friends for granted, really. . . . I rubbed the plastic-covered packet in my hand and began to unwrap it. "So . . . what's this?"

Quinton sat back down and snuggled into the blanket beside me, but his body was tense. Even in the dim light from a handful of candles, I didn't have to look at his aura to know he was nervous about something. "Ben said it's a spell to banish demons. Or *a* demon—I'm kind of unclear on how many. . . ."

It wasn't demons that worried Quinton, though. I suspected he didn't want to talk about why he was really here and why he'd cut his hair, at least not yet. I gave him some time while I removed the plastic and an inner wrapper of brown paper to reveal an intricately folded piece of yellow silk a little larger than my palm. A Chinese character had been inked on one side in red. I remembered what Ben had said about banishing demons, and I guessed this soft little fabric flower was a spell to do just that. It was small enough to shove into a yaoguai's mouth—if you didn't mind the risk of losing a hand.

"Ben doesn't write Chinese," I said, putting the bundle back into its wrappers and tucking it into my shirt for the time being. "I wonder where he got it."

"He said some colleague of his made it."

I wondered what sort of colleague he meant, since I couldn't imagine the college professors he knew suddenly changing their minds about how weird and silly Ben's interest in the paranormal was. "Ah," was all I said.

Quinton tucked me against his side, putting his arm around my waist and pulling the blankets close. I leaned my head against his shoulder. Silence fell between us, deep enough to hear the muffled hiss of the damp sticks burning in the stove.

"Why—" I started, choking off as I realized the question hurt as I tried to say it; it hurt worse than tearing apart a ghost or a god.

Quinton pulled me tighter against him, up into his lap so he could wrap his arms all the way around me. And he suddenly wasn't so wary, as if I'd broken the tension by finally asking the stupid damned question that had been hanging there like Damocles' sword.

"Is that, 'Why have I been avoiding you' or 'Why have I been preoccupied' or 'Why am I suddenly here'?"

"All of those."

"Because I screwed up and I had to fix it and I didn't want you sucked into my mess. That's why I cut my hair off and shaved and why I look like a total dork from IT. And now it's over—mostly over—and I—I just need to be here."

I felt the edge of tears under my eyelids and I hiccuped over them in my throat. "You—you don't look like a dork."

"Then I failed," he said with a sigh, "because I'm supposed to look like the jerk no one notices around the office until he comes in one day with a clanking duffel bag and a long memory."

"Why?"

"Because I owed the FBI a favor."

I sat up so fast and far that I almost burned my back on the stove. "What?"

Quinton shook his head. "I knew you wouldn't like it."

"Like is not a factor. I just . . . Just tell me what you did and why you had to do it for the feds."

He looked up sideways with an anticipatory wince. "You're going to hate me."

I gaped at him for a moment. Then I leaned forward and kissed him. "I will never hate you. I love you. So talk."

He sighed as I settled back on the seat next to him and stole part of the blanket back for myself.

"I love you, too, you know. And that's why I gave myself up."

TWENTY-SIX

I wanted to question him, shake him until he told me what the hell he was talking about, but I knew Quinton wasn't having an easy time telling me his story, so I sat still and held my peace.

"Back . . . back when you were trying to find Edward, you remember I unearthed the video files and I took them to the police."

"Yes."

He didn't look at me but stared at the stove. "Well . . . you didn't want me to go because of the trouble I'd had with the NSA and the cops, and I argued that I was the only person who could convince them the videos were legit and important. But that wasn't entirely why I went. I thought . . . that I could save you. That I could convince them to pick up Goodall and the whole plan would fall apart without him. Then you'd be safe and we could find another way to deal with Wygan that didn't require you to walk into a trap and" — he swallowed hard — "and die."

I wanted to reach out and hold on to him, but his posture told me not to. I bit my lip and waited for him to continue.

"I knew I couldn't just walk in and not have to take the consequences. The paperwork said I was dead, but . . . you know there are only half as many dead spies in the world as there are papers to prove it. The only thing I wanted was to make sure you were safe, and the Feebs just wanted to argue with me about who I was and how I'd slipped off their chain. It was taking too long and I was running out of time. So I called my father."

"The spy? The jerk who 'loaned' you to the NSA in the first place?"

He nodded, but he still didn't look at me. "Yeah. James the First. The big spook himself. I made *them* call him, actually. If you drop the right code words, they'll check it. I wasn't sure Dad would go along. I mean . . . we're not exactly buddies these days, and the way I dropped out made him look bad. But I didn't care. I . . . just wanted to help you.

"Dad, was . . . well, he was a prick about it, but he came through and put the word in for them to take me seriously and start moving." He began babbling a little, talking very fast. "I had to agree to do some work for the FBI and they'd keep me off the books and not let the NSA know I wasn't dead. But they just weren't doing enough and it wasn't fast enough and they wanted to plan an assault and get everything in place and do it all right and I just wanted to get to you! So I ditched them—Solis and Carol helped me get out—and then I went after you. I didn't care what it took to get to you, and I didn't care if I screwed up the plans they were making—all I could think of was you."

His face went pale and slack as if he were seeing something terrible hanging in the air. "And it was too late. I got there and I got in. I went looking for you, down the stairs. There was so much noise and light and . . . it was like walking through hell. These sounds . . . these *feelings* came up like the tide and I—I almost couldn't go. It was as if every nightmare I'd ever had as a kid was pouring up the staircase, every monster that lived under the bed, every bad dream where I could see the horrors happening but couldn't move, couldn't do a damned thing to stop them, where the voices kept whispering in my head what a useless, loveless failure I was. . . . But I could see you and I went forward.

"And it all stopped. You stopped it. The noise, the light, the horror; it all just . . . went away. And you were there and you were fine and I ran toward you. And that *bastard* shot you!" He clenched his fists and ground his teeth. "I wanted to kill him. I wanted to rip him apart, but you were there, bleeding, and I wanted you alive more than I wanted him dead, so . . . I left him to Carlos.

"I don't know what happened after that. I don't remember anything but holding on to you, and there was nothing I could do but watch you—watch you die. They said you were all right, but I saw it: I saw the lights go out and I hadn't helped you. I hadn't saved you at all." There was something familiar and terrible about those words.

He turned toward me suddenly and he seemed to burn from the inside. "I never want to do that again. I never want to see you die again." His body was strung tight and he quivered as if he couldn't move either forward or back from the tension pulling on his bones.

I didn't know if he was going to reach for me or push me away; if he wanted me more than he was afraid of me, so I reached for him instead, praying he wouldn't pull away. I touched his face and he squeezed his eyes closed. I stroked his cheek and his neck, his shoulder, his arm. I took hold of both his arms and stared into his face, waiting for him to open his eyes.

"I'm not going to leave you," I whispered. "I'm sorry I hurt you and let you think you'd failed to save me. You've never failed me. Without you, I would have given up and fallen away forever. But I love you—"

He didn't let me finish, pulling me into his embrace so fast and hard that we were tangled instantly, limbs curling around each other and pressing tight as his mouth closed on mine. Gasping and kissing, we rolled against the edge of the old couch behind us. A rush of hot tears swept down my face and I cried a moment, feeling his own breath catch and shake as he let out a single hard sob of pent-up pain and sudden relief against my neck. Then we melted together and kissed each other breathless, tasting salt and forgiveness.

We would have gone a lot further if something hadn't thudded against the lakeside wall. Then the something groaned and scrabbled at the door, sending skittering shivers through the Grey.

I bolted up to a crouch and reached to the sofa for my pistol while Quinton rolled aside and crawled across the floor toward the shotgun Steven Leung had left behind the kitchen door. I snuffed out the nearest candles. I inched toward the exterior door and Quinton caught up to me on near-silent feet, breaking open the double-barreled shotgun to check it.

"No shells," he whispered.

"Kitchen cabinet with the canned goods," I murmured back. I'd seen the box when we'd unloaded our purchases on arrival.

"What's out there?"

We couldn't see anything except slices of moving shadows from the other side of the shutters, but we couldn't open them from inside. I peered out through the Grey, looking for the shape of the thing outside.

Things—and not human, either. There was only one on the deck so far, but I could see other shapes moving in the water and around the edge of the shore. The energy shapes, shrouded in something dull and inanimate, were pathetic tangles not complex or strong enough to be living humans, but there were at least a dozen of them.

"Not sure," I whispered, "but not people. Twelve lakeside." I turned and looked up, through the gleaming lines of the house, deeper into the Grey toward the hill on the back side of the house and the short wooden walkway that led to the upstairs door. "Nothing landside."

"Upstairs, then—more options."

I wasn't sure the thing on the deck couldn't break in eventually, but Quinton was right: The upstairs gave us a better location to either counterattack or run. Downstairs, all we could do was defend. And it's generally better to be uphill than down in a fight. I didn't know what the things were or how they knew we were here, but I wasn't going to sit still and let them trap us in the house. I headed up the stairs while Quinton fetched the shotgun shells and blew out the last candle.

It was still pouring and even with our boots and coats

back on, the rain felt sharp and surreally wet with an odor like lightning. The loosely pooled energy on the ground seemed to reach up and pull the rain down, flashing colors and sizzling as it hit. Quinton had paused under the porch roof to load the shotgun and I wanted to tell him this rain wasn't natural, but I feared to make a sound that might attract the creatures now crawling out of the water and stumbling along the shore. The mist of the Grey curled around them, rising like ground fog in my view and gleaming with bright streaks of wild magic that powered the things moving toward the house.

We stepped away from the building for a clearer view and even in the wet night, the monstrosities' shapes and shambling movements gave them away. An odor of putrefaction and campfire smoke wafted off them from the lake.

"Those look familiar," Quinton whispered.

I started to reply, but even his quiet voice and our slow-moving presence were enough to draw their attention. The things nearest us turned and showed us rotting faces and death-blinded eyes. Then they started moving our way and the rest followed.

Silence was no longer helpful, so I aimed at the nearest zombie and shot it in the face.

The decomposing flesh tore away, giving no resistance to the projectile. The shambling, undead thing stopped and swayed, the reel of colored light around it dimming for a moment with a high whining sound. Then it continued coming forward with half a head.

Quinton fired the shotgun. The boom of the first barrel going off so close by deafened me. Normal sounds fled, leaving only the ringing of the shot and the whining crackle of the grid as the rain struck into the pools of light on the ground. The monstrosity, barely recognizable as once human, staggered but continued onward. I glanced past it to the shapes coming up the hill from the water and saw that most were the walking corpses of animals, not people. We both fired again, hoping to break the creatures down too much to continue moving, but they kept coming.

In the emptiness of the rain-swept night, no one came to see what we were shooting at; there was no one nearby to hear or care. We'd have to deal with them ourselves, one by one.

I shoved the pistol into my coat pocket and ran to the nearest dead thing. Plunging my hands into the putrid flesh, I groped for the thread of energy that animated it and yanked it out. Two more things had closed in on me and I grabbed for one while the other swiped at me with decaying paws. My ears still rang and I struggled in the buzzing, disorienting silence of the Grey-haunted night to tear the next creature apart while the claws of the other ripped loose and struck through the thick fabric of my coat.

I broke the first one down and turned to take on the ghastly mountain lion corpse that tried to maul me with its dripping fangs. Shuddering, I rammed my hand into its mouth and tore its jaw loose from its half-fleshed skull. I could barely see through its reeking hide to locate the knot of magic that animated it, but I was afraid to drop too deeply into the Grey where I couldn't see the shapes of the things at all and risk being hit or bitten while I was blind to their normal aspect as well as deaf to their scraping approach.

More of the stinking corpse-puppets reached me, and I had to fend them off by feel with elbows and feet while I tore the second one apart. But they still managed to grab me and rip at my clothes, sending bits of cloth fluttering to the muddy ground. There was a flash of yellow silk, but I couldn't spare it my attention as it fell from my torn shirt.

I could smell the gun smoke and see the flashes from the shotgun's muzzle as Quinton slowed the mob down, but he had to reload every two shots and the things were focusing more on me than on him. I was in danger of being overwhelmed if I couldn't clear them off faster. I didn't know what they were going to do to me if they pulled me down, but I didn't want to find out and I knew Quinton wouldn't shoot at anything that was within two yards of me.

I shoved the pressing dead back and cleared a temporary

circle by making a fast series of sweeping kicks that knocked the nearest ones into the ones behind. I followed up by shoving hard on the Grey with the sharp, concussive thrust I'd learned could disperse a ghost or topple a demon.

The shambling carcasses fell down around me in a circle about eight feet wide. It was nice to know how far and how hard the effect hit, but I didn't have time to admire it. I tore off my tattered coat and threw it toward Quinton, hoping he'd take the HK and the spare magazines out of the pockets and use those for a while. It didn't do as much damage as the shotgun, but the 9mm pistol was a lot faster.

There were too many on me to bother trying to see their individual shapes anymore, so I let myself fall into the Grey, concentrating only on the shining skeins of energy that pushed the dead things onward. Knocking them down wasn't good enough, and I didn't know if I could push on them from here or not. I needed to break them permanently.

In the mist-world, the zombies looked like tiny blue lightbulbs wrapped in violet clouds that stretched and deformed as the nightmare things staggered forward. The smell was nauseating. I snatched at the nearest light and felt the creature that contained it tear open like rotten fruit. The process was easier in the Grey, but just as exhausting. The creatures still managed to tear my clothes and pull my hair, and there were so many. . . . There had to be a faster way to deal with them. . . .

I forced my way back up the slope toward Quinton, buying time to get a better look at the situation. The things moved slowly, but with the mindless implacability of idiot machines, each one powered by a core of magical impulse and an unreeling tether to the nearest source of power—the lake. So long as there was water, they'd keep coming.

I couldn't make the lake dry up or set fire to the scraped, hard ground on the hilltop. I'd have to sever their connection to the lake and hope the rain wasn't enough power on its own. That meant giving up the hill, but not yet.

I kept backing up, stepping out of the Grey so I stayed on top of the land, not risking sinking into it.

Quinton was level with me now, still shooting at the on-coming zombies, but he fired off the last of the HK's rounds as I watched. He turned his head as he dropped the smoking automatic into one of his own pockets. I couldn't hear, but I knew what he said: "Out of ammo."

Hoping he could understand what I was saying in my deafened state, I yelled to him, "Draw them into a cluster uphill. I need to get below them, near the water."

I had to take them out in one big push if possible—or at least thin their numbers considerably. I wasn't sure I could gather up the individual threads of energy that pulled from the lake and break them apart, especially not once they'd been bundled together. The combined rope of magic might be too powerful for me to hold and breaking it might not even destroy the power that animated the dead creatures, but it was all I could think of.

Quinton and I fell back together for a few more feet. The undead followed us, packing together into a dense clot of moldering bodies. The rain was slacking off a bit and the zombies seemed a little slower. Maybe there was hope.

Quinton grabbed me and kissed me hard and then spoke against my lips: "Move fast. I don't want to die." He pushed me a little and I ducked into the Grey as he started to swing the butt of the shotgun into the head of the nearest dead thing.

I practically tumbled down the slope to the water, sliding through the mist and cold of the Grey as fast as I could, hoping to avoid the horrors clustering around Quinton long enough to get behind them. A few turned, but most concentrated on him.

As I neared the shore, the gleaming threads connecting the undead to their energy source were bright blue in the ghost world. I grabbed the first one I came to and ran along the water's edge, gathering up as many of the tendrils of colored light as I could. Each one burned with cold that cut into my hands. With each one added, the burn worsened and the racket in my ears grew beyond the ringing caused by the shotgun blasts and into a buzzing howl that rang, not in my ears but in my bones and skull, and riffed through my blood like heroin. Each thread weighed me down, gathering in my arms like fiery lilies from a ghostly bride's bouquet.

It felt as if the power ran through my arms and into my spine. When I snatched up the last visible line, I had to drop to my knees, but I remembered the way Jin had stood with his toes in the water when he raised the car and I put one foot into the lake.

It was like standing on a live wire. Power flowed up through my limbs, but it didn't go into the threads I was holding; it just roared through me and throbbed into my head as if my skull were exploding. I yanked on the gathered threads, twisting them hard together, hard enough to break, and then shoved with all my will, one hard, concussive thrust of the power that flowed in me against the taut rope of energy that ran into my arms.

Magic boomed against the surface of the lake so loudly I could feel it in my chest as if someone had slammed an electric pole into a whole orchestra's worth of bass timpani. Sparks erupted from the lake and it exploded into light that flashed like a mirror in the sun. The rolling sheet of white illumination shot up the hill to Quinton, throwing the shambling dead down like sticks before a hurricane. I could see Quinton drop to the ground and cover his head as it hit.

And it rolled away, leaving the lake black and still, the shore littered with putrefying dead, animal and human. There were no more small blue lamps in purple fog—the lights had gone out.

I crouched, shuddering, on the shore for a few seconds, catching my breath as the broken threads of power faded from my grip and my eyes readjusted to the night.

Rain dripped and pattered lightly on the ground, leaving nothing but ordinary puddles. Even the wild pools of magic that had oozed on the surface like oil were gone, burned away in the outrageous pulse of energy.

Quinton picked himself up and stumbled down the makeshift stair to the water, to me, picking his way as best he could through the swiftly decaying mess that had been an army of animated corpses.

I half expected the ringing deafness in my ears to have magically gone with the flash of energy, but when Quinton tried to say something to me, it sounded as if he were underwater, or as if I were. He gave up and put his arms around me to haul me to my feet, but as soon as he tried to move me, my muscles and joints gave up and dumped me onto the shoreline and into the water.

The icy water of Lake Sutherland made me gasp and thrash, but my movements were feeble. I'd put too much into that last push and I was too weak to help myself. I was also soaked, bloodied, and partially bare from having most of my shirt and sweater ripped away by the claws of undead beasts.

Quinton was only a little better off, but he was able to pull me out of the lake and help me onto the deck of Leung's house. He put my coat over me and bent down, pressing his lips to my ear to tell me he'd be right back. Then he went away.

I looked over my shivering shoulder at the lake, wondering if there was anyone around to have heard the gun battle. The lake was a dark mirror, streaked here and there with light from the moon as it tore a slit in the clouds for a moment before being sewn back into its shroud of rain. Far across and down to my right, I could see a gold rectangle of electric light from an open door, weirdly magnified by the water as the light fell on it. Then the light narrowed and vanished.

In a moment, the storm door to the deck opened up and Quinton dragged me inside, locking the heavy door behind us.

TWENTY-SEVEN

Quinton, adept at getting what he needed while staying off the grid, had turned the water on, but it wasn't warm. There was a generator off the kitchen, but it required gasoline and we didn't have any handy short of a wet slog back out to the Rover. The propane tank for the stove and refrigerator was equally empty. The undead had ripped my clothes, so I was half-naked and I'd lost the packet of yellow silk. I was so cold from exposure, exertion, and the icy water of the lake that I couldn't stop shivering. But I had mud, blood, and bits of dead things smeared all over me and it was too disgusting to leave there, so we ended up washing under the icy tap. Quinton had pulled the old couch up as close to the stove as he could and we snuggled naked together in the blankets to warm up. Quinton curled himself around me and his body seemed to burn my deeply chilled skin. It would have been much more erotic if I hadn't been shaking so hard.

My hearing was still full of low buzzing that made everything sound distant and crackly, like an old radio with a bad antenna, but it was improving slowly. I filled him in on what I'd been pursuing since I had arrived at Blood Lake and what had come hunting us.

"Why haven't the cops shown up about the shooting?" I stuttered between chattering teeth.

"Maybe no one heard it," Quinton suggested. "You said there aren't many people up here this time of year."

"No, but there *are* a few."

"And most of them probably don't want the local sheriffs to come around and interrupt whatever magical nastiness they're up to."

I frowned over that and wondered who'd been at the door that had cast golden light onto the lake.

"How did they know we were here?" Quinton asked.

"Who?"

"The zombies. You haven't stayed here before and you said Newman only gave you the key Monday. You didn't use the place last night or the night before, so how did Costigan know to send the corpse brigade over here to attack you?"

"That's a good question. I'll have to ask the Newmans that tomorrow. I was given the impression they didn't talk — at least not civilly — to Costigan, who seems to be in charge of the zombies around here. I need to talk to him, too. I haven't done anything to attract his ire, that I know of — we've never even met."

"Yeah, but you did tell the ley weaver that Costigan couldn't be trusted, and that might have gotten back to him. And I don't suppose Willow and her pet demon are the most honorable spell-flingers in the area, either."

"More than you might imagine." I paused, thinking, and feeling a little less like a human Popsicle. "What about you?"

"What about me?"

"You said you had to make a deal with the FBI to get their help. What did they want you to do?"

"Oh . . . I can't really discuss it."

"Will they be coming back for more? Are you stuck on their hook?"

"No. Part of the reason I cut my hair — well, it's a little complicated, but I wanted them to think I'm not a good risk. The FBI doesn't use the same kind of people as other agencies. They're really cops at heart and they have less tolerance for rogues and lunatics than, say . . . the CIA does. It doesn't mean my dad won't come after me, but I think I'm done with the Feebs."

"Your dad—he wouldn't turn you in to the NSA, would he?"

Quinton snorted. "No. It wouldn't suit his agenda. I'm an embarrassment that could ruin his career at this point. He's just as glad to have me stay missing."

"Do you despise him?"

"Not really. I just know I can only trust him to do what's best for his career at any given moment. No person is ever going to come ahead of his job. I think that's what made my mother leave him. She said it was the general stuff—the secrets, the tension, the absences—but I always had the impression there was a specific incident that broke them apart. Mom wasn't an angel, either. She had affairs and she ran her life as if the rest of us weren't important most of the time. Not that she made bad, selfish decisions all the time; she just didn't feel the need to discuss them first. She looked after my sister and me all r—"

I shook my head and turned in his arms to put my hand over his mouth. "You have a sister? You've never mentioned that before."

He shrugged and chafed my upper arms, ostensibly to keep me warm, but I thought he just wanted a moment to think before he answered. "She's in Europe, somewhere."

"Just 'somewhere'?"

"I know where, but it's not important. She's married and has kids—none of the family business for her. I think she still writes to my mom and calls her, but she's making her own life without the rest of us and it's probably safer to leave it that way."

That I understood. I also sensed that her decision had hurt Quinton in some way that he didn't want to discuss. I let it slide and leaned against him. "You never told me Solis knew who you really are."

He kissed my temple. "Nope. He swore to tell no one, and that included you."

"So . . . should I start calling you by your real name, now that you're in from the cold?"

Quinton laughed. "What, as if I were someone out of a

John le Carré novel? You do, and I shall be forced to take drastic measures."

"Oh? How drastic?"

"Like this," he said, and swooped his head down to blow a loud raspberry against my belly.

I squealed and wriggled around in the blanket as he tickled me and made more ridiculous noises against my skin. It was silly and it hurt a bit from the pulling of my scars and unevenly healed muscles, but I was more than just warm now and I sure as hell wasn't going to complain.

In a few minutes he stopped tickling and began stroking and kissing my skin instead. It felt strange without the soft rasp of his beard and the silky trailing of his hair, but the heat of his mouth and tongue still wrung a gasp of pleasure from me. He moved lower, sliding his hands and lips down between my legs.

He licked and nibbled, his fingers sliding over moisture, then pushing deep. I put my hands on his head to pull him into me and was frustrated by his short hair. I felt him chuckle against my hot, wet flesh, and the sensation made me moan. He continued, without remorse, building a scalding tension in my body with every touch, driving me tighter, higher, until it burst apart, pushing outward on my cry of ecstatic release.

Liquid and hard, he slid up and into me as I was still gasping. He groaned and buried his face in my neck, biting lightly as he thrust and then licking where he'd bitten. He nipped at my earlobe and then pressed his lips against my ear. "I love you."

I shuddered under him, arching into his movement, and turned my head, capturing his mouth with mine. I didn't need to hear what I knew. I loved the feel of him, the touch and the taste and the depth of his motion inside me, drawing me tight again. I only wanted to feel, without words, to come with him in that breaking, crystal instant.

He gave me my way, making love with only the conversation of our bodies and the upward-spiraling cadence of our gasps and moans, the depth and speed of his thrust and my response. I felt the tension in his body snapping as he groaned and shuddered. A wave of awesome sensation burst into me, like a million sparks dancing over my skin, igniting something that burned across us both. I clenched my eyes shut against the brightness of it through the Grey as I shattered and came with him, feeling our energy twine together, blazing into a circle encompassing us alone and illuminating the world within, then fading softly, slowly. . . .

He laid his head against the crook of my neck once again, breathing deeply, slowing, until his body eased and he slid over to lie beside me. I watched him and smiled until he fell asleep. Then I laid my head down and stared into the dark, feeling his contentment and my own anxiety winding over me. How could I feel warm and fuzzy while I also felt like a lying bitch? I didn't know how I was going to protect him, or how I was going to live up to him. What Quinton feared most, what he had given up his freedom and anonymity for, was all too possible. When my father's ghost had gone, he'd taken away the thing that made me nearly immortal: my deepest kinship with the Grey, the growing inhumanity that had enabled me to hear the song of the energy, to change the structure of the grid and kill a god. That was gone and I had lied to Quinton: I was no longer bulletproof; I could die as easily as anyone and leave him forever.

We got up while the sun was still low and went out to search for the yellow silk banishment and see how much mess the creeping dead had left behind. We had no luck with the missing spell, and I guessed it had probably been carried off by a bird that was now living in the silkiest yellow nest in the world. The remains of the zombies weren't very identifiable except that most weren't human. The stink of decomposition had already attracted scavengers that had done a good job of carrying bits away and spreading the rest around. It was a pain in the ass to scrape up the glop and parts left behind and bury them, but at least none of these dead would be walking again.

Over a cold breakfast afterward, I looked over the lists

I'd gotten from Faith. I swore and laid the papers aside. "Useless. The people on the list are the people I already know about. There used to be more full-time residents, but now there's only a handful and they're all accounted for. I'm still looking for someone who's here, but not here. It's not seasonal renters or even the nonresident owners, because most of the overt violence has happened in the late winter and early spring before they come up here."

"What about Ridenour?"

I shook my head. "I'm not sure. He doesn't seem to have any magical power. He doesn't seem to even see the magical things going on."

"He could be acting. He was married to a demon for a while, after all."

"But he didn't know what she was until Willow told him. And the huli-jing is gone now, so his connection to the grid through her was cut."

"Doesn't mean he can't have started to play with it on his own, if he was so desperate to get his wife back or take revenge."

I nodded. It fit to a degree, but I wasn't quite satisfied with it. Still, it would explain Ridenour's not coming to find me after Willow had escaped from the greenhouse, since he'd have gone after her himself. I respected Ridenour enough that I wanted more proof before I accused him of bashing in Strother's head and killing Leung. Ridenour didn't seem to have any Grey abilities of his own, but that didn't mean he couldn't have borrowed some. After all, whoever had moved the Subaru into the lake had needed help. If the killer wasn't very good at magic, it would explain why the crimes themselves were sudden and violent and why only the aftermath and cover-up had the tang of the Grey. Ridenour didn't live at the lake, but he was around constantly. . . .

Quinton pointed at the other list. "What about that one? Anything there?"

I picked it up and scanned it. "List of what was found in Leung's Subaru." I shook my head. "They're going to have a great time trying to figure out what's significant in this bunch of rotting junk. Not a lot survived the fire in the front of the car, but the stuff in the back was mostly intact until it hit the water. Leung was a real pack rat," I added. Then I summarized the list: "A big lump of wet paper—probably maps—that started to rot as soon as it got into the air; pocket change; keys; a rifle and a box-worth of unfired cartridges to match; a large rock; the remains of what was probably a pair of boots—in addition to the pair he was wearing at the time; a tire iron and jack, badly rusted; a spare coat that was mostly rot and guesswork; a plastic crate of rusted canned goods; a surveyor's transit in a water-logged wooden box; two baseball caps in dubious condition; the remains of two blankets—"

"Sounds like the back of your truck," Quinton interrupted, "only wet."

That gave me pause. The house was neat, orderly, and prepared for a stint of bad weather—if we'd had some gasoline, we could have had the generator running, which would have given us plenty of power to run the water heater as well as the lights. If the propane tank hadn't been empty, we'd have had heat, a working stove, and a refrigerator, all without main power or a gas line. I'd assumed the house had been cleaned and closed up, but Leung's clothes were still in one of the closets and the shotgun hadn't been locked up, but left standing beside the kitchen door in case of aggressive wildlife. Except for removing the gas cans that must have been around and having the propane tank drained and purged, Geoff Newman hadn't done anything to the house but shutter it up and lock it. Leung hadn't been a hoarder; he'd been ready.

"It *is* like my truck. He carried things he thought he might need if he got stranded or in trouble. He even had his old surveyor's transit. I'll bet these are the things he packed when he was still working and didn't see any reason to remove them once he retired."

"So you need to concentrate on what doesn't fit—if anything."

I read through the list again. "This is strange. Even ignoring the dead fish and soda bottles, there are some odd things in this collection. The weirdest has to be the extra finger."

"That's a little gruesome. Where'd that come from?"

"From a grave," I thought aloud, remembering the petty, squabbling dead of Tragedy Graveyard.

"A zombie was in the car?"

"I don't think so. I think someone laid a spell for Leung in his car. I don't know what it did, but that's my guess."

"A spell?" Quinton frowned. "Mara doesn't need bones to cast a spell."

"Not the kind she does, no. But not all magical systems operate the same way. Mara was telling me that one of our mages out here might be using hoodoo, or something akin to it, and that practice definitely does use bones. I'd guess anything involving a human finger isn't a nice thing. The rest of the spell has washed away by now, so no telling what it was. What else doesn't fit?" I wondered aloud, reading the page yet again. "A rock, a pair of lineman's pliers, a screwdriver . . ."

"Aside from the rock, those don't sound too odd."

I looked up. "According to the list, Leung had a complete tool kit in the back. He didn't need to have an additional screwdriver and pliers in the front seat. He certainly wasn't fixing anything while he was driving. Besides those, there's this stone—some kind of quartz and it weighs eighteen pounds."

"Wow. Maybe that's your anchor."

"Maybe, but what was Leung doing with it? The dead near Costigan's house said Leung had been killed for the anchor—or because of it. Jewel said . . . her father was going to do something about the lake. . . . Whatever he was doing, he either didn't do it right or he never finished."

"Not before someone killed him."

"But if the rock is the anchor, then the anchor was in the lake. Why didn't that fix the problem?"

"Anchors don't do much good if they aren't set," Quinton said. "Maybe he hadn't put it in the right place."

"But why would his killer risk putting the anchor back

into the lake at all? The problem here seems to have started in 1989 when the magic got wild. The only person who wants to shut that off is Jewel Newman, and if she'd killed her father for it, she'd have made sure the anchor got replaced properly. The others benefit only so long as the anchor is out of place. I can't see why one of them would risk shutting off the power by throwing the anchor stone back into the lake at all."

"What if they didn't know?"

"You're suggesting an ignorant mage."

"At least one of them is self-taught. Which is sometimes the same as mud-ignorant."

"I don't think Willow killed her father."

"Then it must be the mysterious number five."

I sighed and sipped the weak tea Quinton had made by warming up cups of water on top of the Franklin stove. "I still have no idea who that is. Or if it's the rogue or the child. I can figure out the nexus and the puppeteer—that's Jewel Newman and Elias Costigan. I know the east must have been Jonah Leung or Willow's mother, because they're both dead. Willow could be the child, but she could also be the rogue."

"Think about it from the ley weaver's viewpoint. They're his terms, so the titles are based on his ideas."

"Which is something I can't begin to fathom. And it's not helping."

"Then leave it for now and we'll need to attack a different part of the problem. What's on the last sheet of paper?"

"It's Alan Strother's car log for the day he died. It shows the locations and times where his car stopped. For most of these, I can tell whom he went to see by looking up the residents on the other list. I also see when he clocked back in, how long he was out of the car—that sort of thing. But there are these holes. . . ."

"So he checked out the houses on the list and then what?"

"He drove around. Back and forth a few times. It didn't

make a lot of sense and I'm still trying to figure out the pattern."

"Who's still on your list to talk to?"

"Almost all of them. And now I want another look at that rock, too."

"I guess we're driving back to Port Angeles, then."

Faith was curious about why we wanted to look at the rock. "It's not some kind of precious stone. It's just a rock. Probably fell into the car when it sank." But he pulled out the box of personal effects that weren't too rotted to touch and let us have a look anyway. He did insist on our wearing gloves when we handled the stuff, though. Just in case.

Out of the water, the objects no longer exuded a Grey mist. Most were so inert, they looked like shapeless blanks in my sight—but not the rock. It glowed green and gold with something burning in its core like a banked fire, and it whined and whispered like distant radio signals. If it wasn't the anchor, it was something equally magical. Quinton looked at the rock while I talked to Faith.

"Not much to go on," I commented, stirring the smaller items with my gloved fingers. "Screwdriver and pliers are interesting...."

"We're thinking whoever sabotaged his brakes and fuel line left them—they don't match the set in the back," Faith said, confirming my belief that he was no fool. "It's too damn bad they've been down there so long that we've got no viable traces on them. The cold water preserved a lot more than we could have hoped for, but it's still pretty slim pickings."

"I'm sorry to hear it," I said. I could see Quinton rummaging in his backpack, but I ignored him for now and did my best to keep Faith's attention off him, too.

"So are we all. What do you make of this stuff?"

"Not a lot, I have to admit. Looks as though he was prepared for any contingency except being murdered and dumped in the lake."

"Yeah, Leung was a careful guy, but he was a little superstitious, from what I've picked up. Believed in demons, I'm told—Chinese demons, that is, the sort who can't turn corners and are afraid of the color yellow. You know he always wore something yellow or red?" He nodded to himself. "That's what I'm told."

"It must have made him easy to see in the brush."

"Don't know about that. Never went hunting with the man. Judging by the rifle, though, he wasn't averse to it. Some folks think it's cruel, but round here it can be the difference between making it and going on welfare."

Quinton held up a meter of some kind with a couple of probes hanging off it. "Do you mind if I test this crystal?"

Faith gave him an odd look. "What sort of test?"

"I just want to see if it's holding an electric charge."

"It's been underwater for a while."

"I understand, but some materials don't dissipate electricity in water. If it's charged, Leung might have been convinced it was something magical."

"I'm not sure . . ." Faith started.

"I won't cause it any harm. I'm just going to poke it."

Faith frowned. "Oh, I suppose you can go ahead. But if it explodes or breaks, I'm going to be a mite put out with you."

"Understood." Quinton stuck the probes on the rock in various locations and poked at it in silence until we got bored of watching him and went back to our own conversation.

I started. "But Leung wasn't shot, was he?" I almost hoped Faith would say he had been, and we'd at least have ballistics to catch the killer by.

"Nope. 'Cording to the doc, head trauma would have killed him if the fire didn't. Just waiting on the formal autopsy report to confirm which it was, but it's been pushed back, so it'll be a few more days."

"Why?"

"Murdered cops are a little more important than guys who've been dead for five years."

My turn to nod. Of course they'd push the death of Alan Strother up the priority list.

This was especially true since it was a fresher killing that had a better chance of clearing and might solve Leung's murder at the same time.

Faith didn't seem to notice when something gave out a bright, hard note in my inner ear like a soprano breaking a glass. Quinton yelped.

Faith and I turned to him.

"It sparked. Not a big deal. I just wasn't expecting it," Quinton explained.

"Sparked?" Faith asked.

"Yeah. This thing's mostly quartz and it's electrically active. Most quartz is, but this one might be some kind of conductor. . . . Can I take this rock with me?" Quinton asked. "I'd like to see what else it does."

Faith made a face. "I'd love to get rid of it, but until we have more information, I can't let you."

I chimed in. "You know he wasn't beaten to death with it, so how is it material?"

"Probably not, but it's in the inventory and it'll have to stay. Why would you want it?"

I gave it some thought before I replied. "I think Leung wasn't the only superstitious one around the lake. His killer might have put it in the car to frighten him. . . ."

"You mean all that mumbo jumbo about Elias Costigan laying Voodoo curses on folks to keep 'em away from his place?" Faith snorted. "I think he's managed to put a good scare into a few people, but that's all it is. I'd take it more seriously if one of the Quileutes or Makah were shaking feathers and bones at me."

"Why?"

"I figure the Indians might know a bit about the spirits around here—if there are any. But a self-proclaimed Voodoo witch doctor? He's a crank."

"Even a crank can be dangerous, Faith."

"I don't deny it. But all you've got there is a spare finger and a rock that sparks. Voodoo curse or not, it's no smoking gun."

I needed that rock, but Faith wasn't going to let me walk out with it until the case was solved. I'd have to try another approach. "What's your take on Brett Ridenour?"

"What about him?"

"I've been thinking that if Strother's killer is someone from the lakes and we've eliminated most of the full-time residents, what about the nonresidents who are around all the time? Ridenour certainly fits that description, and he's a little obsessive about 'his' lake and 'his' park. I imagine that if he thought there was a threat to it, he might think he had cause to take drastic action."

"Ridenour? I'm not sure about that ... but he can be a little overzealous, I guess."

"And he has a personal spite for Willow Leung."

"True—he blames her for his wife running off and leaving him. But it's not Willow who's been killed."

"Maybe his dislike is based on more than his missing wife. Maybe he thinks Willow knows something that could incriminate him in her father's death."

"And good luck finding that out. Willow Leung is harder to catch than a snowflake at midsummer. Alan Strother was the only person who ever got close enough and he didn't manage to catch her, either."

"That might have been because he was in love with her."

Faith stared at me. "In love with her? He didn't know the girl except through her jacket and one meeting when he was fresh out of training."

"Not true. They've known each other since high school. Ridenour arrested them and they were in juvenile together."

"No bull? How do you know? Juvenile records are sealed. Did Ridenour tell you?"

"Willow told me."

Faith rubbed his hands over his hair. "Paint me blue. You've talked to that crazy woman? Why didn't you call me, catch her, something?"

"I didn't have any cell service at the graveyard in Beaver and what was I supposed to do—throw a blanket over her and tie her up? She thinks I can find out who killed Strother and her dad. She was willing to talk to me because I'm not a cop."

"Can you get to her again?"

"Not reliably. She finds me."

Faith huffed and frowned. "Damn it. Damn it! You have to get that girl to talk to me."

"She's not going to walk in here and get herself arrested."

"I'll go to her."

"What could she possibly tell you? If she knew who killed her father or Strother, she'd have told me already."

"She knows what happened to her brother and Timothy Scott."

"Scott was the phone lineman she shot?"

"Yeah, but I'm not sure about it."

"She says she did it."

"On purpose? Lying in wait? That doesn't sound like something a nineteen-year-old girl does no matter what Ridenour says about her. If you're telling me the truth, she'd already done a stint in juvie and, believe me, she wouldn't want to go to jail after that, so I can understand her running. But what does a kid that age know? She doesn't have any perspective on the world. She thinks everything is her fault and she blames herself even if it's an accident. She probably thinks she's responsible for her mother's death, too, one way or another."

"You talk as though you know."

"I've seen a lot of screwed-up kids. They come in two kinds: the truly hard and the scared shitless. Willow Leung's crimes aren't the acts of a bad kid, a hard kid; they're wild-kid stuff. Except for the murder, which makes no sense at all. A young woman whose rap sheet is trespass, joyriding, petty B and E on abandoned buildings, and smoking dope doesn't lie in wait and murder a man she's never met. Not without cause."

I knew why she'd really done it, but I was sure Faith didn't; yet he seemed unconvinced of her guilt and that made me curious. "The report she gave was that he raped her and she shot him when he came back to try again."

"Total bullshit. Her dad wouldn't have let that slide if there had been such an incident. He'd have come after Scott himself. But Tim Scott had never been on that route before, so there never was a chance for him to have raped her and come back. I would bet you my salary for a year it was a pure accident. She didn't even know him. I think she cooked up the rape story because she was scared and it's more sympathetic than 'I thought he was a bear.'"

"You don't think she did it?"

Faith shook his head and crossed his arms over his chest. "No, I'm pretty sure she shot him. I just don't think she murdered him. I don't think she killed her brother, either, but I think she does know what happened to him and it's made her scared. Look, her mother died, her half brother died, her dad was a little preoccupied with their deaths, and her half sister ain't exactly Miss Sweetness and Light."

"Hang on. Half brother and half sister? Willow's mother wasn't Jewel and Jonah's mother?"

"Nope. Kind of surprised you missed that in your background on Leung."

"It wasn't a full report—I only spent two hours on it," I objected, stung.

Faith shrugged and he went on. "Leung's first wife, Doreen Fife, divorced him and moved down the hill to town when the two kids were in their early teens. Eventually she moved back east and got remarried. She kind of divorced the whole family, really. Stopped having contact with them once she had a new family to occupy her time," Faith added with a snort of disgust. "Steven married Sula Yu a couple years later and Willow came along a couple of years after that. That house on Lake Sutherland's been in Sula's family since they built it back in the settlement days."

"Sula's family was Chinese?"

Faith nodded. "You don't hear much about 'em, but

there were a handful of Chinese out here as workers when they were building up the railroads. Mostly they left afterward, but the Yus stayed. Dodged the Exclusion Act by keeping to themselves up on the mountain. Mostly quiet, law-abiding folks far as I can tell. Until this generation. Willow's been in j-camp, and she's run a little wild, but—except for shooting Scott—her worst crime appears to have been getting on the wrong side of Brett Ridenour."

"I thought you liked him."

"I like him well enough and I'll give you that he's dedicated to his job, but he's bitter and he's got an inflexible mind. As far as he's concerned, there's Ridenour's way and there's the wrong way."

I considered that and I couldn't disagree. I sighed. "If I can get Willow to talk to you, will you let us . . . borrow that rock?"

"No. But I might misplace it for a couple of days."

I held out my hand. "I'll let you know."

Faith unfolded his arms and shook my hand. "Be careful, Ms. Blaine. You're walking in some damned tricky territory."

I just nodded, and Quinton and I left Faith to his desk and the box full of waterlogged evidence.

TWENTY-EIGHT

"**W**hat do you think?" I asked as we returned to the Rover.

"It's piezoelectric—most quartz is—but it's got some other electrical properties as well. It's a big piece, so I'm not quite sure what the effect would be, but it kind of reminds me of old-fashioned radio crystals. . . ."

"It's very high-pitched."

"I didn't hear anything."

"I think it was a Grey sound. Faith didn't hear it, either."

"Huh . . . I wonder if it's tuned in some way . . ." Quinton mused.

"Tuned?"

"Yeah. Well, quartz has some interesting properties. Aside from the piezoelectric effect—"

"What is that?"

"It produces electricity if you deform it—that's how the pilotless ignition on your stove works—or, if you give it electricity, it deforms in response. It's a useful effect for transducers and—"

I interrupted him. "I'm going to take your word on that. What else does it do?"

"I'm not sure. But given that it seems to be Grey, I'd make a rough guess that it influences the amplitude or direction of magic. When it's in place. Tuned crystals, like the ones in rudimentary radio sets, resonate to a specific frequency. In this case, it might be a specific frequency in the

Grey. I wish I had some of that crystal myself. It might overcome the problems with my Grey detectors. . . ."

His excitement made my own skin buzz, and I could almost see the calculations in Quinton's eyes as he thought about it and made mental schematics for new devices to track ghosts.

I cleared my throat. "I was actually wondering what you think of Faith and his ideas."

Quinton blinked. I rarely ask him his opinion of people I'm working with. "He seems . . . pretty reasonable. Which means he hasn't any idea what's going on."

"What about you? I mean, you don't see ghosts. . . ."

"Sweetheart, we were attacked by walking dead things last night. I may have never seen a ghost, but I've heard them and I have met vampires, zombies, witches, and two-headed sea monsters that turn into homicidal canoes. I think I'm allowed to draw some conclusions from that."

We got into the truck and I started driving up the hill. I kept thinking about the complications around the Leung children and their homes. The Newmans' house sat nearly on top of the power nexus under the lake. That and money explained why people jumped when Jewel said "frog," but the big glass-and-wood house hadn't existed as long as the smaller house at Lake Sutherland with its old, time-etched circle of power and its quiet, old family who kept to themselves, sitting as firmly as Mount Storm King on the deep blue torrent of the east/west leyline. . . .

"What do you think about the *case*?" I asked.

"Well . . . I haven't met any of the suspects, so I can't say for sure. Faith did seem pretty convinced that Willow's not a killer. You seem to agree with him."

"Not entirely—and that doesn't mean she's not a troublemaker, because she is. I know she shot Timothy Scott, but Faith may be right: It was an accident for which she still feels guilty. She told me someone had 'stolen' the magic circle beside the house after Jonah died. It was her mother's circle when she was born and since Willow was her student as well as her child, it should have been *her* circle when Sula died—or at least after her half brother died. Maybe she mistook Scott for the thief, shot him, and then realized she'd made a mistake, but then it was too late. . . . She was still young then. She's powerful, but she's not well trained. She'd already been to juvie and she might not have known at the time that her records were sealed. She probably freaked, thinking they'd send her up as an adult with one strike. Plus her other crimes, she might have believed they'd put her away for life, so she came up with the rape story to buy some time and then she ran for the woods. She seems to have an extraordinary connection to nature here—right down to animals and the plants. Maybe that was why she went to the greenhouse."

"Yeah, I don't get that. Why did she rob the greenhouse of a plant that was growing on the ground outside it?"

"I think she needed to rip the plant apart, but since she's connected to the power there, she didn't want to hurt one that was growing in the living soil around the lake. I've only seen her take things that weren't alive. She knows things she won't tell me, and, as far as I can tell, she takes a positive delight in messing with Ridenour."

"Sounds like mutual hate. It doesn't seem like much of a reason to kill someone's father, though."

"I'm still not sure about Ridenour."

"You kind of like him."

"I do, but that's not a factor in guilt. I'm sure the ley weaver didn't kill Leung or Strother. It's not interested in human problems and it doesn't seem to move away from its . . . sculpture or whatever you'd call it. It wouldn't have to wreck a car since it could just draw the energy out of someone like Leung, and there'd have been no ghost left to tell me a crime had been committed. I'm reasonably convinced Willow isn't responsible, either. That leaves Jewel, Costigan, and Ridenour."

"Unless there's someone else."

I heaved a sigh. "The mysterious Number Five. I just don't know. But I can't get that anchor stone back without solving the murders, and I must shut down the loose power around the lakes. It's not safe as it is and I'm not sure it'll be better back the way it was. Jewel's not the weak and gracious *grande dame* she wants people to believe her to be. She's greedy, and until she got sick, she was powerful and dangerous, and people are still scared of her. But I think she usurped the power when she built the house. I don't think it's really hers, which may be why she's sick now."

"So where are we going now?"

"To find out who knew we were at Leung's place."

Geoff Newman scowled at us when he opened the door, but he spoke in a low voice. "What do you want? And who's this?"

I ignored the latter question. "I want to know who sent a shambling army of walking corpses to visit me last night at your father-in-law's place."

Newman's mouth dropped open and his aura pulsed with alarm. "Who what?"

I pushed past him into the house. Tendrils of yellow and sickly green energy stroked at my legs, but nothing stopped me. Quinton came silently in my wake.

Newman shut the door behind us and stared at me. "I don't know what you're talking about."

"Where's Jewel? Maybe she does."

"Jewel's resting. She had a rough night. The rain—" He cut himself off.

A piece of the puzzle about Jewel's illness clicked into place in my mind. "Rain makes her weaker, doesn't it?" I demanded. Newman hung his head but didn't reply. "At least I can assume she wasn't out directing zombies to my door. But who was?"

He looked back up, imploring. "Please . . . please keep your voice down. Come on in here and we can talk."

He motioned us to follow him toward the unused wing of the house. Well, not entirely unused, since the room we walked into was a kitchen that was plainly an active work area. It was a big space that led into a dining room facing the lake. An ill-advised little dining nook had been built at the end of the kitchen and facing the front of the house where it would never get the sun or a view of anything but the steep road up to the highway. The area had been converted into a makeshift office, and I wondered why Geoff Newman hadn't taken over one of the doubtlessly empty rooms upstairs. I noticed that the writhing tendrils of energy didn't penetrate very far into the kitchen, so maybe that was the reason he'd chosen it—a refuge from the demands of his wife.

He shifted papers aside and closed up an open laptop computer to make room for us all at the small table. He sat in a white kitchen chair and faced us once Quinton and I were seated on the padded bench below the window.

He played with an empty coffee cup, but he didn't offer us any coffee.

"Tell me about Jewel," I prompted.

"Sometimes the rain makes her sick. Not all the time, just storms like last night. I don't understand it. Jewel always says the water is being taken away from her. I don't see how that can be, since the water is falling down on all of us, but that's what she says. Lately she's been pretty sickly, like she just doesn't have any energy at all most of the time."

"When did it start?"

"It's gotten worse over time, so it's hard to say when it started. She's been having troubles since we met and that's why we're here—she said building the house right here would be better for her, so we did that."

"Did it help?"

"A bit, at first. After her stepmother passed was when she first started having bad days. When Jonah died, they happened more often. She talked about demons a lot. At first I thought maybe she was a little . . . touched in the head, but I know that's not true now. I know there's something about the lake that . . . I don't know how to say it."

"It's the source of her power," I supplied. "Right now the power is uncontrolled, so anyone who knows how can take some of it. When they do, they drain power your wife's been relying on and she gets sicker. When it rains hard enough, I suspect the power in the lake gets drawn to the surface, like osmosis, and it's easy for other mages to suck it off and use it. They might not actually be trying to hurt her, but the effect is the same. The system is supposed to be held down by a single nexus point under this house. That's why she wanted to build here, so she could control the nexus rather than drawing power from it at a distance. But right now the nexus isn't anchored properly and others are using the power that Jewel's never truly been able to control. That's what she wants me to fix."

"I understand that. Sort of. What I don't understand is why they have to kill anybody. Is someone going to try to kill Jewel?"

In a bland voice I asked, "Would you care if she died?"

Newman looked appalled, the energy around his head sinking into a clinging, muck green shroud. "Of course I would!"

"Why? Don't say you love her. I know you care about her, but that's not the same thing." There had never been any sign of the dancing sparks between them that I associated with love.

"I do care! She's a hard woman to like, it's true, but she—she makes things better. Do you have any idea what it's like to do good work? To know what you're doing is difficult, but necessary, and that you'll keep on doing it, even if no one notices and no one cares?"

I'd done plenty of "right" things that went without acknowledgment or reward, but they weren't the same. He wasn't talking about Jewel's trying to restore the lake; he was talking about his own part—the silent support. "I've seen it," I replied, knowing it was sitting beside me, and for a moment I felt the same confusion and despair that had kept me awake in the night, studying the ceiling.

"Then you know how I'd care. So . . . is someone going to kill my wife?"

"I don't think so. I'd guess they can't touch her directly and they don't really want her to go away, because then Willow would become the keeper of the nexus and they certainly don't want a rogue sorcerer like her in charge of the power around the lake. She may seem like just a crazy young woman, but, if I'm right, Willow's potentially very dangerous to anyone who is trying to grab power from the lake."

"I don't understand. Why Willow?"

"Willow is Sula's daughter, and, until you built this house for Jewel, the nexus had been husbanded by Sula's family for generations. All the other mages are Johnny-come-latelies, not people who were born here. They aren't connected to the power; they're just leeches. Magic tends to run in families and, in a place like this, old connections mean a lot; Willow, not Jewel, is the rightful guardian of the nexus."

Newman looked stricken, but he kept his gaze down. "Jewel never did like her. She said Sula had made Steven reject her after Willow was born for being half-black, for not being Chinese enough, like Willow. I told her it couldn't be true. Sula always had tried to be our friend and she looked after Jonah like her own son, even though he was— well, he was a bully, arrogant, and mean with it. He and Jewel used to be friends, but then they started to fight like cats and dogs. He used to say horrible things—*horrible* things to Jewel! He'd make her so angry and frustrated, she'd be sick for days. I wasn't so sorry when he died and I'm not going to apologize for that."

"You don't have to. Geoff, did it never seem strange to you that this county's overwhelmingly white, but most of the ... powerful people I've met around the lake aren't? They're black, or Chinese, or mixed like Jewel. . . ."

"Did you ever notice how Western history is mostly white man's history? Even when people of color do something important, it's treated like a fluke or it's buried under the contributions of whites. Washington is full of people who aren't white and they get treated like they don't exist, even though they worked just as hard or harder to make this place a safe home. They built roads and ships and cleared trees and hauled coal out of these mountains. They worked in logging camps and rail gangs and mines."

He looked up suddenly. "Hell, half the workers who made the highway out there weren't white. And where do you suppose they lived while they were cutting roads and laying rails and cooking and cleaning for white folks at the fancy hotels down at the springs and on the lake? They lived out here where there was no running water or sewers or boarding-houses, because the trip up the mountain took too long if you worked twelve hours a day, six days a week. They lived in shacks and tents. And they were mostly black and Chinese and Indians. Why shouldn't they be the ones to find some magic—if there is such a thing? Don't they deserve it?"

So it was a creole magic, shaped by the beliefs and practices of the people who lived here even when the weather was terrible, the ones who couldn't afford to leave. When the magic got loose, it attracted magic users whose skills weren't of the schooled and methodical practices I'd seen with Mara and Carlos. In its current state, it benefited the rogues and inventors more than it benefited the more traditional form Jewel used with her cards and her books.

"Yes, they do," I said, but I was thinking. . . . The natives had stayed away from the lake, fearing the spirits of those drowned under Storm King's wrath. No one had laid claim to the magic or tried to govern and protect it until Sula's family came along, quietly staying below anyone's notice. They must have worked very subtly to keep the lake's power in balance and under control, helping to shape it into a hybrid unrecognizable to most Western mages—until something had happened to set it loose and Sula died without passing that control on properly. Jewel had benefited from the disordered magic, at first, and usurped the nexus. She must have fought with her brother over it and they'd both shut Willow out—Jewel at the source and Jonah at the circle beside the family house. But Jewel wasn't Sula's child; she wasn't the rightful owner. She didn't have the right tools, and instead of controlling the nexus, she was now controlled by it. Whenever someone else used "her" magic, they drained her and she didn't know how to stop them, short of destroying them all.

But someone else was determined to control the lake—someone with little power, unable to oppose Jewel directly. So they got others to ruin her, encouraging other mages to draw on the lake, running her down until Jewel was too weak to stop them. And so long as Willow was on the run, she wasn't likely to grab the power back—she didn't even know it was hers to take.

"Geoff, who knew you'd given me the key to Steven's cabin?" I asked.

"No one. I didn't tell anyone."

"Jewel must have known."

He gave a hard shake of his head. "No. Not even her. I—I wanted you nearby, in case . . ."

"You never wanted me here."

"I didn't. At first. But once I couldn't stop you, I thought . . . well, I thought I ought to get you on my side and get you close at hand, in case things got worse. But you didn't trust me. I didn't know you were at Steven's house. I swear. And neither did Jewel. I didn't tell anyone I'd given you the key because I can't trust any of them, either."

I couldn't see any sign that he was lying in his body language or his aura. Neither of those is foolproof, but Newman hadn't been a very good liar earlier and I had no reason to believe he'd suddenly learned how. "Well, one of them figured it out."

"I'm sorry. I didn't say anything and I don't know what to do now."

I pitied him, but I was also a little angry that he'd snuck around and manipulated and not told me the truth earlier.

"I don't know who tumbled to it, either. But I can find out. Talk to Jewel. Tell her she'll have to lure the other mages here so I can see them all."

"Why would they come?"

"Because your wife is the queen bee. Ridenour told me she runs the community. She's still the nexus keeper, even if she's not in complete control, and they are still afraid of her. She can't trust any of them, but they'll still come, even if they're just curious to see how sick she really is. I don't think the ley weaver to the south will come, but I already know about that thing and it doesn't seem interested in human struggles. She shouldn't waste her energy on it, but the rest . . . Tell her they need to be here tonight. Even her sister. Even Ridenour."

"Why?"

"Because I can solve her problem if she'll do this. It'll be over by tomorrow night if she does."

"You swear?"

"What do you want me to do—prick my finger and sign in blood? Yes, I swear."

I was lying through my teeth, but if I couldn't fix it all by tomorrow, we might have a bigger problem. Whoever was killing people had learned to send the monsters to do the dirty work, which meant he or she didn't have to bash in heads in person anymore. No one was safe.

TWENTY-NINE

From the Newmans', we headed toward the Lyre River and Elias Costigan's house. Although I'd see him later, I still needed to figure out how he'd known about the house, and it wouldn't be safe to try once the sun was heading down.

"What do you think the anchor does?" I asked.

"Um . . . anchors things?" Quinton replied.

"I mean, how does it work? Something to do with its piezoelectric properties?"

"I'm not thinking so, but I can't speculate without data. You're talking about the field interactions of an energy state for which there are no scales or standards. We can theorize based on what we know, but it'll be a pretty rough theory."

"Then what do you roughly theorize?"

"Well . . . is there more than one anchor?"

"Apparently, and I'm led to believe there's a total of four in and around the lake. When they were all in place, the lake's energy was contained and channeled into the nexus where two major leylines crossed—about where the Newmans' house is now, so that would be the top of the T or the middle of the X, depending on how you see it."

"Do we know if the other three anchors are in place?"

"Not by eyewitness, but the general belief is that they are, and my observation of the leylines leads me to agree."

"Hearsay is not very convincing, but I'll accept your observation as being persuasive enough. So one is out of place, and merely putting it *close* to its proper location—unlike in horseshoes and hand grenades—wasn't good enough. I'd hate to see what happens when more than one of the anchors is pulled."

"But that's not going to happen."

"We hope. Because if it did, the system would have no guidance. Huh . . . could it be part of a waveguide?"

"Unknown term, geek-boy. What's a waveguide?"

"Waveguides restrict the radiation of electromagnetic energy into a linear direction. They're kind of like pipes, but not really. Energy naturally radiates in spherical waves—outward in all directions at the same time and rate. That's fine if you want an omnidirectional antenna for radio or television transmission, but some kinds of energy, like, say, microwaves, need to be a little more restricted or they dissipate and do damage. The waveguide has to be specific to the type and wavelength of the energy you're managing. Broadly—and this is really generalized and a little squishy—by pairing the right conductive materials at the right distance, you essentially create an electrical trough for the energy to flow down that constantly reflects the waves back into the trough, rather than letting them radiate outward."

"OK. I'm not sure I get the details, but I get the idea."

"All right, so, if the anchor is part of a waveguide for Grey energy, it has to have an opposite polarity mate creating the 'walls' of the pipe. Removing one of the pair for either directional leyline basically lets the energy at that end radiate without proper control or direction. Since it's anchored at the other end by the nexus and partially directed by its other half, what you get is something like a firehouse that's hooked up to the hydrant at one end and flopping around loose at the other, spraying energy everywhere. With the way this particular energy is influenced by water, I'd guess that the lake itself acts like a conductive sink and lets the energy flow around until the lake's too saturated, and then the magic starts leaching up through the ground wherever it can. Or wherever the thrashing pipe has hit the ground, creating transient hot spots and upwellings.

"Normally, this system around the lake is restricted and the crossing leylines probably created a single sort of well-head at the nexus. Once the anchor was gone, the magic became fair game for anyone who could use it. But, and here's the slippery bit, the wellhead still exists and instead of pumping energy out to whoever's in charge of the nexus, it's now able to suck it back from that person when demand is high, which is why Jewel Newman experiences the sensation of drainage when someone else uses it or when it rains and the lake overflows, pulling more energy out of the sink."

I nodded. "That certainly sounds like our situation."

"You know it'll kill her sooner rather than later if the anchor isn't replaced."

"Yes, I do, and I don't have any great soft spot for her, but if what you're speculating is the truth of the situation, it won't change or get better once Jewel's dead. But how do we figure out where to put the anchor to re-create the wave-guide and fix this damned problem?"

"You can see the leylines, so if we can figure out what the anchors look like in the Grey, we should be able to calculate where the uprooted one goes by the position of the other three."

"Only one problem," I said. "The lake's more than a thou-sand feet deep. I'm pretty sure I can't hold my breath at that depth to go snooping around to figure out where the in-place anchors are."

"Let me give it some more thought," Quinton said while I parked the Rover at the end of the road.

We got out under a threatening sky and began walking toward Devil's Punch Bowl.

Along the way, I didn't see a single ghost or zombie. That made me a little curious, since every time I'd been past the area before, the place had been populated with ghosts. The wayward energy still swarmed around in balls and strings, pooling on surfaces like light on glass, but there were no human remnants, nor animal ghosts, either.

The last stretch was a raked gravel path that was remarkably free of mud and puddles. As we came around a tree-shaded bend a few dozen feet from the house, something shrieked. Then a fireball exploded against the tree closest to us—an actual fireball like the real-life version of a special effect from a Harry Potter movie. It splattered and left smoldering bits of flame on the tree and the path near us.

"Get off my property!" someone screamed from behind the screen of trees.

I edged around and looked out. A skinny man with dead gray hair and skin that looked as if it had never seen the sun stood on the porch of the low log house, tossing a knot of fire from hand to hand as if it were a potato fresh out of the oven. In spite of the frost-edged air, he wore nothing but a sort of sarong slung around his hips and a gold cross on a long chain around his neck.

"I just want to ask you a few questions, Mr. Costigan," I called out.

He suggested something anatomically unlikely and gymnastically ambitious in language so blue I was surprised it didn't hang in the air like fog. "You took 'em! You stole 'em, you sneaking bitch!"

"The zombies? They came after me!"

"You were trespassing! They left you alone once you crossed the bridge, right enough. You didn't have to snatch 'em and destroy 'em! I've been raising those for years! How dare you just go and . . . ruin my work!" And he was off again in a spate of abuse and creative cursing.

One of the curses floated languidly in our direction, a ring of blue-gray smoke and nasty red energy spikes. I didn't like the look of it, and I shoved Quinton backward while I flicked my palm outward in a tiny push on the Grey that sent the thing wafting toward the still-smoking tree.

When the curse touched it, the tree cracked and, with a screech of breaking wood, tore itself into two charred pieces.

Costigan flung the next fireball right behind it, shrieking what I thought was French, but with the way he spat it out, it could have been anything. He made an upward-pulling gesture and the ground heaved in a localized earthquake that spilled Quinton and me onto our backsides. Four glowing green shapes oozed out of the disturbed ground. Humanoid, but not human, they were made of nothing more substantial than colored mist. I still had the feeling I didn't want to touch any of them.

I scrambled up and urged Quinton back toward the truck, but one of the things was remarkably fast and sighed around behind us, cutting off the path back to the parking area.

The green thing reached out toward Quinton with its ghostly hands. I jumped toward them, yanking a bit of Grey shield between the thing and us, but not fast enough to keep it from drawing a finger across Quinton's bare cheek.

Quinton never saw the thing, but he jerked away from its touch with a gasp of pain, and a black line appeared on his skin where the thing's finger had passed. A point of ice seemed to score my own cheek.

Furious, I shoved a hot white wall of energy at the thing, shouting, "Get away from him!"

The phantasm of acid green mist flew backward, shredding into thin wisps that dissipated on the cold breeze from the lake.

Then I turned back to face the other three. I didn't want to expend a lot more energy on this fight and fall apart as I had last night, but the green things had to go. I pulled on the thin shield and pushed my hand through it, keeping the edge of the Grey between me and the nearest thing as I plunged my hand into it.

Even through the layered edge, the horrible vision wrapped around my hand and burned my flesh. I could see the skin and muscle on my hand withering and blackening while an ice-cold pain sucked all feeling from my hand and forearm. But I clutched onto the thing with pain-dulled fingers and shook it as a terrier does a rat.

It had no core of a soul that I could grab onto—at least I felt none—but it apparently did have some sense and a mind of its own, because the monstrous thing of mist fought away from me and zipped back across the distance between us and Costigan, dragging its remaining two companions with it.

As soon as it was gone, the color and shape returned to my hand and arm, but the flesh still felt burned away by cold and my fingers wouldn't straighten properly, as if they'd frozen in their crooked position. I glanced back at Quinton. A bit wide-eyed but still with me, he was clutching his own forearm in sympathy. The black line on his face had widened a little and spread a blue-white pallor onto the skin of his cheek. It looked like frostbite and my own face burned in anger.

Costigan had stopped moving around on his porch and stared at us with his three dire companions huddling around him. "What did you do to 'em? Are you gonna ruin all my helpers?"

"No! I never meant to hurt any of them until they hurt me first."

"You destroyed my work last night. Almost all of 'em. Why? What'd I ever do to you?"

"I destroyed them because you sent them to do me harm."

"I never did!"

"Then who? Who stole your work and sent it out to attack us?"

Costigan gaped, his mouth working as if he were a fish drowning in air. "But, but . . . no. No. I don't . . ."

"If you're done trying to kill us for today, can we come inside and talk?"

Suddenly, he looked old and frail with his pale skin exposed to the inhospitable weather. He nodded jerkily and waved us up to the porch, clearing his misty minions aside with a gesture of one hand. "Well, I ain't gonna waste no more time trying to kill you out here. Might as well come inside."

"Where you can kill us in private," Quinton muttered.

I turned back to Quinton. "Are you all right?"

He started to put his hand to his face but, wincing, pulled it back before his palm quite touched. "Feels as if something burned me, but . . . it's cold. I'm going to be a wuss and admit it hurts. Make that 'fucking hurts.' A lot."

"Anything else hurt or feel . . . strange?"

He paused as if taking a mental poll of his body parts. "No. I'm OK otherwise."

"You don't have to come. Maybe you shouldn't. . . ."

"You're kidding, right? I'm not going to go hide in the truck like a five-year-old and let him kill you—or whatever he's planning to try. Besides, if he did this to my face, I want him to fix it."

"All right, then. Come on."

We walked the last few yards to the house. I kept a wary eye on the Grey, just in case, but nothing molested us.

We stepped up onto the wooden porch, which creaked like a giant cricket. Up close, Costigan's skin was the color of old ivory, as if it had once been darker and had faded under a merciless light, his features slightly flattened. His eyes were ice blue.

Costigan just waited until we were close enough to peer at, which he did. "Lord have mercy, boy. What happened to your face?" he asked, snickering. His accent sounded as if he came from the swampy bits of Louisiana so long ago and through so many other places that he'd forgotten how it should go.

"Cut myself shaving," Quinton snapped at him. "What do you think?"

Costigan shook his head on his scrawny neck and turned to lead us into his house. Up close, he looked about ninety and more like an animated sack of bones than some of his creations had. "Well, I never seen 'em do that before. Not that I ever seen anybody still standing when they were done with 'em, neither. Today's a ponder, that's for sure."

Quinton blinked at me and made a bemused face. "I think he's crazy."

"What would give you that idea?" I replied.

Costigan snorted a chuckle and kept walking ahead of us into the living room.

The room was not what I'd expected at all. With its low roof and long, rambling lines, I'd thought the interior would reflect the same traditional look, but the cabin was a deceptive shell around a modern, cantilevered structure that seemed to hang over the shore from interior braces of white-painted steel. The water-level view filled the wall from side to side without a deck to ruin the illusion that the lake was coming right into the living room. The only thing that seemed to keep the roof from simply collapsing to the floor was a narrow steel fire pit and its collection of hanging organ-pipe chimneys that ran to within six feet of the window on the front and the exterior wall on the back. A folding screen of glass and metal rods held the smoke and fire at bay and reflected on the polished wood floor—where you could see it. Shapeless couches like sleeping buffalo lay here and there on the floor facing no particular direction and in no apparent plan. Small lost ottomans snuggling against the couches made it look like the herd of furniture had just settled itself down for the night. A slab of black granite stood on a pair of trestles beyond the fire curtain, pretending to be a table, its surface dusty with motes and swirls of colored powder and grit. Colored candles stood in slumps of melted wax on the table and lay in pyramid stacks in the corners of the room.

The floor was partially covered by mismatched rugs that had once roamed around as the skins of bears and sheep and now lay about as aimlessly as their sofa companions. I could see traces of chalk and salt on the floor under the rugs, and the air smelled of burning herbs and pine needles, with a faint, clinging odor of dead things under it all. I imagined the furniture could be moved quickly against the walls when needed, the rugs thrown over them to clear the floor for whatever work Costigan got up to. In the Grey, the room breathed slow gusts of dark mist.

Costigan pointed at the sofas as he went toward the

worktable. "You sit. I'll get something for the boy's face." He cackled to himself as he strolled away.

Quinton looked at me and mouthed, "Boy?"

I shrugged and sat on one of the couch lumps, which gave under me as if it were stuffed with down. In spite of the fire in the fire pit, the room was chilly, but the squishy embrace of the sofa made me too warm and I was panting in a minute. Quinton yanked me back up, and I realized the couch hadn't been warming me up so much as smothering me. I gave it a dirty look and stayed on my feet with my coat on.

"Think we can trust whatever crazy thing he's bringing back?" Quinton muttered.

"Not sure. But I won't let him do anything to you," I replied, then added, "That would hurt you."

Costigan shuffled back from the far side of the fire pit, a bowl in one hand and a bottle of rum tucked under his other arm. A thin Grey shadow that didn't bear his shape followed him. He frowned at us. "Whyn't you sit?"

"I think it's feeding time," I said.

"Eh?" Costigan muttered. Then he glanced at the couch I'd escaped from. "Ah. Well, I been busy." He kicked at the sofa in passing and his shadow did the same. The furniture whimpered. "Now, lemme see your face."

Quinton turned his cheek toward the old man warily, watching him from the corners of his eyes as he did.

Costigan huffed. "Looks nasty. You gonna get a scar there. Little scar, but you still be pretty; don't worry." He held the bowl in front of Quinton's face. "Spit." His shadow, flickering the color of budding leaves, reached to stroke the blackened weal and I blinked, conscious of its fingers.

"What?"

"Spit, you fool. Otherwise the spirits think it's me. You don't want them fix you up to look like me, do you?"

Quinton made a face and spit into the bowl. Costigan cackled to himself and poured in a stiff shot of rum before he used his fingers to stir the glop in the bowl around. Then he scooped up some reddish brown paste and patted it on the black line across Quinton's cheek. The shadow did the same while Costigan muttered under his breath. Quinton winced and so did I, which seemed to amuse the old man. "Just poultice, boy. Not gonna kill you, so stop squealing." The crazy old sorcerer shot me a glance, but didn't say anything.

I watched as the old man smeared the stuff on, seeing little green and gold threads, fine as spider silk, weaving out of the goo and settling into Quinton's skin. Where they touched, the skin turned a little rosier and sparkled slightly. The effect spread slowly over the bluish patch on Quinton's face until there was a fine gauze of magic clinging to the injury. I almost sighed in relief and felt the last of the tension drop from my own aching fingers.

But mention of a scar had made me think. "Is that how Faith got his scar?" I asked.

Costigan laughed. "No. I hear he had him a argument with a fella had a rifle and he only had him a dog. Before I come here, though, so I ain't sure."

"Why did you come here?" I asked as he poked at Quinton's face.

He shrugged one shoulder, screwing up his face the way you do when you watch a man shave. "This old lake full of power. I want me some, I come take it. That damned witch 'cross the way don't want no one else round. I say, 'To hell with her,' and I make me some helpers to show her the way to the door." He cut a glare at me. "Until you went and ruined 'em all." He patted Quinton's face aside. "You'll do. You let that set till it get hard and fall off. Or until it start to itch. Whichever." Then he muttered some more words and crossed himself like a Catholic at Mass.

"How long's that going to be?" Quinton asked, looking askance at the half-naked old man.

Costigan looked up again and frowned at him. "Few hours." Then he grabbed Quinton's chin and gave him a fast kiss on the lips before he backed off, laughing. "You gonna be fine, boy. Just fine!"

I think Quinton would have taken a swing at him if I hadn't put a hand on his arm. "He's just messing with you,"

I said, but I wasn't sure of that. The pale green shadow had remained next to Quinton, keeping its head near his. The shadow seemed to breathe its own essence onto the red-painted wound on my lover's cheek, making the delicate fabric of magic brighten and gleam.

I turned my gaze back to Costigan, who'd noticed I was looking at his shadow. He put the bowl down and dropped into one of the sofas with his legs crossed. The bottoms of his feet were black and the position made it obvious he didn't wear anything under his sarong. I tried not to grimace in disgust.

"Now, you say you didn't lure my helpers to you to destroy 'em. I believe you. But who you say sent 'em?" Costigan asked.

"I didn't. That's what I'd like to know from you."

He shook his head adamantly. "If not you, I know who it must be, but I'm not tell you the name."

"Why not? Whoever it was ruined your plans. Aren't you mad?"

"I deal with my child my own way."

"Child . . . ?" I asked, wondering who'd have ever borne this creature's baby.

He cackled again. "Not *that* kind of child, missy. I know what you're thinking. My child been naughty; it up to me to punish him."

"Him." It didn't tell me who I was looking for, but at least I now knew Willow was the rogue and there was one more person to fear. "How long . . . have you had this child?" I asked.

"For a while. Troublesome, but talented."

"Does he live here?"

"I keep to myself. And I prefer that continue," he added, glaring.

"I meant, does he live nearby, your child?"

Costigan shrugged. "Comes and goes."

"On your business or his own?"

"Mine, mostly. I don't care for that city you come from, but time and again, I need send him out there."

"To Seattle?"

He looked at Quinton. "She a bit slow, ain't she?"

"I don't go for fast women," Quinton replied, cupping one hand over his injured cheek. The shadow plucked at his fingers and Quinton shivered before he dropped his hand without apparently thinking about it.

Costigan squealed with laughter. Then he flew to his feet, his face gone as suddenly stormy as the lake outside his window whipped with angry waves from nowhere. He pointed toward the door. His voice came out as a guttural roar: "I done with you. Get out."

We didn't argue; we left as quickly as we could without running.

Outside, freezing sleet had begun pelting down.

THIRTY

The temperature kept dropping as I drove back across the top of the lake. If it continued, the sleet would turn to ice soon, increasing the pressure to finish up my inquiries and get indoors before dusk. I hoped it wouldn't keep the magicians from showing up at Jewel's house later. I stopped at the Log Cabin Resort to use the phone in hopes of finding Ridenour, but the ranger on duty at Hurricane Ridge wasn't sure where the senior ranger was. I needed to find Willow also and see if I could talk her into meeting with Faith. So far, she'd always turned up on her own. I hoped she'd show up at her half sister's house, but earlier would suit me better.

"No luck with Ridenour," I said as I climbed back into the truck. "We'll have to drive around and look for him."

"If he's still out here in this lousy weather."

"He hadn't checked out for the day, so chances are good he's somewhere between here and Sol Duc. With the sleet, he might be checking on the fishery or resort buildings at Barnes Point. The resort people had started opening up the buildings for spring repairs and cleaning when I first came up here, so if this turns into an ice storm, those sites are the most likely to get damaged. Ridenour's the sort who'll jump in and start issuing orders or doing it himself if he thinks something needs to get done to protect his park."

The road was a little slippery already, so I had to go carefully until the Rover was on the comparatively flat and high-traction gravel roads at Barnes Point. I didn't see Ridenour's truck at the Storm King ranger station or fisheries, so I turned around and drove toward the actual resort buildings around Lake Crescent Lodge. The barrier was down, but it wasn't locked, so we lifted it and drove on toward the buildings, which clustered near the shore all along the jutting curve of Barnes Point.

I'd been up to the resort when I'd first come looking for Darin Shea and found its sprawl a little annoying. The old Lake Crescent Lodge had changed owners and names several times, been added onto, acquired outbuildings, and eventually expanded its grounds to include a large meadow and picnic area on the south end, two different sets of old cabins nearby, a new addition of detached condolike things farther north, and the remaining outbuildings and cottages of another resort that had burned down long ago on the farthest-north end, just before the point turned, sticking its stubby bulk into the lake at the narrowest part. The road split past the barrier, directing visitors north to the Marymere and Storm King buildings, or south to the lodge, and the Singer and Roosevelt cabins. The original two-story Singer Tavern was now the Lake Crescent Lodge; it was right in the middle of the shoreline buildings and seemed like a good place to start, especially when I spotted the white park service pickup behind it.

I put the Rover in the slot next to Ridenour's—usurping the spot closest to the maintenance gate that was labeled EMPLOYEE OF THE MONTH with a faded, hand-painted sign. Quinton and I bundled up with scarves and hats against the chilling sleet and got out to walk to the gate, which was locked. Peering over it, I thought the back door of the lodge was a little ajar, but it was hard to tell. The slat-sided two-story building with its weathered white paint was about one hundred years old and most of the doorways and window frames weren't perfectly square any longer—if they ever had been.

As we walked around to the side of the building that

faced the water, I thought about this being where Hallie
Latham Illingworth had worked until her husband had
strangled her and thrown her body into the lake to bob to
the surface years later, turned to soap. I stopped a moment
to look out toward where she'd been found. I could see the
white smudge of the Log Cabin Resort's parking lot and the
evergreen finger of the point above Elias Costigan's house.
From this angle, they seemed to touch and cut off the northwestern end of the lake completely, creating a deceptive
shoreline much shorter and straighter than reality, with
Pyramid Mountain rising straight up and straight out from
the short dock that belonged to the lodge as if the locations
were connected. I stared at the scene.

Quinton put his hand on my arm. "What is it?"

"I'm not sure yet. I can almost put some pieces together,
but they aren't quite clicking."

"Maybe they'll click better inside. I saw light through the
porch windows, so I think someone may be in the lodge."

"The main doors are around on the north side," I said,
remembering the layout from the last time.

The double doors on the entry porch were locked.
Through the tall narrow panes next to them, I could see into
the dim lobby with its Morris chairs and the chandelier of
deer antlers hanging over the fieldstone fireplace. Ghosts
wafted to and fro or sat in the chairs, re-creating endless
loops of memory in the flickering light of long-dead fires
and the glow of wild magic. Shadows and shafts of dusty
light made strange patterns on the wooden floor that looked
a little like body outlines at a crime scene. I shuddered and
we walked farther back to the jutting, many-windowed extension that was now the gift shop. The door was unlocked.

Apprehension tingled over my skin and sent a shiver
down my spine. The lines on the floor seemed like an omen.
I pushed on the door with my forearm, keeping my hand off
it, just in case. The door opened with a squeal. Something
out of view made a scrambling noise on the wooden floor
of the lobby. Then a shadow trailing violet and blue energy
darted across the next doorway and vanished into the

gloom. I started to go after it but heard the kitchen door slam on the other side.

Backing away from the door, I brushed past Quinton and started toward the back, only to find a wooden wall that cut the back of the lodge and the next row of cabins off from the parking lot.

I swore and reversed direction, running around the lake side of the building with Quinton behind me. We dashed around the corner where the path pointed back to the parking lot or toward the low, fieldstone buildings of the Roosevelt cottages on the south end and ran for the maintenance gate, which was now swinging wide, blocking the view of the parking lot and the roads beyond it. We didn't hear an engine, and the noise of the sleet on the gravel parking lot obscured the sound of running steps.

Beyond the gate, there was no one to be seen. I ran several more feet, scanning the ground for a sign of someone's passage, but the sleet and rain had churned up the surface too much to tell, and the Grey, so full of ghosts and colored shadows, was unhelpful this time.

"Damn it," I spat, coming to a halt and glaring into the curtains of icy rain. "How did he get the gate unlocked from the inside?" Probably the same way he'd gotten into my truck to steal my hotel key card, I realized. The same blue, gray, and violet energy I'd seen on the Rover's doors had wound around the borrowed zombies the night before, and now I'd seen it trailing behind our mysterious escape artist. It was unlike the energy colors I'd seen around Willow and Jewel and Jin and not quite like Costigan's, either, though it had the same strange, breathing darkness. We'd just missed seeing Costigan's "child" in the flesh. Whoever he was, he had a way with locks.

There was no way we'd find him in the rain and unfamiliar territory of the forest between the lodge and the road. Our only option was to turn around and figure out what he'd been doing inside the lodge. We went in through the now-open kitchen door, since the gated yard and covered mudroom gave us a place to leave our coats and boots so we didn't track any mess inside. I didn't want to clean up or leave evidence behind that we'd trespassed.

We went through the kitchen to the main lobby. It was gloomy inside, even though the storm shutters had been removed from the ground-floor windows. I couldn't find a source for the light Quinton had seen from outside, but it could have been a flashlight, or a reflection, or even a witch light. What we did find was a gold-colored silk suit, crumpled on the floor in front of the hearth, as if its owner had lain down and vanished, leaving the clothes behind and a thin residue of dust that smelled of camphor and sea salt.

I closed my eyes for a moment and let out an unhappy breath. I'd hoped to get some more help out of Jin, but I didn't think he'd have voluntarily left his suit behind, and that meant he was probably gone for good. I knelt down beside the dim shape of a head above the empty suit collar and picked a scrap of fabric out of the dust. It was about the size of my thumbnail and felt strangely stiff. It was hard to see in the dimness, but it appeared to be a different color on each side. I picked two more shreds out of the mess and put them in my pocket.

"What is it?" Quinton asked.

"I think it's what's left when you destroy a Chinese demon. Or banish it."

"They leave their clothes behind?"

"Maybe they can't take anything with them back to hell—or Diyu, really. I mean, it's not as if you banish the suit no matter how ugly, just the wearer. We'd better sweep this up and take it with us. Willow might be able to tell us more, when and if we catch up to her."

Quinton and I found a broom, a dustpan, and a couple of plastic grocery bags in the kitchen. I folded the suit and Quinton swept up the dust. We put them in separate bags. Quinton carried the bags and the broom back to the kitchen while I continued to stare at the floor for a few more moments. I noticed there were no shoes, but Jin hadn't been wearing any the last time I'd seen him after his original pair had been ruined, so that didn't surprise me, but there were a couple of other things lingering on the floor once we'd gotten the suit out of the way.

Quinton returned and gave me a curious look. "You coming?" he asked.

"In a second . . ." I knelt down to get a look at the shiny things on the floor as the gift shop door squealed again. We both looked up into the business end of a revolver and a very annoyed Brett Ridenour right behind it.

"What in hell are you doing in here?" he demanded.

I kept my hands where he could see them and didn't try to get up. Quinton remained standing, but he made sure his own hands were in plain sight.

"We were looking for you and saw someone inside. The door was open, so we came in, but whoever was in here ran out the kitchen door. We tried to catch him, but we couldn't, and we came back inside to see what he'd been doing."

"You should have stayed outside."

I rolled my eyes. "It's half a step from snowing out there, Ridenour, and we had no way to secure the building. I knew you'd be back this way since your truck's outside, so we figured it was better to wait in here for you and keep any other trespassers out than to go wandering around in the sleet and ice looking for you. We even left our shoes in the kitchen so we wouldn't mess up any evidence."

Ridenour huffed an exasperated sigh and slipped the revolver away under his coat. I wasn't quite sure how he managed to conceal it, since it was big enough to bring down an elk, but maybe that was just my skewed view from the fire-breathing end. "So what did you find?"

"I'm not sure. Looks like jewelry."

I stood up and took a step away, letting Ridenour do the honors, since it was his territory. He crouched and poked one of the small objects with a gloved finger. "Huh." He reached under his coat again and brought out a flashlight, which he clicked on and used to illuminate the nearest of the two shiny things. "Cuff links . . ."

"Not something the cleaning crew is likely to have dropped," I observed.

"Nope," he agreed, picking up the closest one and looking at it. He held the cuff link out toward me. The crest was a silver oval with a blue enameled outline of the U.S. overlaid by a raised silver compass cross. "National Society of Professional Surveyors. You can bet this hasn't been lying around since they closed up in October." He picked up the other one and rose to his feet, leaving the floor bare as he put the flashlight away.

"Has there been a surveyor up here?" I asked.

"Not in a while. They did a survey of the buildings and property a few years ago as part of an assessment for renovation and preservation requirements, but that was more than ten years ago."

"Steven Leung used to be a surveyor . . ." I said.

"Yes, he was. I can't be sure these are his, but it might be a safe bet."

"The trespasser we chased off must have dropped them," Quinton suggested.

"Male or female?" Ridenour asked. Then he looked up and glared at Quinton. "And who are you? I know her, but I've never seen you before."

"Lassiter's an associate of mine," I said, breaking in before Quinton could answer for himself. Not that he wouldn't have said the same, but I wanted Ridenour focused on me, not on Quinton and his red-smeared face.

"Really." Ridenour sounded skeptical.

I gave him a narrow, disgusted glance.

He shrugged it off. "You two find anything else disturbed when you came in?"

"Not that we could see," I replied.

"Uh-huh. What were you after up here?"

"You. I wanted to ask you a couple more questions."

"What about?"

"What happened up here in 1989?"

"'Eighty-nine? Not much I recall. I was the new guy back then."

"No unusual activities? No . . . construction or accidents or fires?"

He frowned, giving it some thought. "Well . . . I'm not sure of the year, but that might have been when they laid the power cable across the lake."

"Was that when they discovered the lake was deeper than they had thought?"

"Yeah, I think it was." He nodded. "It must have been. They had a couple of false starts because they thought the lake was about six hundred feet deep or so and they were laying the cable nearby, where the lake's narrowest. But they ran out of cable on the first try and they couldn't guess how much they needed since they could only measure a maximum of a thousand feet on the reel. They had to pull it back up and start over, and it was a real mess. The cable got caught on some kind of submerged snag or overhang, and they ended up hauling up a bunch of rock and weed that had tangled on it before they could get the cable up and try again."

"What happened to the junk they pulled up?"

"Not sure, now you mention it. Usually that kind of thing is put back where you find it, but the power company might not have done so. They might have just dumped it somewhere off the park property so they wouldn't have to deal with it."

Lake Sutherland was just outside the park boundary. . . .

"Why are you asking?"

"Because I think something they pulled up allowed your wife, May, into this world."

Ridenour's jaw went slack and he stared at me for a second, the normal energy around his body sinking down as if someone had pulled his plug. Then it flashed back in a red glare. "What do you know about it?" He lunged forward. "Who are you to talk about her? Who the hell are you, anyway?"

I had to put my arms up and fend him off as he grabbed at me. Quinton clutched Ridenour's shoulders and tried to haul him back, but the ranger was heavier and had the advantage of traction with his boots on, so Quinton only ended up trapping Ridenour's arms and being pulled across the floor as his socks slipped over the varnished wood planks. I broke Ridenour's grip with an outward sweep of my arms while his leverage was undermined, but we'd come to the edge of the seating area around the hearth and I stumbled backward, falling into a chair as he continued his forward momentum.

The seat was an original Morris recliner and my weight tumbling into it sloped the back down and the seat forward. I brought my left foot up and planted it in Ridenour's chest. "Stop!" I barked.

Quinton hauled backward on Ridenour, pulling him upright and yanking his coat down off his shoulders to trap his arms at the elbow. It wouldn't hold him long, but it brought the older man to a frustrated halt. I put my feet back on the floor with care and got up out of the chair. Ridenour struggled in the confining coat and Quinton let him go. I took advantage of his distraction to turn the ranger and shove him into the recliner I'd just vacated. He flopped into it with a woof of surprise, through the ghost of a sporty-looking fellow in an old-fashioned shooting jacket who paid him no mind and went on reading his memory of a newspaper.

I turned my palms out and raised my hands to chest height. "Calm down, Ridenour. I'm just trying to figure out what went wrong here and caused the deaths of two people. I'm not trying to upset you or degrade May's memory."

"Four people," Ridenour snapped back, wriggling his coat up onto his shoulders so he could free his arms and move the chair back upright.

"Four? How do you count that?"

"Leung, Strother, Scott, and my—and May. It's god-damned Willow's fault."

"Actually, I'm pretty sure it's not," I said, letting my hands fall to my sides. I could feel the pressure of Quinton's presence moving back a little, keeping out of Ridenour's focus. "And I notice you didn't say she's responsible for Jo-nah Leung's death. So don't you believe that anymore, or did you ever?"

Ridenour glared at me for a few seconds; then his shoulders slumped and he hung his head. "I don't know. Ever since you showed up, I just don't seem to think quite right. Or maybe I'm thinking too much. There are moments when I feel . . . connected to something and I think I know things I couldn't know—as if someone whispered them in my ear—and then . . . it's just gone. The same way May was just . . ." He raised his head and looked at me, the watery light through the windows streaking his face with age he hadn't lived. "How did you know about May, anyhow?"

I almost turned my head toward the place Jin's suit had lain, but I gave a rueful smile and kept my eyes on Ridenour. "Weird stuff is my territory, just as the park is yours. Someone told me."

"No one knows. Except Willow. That's why I always thought—well, you know what I think. Who told you?"

"Someone like May."

He squeezed his eyes closed and his face crumpled. He had to swallow hard a few times before he could speak. "At first I didn't know. That she wasn't . . ."

I just nodded. To say she hadn't been human or real would have been too much, and Ridenour was hurting enough by talking at all.

"Why did you believe Willow sent May away? Was it only because she knew about her?"

"No. There was paper . . . yellow paper with Chinese written on it. Folded like a flower."

I crouched down beside the chair, turning a little to keep from blocking the light as I pulled one of the scraps from my pocket. "Were there other pieces around, like this?" I asked, holding out one of the bits of fabric I'd plucked from the floor earlier. In the thin, sleet-battered light it was the color of dry grass.

Ridenour glanced at it and then looked again, longer. "I—think so. That sort of color, scattered around near her clothes."

Now I almost wished we hadn't cleared the suit and the dust away. "How were her clothes arranged?"

"They were . . . in a pile. As if she'd stepped out of them. With the yellow paper flower on top."

"Ridenour, there's no reason to believe it was Willow. The flower was a spell, just like the one that—that sent May back where she came from. Someone wanted you to see it and think it was Willow's work because she's Chinese, but you can't be sure. Whoever did it had two of the papers—one to use on May and one to leave for you to find. What did you do with it?"

"I burned it."

"Who else might have made it? Who else wrote Chinese?"

He shook his head. "I don't know. Jewel, maybe . . ."

I doubted Jewel would have gone to the trouble of implicating her half sister. She didn't like Willow, but she didn't seem to have any grand plan against her. Once again, I sensed the hand of the mysterious child—whoever he was, I'd come to hate him—and I wondered if, on his trips to Seattle for Costigan, the child had stopped in Chinatown. . . .

"Ridenour, who was working on this building today?"

The ranger still seemed dazed. "Some contractors, I suppose."

"Building contractors, renovators . . . ?"

"No, no. The resort is run by a management group that the park service contracts with. The group hires the people they need to do the seasonal cleaning and run the place on short-term contracts."

"What about the building maintenance? Who does that?"

"We do, but, again, we contract for it. It's mostly done as needed, since it's usually odd jobs and immediate repairs, not planned things like the big renovation."

The certainty welled up in my mind so fast I gasped. Ridenour and Quinton both stared at me.

THIRTY-ONE

I looked at Quinton. "I need my boots. We have to get going."

He looked surprised but headed into the kitchen to fetch them. I turned my attention back to the ranger. "Ridenour, how can I find Darin Shea?" I asked.

He blinked at me and shook his head as if trying to clear it. "He's usually around. People leave notes for him on the bulletin board at the Fairholm store and he turns up once he gets them."

"What if no one's home?"

"Most folks have a spare key around if you know where to search, and Shea's got a few keys of his own for the places he looks after regularly."

"I'll bet he does . . ." I muttered.

Ridenour didn't seem to have heard me very well and asked, "What?"

"Mr. Shea's handy with locks, isn't he?"

"He's certainly installed a lot of them round here."

"And I'll bet he's the guy you call when you've locked your keys in your car, too."

"Well, you don't *call* Shea—he hasn't got a phone and mobiles don't work up here, anyway—but he usually comes around the lake a few times a day, working and checking on things. If he's around, he'll always lend a hand with a lockout or a jump start. He carries most of his tools around with him in his truck."

Quinton came back with my boots and his own. We both sat down and started putting them on.

"What sort of truck?" I asked Ridenour while I was lacing up. Shea had been using a pickup truck at the Log Cabin Resort when we'd met, but it hadn't been registered to him, and I couldn't quite remember what color the battered old beast had been. Something pale, but it had been hard to be sure under the coating of road dust and mud.

"Just an old truck, light blue with a shell. Why?"

"Do you know where he is? Was Shea working here today?"

"No, but he's done work here in the past. I think I saw the truck at Rosemary earlier. . . ."

"What's Rosemary?"

"The Rosemary Inn, back along the road here. It used to be a camp and hotel, but it's the Olympic Park Institute now. Not much going on there this time of year and the sign's a little hard to spot sometimes."

I stood up. "Can you get to Rosemary from here on foot?"

Puzzled, Ridenour got up, too. "Of course. There's a trail from the meadow down here all the way up the shore. It's not very far from here to Rosemary—half a mile at most. They bring school kids and Sierra Club groups out here on nature hikes and education retreats all the time. We even show them the hatchery sometimes."

I glanced at Quinton and back to Ridenour. "We have to go."

"No! You know something about May; you have to tell me." He reached for my arm and I deliberately turned aside. I couldn't risk being detained any longer by Ridenour.

"Not now. Come to the Newmans' house tonight and I'll tell you everything."

He tried to object, but I'm fast, and Quinton and I dashed for the kitchen and out, slamming the door behind us to slow him down. We yanked on our coats as we bolted for the Rover. Ridenour wasn't very far behind us, but he didn't give chase for long, returning to the lodge to lock up, I supposed, caught by his duty.

The Olympic Park Institute wasn't very far away at all. It was closer to the Storm King ranger station parking lot than to the lodge, and the sign was heavily overgrown with dead foliage that hadn't yet been cleared off, but I spotted the road easily enough. I turned in and went a quarter mile or so up the muddy road—it was in need of a lot more gravel and upkeep than the rest of the roads in the park—and discovered a round driveway that circled a covered bench and passed a rustic entry gate made of whitewashed logs. The word "Rosemary" was spelled out in bits of tree branch under the peaked roof of the gateway that stood at the front of an open area bounded by quaint little cottages and a tiny schoolhouse with a bell on a spire. But there was no sign of Shea's blue truck anywhere. I figured he'd taken off as soon as he reached it and was now on one of his other errands, feeling smug and thinking we had no way to know who or where he was.

I turned the Rover around and headed back out onto the highway.

"Where are we going to find him?" Quinton asked. "And how do you know it's anything to do with this Shea guy?"

"He's the invisible man," I replied.

"Sorry—I'm not sure I'm following you on that one."

"G. K. Chesterton wrote a short murder mystery where the victim is apparently killed by an invisible man, because no one noticed anyone coming or going. But it's not an actual invisible man who did the murder, but a 'mentally invisible man.' A man so ubiquitous that no one notices his presence. Just like Darin Shea. He's been here off and on for twenty years, but he's not a real resident, he doesn't own any property or rent any, and no one takes much notice of his comings and goings, but they all let him in and out of their property. They even give him their house keys!"

"You think he killed Leung and Strother?"

"I'm sure of it. If we can find his truck, I think I can prove it, and we can get the anchor stone back from Faith to fix the lake. But we have to do it before the gathering at the Newmans'. . . ."

"How did you come to the conclusion that Shea is the one?"

I scowled, trying to put my ideas in order. I thought it would be better if I didn't try to drive at the same time, so I turned onto Lake Sutherland Road and took us to the Leung house where I parked the truck under some trees, looking into the clearing on the west side of the house.

I started speaking my thoughts aloud, trying to make them orderly. "The pattern Strother noticed was the thing that clinched it. I realized that the places he'd driven to for no apparent reason were the same places where I went looking for Shea originally, plus Costigan's house and here, around Lake Sutherland, which Shea himself told me is where he's been house-sitting this winter. I told Faith we were looking for an invisible man, which Shea is. We know that invisible man has to be the killer and he has to be an ambitious but ignorant mage. All the magic users are accounted for: the puppet master, the nexus keeper, the east, the rogue, and the ley weaver, but not the child. So Shea has to be Costigan's so-called child. I know Shea's been to Seattle several times—he's a potential witness on the corporate case I'm working on for Nanette Grover that's based in Seattle—and Costigan said he sent his child to the city on his business. It would have been no trouble at all for Shea to find someone either foolish or unscrupulous to create the banishing scrolls for him. Someone like Ben's colleague who made the one you brought to me. Shea used it to encourage Ridenour's animosity toward Willow by banishing May and then telling the ranger it was Willow who did it. He's probably been Ridenour's little snitch ever since.

"Once Shea had Willow on the run and could manipulate Ridenour out of his way, he had a free hand to try to control the lake. He wasn't in any hurry about it since he had to learn how to grab the power and use it. Until Steven Leung got the idea to 'fix' the lake. I don't know why Leung

waited or what he meant to do that didn't work, or how
Shea knew what he was planning—"

Something rapped on the rear window. Quinton and I
both twisted around to look. A tree branch swung down to
tap the truck again; there was no wind to move it.

I got out so I could see into the Grey more easily. The
green streaks and pools were brighter and thicker than I'd
seen in a while, and I was surprised after so much
energy had been spent the night before. Quinton tried to
get out of the truck and join me, but the trees shifted and
moved their branches in the windless air, barricading the
doors closed.

Willow stepped out from behind one of the trees. Wearing her black dress, she was barefoot as usual, even in the
icy slush. "Who's your friend?"

"Boyfriend, to tell the truth." I could sense Quinton's
anxiety, but I wasn't going to tangle with Willow until I
knew what she wanted.

"And you let Elias doctor him? You can't be too fond of
him. . . ."

"Since it was Elias who hurt him, I figured he owed me
a few repairs. Besides, he didn't do much—his shadows did
the real work."

"The loa. I hope it was Loko, not Ghede, who cured
him."

"They didn't give their names."

"Was the shadow you saw black or green?"

"Green."

"Loko. It will be all right, then."

"How do you know?"

"I've been watching and . . . borrowing from Cheval
Elias for a long time. He's not so much a houngan or even
a bokor as he is a mount for the loa. He has the delusion of
power, but he doesn't control his actions so much as he
thinks he does. He's very dangerous to know."

"His child is worse."

"Shea? He's a fool."

"Apparently that's your part." Her face grew stormy and

she started to raise one hand, but I put up both of mine and said, "Hear me out before you smite me—or whatever you're thinking of doing. How well did he know your father? Would your father have, say, given him a gift?"

She watched me with a narrowed, angry expression, but she let the gathering power in her hands slide back to the ground as she answered. "They were friendly, but not like that. Daddy was lonely and Shea liked to sit and talk to him instead of working. It seemed harmless."

"He's a better actor than anyone would have credited. And good at masking his abilities—he fooled me, too. What did they talk about?"

"I don't really know. I wasn't around much—too busy staying out of Ridenour's hands and trying to teach myself the Way."

"I think your father must have told Shea how he meant to fix the lake. I don't know how he got it, but he figured out that the anchor stone was the key to the problem. Unfortunately, he didn't know how to use it properly. I think he was going to take the stone away from the lake. He didn't know that would have just made things worse. Shea didn't know, either, and he thought he had to stop it. So he killed your father and hid his body and his car in the lake. The anchor was in the car the whole time, ironically, but it never redirected the leyline as it should have done, because it wasn't in the right place."

Willow blinked at me and a tear rolled down her blank face, leaving a streak. "Shea can't have done it. He's not strong enough."

"He was strong enough to steal your mother's circle."

"Why do you think it was him? It could have been—"

"Nobody else. No one else needed it except you and no one else who could use it is still here except Shea. It has to be Costigan's child—who turned up as soon as I found the circle—Shea. He steals magic; that's why he's here. I can tell from the color of the energy he leaves behind. He uses Costigan's hoodoo and he 'borrows' your family's energy, too. I think he gave the ley weaver the hand-spiders and said they were from Costigan. Then he could get help from that creature, too. I think he's used his access to people's houses to set traps and drive other, weaker mages away now that he's getting closer to his goals. He comes and goes wherever he pleases and no one pays him any mind—they even *ask* him in! He must be clever enough to get his master's loa to help him hide the Subaru after he rigged the brakes and set it on fire when it crashed. I saw the memory of it in your mother's circle."

"He used my mother's circle to kill my father?" Willow looked appalled and started shaking her head desperately. "That can't be. The divine horsemen would never obey Shea. He's only a hoodoo-man, not a real votary of the loa."

"He's not 'only' anything. That's how he's tricked all of you for so long. But if not the loa, then it must have been Jin who helped him. Which might be why Shea banished him."

Willow stared at me. "Banished Jin? He couldn't. . . . He wouldn't know how. . . ." She put her hand on her chest and closed her eyes, whispering words that circled into the air and died. Her eyes flashed open in shock. "Jin's gone!"

I nodded. I wished we were having this conversation somewhere warmer, but I suspected she'd never agree to sit in the Rover where the steel and glass would cut her off from the streams of magic that flowed underfoot.

"Willow, how would you banish a demon like Jin? Or May?"

"I'd cast it out by force. I can. Now. But I didn't banish May. I liked her, and I wasn't strong enough then to force a demon. I barely managed to bind Jin so he wouldn't kill anyone after Jonah."

"Couldn't you have used a spell on yellow paper?"

"If I could have bought one. I never learned the characters for a major banishment. The best I could do with the Chinese I can write is scatter the stupid guai. It's much easier to just shove them out."

I knew it wasn't easy to shove anything in the Grey, but Willow seemed to have a greater command of the local power than she realized. Shea had been wise to keep her distracted for a while, but he'd been terminally foolish to let her stay alive so long. I imagined he had plans to change that soon. "You must have learned more since then...."

She cocked her head and pulled a sarcastic face. "It's not like English letters, where it doesn't matter which stroke comes first. Especially for magic, the characters have to be made right. Who would teach me? Jewel? One of the old women—oh, but I forgot: There *are* no old Chinese grandmothers left here. I know—I could have gone to Olympia! Except I can't leave here for very long; the magic owns me."

"Maybe, but you also command it. It's yours—or it should have been. Your mother's family have been taking care of the magic here for generations. I'm guessing you should have been next. Shea knows it, and he's been perfectly happy to keep you from learning what you needed to, to keep you on the run and unable to repair the damage to the leylines that were your mother's legacy while he played games and set everyone against one another. He got the other sorcerers around here to fight and waste their time while he became stronger, keeping Ridenour occupied with May and then with hating you. Now he's got to make a move, and banishing Jin must have been his first step to weaken you."

"I knew the demon worked for others, but I didn't know who. I didn't have the skill to bind it exclusively to me, but so long as it didn't kill anyone else, that seemed good enough. But Shea..." She shook her head. "I told you he couldn't possibly banish Jin."

"I'm pretty sure he did. First he bribed Jin to do work, and then he got rid of the demon now that push has come to shove."

She scoffed. "How? He has no power over the gate to Diyu."

"He only needed a banishment that he stole from me last night. Anyone can use one, right?"

"Yes," she replied, slowly, as if waiting for the "gotcha."

"I thought the purpose was to kill us, but now I think he

just wanted this." I pulled one of the scraps from my pocket and held it out to her. She took it and gave it a wary look for a moment, as if she could read what had been written on the vanished silk. Then she handed it back to me.

"How did he get it from you?"

"He borrowed Costigan's zombies and attacked your father's house last night while we were sleeping there. The zombies tore it out of my pocket and Shea picked it up in the aftermath. He probably stole things from this house to bribe Jin with, too—Jin had a pair of your father's cuff links. And when that wasn't enough, Shea gave him information gleaned in Seattle, where Jin couldn't go."

Her face grew dark with fury and she muttered under her breath.

"Don't waste your time on him just yet," I warned. "There's a party at your sister's tonight and I want you to crash it. Then you can raise some hell for Mr. Shea. Of course, I imagine Jewel and Costigan will have some of their own to sling around, so hold on to your resources until then. In the meantime, I want you to get in touch with Soren Faith—he's the man investigating Alan Strother's murder."

"Why should I? He can't help—"

"Don't be an idiot. He has the anchor stone and he said he'd give it back if you would meet with him."

"He only wants to arrest me!"

"He said he'd come on your terms to whatever spot you designate. I think he really does just want to talk. He doesn't believe you meant to kill Tim Scott," I added.

She stared at me, conflicted and confused.

"Come into the house where we can speak in private," I suggested. "We need to get that rock back and I'm afraid it's up to you. But if we keep talking here, someone is bound to overhear us. . . ."

"The trees will keep them away," she objected.

"Maybe, but I'd still prefer somewhere drier and more private."

She rolled her eyes and sighed. "You're very soft for such a hard-ass."

"Yes. I have a lot more to do today and hypothermia won't help."

The trees swayed away from the Rover, and Quinton jumped out to join us, apparently relieved to get out of the truck at last. Willow gave him a crooked smile and shot a funny look in my direction before she shrugged and started walking to the house, letting us fall in behind her.

THIRTY-TWO

illow seemed a bit uncomfortable indoors, glancing around continually and unable to sit still. She walked around the living room, noting the repositioned couch and the ashes in the Franklin stove, and grinned at us. "What have you two been up to in Mother's house?" she quipped, not really expecting an answer and not getting one. I bit my lip and brushed absently at my cheek with the back of my hand.

Quinton came back into the living room from starting up the generator—he'd taken the gas can from the Rover. Since the cat was already out of the bag that we were staying in the lakefront house, it seemed pointless to live rough. There was nothing we could do about the propane stove and fridge, but electricity did make things a little cozier and helped push back the Grey fog and swirls of color that seemed to be seeping into the building, deepening, and growing thicker since we'd followed Willow inside.

"The water heater's electric, and there's a microwave, so it's not going to be cold food and baths like last night," he announced, sitting next to me. He rubbed at the dried poultice on his cheek, knocking some of it off.

Willow hopped up from the chair she'd barely perched on, announcing, "I'll make tea!" and darted for the door, giving us amused looks as she went to the kitchen.

"What the hell is that about?" Quinton asked.

"Your goop is flaking," I said, touching the crusted wound on his face with my fingertips.

"About time. It itches." He scraped his fingers over it again, loosening more of the dry muck Costigan had plastered him with. Outside, the shadows were deepening under the cap of clouds as the sun headed for the ocean. I hoped we'd be able to talk Willow into meeting with Faith before things got crazy at the Newmans'—and it was a good bet they would get weird once we showed up.

I studied Quinton's face. The dead color had vanished, leaving pale but healthy-looking skin under the fading gauze of magic that had covered most of his injured cheek. The tiny tendrils of energy were retracting into the dried cake of glop that hid the ugly black line that had appeared when the spirit thing had touched him. "Well . . . it looks a lot better," I offered.

"Maybe I can wash it off, then. You think?" He raised his eyebrows in hope. "I shudder, imagining what might be in this stuff."

"Something worse than rum and spit?"

Willow stuck her head around the kitchen door. "It's mostly comfrey, red pepper, and bearberries, maybe some boneset, definitely some garlic. It brings the blood to the skin and warms it up, wards off infection. Since it was Loko who came to help, there isn't any graveyard dust in it—you're lucky."

"Garlic and red pepper," Quinton said. "That explains the smell. . . ."

"I wouldn't use it," she added with a raise of the eyebrows and a smug-cat smile, "but it does work when you're getting some help from the loa." Willow vanished from the doorway and went back to making tea.

"I begin to see why she's a loner," Quinton whispered.

I poked him with a finger in the ribs. "You could just go wash it off."

"What, and miss my chance to imitate a spicy Italian sausage?" He waggled his eyebrows at me in a way that was too silly to be suggestive.

"You are a danger to morality," I said, smiling.

"I try."

I flapped a hand at him. "Go wash that stuff off. Costigan said it was done when it started to itch."

"All right, all right," he agreed, getting up from the couch and heading for the kitchen.

Willow redirected him up the stairs to the bathroom, saying she didn't want Costigan's concoctions dirtying up the place. In a few minutes, she came into the living room with a teapot in one hand and a cluster of mugs threaded on her fingers by the handles.

"You said he was your boyfriend," she said, putting the tea things down on the nearest table.

I frowned. "He is." Then I felt a sharp, cutting pain across my cheekbone. "Ow!" I gasped, clapping my hand over my face.

Willow shook her head. "Mates."

"What the hell . . . ?"

She stopped what she was doing and peered at me. "When did it happen?"

"What happen?" I asked, looking at the palm of my hand and expecting to see blood, but there wasn't any.

"When did you marry?"

"We're not married."

"Not by the state. The soul-bond. It must be new—it looks new."

"We haven't done anything like that. No ceremonies, no rings, no blood, no . . . whatever it takes." I found myself glancing over my shoulder, half expecting some Chinese ancestor to materialize and chastise me for abusing their hospitality. No one did, but that funny feeling remained. . . .

Willow looked around the room. Her gaze paused on the neat pile of blankets beside the couch, then on me. She looked me up and down again. "Did you two have sex in this house?"

I blushed and gaped at her, feeling like a naughty teenager.

She gazed around the room again, but this time with

fondness. Then she shrugged. "It's my parents' house. It knows these things. You really have to be careful on top of a leyline." Then she giggled. "Lay-line. That's funny."

Quinton came clomping down the stairs and into the room. "What's funny?"

"You're bonded and you didn't know it," Willow said, chuckling.

"What?"

"It's sort of adorable," Willow added, "in a sickening way. You two." She started laughing. "You had sex. Here."

"I'm confused . . ." Quinton said. "Are we in trouble?"

"Willow," I growled in the most quelling voice I could, leaning hard on the Grey.

She snapped her head up, spinning away from me and into a crouch near the door, her expression feral and her hands curling into the rising tide of energy that flooded suddenly into the house. "Don't do that! Don't make me!"

I let go of everything and sat back against the couch, keeping my own hands relaxed and in plain sight. "I'm sorry. I didn't mean to startle you."

Willow was still tense, but she stood up, slowly, unbending and releasing her grip. She let the magic pool around her feet, though. "All right, then." She turned and looked at Quinton and pointed at a raw patch on his cheekbone where the red glop had been. "You are impatient—just like a man—and pulled the poultice at the end instead of soaking it off. It stung, didn't it?"

Quinton touched his fingers to the redness on his face. "Yeah. So?"

Willow pointed at me. "She felt it." Then she glared at me. "Didn't you?"

I frowned. "Yes."

"It will fade. You won't feel the minor things after a while, but the major hurts, the physical and the emotional, you will. You're bonded. Mated. When your souls were in tune and open, when you were soft and alight with love, you gave a piece of yourselves away to each other. It's still there, knitting itself into you. You can tear it out now, while it's still young and soft. You don't have to . . . remain this way. If you don't want to." Darkness flitted across her face. "You have a few days to end it, if you change your minds."

Quinton looked shaken and I could feel the trembling of his emotions like a distant earthquake in my body. "Why would we?" he asked, glancing at me.

"Because it makes you weak! It makes you vulnerable!" Willow shouted back. "It ties you to another person who can be hurt and hurt you! You're a dependent, a thrall, a . . . an adjunct."

"But it's mutual, isn't it?" Quinton asked. He didn't sound unsure; he was just being polite by framing it as a question. "What might be a weakness could also be a strength. We're together. We share—"

"Not like that, you don't," Willow snapped. "It's not the powers you share, just the tugging—the horrible, horrible tearing apart when they leave you! The hollowness, the pain . . ." She curled on herself, sinking to the floor as if in agony. "Tear it out now. Get rid of it. It's just a little pain, a little dead spot, like a place where the nerves died. You'll never notice after a while and it's so much better than—than . . ." She slumped against the hearth, sobbing and shaking. "In my parents' house. My parents' house . . ."

Quinton looked horrified and started to kneel down beside her. I shot off the couch and reached Willow first, tugging her into my arms.

"Who was it, Willow? Who . . . ?" She wasn't a child now, but this was the house where she had been and it brought everything with it.

"All of them." She breathed against my neck. "My mother, my father, my . . . friend. All of them. Tearing pieces of me away . . ."

I looked over her shoulder to catch Quinton's eye. He made a frustrated little twitch, unsure what to do. I jerked my head upward, glancing toward the bedrooms upstairs, hoping there really was a connection between us, that he'd figure out what we needed to do. He blinked, then scrambled away, up the stairs. I heard him moving around and then the wheezy rattle of the electric heaters coming on for the first time in years. The house seemed to sigh and the shadows in the corners stirred.

In a few more minutes Quinton returned to the living room and scooped Willow out of my hold and into his arms. She nuzzled against him, exhausted and trembling as he carried her upstairs. I came along behind. When we reached the top of the stairs, he turned and carried Willow into what must once have been her own bedroom. A cloud of raw ghost-stuff trailed them, passing through me and leaving a strange tingling warmth on my skin as it went. The green light that had welled up at her feet downstairs flowed up and oozed across the floor into Willow's bedroom, spreading out to touch all the walls and send glimmering fingers up to frame the door and windows. Even asleep, the magic looked after her.

Quinton left Willow tucked into bed with an extra blanket over her, against the chill he felt as ghosts began filling the room with swirling fog that seemed to fall from the ceiling. I turned away and preceded him down as he returned to the stairs.

He caught up to me in front of the Franklin stove and pulled me gently back around to face him. "We're screwed, aren't we?"

"Well, I wasn't counting on a breakdown from the only mage on our side."

"That is not what I meant."

"I know, but I can't solve that problem right now and this one, too. This business at the Newmans' will be happening soon and, without Willow, I'm not sure how it will come out. I can't let any of them get an advantage before we figure out how to put the anchor stone back in its proper place. Of course, we have to get the stone first, which won't happen with Willow passed out upstairs. Why can't the damned Guardian Beast look after this stuff him—*it*self? It can shove me through a wall. Why can't it pick up a rock and put it back where it came from?"

Quinton shook his head and made an exasperated face.

"Harper, stop. You're frustrated because you're too focused on one path instead of on the goal. It doesn't matter if they all destroy one another. Or not. It's not up to you to pick the one-mage-to-rule-them-all. You're already more than half-done with your job: You found out who killed Leung and Strother and you can turn him over at any time. Then we can get the anchor and put it back in the lake. And I have an idea how to find the place for it." He glanced aside, and then back into my face. "This other thing . . . I guess we'll have to figure out later what we're going to do."

I bit my lip. I didn't know what would happen and I shouldn't have anticipated the worst, but I admit that Willow's hysterics weren't too far from my own thoughts, and Quinton knew it.

"Then I guess we fall back and punt."

He snorted. "Please, no football analogies. Now I have an ugly vision of zombies in shoulder pads and tight pants doing wind sprints on the lake."

I laughed in spite of myself. "Then, so long as we're at loose ends, tell me your brilliant idea about the anchors."

"You said it made a high-pitched sound, right?"

"The anchor stone? Yes, when you sparked it, it did."

"All right. Sound waves travel very efficiently through water, so if we can isolate that sound and get an electronic sample from the anchor stone, I should be able to rig a rudimentary sonophone that will help us physically locate the area where a matching tone is being emitted. That'll be where we have to drop the rock."

"How are you going to get the waveguides to sing in the first place?"

"That's a little trickier. You should be able to see the line of both the intact and broken waveguides. Once we have the line, we can find a place to apply a current to the broken one and then follow the sound into the lake."

"But . . . ?" I asked.

"But since the sound was emitted in the Grey, I think you're going to have to apply a Grey current. You'll have to pull a bit of energy to the waveguide."

"I can't do that anymore. I don't have that ability to simply . . . pull the grid around."

"We don't need a grid line. Just a thread. Like an extension cord. You managed threads last night. We don't need more than that."

"I broke them—I didn't put them together. I can't make things of the Grey—I can only . . . break them."

Quinton sighed and put his arms around me. "I don't think that's true. You don't just break things; you fix them. We'll figure out a way to fix this, too."

"We?"

"Hey, we're bound together, babe. Remember?" He struck a noble stance, showing me his profile as if posing for a dramatic movie poster, and declaimed, "Soul to soul, heart to heart, together forever!" He looked like Val Kilmer in *Real Genius* when he introduced the student beauticians.

I scoffed and shoved him gently backward. "Goofball."

He exaggerated his loss of balance and fell on his ass, taking me with him, laughing all the way down. I landed on his chest and he let out his breath with an *oof!* Then he pulled me hard against him, wriggled a little, and caught my legs with his so I was pressed against him full length. "Mmm . . . That's nice."

A voice floated down from above. "You have no time for that."

It wasn't Willow's voice, exactly, but it was something like it. More resonant, but not loud, as if the speaker were standing in a hollow place that reflected the sound slightly out of sync. A small cloud descended from the ceiling, filtering straight through the floor from the master bedroom rather than coming down the stairs.

Quinton didn't quite focus on it, but he had turned his head in the right direction and was squinting like a man trying to see against the glare of the sun. He kept his arm around my waist as we struggled back up to our feet to face the apparition. His breathing was a little fast, and I could feel his excitement and apprehension tingle across my skin and shorten my own breath. I worked to keep my own emotions calm.

"Ghost?" he whispered.

I nodded.

The mass of Grey-stuff billowed and tumbled, changing shape on its surface, but staying about the same dimensions—a tapering column about five feet tall and two feet at the widest point in the center. It sank to within a foot of the floor and stopped, floating and churning in front of us. A broad-cheeked, almond-eyed face pushed out of the mist and was replaced by another and then another—a company of spirits taking turns looking us over. A dragonlike head extruded from the cloud for a moment and thrust toward us, its ghostly jaws agape. Quinton flinched.

The first face returned. "She is leaving."

"Willow?" I asked. "But—"

"We awaken to our own. We have told her she must talk to your policeman. It is right."

"Ancestors," I whispered.

Quinton nodded. He wasn't scared, just excited. I would have interrogated him to find out what he was experiencing, but the spirits of Sula's family spoke again.

"When the stone was here, we could not be heard. Our daughter died without our voice in her ear. Our granddaughter lost her way. It must be made right. Willow will help you. Go to the sister's house and tell what you know."

The collective spirit began fading, sparkling into dust and water vapor wafting on curls of colored smoke that rose off the grid. I felt I was supposed to do something, but I couldn't think what.

"Bow," Quinton whispered. "Be polite."

Hastily, we bowed together, his arm still around my waist. "Thank you," I murmured.

The house flickered and seemed to dim into ghostlight and fog, leaving us an instant's impression of being surrounded by hundreds of ghosts who looked at us and laughed. "Love has brought power back to our house." They bowed to us in return and vanished in the sudden drawing of a breath.

Quinton staggered against me as we found ourselves alone and back in the small house at the lake's edge. I wasn't so startled; I'd gotten used to the sudden comings and goings of ghosts.

"Did we actually move or did I imagine that part?" he asked.

"Not physically," I replied. "Did you see them?"

He seemed a little dazed, nodding. "I—I certainly did. They were kind of vague at first, so I wasn't sure. . . . I could hear them better than see them, and even that was kind of lousy. And then they were . . . they were *here*. Or we were there. I'm a little confused."

"No, you're spot-on. It's here and there at the same time. Makes you a little seasick at first."

Quinton let go of me and flopped into the nearest chair, blowing out a long, slow breath. "Yeah. Am I going to have to get used to that?"

"I don't know. What do you see now?"

He glanced around. "Um . . . the living room."

"Look very attentively out of the corners of your eyes. Sounds crazy, I know, but give it a try."

I watched him struggle with it, shifting his eyes as he turned his head.

"This is giving me a headache. . . ."

"But do you see anything . . . unusual? Sort of sneaking up in your peripheral vision."

"Some flashes, but nothing I can identify or focus on."

I heaved a sigh. My relief was almost embarrassing. I smiled. "I think you'll be fine. Well, normal at least. Most people can see the Grey once in a while, just around the edges. If you start seeing it easily, right in front of you, then you need to worry."

He looked up at me and cocked his head to the side. "I don't know if I'm pleased or disappointed."

"I think I prefer you normal."

"I object to being called something as boring as 'normal.'"

"Will you settle for 'within a standard deviation of deviant'?"

He gave it a token thought. "I guess," he replied with a shrug. "Now I'd better go shut that generator down so we can go back to hunting killer mages."

THIRTY-THREE

The parking area in front of the Newmans' house was crowded once we added my Land Rover to the mix. The sleet and rain had hardened into ice as the sun had tilted down, but this time there was no red flash across Blood Lake at sunset; the clouds were too heavy and black overhead, leaking fine flakes of ice-sharpened snow. Even in the premature night, I recognized Ridenour's park service pickup, carefully turned tail in so leaving would be easier. Beside it was a pale blue truck I recognized as Shea's, its paint so oxidized it looked dusty, the low white shell over the bed gone rusty at every corner. As we headed for the door, I wondered where Willow was, and, not seeing any sign of a sheriff's car, if she'd bring Faith with her whenever she arrived. There were a couple of small boats tied up at the dock now, too, and I didn't envy their owners the cold trip home.

A wind had started up as the clouds blackened and the lake seemed to boil, throwing harsh reflections off wave tops where the light from the living room windows fell on the water. Even if there hadn't been random streaks of energy and the fog of discorporated spirits all around, the lakeshore would have seemed haunted and dark with menace. I shivered and tightened my red scarf around my throat—red was lucky, wasn't it? I hoped so.

Quinton's coat flapped, giving him the aspect of a crow as we climbed the steps to the porch. Geoff Newman opened the door before we reached it, staring out at us with anxiety clear on his face. He rushed us inside, taking our coats and whispering into my ear, "I hope you know what you're doing. Jewel's so wrought up, I don't know what she'll do."

I frowned at him but couldn't get a word out before I heard his wife spitting out angry words behind us. I kept my scarf, draping it over one shoulder like a sash of rank. These were people used to having their way and I hoped the bloodred cloth would warn them off trying it.

Turning, I stepped down into the living room. Jewel was seated in a large high-backed chair deeper into the center of the room, dressed regally in long layers of silk dyed the colors of evergreens and strong tea. She swore at Costigan, who stood nearby in his sarong and cross. He glared at her as the words fell like red thorns between them.

At first I couldn't see him, but I soon spotted Ridenour hunched on a piano bench near the windows as far from Jewel and Costigan as he could get. He looked so miserable, I could almost imagine the ghost of his demon wife hovering at his shoulder, pouring crocodile tears. Beyond him, hidden from the doorway, Shea leaned against the curve of the walnut baby grand and watched them all, looking incongruous in his Noel Coward pose while wearing grubby work clothes. The energy in the room strobed and banged against the walls in dizzying colors. Through the huge windows I could see a tower of coruscating light far to the south that seemed to reach and bend toward us. The ley weaver hadn't left his creation, but he was watching everyone in the room nonetheless.

And they were all, suddenly, watching me. Quinton kept to my side but a step back, letting me lead and giving the strong impression no one would get to me without going through him first.

Jewel sent me an imperious glance that was only a little spoiled by the sickly olive color of her aura and a sudden fit of coughing. Geoff darted to her side and tried to help, but he only got pushed aside for his pains.

Costigan cackled.

"Shut up," I advised him, stepping closer to the middle of the room. I leaned a bit sideways and waved out the window.

"What are you doing?" Jewel sputtered, covering her mouth with a handkerchief that was already spotted brown and red.

"Just making sure everyone's paying attention," I replied. The light of Beauty flushed blue and then gold. I turned around. "But we are still missing someone, so let me start with the easy part."

"Sure of yourself . . ." Costigan started.

"I generally am," I lied, cutting him off. "You can take it up with your loa, if you feel slighted . . . Elias." I swept them all with an unblinking stare before I started in again. "You all came to the lake for the same thing: power."

Jewel began to object, "This is my lake."

"Only by theft. This was Sula's lake and it should have been her daughter's lake, but Sula died and you grabbed the power while you could. Because you were the oldest and the biggest bully."

"You can't talk to her like that," Newman sputtered.

"I wouldn't have to if you did it. She bullies you the most, Newman. She bullied you into marrying her so she could build this house on the nexus, and she bullies you every day until you've forgotten what it's like not to be pushed around. Except for you and the rightful owner, the lot of you are a bunch of opportunists and johnny-come-latelies. There used to be just one lake keeper—that's the way the system was meant to work since Storm King threw his peak down and drowned the whole valley. When the magic got loose, you all came to feed, like vultures on carrion."

I noticed Ridenour staring at me, a sick, dazed expression on his face. I turned to him. "Even you. You didn't see it that way, but you still grabbed onto the power with both hands when it was offered, even when you didn't know what it was or how to use it. You didn't really care what May did to get you promoted so fast; you were just glad she did it."

"No!" he croaked, starting to rise but sinking back down as if his legs wouldn't hold him.

"Oh, you did. You all did. But none of you latecomers were so greedy that you tried to get it all for yourself. You didn't challenge Jewel, not at first. You just gathered what you could and used it. That was enough for most of you." I could feel the energy in the room flux and change as someone opened the door. I hoped it was Willow, but I couldn't look back to be sure. Then a burst of confidence that wasn't mine pushed through me and seemed to ground me against the rising fury the spell-flingers were building as they stared at me.

Quinton must have seen Willow come inside, I thought, but there was more to the sensation of solidity, a vibration in the floor that was different. . . .

I went on, shifting my subject and hoping Willow had brought Faith with her.

"But one of you was a lot more ambitious than he let on. He wanted everything, and, when he couldn't have it, he found ways to steal it. When Darin Shea thought someone would take it away, he killed that person. Killed Steven Leung, killed Alan Strother—"

"No!"

The room seemed frozen, teetering on a fulcrum.

I turned to Ridenour, surprised it was he. Or was I? I raised an eyebrow, but I kept Shea in sight at the same time. "Are you confessing to it yourself or do you disbelieve me?"

Ridenour looked dizzy, and his eyes didn't quite focus on me, but he was on his feet, clasping his hands together so tightly, the knuckles were white. A thin violet thread winked over his shoulder, twisting back to Darin Shea—he'd picked up a lot from his mentor.

"Why are you accusing Shea?" the ranger mumbled. "You don't have evidence, or cause. . . ."

"I'm quite sure there's more than enough evidence in Shea's truck. Such as a watch he couldn't begin to afford and that never belonged to him, just like those cuff links you found today . . ."

Shea's eyes widened behind Ridenour, but he didn't move otherwise. And something new rippled across the Grey, two moving forces that collided near my feet, making the room shiver. I couldn't look back yet. Let it be Soren Faith, even if he thought I was insane for what I was going to say, please let him listen to the rest. . . .

Ridenour swayed. "You came here looking for something against him. . . ."

"Yes, I did," I replied. "I came up here to interview Shea for a court case, but I never could find out anything about his background. He's slippery as a fish and as hard to find as the invisible man—someone who could commit murder and never be noticed. But no matter how hard he tried to conceal it, he *does* have a past and some of you know it, if you just stop and think. He killed Steven Leung and he sank his car in the lake. He killed Alan Strother so no one would put the pieces together about where he went and when. He also sent your wife back to hell."

"He's—he's not like that," Ridenour objected. He looked mesmerized.

"Why not? Why are you defending him? Because he's been around for twenty years? Because he's cheap and friendly and always willing to help? Or because he spied on Willow and told you she was up at the greenhouse so you could ambush her? He played on your hate, but he's the one who created it when he made you think it was Willow who drove May away. Who was he friends with?" I demanded. "Who did he do extra work for and spend extra time with?"

"Everyone!" Ridenour shouted. I could see Shea mouthing the word behind his back.

"Not everyone," I snapped back. "Newman won't have him around. One thing I've learned about the rich is that they stay that way by holding on to their money. So why wouldn't the richest man in the area use the cheapest labor he could find? Because he knew he couldn't trust him. Newman knew Shea was a thief, a liar, and a sorcerer."

"A what?" The words came from in front and behind me at the same time. I'd shocked Faith, but he *was* listening. I kept my concentration on the men in front of me. They were the dangerous ones.

"You heard me! Don't play stupid, Ridenour. You already know there's something strange here, and you believe in it enough to have lived with a fox-demon as your common-law wife for years. You didn't know she came by magic, but you knew magic sent her away, and you believed Willow had done it because you knew Willow wasn't just a hell of a woodsman, as you told me. The woods literally love her; they do what she says, even the bears and the mysterious white 'deer' that came down to the ranger station. Did you really think they were just passing by that night they attacked the station at Hurricane Ridge? I was with you, and all you could think about was catching Willow Leung. You didn't even worry about your man trapped in the station. Or me. You left me here to break the news about finding Steven Leung's body in the lake. Me, a stranger you didn't even question about how I'd found a vehicle that had been missing for five years. You didn't care about anything but taking revenge. And that's how he's played all of you. By your weaknesses, by your greed, and vanity, and laziness.

"He was right in front of you all the time, taking away everything you really cared about. And you, none of you, saw what he was doing. You saw only what you wanted. Even the way he *looks* is a mirror of what *you* want to see. He *played* you!" I roared at them.

They all stared back and the floor shook, but it couldn't knock me down. I could hear something in the Grey, something singing and whispering.

Then Faith brushed past me, striding toward Shea. He had his handcuffs in one hand and the license plate from Steven Leung's Subaru in the other. Shea backpedaled toward the window. Faith threw the plate onto the piano and reached for Shea, saying, "You're under arrest for the murders of Steven Leung and Alan Stroth—"

The song broke and something black shrieked past my ear toward Faith and Shea. I whipped back to see where it had come from and saw Willow at the edge of the room, her hands flung out and a fierce expression on her face. "What you took, you now will lose," she spat. She twisted her hands as if tightening the lid on a jar.

Behind me, Shea screamed. I spun around to see the spiked, black torus of Willow's curse spin and fall around his head and shoulders. His shriek shook the room and he wrenched one hand loose from Faith's closing handcuffs. Then he threw himself back against the glass, howling words that made no sense.

The window exploded outward and Shea was propelled through with the force, into the lake, which heaved upward as if it meant to embrace him.

To the south, Beauty burst into screaming red light that turned the waters of Lake Crescent a bloody crimson. Light rushed up from the depths of the lake with a rage of noise; shafts of impossible color pierced the water and the sky like swords and batted the tumbling shape of Darin Shea sideways through the air. He skipped and tumbled over the surface for a moment, then dropped into the shallows where Jin had raised the wreck of Steven Leung's car.

Illuminated by the howling lights from Beauty and the lake, the shoreline was as bright as day, and we all saw Shea stagger to his feet and vanish into the scrub. A crying laugh and the flicker of shadows followed him.

Behind me I felt the press of others as I leaned out to see the lake. Willow's voice muttered in my ear, "I'm going to make sure he dies powerless and screaming. Like my father."

"No, you're not."

THIRTY-FOUR

Soren Faith put his hand on Willow's shoulder as if he were keeping her in touch with the floor when she might have levitated out the broken window after Shea. He squeezed his eyes shut against the flaring lights off the lake for a moment and then blinked until he could see her more clearly. "I don't know what's going on here. In a year I'll probably have convinced myself I never saw or heard any of this—or I hope to God I do—but right now we are going to pursue and apprehend a killer in the perfectly normal way." He glared at Willow and then at me. "And you all are going to sit tight and wait until we do and not go running around in the dark . . . doing whatever you're doing. And that means all of you," he added, shouting at the rest.

Then he let go of Willow and grabbed onto Ridenour's arm. "You and me, Ridenour. Now!"

The ranger trembled and resisted Faith's tugging. "No, no . . . I can't." His face was streaked with tears and he hunched as if broken.

"You're going to have to. This is your territory, Ridenour, and you're the senior officer. You're coming with me if I have to drag you. And besides, that bastard's got my handcuffs." Faith put his hand under Ridenour's armpit and hoisted him to his feet, forcing the other man toward the door until his legs started to work on their own.

Costigan cackled and muttered, dancing side to side where he stood and casting weird, energy-tailed gestures at

Jewel Leung, who was cowering in her seat, gasping and clutching her chest. Geoff groped for an oxygen cylinder and mask under her chair, but he seemed afraid to take his other hand off her and couldn't quite reach it.

Faith paused in frog-marching Ridenour to shout at the old man, "Cut that out!"

Costigan spat at him. Faith rammed his free fist into Costigan's belly, knocking the breathless bokor to the floor. "I'll be back for you later, you damned lunatic." He wiped the spittle off his face and shot a scowl at me. "Help Newman with his wife. Then stick this idiot somewhere he won't scare anyone else. And you," he added, pointing at Willow, "stop acting like a juvenile delinquent and don't break into any more trucks!"

He grabbed Ridenour again, but the ranger now seemed to be all right on his own. The two men headed for the door. Faith cast one more appalled glance at the light and noise still rioting above the lake and shook his head, muttering, "I miss my damned dog."

Quinton was closest to the Newmans, so he crouched down and dragged the oxygen from under the chair, handing it to Geoff. While Geoff helped his wife, I grabbed onto Willow's elbow and pulled her with me toward Costigan. Quinton joined us in wrestling the writhing bag of bones and spite to his feet.

"I guess a punch in the stomach works pretty well," Quinton said, patting his pockets. "Not as messy as a knife between the shoulder blades, either."

I frowned at him, but Willow laughed. Obviously I was missing the joke.

Willow started to make a gesture over Costigan, but I stopped her. "There's no telling what's going to happen to magic right now. Better stick to the mechanical means of keeping him out of trouble."

"Oh," she murmured. She reached into her pocket, pulled out a wadded handkerchief that didn't look like hers, and stuffed it into Costigan's mouth.

Quinton found a roll of duct tape in his endless pockets

and put a patch of it over the hanky before using most of
the rest to bind up Costigan's arms and hands so he wouldn't
make any more interesting gestures. For good measure, Willow removed his cross, but it crumbled away to a twisted
handful of rust, bones, and thorns in her grip as soon as the
chain was clear of his body.

She gave him a sly look. "Oh, you are a nasty little man,"
she whispered. Costigan's eyes widened with fear, and he
squeaked through his gag as she waved one of the bones at
him and sang in a low voice that slid and rattled on the
spine like blues, "Black cat bone, black cat bone, think my
woman done took my black cat bone. . . ." She snapped the
bone in two and threw both parts into the fireplace. Costigan whimpered and slumped in our grip, shivering, his skin
suddenly wrinkling with goose bumps in his undressed
state. Willow glanced at me with overly bright, defiant eyes.
"It wasn't his," she said.

The sound of the lake changed, the roar pitching upward
and then booming while the room filled with searing white-
ness. The house shook and waves battered the windows,
flinging gallons of icy water into the building. Jewel made a
panicky moan behind her oxygen mask while Geoff lifted
her out of the chair and tried to rush her to the door.

"We'd better get that lake fixed soon," Quinton yelled,
"or there won't be much left around here."

"We need the anchor stone!" I yelled back over the
noise. The hot light was fading a little, but it left normal vision stunned and dim. "Get the Newmans and Costigan out
of here and into Geoff's SUV. He can drive them someplace
safe while we try for the anchor—"

"It's here," Willow said, her voice cutting through the
roar of the lake's power with silky ease. "I left it by the
door."

So I *had* felt the stone enter the room. Good to know I
wasn't imagining things, but we still had to figure out how
to get the stone back in place.

Quinton and I helped Geoff move Jewel and her oxygen
into the Mercedes. Then we hauled Costigan to the SUV as

well and locked him in the cargo area at the back. He made no protest, but we didn't trust him, even if he had started shivering violently. Geoff called him a mean old bastard, but he threw a blanket over the man anyhow.

Willow met us at the dock with the stone in her arms. The agitation of the water had died down a little, but the lake's surface was still chopped into rough waves and icy spume that had coated the short dock in a thick layer of frost. Hard, sharp shards of snow stung our faces and hands as the wind cut into us, even through our coats. One of the boats had been rammed into the dock with such force that the bow had knitted into the nearest piling in a shredded mess of fiberglass and wood. The remaining boat was small but looked sound, if somewhat waterlogged, since it didn't have any real cabin, just a partial enclosure and windshield over the steering wheel near the front.

"How are we going to do this?" I asked over the howling of the magic-fed storm.

"I'm driving," Quinton replied, "while you look for the broken waveguide. It has to be near Barnes Point, since that's where the stone was hauled up."

I glanced in the direction of the hatchery building where I'd first met Ridenour. It looked a dreadful, cold distance away.

"It'll be OK," Quinton said, seeing my worried look. "This little boat is seriously overpowered, even with three people in it," he added, reaching to pat the massive outboard engine and nearly slipping into the lake as his feet slid on the frozen dock. "Whoa! We'd better get to it."

We climbed in, trying to keep our feet out of the chilly water in the bottom. Quinton struggled to get the frost-crusted engine started, but after a minute it roared and then settled into a throaty burbling.

Willow had put the stone down in the bottom of the boat where it glowed bright green and gold once it was in the water. Then she'd dug into a cabinet under the seats and found what looked like pairs of padded suspenders, which she handed out while Quinton was coaxing the engine.

"Self-inflating life preservers," she explained. "You pull the cord if you go in the water."

I didn't think we'd have enough time to do anything but drown in water that cold, but I didn't say anything and struggled into the weird-looking garment anyway. I'd never spent much time on boats, but I guessed Willow had since she had grown up near the lakes, and I'd take her word that even a powerful mage might need a little help if they fell in.

Quinton cast us off and then eased the boat out into the lake before opening the throttle and sending us slamming across the waves toward Barnes Point. We all huddled under the little shelter to avoid the worst of the storm and spray.

"Why is it so bad?" Quinton asked, looking at the lake that still shot light and streamers of energy into the sky, illuminating the boiling clouds overhead. "It's as if the lake got pissed off. . . ."

I looked to the south. "I think I underestimated the ley weaver," I replied, "or its connection to Shea. The power jumped up exactly when Shea broke the window. Can you see how Beauty is getting smaller and changing color? I think it's pumping accumulated power back into the lake, either to help Shea or to create an overload that might kill all of the other mages."

"Is re-laying the anchor actually going to help?" Quinton asked. "I mean . . . that's a lot of energy. . . ."

Willow cut in. "No more potential than the lake has always had. The leylines always managed the storms in the past. They channeled the wrath of Storm King; they can manage this."

"If we can repair them," Quinton replied. "I'm not sure how we're going to do that. Harper can find the broken line of the waveguide— at least I think so—but I don't know how we're going to find exactly the right place to put the anchor back down or make sure it goes into place."

"I'll sing."

"What?" he asked, peering at her.

"Listen to the stone. I'll sing that note and the lake will

answer. When we are in harmony, we'll have found the stone's proper place."

"How are we going to hear the lake singing in all this noise?"

Willow shrugged. "I don't know. If we could send energy back to the . . . waveguide? It would sing louder, but all the energy flow is up right now. We need down."

"I'll have to push, then," I said. "It won't last long, so we'll have to be close, and if we're off, we'll have to reposition and try again."

Willow nodded, her uncovered hair straggling like ink around her face. She looked as chilled as I felt and I hoped we'd be in the right place soon.

As we neared Barnes Point, I crouched down on the seat beside the little boat's side rail and let myself sink deep into the Grey, as close to the grid as I dared. I fell through chaos, the mist and color of the Grey roiling and slashing at me as I went deeper. Streaks of light and hard knots of ghost-stuff ripped through me, making it difficult to concentrate and look for the straight, sharp line that would mark the waveguide's edge among the roaring cataracts of magic.

I could see the brighter, stronger lines of the dominant power flow below us, rippling in ever-changing shades of green sparked with gold, but it lay deep under the flooding wash of red and gold belched into the lake from the ley weaver's dwindling construction. The closer we got, the more the tiny boat pitched and squirmed against the thrashing surface. I tried to grab onto something to keep myself in the boat that looked from within the Grey like a spiderweb cupped around a tiny green gem that was the anchor stone, but I was so thin in the normal world that my hand passed through the upright I tried to clutch for. I hoped I wouldn't be thrown out and drowned, but I'd spotted the sharp razor-cut line of the waveguide—a weak emerald glow in the depths—and I couldn't waste my concentration on anything else.

"There," I tried to say, but my voice didn't seem any more substantial than a ghost's.

Then I felt a soft touch against my palm, a delicate brushing like butterfly wings, light but real. "I've got you, Harper," Quinton's voice whispered into my head. He'd never been able to touch me in the Grey before and I'd been able to hear him only as if from a great distance. But now, it was almost as if I felt him inside my own skin.

I pointed at the line. "There." I felt the boat turning, rocking, as we moved closer. I kept pointing and giving directions as best I could until we were right over the line and Quinton brought the boat to a halt. Deep below the surface, the wild stream of the leyline rushed and roared, drowning all other sounds in the Grey. I came back up, through the red battering and clatter of Beauty bleeding into the lake and away from the boiling mist, back into snow that had turned to sleet from angry, flashing clouds that seemed to scream and tear themselves apart over and over.

Quinton tightened his grip on my hand and hauled me closer to him. I felt bruised from my brush through the fierce energy the ley weaver was pouring back into the lake. "It's right below us," I said. I wasn't sure my voice was loud enough to hear, but they both nodded.

Willow picked up the anchor stone. "We need to find the proper place for this."

"Wait a minute. Harper needs to rest."

"We can't wait! The storm won't let up until we're done, and I can barely feel my fingers and toes now. I won't be able to sing for very long. We have to do it *now*."

Quinton would have objected, but I pulled away from him and nodded, catching my breath. "We can't wait. We have to try now."

Willow held up the stone near her ear. "I can barely hear it."

I flicked a passing bolt of blue energy toward the stone. It felt ridiculously heavy and sluggish, not at all as it had when I'd pushed on the energy to stun Jin or dissipate the ghosts in Tragedy Graveyard.

The stone rang, sending ripples into the Grey. Willow sang back.

A distant note answered from the lake and the surface of the water broke into hard waves that rushed at our little boat, driven by a surge of red energy from Beauty.

"Down there," Willow said, pointing west toward Fairholm.

Quinton let go of me to maneuver the boat farther down the lake until we reached the spot Willow liked. The boat pitched violently, like a dog shaking off water, and Quinton pulled me in under the canopy, nearer to the wheel. Willow locked one elbow around the nearest railing and sang at the stone again, having difficulty staying on pitch as the cold dug in its claws. I pushed as hard as I could, shoving the loose energy at the surface down to the waveguide.

The water exploded upward with a blast of sound, knocking the boat into the air and shooting toward the clouds with a shout as if from a giant throat.

Willow shrieked as she tumbled overboard, the anchor stone flipping through the rain and reflecting flashes of lightning from the storm. Something in the clouds answered, screaming and diving toward us. Quinton and I sprawled in the sloshing cockpit and then struggled to the rail, calling out and looking for the black shape of Willow's flapping dress.

Willow hit the water several feet away. She'd pulled the cord on the life preserver, but her movements were weak and we could see the anchor stone sinking into the water, gleaming. We had no way to know if it was heading in the right direction or not.

"Oh gods, no," I muttered.

The screaming thing from the clouds ripped its way loose and dove toward Willow. The long flashing shape, resembling a slender fish with a monstrous, tooth-filled snout, let out a screech, and lightning leapt from its mouth, curling along the shredded bottom of the clouds. A second scream came in reply and another lightning fish tore from the storm.

Willow, floating in the ice-cold water, let her head loll back, using the last of her breath to sing something that rose in pink and green smoke toward the lightning fish. The last wisp of color slipped from her and spun upward.

Quinton restarted the swamped engine and spun the boat toward Willow.

Willow's song brushed the first lightning fish and it writhed around, coiling and leaping in the storm-slashed sky before it dove straight down, toward her, toward us, toward our tiny, fragile boat. . . .

The lightning fish plunged into the water, massive as a bus. The wave it sent up shoved Willow toward the boat and the boat toward the shore. Quinton fought to keep the boat in a safe line and turned back to come around without hitting Willow.

"There has to be a life ring or something in the lazarette!" he yelled at me.

"In what?"

"The seat locker. Look under the seat!"

I slid back into the rear, scrambling to get the seats up and look in the compartments under them. I found a life ring on a line and held it up for Quinton to see. He nodded and steered the boat in a circle around Willow. Overhead, the second dragon-thing screamed lightning into the sky and thrashed the air with its tail, chasing the shadow of its nemesis thrown on the surface of the water by the gruesome light of the lake's corrupted power.

I threw the ring at Willow and the movement of the boat brought it slowly around to her, but she barely moved and it slid past her.

"She's too cold," I shouted back to Quinton. "She'll pass out in a minute!"

I tore off my coat and threaded the stupid red scarf under the straps of my life preserver. Then I dove into the water toward Willow.

Below, the first lightning fish grabbed the anchor stone in its mouth and flipped around, shooting toward us. I swore and swam through the freezing water to Willow. I grabbed on and wedged my arm through one strap of her life preserver before I tugged on the cord of my own. The sudden added buoyancy as the packed straps bloomed around my chest and head popped us upward for a second. She murmured in distress, her face pale blue in the storm light as the lightning fish leapt from the water, spitting fire at the clouds. I could hear the stone singing as the lightning flashed past it.

I wrapped the sodden scarf through the front straps of Willow's life preserver and tied her to the ring as it floated by again. She held on to me with sudden strength. "Bring it back. Make it sing again," she croaked, barely intelligibly from between stiff blue lips.

"Just get back in the boat," I snapped, pushing her away and waving at Quinton to haul her in.

Willow made a weak noise of protest, but Quinton was already reeling her back in. In the clouds, the two lightning fish fought and squabbled over the anchor stone, lashing at each other with their tails and lighting up the clouds with their fury.

I was barely warm enough to keep treading water myself, but I caught my breath and gathered my strength. Then I *pushed*. I shoved as hard on the boiling energy of the Grey as I could, thrusting it downward to the broken waveguide of the lake, hoping, praying even, that it would work.

Bright green light pulsed in a hard, straight line from the water below me and shouted into the sky, knocking the battling lightning fish across the storm like jackstraws. The first dragon spun in the air, spiraling like a falling maple seed, the stone singing in its mouth and shining the same bright green. The lightning fish dove toward the water again as if the line of energy below were pulling it down.

Then it spat the stone out. The light seemed to snatch the tumbling rock and drag it into the depths, the sound of the two songs forming a single soul-shaking note that boomed into the air and then faded into the depths.

The light ebbed down, the screams of the lightning fish receding as the storm eased and the clouds drifted open enough to let ordinary moonlight slice onto the suddenly becalmed surface of the dark lake. The silence breathed around me and I shut my eyes a moment. There were no wild streamers of energy or pools of magic screeching into the sky, no piercing red light from Beauty, just the moon and the distant lap of the lake on the shore.

And the burble of the outboard engine drawing closer.

EPILOGUE

You never would have known there had been a magical battle on the lake if you hadn't been in it. The shore looked a little storm ravaged and the Newmans' house needed some new glass the next time I saw it in daylight, but there was nothing you couldn't explain as the action of unpredictably bad weather. Faith and Ridenour had spent a long night pursuing Darin Shea in the downpour and wind until they found him lying on the porch of Steven Leung's little house on Lake Sutherland, barely breathing and blue in the face from hypothermia.

They would have found him dead if Willow had had her way. In spite of our mutual dousing in Lake Crescent, she seemed to feel no ill effects—which I credited to the restoration of the nexus's proper position and structure. I was sure I'd never be warm again.

She had insisted on going back to her parents' house before going anywhere else and she didn't seem surprised to encounter Shea, still upright and still angry as hell, when we arrived. Like the rest of the lake's magic stealers, his powers had been drastically reduced, so he'd lunged at her. She'd sidestepped him with no real effort. Then she'd tightened the grip of the curse she'd laid on him and he went to his knees.

Willow leaned down and, drawing her fingers over his face, plucked away the violet and gray cowl of his stolen and patchwork magic. "Powerless," she whispered to him. "I'm still working on the 'die screaming' part."

She drew something in chalk on the door of the house and led us away, leaving Shea where Faith and Ridenour found him an hour later.

We'd sat in an all-night restaurant by the ferry dock in Port Angeles for a while, waiting for me to warm up and trying to put the whole mess together. Willow explained how she'd found Faith and told him most of the truth about shooting Timothy Scott—as I'd guessed, she'd thought he was the one who'd stolen control of her mother's spell circle, but she'd only said "thief" to Faith, and nothing about what had really been stolen. Then she'd told him what I'd put together about Shea. Faith wasn't too keen on the "mumbo jumbo" part of the explanation—as he called it—but he'd believed her enough to hand over the anchor stone and drive to the Newmans' house with her. Willow had circumvented the need for a warrant by breaking in to Shea's truck right in front of Faith. He'd tried to arrest her, but the license plate was in plain sight.

Anyone could see there was no place for Willow to have concealed the large metal rectangle in her thin dress, so Faith was left to conclude it had been there all along. He'd gone with Willow into the house just in time to hear me saying true—if crazy-sounding—things about how and why Shea had done what he'd done. That was all Faith had needed.

Faith never did feel quite comfortable with all the weird things he'd seen and heard, but he still put together a fine case against Shea, making the magic out to be a figment of everyone's cabin-crazy imaginations. The last time I talked to him, he was back out with his old partner and his dog, investigating bodies that floated in on the U.S. side of the Strait of Juan de Fuca and he liked that fine, thank you.

By the time things were straightened out at the sheriff's station and Shea was judged well enough to be in jail instead of the hospital, Faith had tracked down Shea's real identity from fingerprints and other evidence found in his truck. It wasn't any nicer than his fake one. Theft, burglary, assault, and fraud were all frequent charges on the list Faith compiled from records in Maine, Connecticut, Rhode Island, North Carolina, and Oregon—places Shea had passed through in his younger days or retreated to in the summers when Lake Crescent was too populated for his taste. He hadn't started out as cruel and calculating, but he'd become callous as he edged closer to real power. By the time the Clallam County prosecutor's office had built a case they liked enough to take to court, Shea confessed from sheer vanity and frustrated the lawyers who'd worked so hard.

Speaking of lawyers, as soon as I could, I'd called Nan Grover and told her her witness was a murderer who wasn't quite mentally stable, considering he claimed to be a sorcerer. I don't think she minded losing him on the stand so much as she hated having her case unbalanced. She even paid my expenses, though I said she didn't need to, and passed along a message from Solis: He'd asked her to tell me that he'd closed the file on Will Novak without arresting anyone—it was just another sad disappearance of a sick man and Michael was free to go back to England, if he wanted. And I assume he did.

The night of the storm, Geoff Newman had driven his wife and unwilling passenger to the hospital in Port Angeles. Elias Costigan was too sick to move by the time they arrived, and died in the hospital two days after he was admitted. No one could really say which of the many diseases they identified had finally killed him, though they absolved us all of duct taping him to death. Faith claimed it was "old age and being bug-nuts crazy." Jewel had been told she couldn't return to her house until her condition was stabilized. So far as I know, she never has gone back to Blood Lake. Willow has.

Of the ley weaver, Willow claims never to have seen another trace. I doubt her story, but not to her face. I have no idea what the creature was or where it came from, and I hope I never see it again; I have no desire to be part of its next "work of art."

Ridenour requested a transfer out of the Olympic National Forest. I don't know where he went, but he went fast.

In spite of having unnaturally good health most of the time, I caught the worst cold of my life and stayed in bed for a week—not alone, of course. Sometime in the middle of that week, Quinton and I lay together, staring at the ceiling while the ferret romped over our bellies, chuckling to herself.

Quinton took my hand a little tentatively. "Are you thinking about what Willow said?"

I nodded. It was still a little eerie the way we sometimes knew what the other was feeling or thinking or if the other was hurting. The sensation of connection wasn't as strong as it had been and I could barely feel it at all when Quinton wasn't right next to me, but it was undeniably there, if fading slowly.

"Yeah."

"Do you . . . wish it hadn't happened?"

"No. I'm just not sure we should let it remain."

"Why? Most people in love don't have this kind of connection. Is it the 'in love' part that worries you?"

"It's the 'hurting you' part that scares the living hell out of me," I confessed. "I have been taking you and my friends for granted and causing all kinds of harm and upset by that. Phoebe's pretty much not talking to me and the Danzigers are friendly enough, but I can tell they're more wary around me than they used to be. That's all bad enough, but I hurt you when I died and I can't stand the thought of hurting you again—especially by some magical remote control because of this . . . tie between us. Even if it's not anything as dramatic as getting shot, I'm not going to live a quiet, safe life. Terrible things are going to keep on happening around me because . . . that's part of my job—both jobs. I'm a walking time bomb of pain for you. Will couldn't even handle the *idea*. You'll have to live with the reality."

"I'm not Will."

"I know that, but—"

"Harper, you think you have to save the world, that you have to be responsible for more than any person should have to bear."

"I do have to save the world . . . once in a while. Or just a lake full of crazy people."

"All right, that's true. It does go with the job. But it isn't ever going to be easy, even if you only had to save the loonies from themselves. Isn't it going to be easier with someone who can help you stand up to it? You know, suffer the slings and arrows and all that jazz?"

"But they aren't *your* slings and arrows. They're just mine."

He rolled on his side and scooped me closer, displacing the ferret, who tumbled onto the floor and bounced around in tiny fury while we ignored her. "Sweetheart, your slings and arrows are always going to be mine, too. It would be that way even if you were just an ordinary person with an ordinary job. I love you, and that goes with the territory. What if it were me? What if it were my crazy job that hurt and raged and flung us against the rocks? Would you want to not know, to not help me get through it?"

"No!" I replied, outraged that he'd even ask.

"It's safer," he offered. "It doesn't hurt so much. . . ."

"I don't care about that. People have hurt me, knocked me down, *dragged* me down, torn me up long before I ever met a monster or a ghost or a lake full of magic. I can manage that. I can manage to keep getting up when it's just *me* who's been knocked down. But when it's you, I—"

He put his fingers across my mouth. "You don't have to pick me up. I'll get up on my own. Right next to you. Every time."

"Every time?"

"Yep."

"Even if I have trouble getting up? Even if it hurts so bad you don't even want to?"

"Even if." He kissed my nose. "Because you'd do the same for me."

I blinked at him and a tickle of joy expanded inside me, pushing happy tears over my lashes. "Yes, I would," I replied. "Even if."

AUTHOR'S NOTE

I seem to take liberties with real places. In this case, although Lake Crescent, Lake Sutherland, and the surrounding areas and landmarks do in fact exist exactly as and where I described them in the text, they never were referred to as "Sunset Lakes" or "Blood Lake." I made up these nicknames to serve my story. And the houses at East Beach and Devil's Punch Bowl that I described do not—and never have—existed.

The town of Beaver, with its "Tragedy Graveyard," is real, and so is the fire that destroyed the Sol Duc Hot Springs resort in 1916 while the automatic organ in the ballroom played Beethoven's Funeral March endlessly until it, too, burned to the ground.

As fantastic as it sounds, the story of Hallie Latham Illingworth and her death and bizarre reappearance is also true. Strangely enough, I discovered that I had a glancing connection to the story of Hallie: Her murderous husband was arrested in Long Beach, California, which is where I attended college and where I first heard about—but dismissed as too weird—the arrest and trial of Monty Illingworth. So you never can tell what will turn out to be of use—save those newspaper clippings!

I culled a lot of my background history from the archives of the Clallam County Historical Society. Alas, some of the most interesting bits of Clallam County history didn't fit in the tale I was trying to tell—the full story of Anna Petrovna, for instance, or the real-life horrors of Starvation Heights—so I guess I'll have to save them for another book. I owe the ladies in the archive endless thanks for their time, patience, and tales—including some about the ghostly orbs that are occasionally seen floating through their own haunted school building.

I also took huge liberties with the investigation of crimes on federal park property and with the administrative structure of the park service in the interest of both a better story and a lot less faffing about with details that would make the story needlessly complicated. I hope the park and forestry services will forgive me. On the other hand, Clallam County does have a renowned K-9 investigative unit that has often worked closely with the Canadian authorities. Also, the "floating feet" is a true story. And the rangers at Hurricane Ridge were quite friendly and have no idea how I abused their very nice visitor's center with bears and demons. If they knew what I was planning, they probably wouldn't have let me in. If you visit Olympic National Park, be sure to drop in and check out the place.

If you have noticed that some things about this story seem a little familiar, they probably are. I leaned heavily on Dashiell Hammett's book *Red Harvest* for the basic plot structure—which he stole from previous authors, so I figured he couldn't complain, not least of all because he's been dead for quite a while.

I suspect I got a lot of details about hoodoo, Voodoo, Chinese demons, and geology wrong, since I am not an expert and become a gifted amateur only for a limited time during the writing of these books. I also have used the names of real people with their permission, but the characters I've created around them have no relationship to, nor are they meant as reflections or comments on, any real people, living or dead. Whatever I got wrong, wherever I went astray, it was an honest mistake and not an act of malice or the fault of those who gave me help, advice, or coffee.

Read on for an exciting excerpt from
the next Greywalker novel,

SEAWITCH

by Kat Richardson
Coming August 2012 from Roc.

The news called it a "ghost ship." I didn't detect any ghosts from the outside, but the boat was enshrouded in thick, colored skeins of Grey fog and ghostlight in gleaming, watery shades: aqua and cerulean with thin whispers of violet twining through them all. I didn't see any ghosts per se, but there was definitely something paranormal going on—more than any reporter was likely to credit.

I stood in the fog near the end of "B" dock, waiting, looking at the *Seawitch*. The insurance paperwork called the old wooden boat a "fantail motor yacht" designed by someone named Ted Geary—which I guessed was a big deal. I've dealt with boats before, but I'm certainly not an expert and a lot of the technical information about this boat meant nothing to me. It had a long, low profile—relatively speaking—with a round stern and rakish angles that exuded a Jazz Age sense of power. I knew the family had money— the boat wasn't the only expensive object the insurance company that had hired me had covered for them—but the vessel wasn't flashy; in its current derelict and stained condition, freighted with mystery, it was grim.

By all reports—official and speculative—the *Seawitch* had cruised away from its berth in this same marina twenty-seven years earlier and vanished from the knowledge of men, taking four passengers and one crewman with it. They had never returned, but the boat had; suddenly and without any sign of hands aboard, it had simply been found one recent morning standing at the end of her old dock. The derelict boat had been moved to "B" to rest with the abandoned, broken, seized, and foreclosed vessels until the truth of its reappearance could be ascertained.

The story in the newspaper claimed that the boat had sailed into port under its own power, but, really, the *Seawitch* seemed to have arrived under cover of the strange, low-hanging morning fog that swelled around the edges of the Sound and skulked below the bluffs every June morning in Seattle that year, making the hills and spires of the city appear as islands afloat in a haunted sea. Here it was: a lost ship piloted by no one living, returning to its berth after being presumed lost at sea with all hands. Of course, that wasn't quite the truth of the matter but it was close enough. And it raised the hit rate at the news Web sites by a thousand percent, which was far more important than veracity: Advertisers pay for eyeballs, not for unvarnished truth.

The insurance company had paid the claim long ago, and when the *Seawitch* reappeared, they were far more interested in where the boat had been all this time and why it wasn't a hotel for fish at the bottom of Puget Sound than in unraveling any ghostly sea stories. They felt it far more likely that someone had defrauded them than that the boat and her crew had somehow vanished and remained hidden for all this time. They wanted prosecutable answers.

The case would have landed back with the original investigator, but he'd retired and since freaky circumstances are my specialty it didn't take long for the file to end up on my desk. This case had the smell of something that would taint your life and haunt your dreams for years afterward, so I wouldn't have blamed anyone who passed on it, especially since insurance investigations of this kind don't come with high-end recovery fees—just lowball hourly wages and the occasional dinky bonus. Insurance investigators are sometimes known to play fast and loose, so once the cops got involved, my colleagues were even less interested in contesting my assignment.

Lucky me: I not only got the case, I knew the cop.

And so I stood in the shreds of morning mist, waiting for Detective Rey Solis to arrive, show me aboard, and explain why the Seattle Police Department was involved in what should have been a matter for the maritime lawyers and insurance actuaries to scrap over in court. Something large and dark—maybe an otter hunting in the salmon run—splashed in the water beside the dock and made me jump.

In the swirling fog, the sound of footsteps on the floating cement dock bounced off the water in disorienting directions. I turned my back to the boat and the unseen otter and stood still, waiting for someone to emerge. Solis, looking like a specter in his dark raincoat with his dark hair clinging wet against his head, seemed to resolve from the murk as he drew close enough to see me—and I him. He nodded to me and stopped at the foot of the steps someone had provided for boarding the *Seawitch.*

"Good morning."

I wasn't so sure of it, but I nodded back. "Morning, Solis. How did you get stuck with this one?" I knew he'd been promoted to detective sergeant not long ago and he probably had the seniority to avoid an assignment like this one. Homicide had been separated from other major crimes a few years back and this sort of thing wasn't their usual beat; they were still top dog where any suspicious or violent death was concerned, but the vagueness of the jurisdiction might have put it in some other agency's bailiwick or given a senior officer an excuse to push it onto someone else.

He cocked his head in what I thought of as his half shrug, but didn't explain himself. His aura didn't give him away, either, but it rarely does.

I can't say I was unhappy to be working with Solis—he's a good detective and I respect him—but I'd never thought Solis was comfortable with me or the creepy cases I seemed to attract, so this was going to be interesting, most likely in that Chinese-curse sort of way.

"Well," I started, not sure what I should say, "*I'm* glad it's you—better than working with someone new."

He gave another small nod and turned to look at the *Seawitch*. "She does not look like a ghost ship, does she?"

"Looks solid enough," I replied. The structure was intact so far as I could tell. I was more than ready to go aboard and not worried about the physical side of the boat: I couldn't recall ever being seasick except when experiencing the sensation of the world heaving underfoot when I'd first been introduced to the Grey. I'd gotten over that eventually.

Solis led the way on board up a set of plastic stairs that were a little too short—the last step to the deck was about eighteen inches above the steps and a couple of feet away across empty air. With my long legs it was only annoying, but Solis—being five inches shorter than I—had to stretch a bit. He then used a key on the padlock affixed to a makeshift hasp on the main hatch. Someone had taken a drill to the original lock inset in the narrow wooden door and the remains sat loosely in their case, making a metallic rattle as Solis pushed inward.

"Did your guys drill the lock or was it that way when you got here?" I asked.

"We believe it was one of the Port Authority employees," he replied, stepping inside, since there was no room to move in any other direction with me standing on the side deck behind him.

"They can just do that?"

"Yes—if safety is in question."

The boat didn't seem like a hazard—just a bit old and abused—but in this day of terrorism, I suppose the thinking was, Who could be sure that it wasn't a bomb or a floating biological attack waiting to happen?

I nodded as Solis watched me slip through the doorway. I nearly recoiled at the smell inside.

The room reeked of mildew and wood rot. We'd walked into a huge upper salon with scattered sofas and tables around the room and sturdy wooden cabinets and shelves built into the walls below the window line. The cream-and-blue upholstery on the seats was striped with green and black stains, and the filthy blue carpet felt moist and spongy underfoot. The matching blue curtains had rotted to shreds and the tables and cabinet doors were warped and discolored. From inside, I could see out in almost any direction between the ruined hangings. I would bet the sun shining on all that glass had done its part to advance the rot, and at the same time, the spotted windows made the room seem both open and trapped in its own personal fog bank.

I sneezed and coughed a little as the smell aggravated my nose and throat. "Ugh," I muttered. The movement of the boat was barely noticeable, but the stink was compensating for the lack of mal de mer.

"It is unpleasant," Solis responded. "It's worse below."

"Oh ... goody," I replied, turning my attention back to the room around us.

A squared-off arrangement of the furniture defined a lounge area that faced the rear of the living room–like space—I knew real hardcore boat people would have called it "the saloon," as it was labeled on the plans, but damned if I would. I wondered why the seats were oriented to the back until I figured out that the entire rear wall was made of wood-and-glass panels that folded aside to open the back of the space to the round, covered aft deck. Passengers could sit inside reading, chatting, or eating while enjoying the outdoors without having to be in it—back when the interior was still clean and dry—and still use the area if the weather went sour just by pulling the doors across. Judging by the moisture level, the weather had invaded at some point, doors or no doors.

"Could we open those up and air this place out a bit?" I asked.

Solis considered it, then nodded and went to open up the doors himself, scowling at me when I moved to help. I ignored him; the sooner we had the boat open and full of fresher air, the better, as far as I was concerned. It wasn't as if we were trampling up a clean crime scene, here. Whatever had happened aboard the *Seawitch*, it hadn't taken place recently.

I touched the nearest of the folding doors and felt a cold frisson race up my arm and across my scalp. I must have gasped or twitched, because Solis cocked his head and glanced at me from the corner of his eye.

I shook him off. "Just one of those creepy feelings."

He grunted, nodded, and went back to opening doors. Once we had the back of the boat open, fresher, cold air rushed in, swirling around and, to my eyes, raised filaments of violet, blue, and green energy off the floor and furnishings as if the magical residue of whatever had happened in the boat had dried out like sea grass left on the shore. The fine threads were the same colors I'd observed outside. I helped Solis shove the last of the resisting, warped doors aside and took a moment to peer harder at the Grey—that thin space of magic and possibility lying between the normal and the paranormal worlds.

The misty material of the Grey was acting stranger than usual here: Instead of the foggy, airy movement I normally saw, the boat seemed to be filled with two separate Grey fluids that refused to mix. The brew flowed and crested in the space as if held in an agitated fishbowl, the walls warped and rough around it. At the far end and to the right was a staircase where one of the substances flowed down, taking all the amethyst color with it as well as the cerulean and emerald, while the other remained above showing only thin watery shades of blue and green. The air felt colder in that area, piercing right through my jacket like winter ice.

I stared a moment longer at the strange tide of the Grey. It looked . . . as if something powerful had passed through the boat from back to front, sinking down where it found access, and leaving this lingering stream as a reminder. How long ago had it been at full flood?

I turned my attention back to the normal world, to Solis, who was frowning at me nearby.

"This . . . evidence of something foul that brought you here, is it downstairs?" I asked, thinking about the direction and flow of the energetic traces.

He raised his eyebrows. "Yes. Come with me."

He continued to frown as he turned to lead me to the scene of whatever crime the SPD suspected had happened aboard. Judging by the way his usually-quiet aura spiked and jumped, I'd rattled him—which was no mean trick.

We bypassed the rest of the upper deck and I followed him down the narrow staircase—a "companionway" to sailors—submerging into the oily, swirling Grey. For an instant I thought I was drowning, the rising spectral liquid bringing a cold recollection of a certain teenage summer when I'd gone swimming with my cousin Jill and not entirely escaped my first brush with death—Jill had not escaped at all. I was glad I was behind Solis and he couldn't see me jerk my head back in suddenly-remembered terror as the uncanny fluid seemed to rise over my face and push into my mouth and nose. In a moment, the sensation passed as I continued to breathe normally, but my heart was still racing for a while afterward and the scent of the sea stayed in the air around me as long as we remained aboard the *Seawitch*.

From the foot of the stairs, Solis lead me forward along a narrow corridor that ran about a third of the length of the boat. As we walked, I felt colder and colder and the sense of damp became oppressive. I realized I was slowing, as if I were fighting a current, and feeling tired from it. Nearly to the end of the hall, Solis, who was several steps ahead of me, stopped and turned toward a narrow door on his left.

I moved to catch up with him—he hadn't even opened the door yet—but a sudden blast of wet cold smacked me down. I stumbled to one knee, bowing my head against what felt like a deluge of icy water. Solis whipped back to stare at me and took a step away as I planted my hands on the walls and shoved my way back to my feet. Keeping my hands braced, I stood firm and shook back my hair with a sharp flip of my head. Water from my drenched locks spattered against Solis's coat and face—seawater that reeked of dying things struggling in poisoned currents.

He caught his breath short and stared at me, his head pulled back, murmuring under his breath, *"Madre—"*

I took a couple of steadying breaths and fought off the sense of being battered by a riptide only I was caught in. "Welcome to the freak show," I muttered.

New from

Kat Richardson

SEAWITCH
A GREYWALKER NOVEL

A quarter century ago, the Seawitch cruised away from her dock and disappeared with everyone on board. Now, the boat has mysteriously returned to her old berth in Seattle and the insurance company has hired Harper to find out what happened. But Harper is not the only one investigating. Seattle Police Detective Rey Solis is a good cop, albeit one who isn't comfortable with the creepy cases that always seem to end up in Harper's lap. As Solis focuses on the possible murder of a passenger's wife, Harper's investigation leads her to a powerful being who may be responsible for the disappearance of the Seawitch's passengers and crew.

"[Harper Blaine is] a great heroine."
—#1 *New York Times* bestselling author
Charlaine Harris

Kat Richardson

The Greywalker Novels

A detective series with a supernatural twist,
featuring PI Harper Blaine.

ALSO AVAILABLE IN THE SERIES

GREYWALKER
POLTERGEIST
UNDERGROUND
VANISHED
LABYRINTH
DOWNPOUR
SEAWITCH

"The Grey is a creepy and original addition
to the urban fantasy landscape."
–Tanya Huff

**Available wherever books are sold or at
penguin.com**

R0113